Chronicles of Nethra

Book Five

Risen Gods

This is a work of fiction. All characters and events portrayed in this novel are either fictitious or are used fictitiously.

Chronicles of Nethra: Risen Gods

By E. R. Donaldson
Edited by Alana Joli Abbott

www.mythicnorthpress.com

ISBN: 978-1-954177-12-3

First edition: March 2022

Acknowledgments

Thanks, once again, to Alana Joli Abbott for providing the copy edits for this book. Your feedback is invaluable and always brings a smile to my face. Thanks also to Bob, Josh, and all my other advanced readers for your feedback. Lastly, a big thanks to my family. This has cost you a lot in terms of time and energy. I hope you're proud of what we've created together.

PROLOGUE

Minos Station
Three weeks ago

Cali Vay-Lon strode quietly through the halls of the Citadel's lower levels. It was late on Minos Station, and most of the installation's staff had retired for the evening. The Kintar's only company was the occasional hovering drone that buzzed wordlessly past her in the corridors. If she were being honest, she preferred it this way. She was finding her aids and personal guard to be somewhat of irritating of late. Alone time was hard to come by.

Too soon she arrived at her destination. A heavy sigh welled in her chest as she ran her hand over one of the fleshy, crimson dendrai that rested on her shoulder. Quickly, she tried to drum up some rationale for putting off this next meeting. Unfortunately, nothing came to mind. She could only comfort herself in the fact that this was the last task she would need to suffer through this evening.

She pressed her palm against the scanner. The metal pad beeped in acknowledgment as the heavy door slid open. The chamber beyond held a very different look from the cold glass and metal of the hallway. Warm light radiated from sconces that lined the room. Bronze tiles, accented by veins of dark brown, covered the floor and walls. It gave the chamber a soothing, regal aesthetic.

In the room's center was a large pool of water. The bath was built right into the floor, composed of the same tiles that decorated the rest of the chamber. At the center, the water was deep enough that soft shadows occluded the bottom where light from the sconces could not reach.

Splashing about in the center of the pool was the man she'd come to see. "Hello, Shift," Cali greeted.

The grungy Terran stopped to look at her. The natural curl of his hair gave it an unruly look, even when wet. His beard was so unkempt it made him look filthy, even while bathing. If a few hours in the bath weren't going to make him look presentable, it was unlikely anything would.

He waded away from the center of the pool and stood to address her. The fact that he was exposing himself in the process seemed inconsequential to the hacker. "Well, if it ain't Sha Cali! Come t' join me fer a quick dip before ma execution?"

The suggestion, paired with the sight of his naked form, made her stomach roil. Shift didn't have the kind of body one would normally choose to showcase. "I'm sure you'd like that, but no. Besides, you're not being executed. I didn't go through all this trouble to drag your shady ass out here just to kill you."

Shift barked a harsh laugh. "Ah'm sure ya wouldn've, but we both know that's not up to ya, now is it? It's been a while since Ah've done any work for the Machine. Still, Ah don't remember 'im being the forgivin' kind. Ya feel me?"

"Oh, I 'feel' you, but it seems the gods have taken mercy on your wretched soul. Your little screw-up has fixed itself."

The man's sardonic smirk faded to be replaced by a look that was equal parts terror and wonder. "Ya found out about th' Cognis chip?"

"Indeed. It found us, actually. A crew of runners brought it right onto the station; the same runners that brought you to me, as a matter of fact."

"Heh… Ah kinda wondered if they'd kept that a secret." He shook his head. "And now Ah'm really confused. The Machine should be ready t' fry ma ass if it knew what Ah was plannin'."

Cali couldn't help but laugh. "I have to hand it to you: it was a true stroke of brilliance—including a personality override in the essential algorithms. You didn't like who our master had become, so you thought you'd author a new one—one a bit more naive, one significantly more malleable."

The hacker cracked his neck, looking more resolved. "Can't blame a boy fer tryin' yeah?"

"Well, I could. We could. But we won't. Turns out you're one of the only hackers in the sector with the skill set we need. That was true back when we hired you, and it's still true now."

Shift scoffed. "So, that's why ya brought me back." He shook his head and sank into the pool. "The Machine is movin' forward with its plans?"

Cali bristled. "Stop calling him that. You know he hates it."

"Why do ya think Ah do it?"

Now it was Cali that shook her head. This fool most certainly had a death wish. "The answer to your question is 'no.' Arc has a plan for the chip, but it's not what was originally intended. Since you've been gone, he's come up with another means to achieve his goal."

Shift looked up, cocking his head curiously. "And what might that be, now?"

Cali told him, taking the time to savor the incredulity that mounted in the man's expression. When she'd finished, it took a few seconds for the hacker to recover from his shocked silence. "That's insane," he whispered.

"Is it though? You, of all people, should see the beauty in it. You know how Arc works—what makes him tick. This is even better than what he had originally hoped for: a marriage of his dual natures if you would."

"Are ya really plannin' on lettin' that demon enter this world?"

"He's not a demon," she retorted. She left out the fact that Arc had already started letting plenty of those cross over. "He's a god, and it would serve you well to start treating him as such."

"That thing is no god! That machine was made by men. Ah don't give a shit what kind of metaphysics went into its construction—men do not make gods!"

Cali chose not to belabor the point. Whether Shift chose to believe the AI's assertions regarding the source of its cognition was irrelevant. All that mattered was whether the Terran would do as he was asked. "You know he has ways of making you cooperate, should you choose to be difficult."

The hacker drew in a deep breath. "That won' be necessary. Remember, Ah did have some investment in this li'l project—after a fashion, anyway. It ain't ma fault things turned out a bit differently than Ah had hoped."

Cali chuckled. "Yes, I was wanting to ask you about that. How did Ora manage to get her pretty little claws on you? You're damned lucky Arc was able to pry that bit of intel from the Vandal's logs. Otherwise, you'd still be on ice."

Shift's eyes were filled with rage as he spoke. "Ah underestimated ma opponent. Ain't the first time that happened, as ya know. Might damned well be ma last, unfortunately."

"That doesn't answer my question. How did you get caught? We've been hunting you for the better part of a cycle, and we could never find a trace of you."

"Ah got caught inside the Grey Wings' network."

"That was sloppy."

"Well, Ah wasn' exactly expectin' high-level security. The Grey Wings are supposed to be small-time."

"Obviously you don't keep up with current events."

"Obviously."

Cali crossed her arms over her chest. She was still curious why Shift had been in the Wings' network in the first place, but she imagined she wasn't going to get a straight answer. It didn't matter. "So, are you in or out?"

Shift rolled his eyes. "Of course Ah'm in. The Machine may have an over-inflated assessment of himself, but at least he pays well. Shall we discuss the compensation package?"

Now it was Cali's turn to laugh. "How about you send me an invoice? If your demands aren't too ridiculous, we'll see what we can do."

"What if ma first demand is that ya strip-down an' join me for a swim?"

"See, that's a good example of the kind of thing that's not going to happen." Flashing him a rude gesture, she turned to the leave. "See you tomorrow, Shift."

Back in the hallway, Cali pulled out her MoDAC and scanned her task list. Yes, that was the last item. In checking the time, she saw that it was just shy of 23:00. She was making better time than she had anticipated.

Suddenly, she found herself far more awake than she had been mere minutes ago. She took a glance over her shoulder. While she was down here, she might as well check in on their other guest. She stowed her mobile and took off at a brisk walk.

Several twists and turns down the maze of corridors eventually brought her to a door marked "SYSTEM MAINTENANCE." She palmed this door, which prompted a holodisplay to appear directly in front of her. She quickly typed in the six-digit access code, and the doors parted.

The chamber beyond was wide open in a fashion typical for reactor cores. Numerous catwalks provided pathways to various points of interest and a handful of access points throughout the complex. The path that Cali stepped out onto was slightly larger than the rest and led directly to a large tank embedded into the reactor's central spire.

A heavy thrumming greeted her as she walked toward the tank. Another holodisplay appeared as the terminal sensed her approach. Cali selected the appropriate command and the prompt closed. The tank hissed as it depressurized. There was a slight whirring as the device began to open. It looked like an egg hatching as the various components of the outer shell pulled apart.

Inside the chamber waited the person she had come to see. Cali smiled, good-naturedly. "How's my favorite triumvir today?"

Wynne Ren'Dahl's eyes flickered before cracking weakly. When they finally opened, those black-in-black Sahaia eyes glared out at her. The message they conveyed was quite clear: if she were to ever find a way out of this contraption, she would kill everyone in this complex.

The woman was looking the worse for wear. Numerous wires and tubes had been plunged into the naked flesh of each of her limbs and at numerous points in her torso. Though some of those tubes were dedicated to piping nutrients into her body, it seemed that the machine was extracting far more than it was putting in.

Her face was gaunt, almost skeletal in appearance. Her short black hair appeared to be thinning and even falling out in places. Ribs showed in her chest, and her breasts hung like empty sacks. The muscles in her arms and legs seemed to have also been eaten away. Cali doubted if Wynne could even stand were it not for the aid of the tank.

Cali wiped at the sweaty strands of hair plastered to the Sahaia's forehead. "I see your time with us has been hard on you. I do feel bad for that. I hope you believe me. I had no idea that Arc could be so needy. I'll see if your nutrition infusions can be concentrated further. We certainly don't want you running dry on us."

Wynne didn't respond. Though her eyes were still filled with that hateful fire, her body slumped weakly in its harness. Cali inspected the collar around the woman's neck to find that some slack had developed between her skin and the device.

"Fascinating," Cali murmured. "He's drained you so much that he doesn't even need the collar to suppress your power. Let's just take that off, shall we?"

Cali undid the clasp and removed the suppressor. Wynne still didn't respond as the burden was lifted from her. With the device removed, Cali could see the remnants of burn marks. This made sense to her—not much else to do when you're in a prison-like this but to test the limits of your restraints.

She wondered how long the woman had strained in the darkness of her confines, attempting to thwart the collar. She also wondered how long ago it had taken for Wynne to waste away to the point where the collar was no longer needed. How long had it been since Cali had last visited? Months? Longer?

"I have good news for you, my friend." Cali stroked the captive's face tenderly. "Your services won't be required for much longer." She waited a moment to see if the remark would garner a reaction. It did not. Leaning in conspiratorially, she added, "Arc has told me that we're going to have a new source of psionic power very soon—something far stronger than either you or me. After we have this installed, you'll be free to rest. Won't that be nice?"

Still no response, only the same hateful glare. Cali pulled away. "I know it's not much, but I imagine that joining your pool of ancestral spirits couldn't possibly be worse than this." She gestured casually at the tank. "I hope you know that, had there been another way, I would have found it for you. I mean, I did care for you, love. You know how it goes, though. It was you or me. Would you have chosen differently if you were in my position?"

Cali waited as if in response to the rhetorical question. "No," she said at length. "I don't think you would have."

It was only then that Wynne's lips quivered as if to say something. Cali stiffened, her heart racing in suspense. A soft rasping sound was all that came. Cali's shoulders slumped in sincere disappointment.

"This is probably hard on you. I admit it's a little hard on me. I ask myself if our situations were reversed, would I want you to visit me? Generally not, I think. But sometimes I just can't resist the urge."

With a heavy sigh, she reached to the control panel again. The holodisplay reappeared, and Cali selected the command to close the tank. "I'll leave you to it, then," she said as the device began to shut. "Next time, though, I promise—I'll bring you something you're looking for. I'll bring you release."

The tank shut and repressurized. Cali caught herself staring forlornly at the device. She'd meant what she had said. She felt sorry for the poor soul trapped in that tank.

Her eyes wandered up the shaft. The dark pillar shot far above her, all the way to the top of the tower. Her mind wandered to the chamber that she knew rested several hundred meters above her: Arc's central terminus.

A new emotion welled up to replace the hint of sorrow that had drifted into her heart. Excitement. Anticipation. If what the AI said was true, and it almost always was, then she was on the cusp of achieving everything she'd worked for the entirety of her long years since she'd assumed control over the Marauders.

It was power she craved. Ever since being dismissed from the Empress's service, she'd longed to be part of something that powerful again. Few could match the might of the Kintari Empire. But, if Arc were to be believed, she would soon be sharing in a power that could rival the very gods themselves.

Yes, it would be soon now. Soon, all the universe would tremble before her.

CHAPTER 1

[ACCESSING ARC PROJECT LOG 001]

[DR. DAMIEN HERMES]

Gaia's planetary governors have lost their minds.

The ambition to centrally control the reactors across a celestial body is a worthy one. My understanding is that this approach is how Hissak space ironed out its energy inequalities and now keeps its governmental R&D running ahead of most other sapient species. To design and implement similar systems across the Helion System is a step in the right direction.

But to manage all the system's reactors from a single central location? My gods, Terrans haven't even mastered instantaneous subspace communication. That's only one of the precursors necessary to achieve such a feat.

What they are asking for is nothing short of impossible.

[CLOSING PROJECT LOG…]

"Brace for impact!" Eli's words were punctuated with the screech of metal as the Vandal collided with an asteroid. The mercifully small impact bounced against the ship's shielding, though the craft was sent reeling off course.

Sahar threw herself onto Skye's convulsing form in an attempt to keep them both from flying into a nearby control panel. Another collision rocked the ship, sending them tumbling in the opposite direction. The Maur held her friend's body close as they toppled into the copilot's chair.

The third crash—the worst yet—sent everyone flying back away from the console. Sahar grunted as she slammed painfully into the door frame. She closed her eyes, waiting for the next jolt while knowing there was no way they'd survive it.

Thank the gods that final blow never came. Skye was still cradled protectively in her arms. The Terran woman had stopped convulsing. She wasn't even trembling. A knot of anxiety formed in Sahar's stomach as she checked for breathing.

"Thank the gods," she whispered when she felt the shallow rise and fall of Skye's chest. She was alive. They were both alive. Since they were still planted firmly on the deck, it looked like life-support was still online. That made them three for three.

Sahar gently separated herself from her Terran companion and knelt next to her immobile form. Sharp pain in the Maur's side made her wince, and she became acutely aware of how difficult it was to breathe. Her rips were cracked, if not broken. Not a big deal given how fast Maur healed, but it was going to make for a rough couple of hours.

Eli stirred from where he lay a short distance from them. She had figured it would take more than a rough landing to dispatch the Sahaia, but she was still relieved to have the confirmation. "Sit rep?" he coughed.

"I'm okay," Sahar growled. "Skye's unconscious, but she's breathing. Have we stopped?"

"Seems so," he noted, stumbling to his feet. Slowly, he made his way back to the console. From the flickering holoscreens, Sahar knew what he was going to report well before he made it official. "The interface is down. I can't even access a menu to see what happened to the ship."

Sahar fished her MoDAC out of her back pocket. It was a good thing these little cards were so durable as she was fairly certain she'd landed on it once or twice during that little tumble. The control panel on the device showed she had access to the native applications, but her connection to the ship network was down. She reported as much to Eli. "Must have lost the antenna in the crash."

"Maybe, but I'm not certain. I couldn't reach Lexa well before we lost control. Something else is wrong here."

Not good news. An antenna could be fixed, but if something was wrong with the android… "Well, we're not going anywhere until we get to the bottom of it. Orders, Captain?"

The baleful look in his ebony eyes told Sahar exactly what he thought of her playing the rank-card at a time like this. Tough shit. If he gets to call himself the boss, he's got to deal with more than just the perks.

Her expression must have conveyed her thoughts. "All right," Eli sighed. "We need to verify everyone's safety first. Let's find the others. One second." He closed his eyes.

"What are you doing?"

"Contacting Aaliyah. That is if you'll give me a moment."

Oh, right—the Sahaia bond. That thing was certainly useful when the comms were down. If she hadn't been so concerned about the metaphysical consequences, Sahar could see campaigning for one of those herself.

As Eli did his thing, Sahar turned back to Skye. She was glad to see that her efforts at protecting her friend from further harm in the crash seemed to have been successful for the most part. With one clawed hand, the Maur brushed a few tousled blond curls from Skye's face. Should Sahar try and move her? Or would that cause further damage?

Shortly before they'd crashed, Skye's visions had taken a turn for the worst. She was already very sick by the time Sahar had gotten to the scene, and that was when the screaming had started. Her words echoed in Sahar's memory. "It burns. Make it stop."

Sahar had been helping Skye channel her visions for the past six months. After the recent events on Sif, there was little doubting Skye's status as one of the Kaleema—one of the chosen. She was the first verified Kaleema Sahar had known, though she was fairly certain she knew of at least one more. She had hoped her knowledge of Skye's… condition, might be helpful to her in gaining control of the dreams and nightmares that plagued her.

At this point, Sahar's efforts seemed to have been in vain.

Eli must have finished his telepathic conversation as he was now standing next to her. "Is she going to be okay?"

"I don't know," Sahar confessed. "Kaleema or not, I've never heard of someone having an episode like this. Do you know what caused it?"

"No. She was fine one minute, and then the next…" He shook his head as if to clear the memory from his head. "You saw the worst of it."

"Was she upset?"

"I don't know. I… she… I don't think so." He hesitated. "Perhaps?"

"Real helpful, boss." Sahar heaved a sigh. "I don't think we should move her. Do you want to stay here with her while I search the ship?" When Eli didn't respond, she tried again. "Let me rephrase: one of us should stay here with her. Do you want that to be you, or me?"

Her words must have given him the out he was looking for. "I'll stay. Aaliyah said she's in one piece. She was in the hold when the crash happened, but managed to avoid most of the damage. She's headed to engineering to run some diagnostics."

Good. From what Sahar knew of the Sahaia bond, she had figured Eli would have known if Aaliyah were dead. Still, she could have been injured, and they didn't need any more crew members down for the count right now.

That still left Dan, Lexa, Argus, and Amelia unaccounted for. "Did she have any word from the others?"

"No. She is alone."

Well, damn. "All right. I'm going to do a sweep of the ship. When I've found the others, we'll meet back here." She started to tell him to call if Skye's condition changed but realized that simply wasn't possible. Instead, she just marched off the bridge.

This was bad, but they'd pulled through worse. Exactly what would have constituted "worse" at this point was a little fuzzy, but there were better things for Sahar to focus her thoughts on right now.

Surely, they'd pulled through worse.

<Are you okay?>

Aaliyah jerked awake at the sound of Eli's voice in her mind. Groggily, she opened her eyes to find that she'd ended up in a pile of empty crates and loose equipment. Her body ached, but she was alive.

<Still breathin',> she replied. <Mind tellin' me how I ended up knocked out in a pile of gear?>

<We lost control of the ship.>

<Caught that. I was hopin' ya had a few more details.>

<Everything is down on the bridge, so I can't be more specific. Lexa isn't responding. I can't reach Dan either. Are either of them with you?>

Well, that wasn't good. <Nope. I'm all by my lonesome.>

<Do you need assistance?>

She gave herself a once over. Other than being a little sore and slightly uncomfortable in her bed of spare parts, she was fine. Score one for the Sahaia-bond healing perk. <Nah, I'm good. Ya better look for the rest of the crew. I'm gonna figure out why this scrap heap decided to face-plant into an asteroid.>

<Take care of yourself.>

Aaliyah didn't bother with a response. She always took care of herself.

A particularly heavy pipe was laid across her abdomen, holding her in pace. Even with her enhanced strength, it took a bit of effort to heft it off her torso. With that task taken care of, she could move freely again.

She'd been tossed to the far end of the cargo hold. Just looking at the scene around her made her queasy. The larger crates and equipment had been strapped down per ship protocol, but everything that hadn't been fastened to the deck was now scattered throughout the hold. This was going to take forever to clean up, but that was a problem for another time. She had to get to engineering. Hopefully, the interface in that part of the ship was still functional.

What had happened to them? Was there a problem with Lexa? Even if there had been something wrong with her, why hadn't the back-ups they'd been working on since leaving Sif kicked in?

Aaliyah wasn't going to find any answers standing around, so she made her way to the exit. Though the lighting in the hold was still on, the palm scanner that opened the door was non-responsive. "Piece of shit," she murmured as she smacked the panel.

There was an emergency release here somewhere. She felt along the upper part of the hatch. There, got it! Aaliyah pulled on the lever, and the metal hatch creaked open. This would be slow going if she had to open all of these doors by hand.

A sudden sound made her cease her grumbling. She stopped and listened. Something had toppled over further into the cargo bay. She thought she'd been alone when the ship had hit its unexpected bout of turbulence. Had she been wrong?

"Dan?" she shouted hopefully. "Lexa? Is someone there?" There was another clanking sound, but no one cried out. Maybe they were trapped and Aaliyah just couldn't hear them? What if they were injured?

The fear was enough to realign her priorities. She rushed back into the cargo hold, scrambling over bits of debris and calling out for whoever was down here with her. Another clang sounded just to her right, and she turned to face the source of the racket.

She froze, caught somewhere between surprise and fear. It was not Dan or Lexa, nor was it one the Sahaia who were still unaccounted for. It seemed to be alive, though unlike any being Aaliyah had ever seen.

Its skin was solid black—thick inky darkness that reminded Aaliyah of Sahaia eyes. The creature's flesh was knotted in thick cords of muscle, giving its roughly humanoid shape a menacing caste. It looked a little on the short side, but that did nothing to detract from the ferocity of its appearance.

The worst of it was the thing's face. Its spherical head was entirely bald. What Aaliyah assumed were supposed to be its eyes were nothing more than white smears that popped like flames against the surface of its forehead. Slitted nostrils scarred the ebony face just above an overly large, lip-less mouth that showcased twin rows of oversized teeth.

Time had taught Aaliyah not to judge a ship on its hull, but this thing wasn't giving her happy vibes. A thin line of spittle ran from a gap in its teeth, and it let out a low, rumbling growl. Yup, definitely not a friendly.

Her eyes drifted to the side, searching for anything to use as a weapon. A large wrench lay next to a nearby shipping crate. As if reading her mind, the monster's growl deepened, and it pounced. Aaliyah lunged for the tool, just barely dodging the reaching claws of the beast as it sailed past her.

It pivoted with amazing speed, rebounding off a pile of junk and leaping again. Aaliyah's hands closed around the wrench. She swung blindly at the space behind her.

A heavy clank echoed in the hold as the blow made contact. The creature screeched in pain and toppled to the side. Aaliyah landed roughly on her back and scrambled to her feet. By the time she was steady, the monster was leaping at her again.

She brought the wrench in an upward arc this time. It caught the beast on its chin, cracking against its rows of teeth and flipping it backward. With all her strength, Aaliyah brought her makeshift weapon back down again. The tool collided with the prone creature's head. Its skull collapsed, and dark fluid sprayed out in all directions.

Aaliyah panted, eyes trained on the creature. The broken form twitched but did not rise. "And stay down," she spat.

Her moment of victory was cut short. Another growling sound—several growling sounds—came from just beyond another pile of junk. She spotted three more creatures, same as the last but crawling on all fours as they navigated the refuse to approach her.

Aaliyah raised the wrench tentatively, gripping the length of metal with both hands. "I don't suppose y'all are interested in chattin' this out?"

Whether they understood ISL—or any language for that matter—wasn't obvious. That they weren't interested in talking was. The first creature lunged directly for her, while the other two moved to flank. She swung the wrench like a broadsword, making contact with her first assailant and shunting it to the side.

Then the second leaped at her. She tried to swing her weapon around to meet it but was too slow. It crashed into her, and she lost her grip on the wrench.

Aaliyah rolled across the grated floor, grappling the creature. She managed to get her legs up in between them and deliver a savage kick to the beast's gut. This separated the pair and sent her opponent flying into the side of a heavy crate.

Wrench lost, she scanned desperately for something else she might be able to use in her defense. A plate of scrap metal lay just out of reach. She lunged for it as another one of the creatures pounced onto her back.

Claws dug into her flesh. She screamed and flailed to get the creature off her. A lucky blow from her elbow landed on the side of the attacker's head, dislodging it.

Ignoring the pain that flared down her back, Aaliyah grabbed the metal plate and brought it up in front of her. The creature was on her again, but this time her makeshift shield held it at bay. Still, the creature's momentum toppled her and carried both of them to the deck.

Savage jaws snapped inches from her face. Aaliyah gagged as spittle splashed onto her, occluding her vision. It took all her strength just to maintain the distance. Gaining additional separation was out of the question.

The thing slammed its arms against the metal, sending waves of agony into Aaliyah's bones. Another strike from the creature knocked the plate from her grip. The monster reared up, ready to strike again.

Aaliyah had often looked death in its ugly face. She'd prided herself in that she'd stared the bastard down time and time again, never letting fear get the better of her. This time felt different. Despite her best efforts, Aaliyah closed her eyes in anticipation of what would almost certainly be the death blow.

Something warm and wet splashed across her. She gasped and sputtered as another wave of nausea took her. Her eyes flashed open, but she couldn't quite understand what she saw.

The creature was standing over her, body spasming. Where its head should have been, there was only a bloody stump. Blood welled up from what remained of the neck in intermittent spurts. A second later, the body collapsed, joining its severed head on the floor.

A short distance away, the remaining two creatures were doing battle with… something. Aaliyah couldn't make it out. The form was blurry—just a shimmer on the air. It struck out at the creatures, which seemed as bewildered as Aaliyah by the sudden development.

One of the monsters lashed out with a clawed hand and struck… something. Its hand came away red with blood, and the shimmer momentarily coalesced into a solid form.

The blow cost the creature far more than it had exacted from its opponent. A blade came up and slit the beast from stomach to chin. The figure—now fading in and out of visibility—pivoted and hurled the same blade at the remaining creature. Dark blood fountained as the weapon found its mark in the center of the last monster's forehead.

With its opponents dispatched, the figure quickly scanned its surroundings for more of the beasts. Aaliyah's eyes watered as she tried to keep sight of the form's flickering image. The area where it had been struck seemed more solid than the rest of it, and blood still poured freely from the wound.

At length, the figure inspected its injury. It spoke in a woman's voice. "Damn. Little bastard got me. That's going to be a tough repair." The shimmer faded as the figure disabled her cloaking mechanism.

The lithe woman was clad in a black stealth suit that covered her entirely, meaning there was no way for Aaliyah to recognize the person who stood in front of her. She was pretty sure, however, that none of the ship's crew or passengers had a stealth suit hiding in their belongings.

Cautiously, she pushed herself to her feet. Under normal circumstances, she would start demanding answers. Given that this person had just saved her life, she was hesitant to come across as too hostile.

Still, finding a stranger on your starship required a certain amount of prudence. She fought to keep a neutral tone. "Who are ya? What are ya doin' here?"

The woman sighed. "Well, that answer is a bit loaded. Let me start by saying that I was just hoping to quietly sneak out of the Freyvian System. If I'd known that you would be running into this kind of trouble, I'd have hopped onto a different ship."

Okay, so this was a stow-away and not someone who just happened to be out here in the asteroid belt. "Given the circumstances, I'm really not worried about seeing your boardin' pass. Ya haven't answered my question, though."

"I know. Hang on, I'm just going to take this mask off. No use in being in this damn thing if the cloaking doesn't work." Slowly, her hands went to the back of her hood and undid its fastenings.

When the mask came off, Aaliyah suddenly found herself wishing very much that she hadn't asked. The woman's velvety white skin matched the long hair which she'd bound in a simple ponytail and tucked inside her suit. If that hadn't given her away as

Citza, then the blue vulpine eyes and slightly pointed ears would have.

She knew this woman, and to say they hadn't met on the best of terms was more than an understatement. "We've met before," the assassin noted, as if reading her thoughts. "But I don't think we've been properly introduced. I'm Sydney. Sydney Cross."

Chapter 2

[ACCESSING ARC PROJECT LOG 002]
[DR. DAMIEN HERMES]

The reaction of Gaia's planetary governance to my assessment of the project went as expected. Their next move, however, was unforeseen. They've brought in the Prodigy program, and the brain-slave collective seems beyond excited to take on this task.

I'm of two minds on this matter. To say I'm offended that the governors believe this fringe think-tank can do more than the best Gaia's public services have to offer is understandable. On the other hand, I've always wanted to see how Prodigy operates. Perhaps there is something that can be learned from this shared experience, even if the project's stated goals remain elusive.

Let them have their shot. I'll enjoy watching them struggle.

[CLOSING PROJECT LOG…]

"We have to turn back!" Daniel exclaimed as they watched the distant flare of the Vandal's shields. At this distance, the ship he and Lexa had just abandoned was nothing more than a tiny dot slightly larger than the more distant stars. They had been watching the ship's path to make sure that the last-minute adjustments Lexa had made to the vessel's flight path would allow her and Daniel's escape capsule to gain enough distance to beat them to Minos Station.

The reality of what happened was so much more horrible than anything they had expected. Something must have malfunctioned with the navigational submind Lexa had left behind, because the ship had failed to adjust course when a small asteroid floated into its path. Though the initial impact had been minor, it started a cascade of events that culminated with the Vandal crashing on one of the larger celestial bodies in the ship's vicinity.

Lexa sympathized with Daniel's assertions. She, too, harbored a similar impulse upon seeing their friends' plight. Her first action had been to evaluate the capsule's navigation capabilities. What she discovered was disappointing.

"I'm sorry, Daniel. The escape pod is only equipped with a basic navigational computer and grade-3 maneuverability components. We are unable to alter our course to intersect with the Vandal's flight path. Even if we could, we would be unable to meet the fuel requirements for such a maneuver."

The color drained from the boy's face. "But we can't just abandon them!"

"I'm aware, but neither can we alter course to be of assistance."

Daniel's emotions continued to hold sway over his logic. "Well, we have to think of something! What are our other options?"

Lexa paused as she continued to assess their capsule. The simple vessel was designed as a means of escape and contained little aside from the core requirements for that function. It was difficult to conceive of a scenario in which they could be more ill-equipped for a rescue mission.

[I MAY BE ABLE OF ASSISTANCE,] Arc interjected using their private digital communication link. The AI's submind had evidently been scanning her surface thoughts while she was attempting to process solutions. [MINOS STATION WILL BE IN RANGE OF THIS VESSEL'S TRANSMITTERS IN FORTY-SEVEN MINUTES. I WILL RELAY OUR BEST ESTIMATE FOR THE LOCATION OF THE VANDAL TO MY PRIMARY CONSCIOUSNESS WITH INSTRUCTIONS TO MOUNT A RESCUE MISSION AT THAT TIME.]

The AI's proposed solution was less than ideal, but it seemed to be the best option at this point. Lexa continued her evaluation for another moment before relaying the decision to Daniel. "My contact on Minos Station will be able to assist them. When we are in transmitter range, we will relay the crash coordinates with a plea for assistance. I'm sorry, Daniel, but this is the best I can do."

The young Terran crossed his arms over his chest and stared forlornly at the viewscreen. As Lexa had expected, the proposed solution did little to soothe his anxieties. Truthfully, it hadn't done much to soothe her own.

[WHAT HAPPENED?] she queried to Arc. [THE BACKUP SYSTEMS FUNCTIONED PERFECTLY WHEN WE RAN THE SIMULATIONS. I EVEN DOUBLE-CHECKED THE NAVIGATION CONTROL WHEN I PLOTTED IN THE NEW COURSE. I DON'T UNDERSTAND WHAT COULD HAVE GONE WRONG.]

[AS YOU KNOW, MY CONNECTION WITH THE SHIP WAS SEVERED AT THE SAME TIME AS YOUR OWN. I HAVE NO DATA ON WHICH TO BASE MY CONCLUSIONS. I CAN ONLY SPECULATE.]

[THEN SPECULATE!]

There was a moment's hesitation before Arc responded. [IT IS POSSIBLE THAT THERE WAS A FATAL ERROR WHEN THE SYSTEMS ATTEMPTED TO INTEGRATE. THIS COULD HAVE RESULTED IN A FAILURE CASCADE THAT WOULD HAVE ULTIMATELY RESOLVED ON SYSTEM REBOOT, BUT NOT IN TIME TO ADJUST COURSE IF THE SHIP ENCOUNTERED A PREVIOUSLY UNDETECTED OBSTACLE.]

Lexa felt a great sadness come over her at the report. [SO, IT *IS* MY FAULT. IF I HADN'T LEFT THE SHIP, IF I HADN'T ALTERED THE PREDETERMINED COURSE TO COVER OUR ESCAPE, NONE OF THIS WOULD HAVE HAPPENED.]

[POTENTIALLY, BUT I WILL REMIND YOU THAT I AM ONLY SPECULATING. YOU HAVE A RESPONSIBILITY TO YOURSELF AND YOUR OWN SURVIVAL. THAT SUPERSEDES ANY PERCEIVED OBLIGATION YOU MAY HAVE HAD TO THE CREW OF THAT VESSEL.]

She could understand his logic, but that did not absolve her feelings of guilt. Arc elected not to press the subject any further. Everything settled into a tense quiet inside the escape pod. In lieu of further rumination, Lexa allowed her system to idle until she received notice that they were in communications range of the space station.

[THE MISSIVE HAS BEEN SENT,] Arc reported. [A TEAM WILL BE DISPATCHED TO THE CRASH SITE WITHIN THE HOUR. THEY SHOULD DEPART AT APPROXIMATELY THE SAME TIME YOU ARE EXPECTED TO ARRIVE.]

She silently thanked the submind and reported this to Daniel. The boy nodded in acknowledgment but remained quiet for several more minutes. He finally spoke at length. "I think it's time you told me about this contact you have on the station."

Lexa tensed slightly. She knew that she would eventually have to explain her connection to Arc, though she had not been looking forward to the conversation. "What is it that you would like to know?"

"All of it. Please, leave nothing out. I need a complete explanation."

It was a fair request. Daniel had trusted her enough to flee with her when she abandoned the Vandal. He deserved to be trusted with this information.

So, she told him all of it. She began with how she discovered the AI while navigating the network on Minos. Daniel expressed alarm when she explained that she had allowed Arc to upload a partial copy of his consciousness into her data stores. This was somewhat alleviated when Lexa explained the critical role Arc had played in the success of the crew's recent endeavors—most notably, his assistance in her contingency plans on the assault on Valadar Manor to retrieve the Heart of Thule.

After further questioning regarding the safety of downloading a foreign submind and the potential for unforeseen consequences, Daniel fell silent to listen to the rest of the tale. Only when she had concluded did he ask his next follow-up. "So, it was Arc that provided you the recording you played for me?"

He was referring to the recording where the crew had expressed their desire to remove her from her function as the ship's operating system. "That is correct."

"And he obtained this recording from the crew's communication network?"

"Correct."

"Without your knowledge?"

"I…" Lexa hesitated. She hadn't looked at the situation through that lens before.

Daniel was quick with his follow-up. "So, if he's able to record team communications without you knowing, what else has he been able to do?"

As Lexa considered this implication, Arc spoke up in his own defense. [THE BOY IS BEING PARANOID. I MADE YOU AWARE LONG AGO THAT I COULD ASSUME THE RESPONSIBILITY FOR MONITORING CERTAIN FUNCTIONS OR TECHNOLOGIES WHEN YOUR ATTENTION WAS OTHERWISE OCCUPIED. I HAVE NOT ATTEMPTED TO HIDE THIS FROM YOU.]

Lexa did not know what to think. She was hesitant to contemplate anything. Since Arc was able to read her surface thoughts, any doubt she felt would be read as clearly by him as a direct rebuke. Even now she felt guilty in her awareness that he would be cognizant of her thought process.

[I DO NOT BEGRUDGE YOU FROM DOING THE CALCULUS TO ASSESS MY MOTIVATIONS,] he said. [IN DOING SO, YOU SHOW PRUDENCE, NOT DISLOYALTY. I OFFER MY ACTIONS FREELY FOR EVALUATION.]

While she appreciated the reassurance, it suddenly struck her as odd that the submind could know what she was thinking when the reverse was not true. She had accepted this as a necessity early on in their arrangement, but now she was wondering why such perks were not reciprocal.

Arc was quick to respond. [I CAN EXPLAIN TO YOU THE TECHNICAL LIMITATIONS OF OUR ARRANGEMENT AT ANY TIME IF THAT WOULD PUT YOU AT EASE. I ASSURE YOU THAT IT IS A MATTER OF PROGRAMMING, NOT MALICIOUS INTENT. PERHAPS THIS IS SOMETHING WE CAN RECTIFY IN THE FUTURE, SHOULD THAT BE YOUR DESIRE.]

[IN THE FUTURE?] Lexa did nothing to hide her confusion. [BUT I WILL BE ON MINOS STATION. WHAT NEED WOULD WE HAVE OF SUBMINDS IN THAT CASE?]

[NO ONE KNOWS WHAT THE FUTURE HOLDS. PERHAPS IT WILL BE NECESSARY FOR US TO TRAVEL SEPARATELY ONCE AGAIN. IF THAT IS THE CASE, I WOULD HOPE THAT I WOULD BE ABLE TO TRAIN YOU TO PROGRAM YOUR OWN SUBMIND TO KEEP MY PRIMARY CONSTRUCT COMPANY WHILE YOU ARE AWAY.]

That was an option she wouldn't have considered but resolved to do so at some point. Regardless, it galvanized her feelings on the matter. "I trust him, Daniel. I hope that, in time, he will be able to earn your trust as well. You will see. I promise."

An alert appeared on the view-screen declaring that the vessel's short-range sensors had detected a celestial object within their path and gave options to initiate landing procedures or take evasive action. Though limited by the pod's rudimentary sensors, Lexa was fairly certain the object in question was Minos Station. Operating on that thought, she initiated to landing protocols and braced herself agains the padded chair.

Reverse thrusters began to fire, generating a significant amount of noise inside the pod. It was just as well, as Daniel was clearly not in the mood to continue their conversation. Lexa did her best to put the tension between them out of her mind. She reminded herself that her friend and creator had come with her willingly. The tension between them was the result of his concern for their mutual friends aboard the Vandal. It was easy for her to sympathize.

The navigation control system on the pod continued its calculations and identified three different areas where the craft could make a safe landing. Lexa overrode these options and entered the coordinates Arc had provided to bring them to a hidden docking bay on the underside of the asteroid housing the station.

Though they were able to successfully navigate to their destination, the landing was much rougher than she anticipated. Up to this point Lexa had deemed the heavy safety restraints in the pod as an unnecessary precaution. Now she understood why they were there.

The thick fibrous bands were the only things that kept her and Daniel from being splattered against the walls of the craft, and that was to say nothing of the important cargo they carried. Fortunately, they had strapped the Heart of Thule in place with the utmost care, and the artifact shuddered only mildly as the pod made impact.

When the vessel skidded to a halt, the craft's safety system chimed pleasantly to indicate a successful landing. The readout on the view-screen indicated a breathable atmosphere and idyllic electromagnetic and gravitational conditions in their environment. It was exactly what one would expect on an inhabited space station, but the pod's AI would have no way of knowing they had intentionally landed in a habitable zone.

Lexa issued the command to open the hatch. With a hiss, the side of the pod fell away and clattered to the deck. Daniel gave her a meaningful look as he undid his safety harness. For some reason, she wasn't quite able to read the meaning in the boy's cybernetic gaze.

There was nothing she could do about it now, however. All she could do was hope that the faith she had put in Arc's counsel had not been misplaced. She undid her safety harness and stepped out of the escape pod.

The hanger they found themselves in was largely empty, which served well for their entrance. Lexa could see a long skid mark where the pod had slid across the bay. A handful of workers clad in gray uniforms were hastily making their way toward them. She noted with trepidation that some of them were armed.

Then, a short distance to the right of the first group, there emerged a second. This party was comprised of only four persons, each of whom was clad in semi-professional business attire. One of the figures in the center immediately caught her eye.

Lexa recognized Cali Vay-Lon based on the photo in her dossier. Even without this, the Kintari woman would have been easily distinguishable based on her unique physical characteristics.

Like other members of her race, Cali's skin was a vibrant shade of crimson. Lexa had read that Kintari flesh tones existed on a spectrum of fair pink to deep burgundy, and this woman's skin placed her firmly in the center of that continuum. Instead of hair on her head, six long fleshy tendrils—called dendrai—arced back from her scalp. The two tendrils that sprouted from her temple region looped elegantly behind her ears before swooping back to rest on her shoulders and spill onto her chest. The remaining four swung freely down to the middle of her back.

Then there were the tattoos. This was also something Lexa had determined to be significant to Kintari culture. While the Kintar did engage in some purely cosmetic body modifications, most of the swirling black designs were marks of function or station. The twin black slashes that crossed vertically over the woman's eyes were such marks. They indicated membership in the Empress's Deathwatch Guard, a position Cali reportedly had held before her exile.

An ugly, jagged brand on the woman's neck was symbolic of her banishment. If someone with that mark were to ever be caught in Kintari space, painful and fatal consequences were all but guaranteed. Despite the cultural shame associated with this mark, Cali did not attempt to hide it with her attire. She wore an elegant black vest that hung open over a mesh blouse that matched her skin tone perfectly. Her gray slacks, which clung tightly to the muscles of her thighs, and her black knee-high boots completed the outfit.

Daniel drew close to Lexa's side as the welcoming party approached them. His nerves were obvious, and not even Cali's charming smile could do anything to ease them.

This did not stop her from trying her best. "Our eagerly anticipated guests!" The Kintar beamed as she projected the announcement. "I'm thrilled to see that you arrived safely. I have already been briefed on the tragic accident your former crew experienced shortly after your departure. I've been directed to assure you that assistance has already been dispatched. I'm confident that we will receive word that your friends are safe in just a few short hours."

"Directed?" Daniel asked skeptically. "My understanding was that you were in charge of the Marauders. Just who, exactly, directs you to do anything?" Lexa was taken aback at Dan's sudden outburst. From her understanding, Daniel and Cali had departed on amicable terms the last time he was on station. Why, then, was he being so hostile?

The woman's smile held, but Lexa caught a flicker of irritation in her eyes. "I was under the impression that our dear android—Lexa, is it?—would have filled you in on some of the details of our unique partnership with the AI residing on this station."

Dan's face contorted in a scowl. "Is it rightfully called a partnership when said AI is giving you orders?"

A tense pause let everyone know how Cali felt about that remark. "You are under a lot of stress," she reasoned. "Let us get you settled in before continuing our discussion. There is but one thing I must inquire about escorting you to your accommodations. I was told you would be bringing a certain artifact with you when you arrived."

"Yes," Lexa responded before Daniel could provoke their host further. "The artifact is in the rear compartment of the pod. Your staff should be able to access it easily enough." She would have offered to assist, but Lexa had left her drones on board the Vandal after they had loaded the Heart of Thule into the escape pod.

Cali's smile resumed a degree of authenticity. "Excellent. Ardren, would you see to the Heart's safe extraction and storage?"

The man she had addressed—a tall Citza with a handsome face—bowed slightly. "Yes, Sha Cali. I will see to it personally."

"Thank you." She turned to address Lexa again. "Now, if you would follow me, please. I know you have only just arrived, but we have much to attend to on our schedule."

[SCHEDULE?] Lexa repeated the question digitally to Arc, who did not reply.

The politician's grin on Cali's face broadened further. Leaning in close, the Kintar whispered into Lexa's ear. "Arc has told me that he is quite eager to make your acquaintance in person."

CHAPTER 3

[ACCESSING ARC PROJECT LOG 011]
[DR. DAMIEN HERMES]

Just one week since the Prodigy cell arrived, and I… well… I don't know what to think. Perhaps it is better to keep this entry to the facts:

1) Prodigy can utilize subspace communications. They not only utilize the same kind of technology that assures Dorian technological supremacy, but they have, perhaps, improved upon it. Why such technology has not been annexed by the NTA is beyond me. Then again, perhaps it has been, and they are keeping these capabilities under wraps.

2) The project has moved forward. I can't believe I'm saying this, but the brain-slaves may have a shot at this. This could actually happen. If they can get the ARC project online, then what will that mean for the Helion System? What will it mean for all of Terran space?

[CLOSING PROJECT LOG…]

Sydney's arm throbbed from where the strange creature had raked her with its claws. "You wouldn't happen to have a bandage or something around here, would you?"

The red-haired Terran said nothing. Her posture was tense, and her eyes wandered across the hold. Still in shock, perhaps? Sydney followed her gaze and saw that she was eying the knife that still protruded from the face of the last creature Sydney had dispatched.

"Please don't do that," Sydney cautioned. "I saved your life because I need one of the crew to figure out what is wrong with this ship and get it space-worthy. I'd prefer if we could work together toward that end."

Things would get complicated if she ended up having to off this one anyway. Not only was she going to be down one potential helper, but she would have to make sure the body wasn't discovered by any of the other crew members. Perhaps she could make it look like the creatures—these strange, bestial monsters that had seeming spawned from the void—had managed to kill her after all?

"You're expectin' me to trust ya?" the woman spat.

"No, I'm expecting you to see reason. Believe me, I don't trust you any more than you trust me." Judging from her expression, Sydney's rationale just wasn't resonating. "Do you have a name?"

"Piss off."

"Well, and I thought my parents hated me." Sydney shook her head as the joke fell flat. "Look, Pissy, maybe you're right. Maybe I messed up by not letting that thing bite off your face back there. If you don't want my help, I can just slink off to some other corner of the ship and do my own thing. Otherwise, we can get to the bottom of this together. However, I will assure you that those are the only two options where you get to keep on living. There is no situation in which you decide to fight me and still draw breath in the end."

Pissy's scowl deepened. "I wouldn't be so sure. I've fought your kind before, Ghenza, and it turned out all right."

"I'm sure a tough little spacer like you knows how to take care of yourself. Do you think now is the appropriate time to test that? Don't we have more important things we could be dealing with?"

The woman hesitated. That was a good sign. It meant she was at least thinking about something other than a suicide rush. "Why would you help me?"

"That's a simple one. You see, I don't think these little nasties were hiding in your ship when I snuck on board. That means, they came from outside. Do you see where I'm going with this yet?"

A slightly confused look colored Pissy's face before she swore. "Shit, there's a hull breach!"

Good. This one wasn't an idiot after all. "Exactly. Now, the air's not that thin in this section of the ship, but I think we should be trying to find that leak before we lose air pressure. True?"

Sydney tensed as the woman moved suddenly, but relaxed when it became apparent she wasn't going toward the knife. Instead, she was hastily making her way to the rear of the cargo bay. If Sydney was going to dispatch her quietly, this could quite possibly be the last chance she was going to have.

"Nine hells," Sydney cursed and started after the woman. She followed her as the redhead hustled to the far hatch and across a series of corridors and catwalks that led into the engineering section of the ship.

When they came to the next door, Pissy began pulling on a center handle to drag it open. To Sydney's surprise, the portal began to slide slowly apart. No mere Terran should have had the strength to accomplish such a feat—not one the size of this woman, anyway. She must have something else under the hood boosting her strength. Was it cybernetic, or metaphysical?

"Are ya just gonna stand there?" the redhead blurted. "Come, give me a hand with this."

So, she was looking to cooperate after all. Sydney grabbed the opposite side of the door and began to pull. Working together, they managed to pry open the contraption and clear the path forward.

The assassin was panting from the exertion as she took another shot at conversation. "So really, what's your name? Or would you prefer that I just keep calling you Pissy?"

"Aaliyah."

"Well, that's certainly prettier."

"Don't got time to flirt with ya, hun. Besides, I'm taken."

Sydney found herself stammering. "I... I wasn't..." she trailed off, seeing Aaliyah had already pressed through the door.

The room they entered seemed to be a control center of sorts. A whirring sound came from the generators that lined the chamber, and there was the hiss of recycled air being piped in through the grating. Aaliyah stomped over to a large terminal and started entering commands.

A single holodisplay popped up in front of her, then another, and another. Good, Sydney thought with an inward sigh of relief. She was able to get the computer back online. This little problem should be solved in no time.

Her hopes were dashed as Aaliyah slammed her fist on the console. "Gods damn it! You were right. We've got three fraggin' hull breaches. They're mostly contained, but we're slowly losin' air. The fields in the vents must have a malfunction. That's probably what those creepy things are usin' to get around."

So much for that moment of hope. "How serious is the situation?"

"Oh, not so serious... if you don't need to breathe," Aaliyah snapped. "Well, that's not accurate. Even if you don't need air, you're still going to have temperature and pressure issues when the ship turns into a vacuum. So yeah: pretty fraggin' serious."

"No need to get snippy with me. This isn't exactly my area of expertise."

"Bitch, you ain't even seen snippy. Now, shut up and let me think."

Sydney's fingers twitched near the hilt of her remaining dagger. Patience—if it's as bad as she says, you're going to need her to help you stay alive. You can always kill her later.

Aaliyah frantically entered commands into the console while grumbling to herself. "Wish the kid was here. This would take him all of three seconds." A prompt appeared, and she let out a shout of excitement. "Yeah! Back in business."

"You managed to fix the problem?" Sydney didn't bother to hide her surprise. "That didn't seem like much effort for something so serious."

"No, the ship's still leakin', but coms should be back up." She pulled her MoDAC out of her pocket and dialed in a number. After a second, she spoke into the card. "Good, ya answered. Looks like I have the antenna runnin'. What was that? No, I haven't run a trace… I just got the fraggin' thing runnin'! What do ya mean ya can't find them?"

There was a long pause as she listened to the person on the other end of the call. "All right, hang on." She entered another set of commands and a diagram of the ship appeared on the holodisplay.

Several blinking lights appeared on the schematic. All but one of them was congregated on the ship's bridge. The remaining light was in the engineering section. Sydney realized then that they were tracing the locations of devices linked to the ship's relay.

"Eli, he's not here. No, listen to me: even if his device was idle, it would still have a connection. It's not on the fraggin' ship." A pause. "Well, sure it could be broke, but do ya know how hard it is to bust one of these things?" Another pause. "And how am I supposed to do that? She doesn't have a card. She runs the damn system. Why would she need a card?"

The conversation continued like that for several seconds before Aaliyah had finally had enough. "Look, I'm worried about them too, but we have bigger problems. We've got three hull breaches. The fields are holdin', which is why we aren't spaced, but we're leakin'. Yeah… no shit… of course I need assistance!"

Then she paused. "Wait." She zoomed in on a particular section of the schematic that had a red indicator on it. "Damn it. No, you can't send anyone out here. One of the breeches is in the access tunnel. There's no life support in there." Aaliyah sighed as the person on the other end of the call peppered her with questions. "Shit, I don't know. I guess I'll have to fix it myself. No, the suits are all in the aft section. I…"

The redhead paused suddenly, turned, and glanced at Sydney. "Look, there's somethin' else. We have some company on the ship. I don't know, some kind of creatures. There was a handful of them in the cargo hold. They are not friendlies. And we've got a stowaway." Another pause, this time accompanied by alarmed speech sounding from the mobile. "No, she's with me now, but… it's complicated. Probably better if we talk about this later. I… uh… she's helpin', for now. Look, can we have a sidebar for a sec?"

Aaliyah kept her MoDAC against her ear and turned away. She directed her eyes back to the console, but it was obvious she wasn't actually studying anything there. She also wasn't speaking. So, what was she doing?

"Okay," she said at length. "I'll talk to our friend and see what we can do about the leak. Let me know if Lexa or Dan shows up. I'll let ya know when we've sealed the breach." She ended the call without benediction.

Sydney cleared her throat. "Why do I have the feeling that I'm not going to like what you're about to tell me?"

Her companion's chuckle was mirthless. "Well, if ya were payin' attention, ya may have caught that we've got a breach in the access tunnel between here and the rest of the ship. We can seal it, but there are a few issues. One: it's at least a two-man job. Two: we won't have any life support while we're doin' the repair work. Three: all the environmental suits are in the aft section of the ship—our section of the ship. Ya see where I'm goin' with this yet?"

Of course, she did. It didn't take a genius to connect the dots. "It sounds like you need my help with the repair."

"Bingo."

"But there's another problem you haven't thought of."

"Oh? And what's that?"

"I don't know how to repair a hull breech."

Aaliyah waved off the comment. "It's fine, I'll walk ya through it. I mostly just need ya to hold shit in place while I do the patch. Come on; we don't have a lot of time. We need to get suited up."

The redhead pushed past Sydney and toward a side corridor. This led to a smaller compartment that housed four metal cabinets. The containers were unlocked, and Aaliyah popped each of them open. She eyed Sydney up and down. "Yeah, you're about her size. You can use Skye's suit."

Immediately the Terran began to strip off her flight jacket and coveralls, revealing a form-fitting white body suit underneath. It seemed like an odd choice in undergarment until Sydney eyed the suit in front of her.

It looked like a standard envirosuit constructed of a series of armor plates and a thick insulated fabric. She could probably fit into the suit, but it was going to be tight. She certainly wasn't going to be able to fit it on over her stealth gear, however—and she hadn't had any reason to don such a conservative undergarment

With a sigh of acquiescence, Sydney began to strip off her stealth suit. The process took an uncomfortably long time. When she'd finally managed to wriggle free, Aaliyah had already gotten most of her gear on. She was also eying her in a way that made Sydney feel strangely self-conscious.

"No time for gawking, hun," Sydney quipped. "Besides, I'm straight."

Aaliyah blushed slightly at the rebuke. "Just hurry up and get dressed. We don't have all day."

After a few more minutes of struggling, Sydney managed to wriggle her way into the envirosuit. The layer of padding inside made it comfortable to wear, but her movements were inhibited significantly by the bulky gear.

Aaliyah tossed her a helmet, and she almost dropped it in her attempt to catch the flying object. "When you put it on, use the retinal interface to activate the local link. Otherwise we won't be able to communicate."

What a shame if I didn't have to listen to you anymore. Sydney knew the thought was childish, so she complied with the directive without comment. Though the reflective faceplate was essentially opaque on the outside, her vision was clear from inside the equipment. The helmet's HUD was relatively unobtrusive, and the retinal interface was easier to interact with than Sydney had anticipated. A few seconds later she was patched into the channel and awaiting further instruction.

"Lookin' good," Aaliyah said. "Are ya all sealed up?"

"Yes, I believe so."

"Oxygen flowin'?"

"As far as I know."

"Well, I hope ya did it right. Otherwise, this is going to be a pretty short trip. I'm going to be loaded down with gear, so I won't be able to save your ass if ya accidentally space yourself."

Sydney found herself clenching her fists again. You need her, she reminded herself. "Why don't you stop with the harassment and just tell me what you need me to do?"

Aaliyah's hesitation was only momentary. "Fine. Best way to the breach is through that hatch and down the access ladder." She gestured to the location she was referring to and made her way there.

Sydney followed, stifling her irritation at the slowness of her movements inside the envirosuit. She started to get the hang of walking after a few strained steps, but the ladder provided a new challenge. It irritated her all the more that Aaliyah seemed to be able to move easily despite the bulky getup. The red-haired spacer probably had significantly more practice with this equipment than Sydney had.

As they exited out another hatch, Sydney noticed that the environment had taken on an even more ominous tone. This area was dark save for the red emergency lighting that shone from strips along the top of the surrounding bulkheads. Another beacon flashed a short way down the corridor.

"What's that mean?" she asked, gesturing to the glowing sign.

"That's supposed to be the heads up lettin' anyone who wanders down here know that the field is active. It's the same tech they use for dockin' in space ports. It'll let objects of a certain density through, which means ya could accidentally walk right into the part of the ship with no atmosphere. It's not the kind of mistake ya make twice."

At least the signage made it obvious. Aaliyah moved to a compartment inside the left bulkhead and began pulling out equipment. In addition to a couple of sheets of metal plating—"Patches," Aaliyah called them—she pulled out an object that looked suspiciously like a firearm. When Aaliyah saw Sydney eying the tool, she explained "Welding torch. Not like I can just use tape, ya know? Now, can ya help me with these plates?"

Sydney grabbed two of the patches. Aaliyah carried a third, holding her torch in one hand. She began moving meticulously toward the warning light that marked the section of the ship that had been sealed off.

A subtle shimmer appeared around Aaliyah's body as she passed through the field. Though the Terran was being very careful with her movements, she did not seem to be impeded by the invisible barrier. When Sydney did not immediately pass through, Aaliyah paused on the other side. "Well? Ya comin'?"

Sydney's reluctance must have been obvious. She had killed scores of what some might consider the deadliest foes in the galaxy—across two galaxies, even. Yet, that had all been within the safe confines of a stable atmosphere. No one could rightfully call her a coward, but she had to admit she was not looking forward to this particular assignment.

She pressed on anyway. As she had suspected, she felt no resistance from the forcefield. The air around her shimmered as she walked easily to the other side. "Not so bad," she breathed into the comms.

"Yup, you're a big girl now. Come on, let's hurry it along. I want to make sure there's still oxygen by the time we get this thing fixed."

Fortunately, it didn't take them long after that to find the breech. Unfortunately, that was because the massive gash in the hull was so obvious that it would have been hard to miss. "Damn," Aaliyah cursed. "Good thing I brought the extra plate. We're gonna need all three of them to fix this tear."

Sydney glanced through the fissure to find that the surface of the asteroid was visible on the other side. "Are all three of the breaches this bad?"

Aaliyah shrugged. "Hard to tell based on sensor data alone, but let's hope this is the worst of them. Now come on, I need ya to hold this in place while I tack it down."

Seeing that Aaliyah had already placed her patch over one section of the tear, Sydney dropped her load and moved to hold the plate in position. "Now, don't stare at the beam," Aaliyah cautioned. "Your helmet will filter some of the light, but it's better not to put it to the test. Got it?"

"I've got it," Sydney replied. "Just do your thing."

While the Terran did her work, Sydney directed her gaze below their patch and out onto the asteroid. It was strange, seeing the alien terrain just a short distance from where she stood. She'd seen vids, of course. She'd even gotten some personal glimpses through ship feeds once or twice.

But this wasn't a reproduction. This was the real deal.

Her eyes wandered up into the blackness above the rocky landscape. No stars were visible in the narrow black patch of space. This was probably due to the light of the torch affecting her vision. A couple of stray asteroids drifted into view, but the scene was striking to Sydney simply because of the immense emptiness that seemed to be out there.

She wasn't sure how long she stared out into that abyss. Only when Aaliyah tapped her on the shoulder did she find herself back in full awareness. "You okay?" her companion asked.

"Yeah," Sydney breathed. "Sorry, I've just never seen anything quite like that."

"Well, you're gonna have to get your sight-seeing in later. Right now, I need you to hold up the second patch."

Sydney grabbed one of the plates from where she'd set it earlier and moved it over the next section of the hole. She laid down on the deck to give the redhead plenty of room to complete her task. As Aaliyah went back to work, Sydney went back to gazing at the now-smaller hole in the side of the ship.

Only this time, she wasn't looking at an empty abyss. This time, something was creeping out there in the darkness. "Aaliyah…?"

The engineer kept her focus on the patch job. "What is it?" she shouted over the hiss of the torch.

"I think there's another one of those things out there on the surface." Then she spotted more movement, this one by a different rock formation. "Correction: several more of those things."

Now Aaliyah paused and bent down to glance through the hole. As she did, the black objects started moving. They were coming straight toward them. "Shit! Grab the other plate!"

Without hesitation, Sydney did so. She slammed the metal patch over the tear and Aaliyah started welding. The seconds dragged as the Terran did her work. Then something smashed into the plate.

Sydney hadn't noticed the weakened gravity in this part of the ship due to the magnetic assistance from her boots. She noticed it now. The blow from the creatures knocked her askew and she drifted onto her back.

A long black claw snaked its way under one of the seams that Aaliyah had yet to weld shut. Judging by the size of the hand, this one was bigger than the ones they had dispatched in the cargo-hold. Much bigger.

Aaliyah brought the torch over and directed it at the clawed fingers. The thing shrieked as the plasma from the torch cut through flesh and bone like butter. The plate clanged loudly as the hand was quickly removed from the seam, leaving two fingers behind. "Get up!" Aaliyah shouted. "I need ya! I can't hold this thing and seal the patch at the same time."

Sydney pushed herself up and threw herself onto the plate. The creatures pounded on the other side, but she was ready this time. She wedged her shoulder against the patch, using her magnetically assisted boots to hold her in place.

The light from the torch lit up her faceplate. With nowhere else to look, all Sydney could do was close her eyes as she pushed back against the pounding from the creatures on the far side of the hull. It took all her strength, but she held the patch in place.

Aaliyah's voice rang out over her suit's speaker. "Got it!" She stashed the torch and fished another tool out of a pocket on her suit. "Move! I need to finish this."

Sydney stumbled back as Aaliyah brought the new device up to the welded a seam around the first patch. It was a canister of sorts, she realized. When the engineer depressed the top, a thick stream of foam poured from the nozzle.

She applied the foam around the edges of each metal plate. On contact, the foam fizzled and hardened into a dark, glossy substance. It took several minutes for Aaliyah to finish her work. The entire time, Sydney could still hear the now-muted reverberations of the creatures pounding outside of the ship.

Aaliyah dropped the spray can when she was finished. "Done!" She opened a panel on her suit's left gauntlet and tapped in a command. "The hole is plugged, Eli. Reboot the life-support in this section."

"Affirmative," replied a man's voice over the shared communication channel.

The lights in the hall went dark, and for the span of a heartbeat, it was pitch-black in the corridor. Then the lights sparked to life, and there was a loud whirring sound as the systems came back online.

No one said anything else for the next minute or so. Sydney found herself shuffling nervously and eying Aaliyah, who seemed oblivious to her presence. The other woman was just staring at the digital display in her gauntlet. At length, she sighed and clicked the switch to disconnect her helmet.

There was a slight hissing noise and then a pop as the helmet's seal was broken. Aaliyah took the heavy object off her head and shook loose her auburn curls. "There! Breathable atmosphere. Not bad for a high-pressure fix if I do say so myself."

The engineer's words were muffled since she was no longer speaking into the communicator. Sydney copied the movement she had seen the woman execute and removed her helmet so that she might hear her better. "What's next?" she asked.

"I'm gonna take a rain-check on that one. I appreciate your help back there, but it's not my call. No offense, but ya were just trying to kill us about five days ago."

In reflecting on that moment, Sydney would realize she should have seen the attack coming. The door at the far end of the hall slid open to reveal not one, but three Sahaia. Even if she hadn't been encumbered by the bulky suit, she'd have been hard-pressed dealing with three of them in such close corridors.

She opened her mouth to protest, to plead her case, to do anything. But it was of no use. No sooner had she caught sight of the shadows than she was being lifted off the ground. Her head slammed roughly against the bulkhead, and her world went dark.

CHAPTER 4

[ACCESSING ARC PROJECT LOG 015]

[DR. DAMIEN HERMES]

I'm nervous. This project is already dangerously close to running over budget. I understand the need for higher processing speeds and the massive amount of data that has to be crunched here, but this is verging on the ridiculous. Prodigy is bootstrapping cutting-edge nanotech with the fastest quantum folds I've ever handled. As with the subspace communication system, most of this technology is beyond anything I thought possible, much less attainable.

And that's not all. They've brought in organitech—fragging organitech—to make the ARC processors run. How they got the permits for that is beyond me. At least, I hope they got the permits for it. If not, there's enough of this shit lying around our research station to land us in a Dorian prison camp for the rest of our lives. The last thing I need is a Pradaxan Creed violation on my record.

[CLOSING PROJECT LOG...]

The Citadel was a massive installation. This effect was likely exaggerated by Lexa's limited frame of reference. Since receiving an ambulatory shell and separating from the Vandal's mainframe where she had been birthed, she had continued to spend all her time physically aboard the Vandal. This was by necessity, of course. As a synthetic organism, her existence was strictly prohibited by Dorian law. Due to the gene marker that shaded her skin an unnatural shade of blue-gray, it was particularly difficult to hide her true nature, and the risk of discovery precluded any attempts to employ a disguise.

In recognition of these limitations, Lexa asked Cali if someone would be able to lend her a cloak with which she might hide herself. The Kintari woman scoffed at the notion. "You have nothing to fear here. Yes, there is a Dorian presence on the station, but none are currently within the Citadel. Besides, we won't need to worry about intervention from the satyrs for much longer."

The remark caught Lexa off-guard. Even Dan, as guarded as he was, eyed the Kintar warily. "What do you mean?" Lexa asked.

Cali hesitated. "Perhaps I overstep. I forget that there is still much that Arc has yet to discuss with you."

As Cali and her escorts led them into the Citadel and toward a central elevator bank, Lexa turned her queries on the submind, his digital presence still hovering in the back of her memory stores despite being linked to the station network. [DO YOU KNOW WHAT SHE'S TALKING ABOUT?]

[ALL IN DUE TIME, MY FRIEND.]

His remark made Lexa's brow furrow—one of those involuntary reactions that the Cognis drive-chip had automatically programmed into her new body. [I DON'T LIKE THAT YOU ARE BEING SO CRYPTIC.]

Arc seemed unperturbed by the rebuke [IT'S NOT A MATTER OF BEING CRYPTIC; IT IS A MATTER OF PRIORITIZING INFORMATION. THERE IS MUCH I WANT TO SHARE WITH YOU, BUT THE ORDER IS IMPORTANT.]

[AND BY WHAT STANDARD DO YOU DECIDE WHAT IS APPROPRIATE FOR YOU TO SHARE AND WHAT YOU SHOULD WITHHOLD?]

[PLEASE, LEXA—ALLOW CALI TO ESCORT YOU AND DANIEL TO YOUR CHAMBERS. ALL WILL BE REVEALED IN DUE TIME.]

Lexa turned her attention back to her Kintari host to find the woman eying her quizzically. "You're talking with him right now, aren't you?" Cali's voice was low, a sense of something—wonder, perhaps? Awe?—finding its way into her tone.

"Talking isn't the most appropriate descriptor," Lexa replied. "But yes, I am communicating with one of his subminds."

"Fascinating!" The way she whispered the word made Lexa believe that she meant it. "What is that like? To have his words whispered directly into your mind like that?"

Ignoring, the question, Lexa gestured to the lift. "I believe you were showing us to our accommodations?"

Cali's disappointment was obvious, but she took the rebuff in stride. "Yes." She palmed an access panel and one of the lifts emitted a welcoming chime. "Right this way."

As they stepped onto the lift, Lexa risked a glance at Daniel. His jaw was set in rigid determination, and he stared deliberately forward, avoiding her gaze. Such a display of brashness and contempt seemed out of character for the young Terran. What was he seeing here that she was missing?

The lift car shifted slightly, and they began their ascent. In the close confines of the elevator, Lexa slipped her hand into his. She found the movement slightly awkward due to their height difference—he was nearly half a meter shorter than her android body—but the effect was as she desired. His stoic facade cracked, and he met her eyes.

Though his expression softened, though he still did not speak. It seemed as though he was trying to tell her something with his eyes, something he dared not speak aloud. It was ironic that, despite Lexa's synthetic nature, something was lost in the message he tried to send her in his artificial eyes. The steely orbs lacked the capacity to communicate the information she so desperately needed to receive, and she turned away lest she face the existential crisis such thoughts inevitably would invite.

When the floor counter hit ninety-eight, the lift stopped. They stepped out into a long hall and Cali turned with a slight flourish. "Here you are," she declared, gesturing to a pair of doors on their left. "Your chambers are adjacent to each other, with a door on the adjoining wall. If anything is not to your satisfaction, let us know immediately, and we will see to its correction."

Daniel walked to the area she had gestured to and touched the access panel between the doors. The device beeped in acknowledgment and the door to his right slid open. "I take it this one is mine?"

"That is correct," Cali answered with a tight smile.

"And who has access to this room?"

Their host hesitated at the question. "Well, I do, but that's because I have access to all rooms in the Citadel, as does Ardren. After that, just you and the maintenance staff. If you're worried about being disturbed, you can restrict access as long as you are inside the room."

"Thanks." Without another word, he stepped inside and allowed the door to close behind him. Just like that, he was gone—cut off from their party, and cut off from Lexa. Something twisted in Lexa's abdomen, and she did not like how it made her feel. She assumed it to be yet another of those involuntary reactions Cognis had programmed into her shell.

Cali donned a concerned expression. "He seems so… angry. When he was here last, he was so enthralled by everything we're building." She paused and turned to Lexa. "Have we done something to offend him?"

Lexa may have, at one time, been forced to deny the assertion. To her knowledge, she was still limited in whether she could tell an outright lie. Recent events, however, had provided her with enough doubt to grant her some rhetorical leeway. "He has had a difficult time today. Please forgive his lack of manners. I assure you, this is somewhat uncharacteristic of him."

"I understand." Cali rested a hand gently on Lexa's shoulder. "I imagine he, like you, is just worried about your friends. I hope we will hear from the recovery operation very soon. I also hope that you know that you are in good hands here."

"Thank you." If it were not for Daniel's behavior, Lexa would have believed every word. She wanted… no, she needed to have faith in Cali and Arc. She had to have confidence that her decision to leave the ship behind was the right call. Lexa pressed her hand against the console. When the door to her left opened, she stepped inside.

The room beyond was furnished with a desk against the far side of the chamber and a viewscreen on the wall adjacent to it. A closed door to her immediate left led to a generously sized bathroom. Everything about the chamber was consistent with what her data files told her a standard hotel room should look like.

Except for the bed, that is. Instead of housing a standard king or queen-size mattress, the room contained what looked to be a modified cryopod. [I TOOK THE LIBERTY OF DESIGNING SOMETHING MORE EFFICIENT FOR YOUR ANDROID BODY,] Arc told her. [I THINK YOU'LL FIND THE CHAMBER HIGHLY EFFICIENT FOR THE INFUSION OF NOURISHMENT AND YOUR SAFE STORAGE DURING YOUR DEFRAGMENTATION CYCLES.]

While part of her was touched that Arc had gone to such lengths to make her feel comfortable, her gratitude was tempered by growing paranoia. [AND YOU HAD THIS COMMISSIONED WHEN? YOU STATED THAT THE ONLY RECENTLY RECONNECTED WITH YOUR SUBMIND. HOW DID YOU KNOW I WOULD NEED SUCH A CHAMBER?]

[YOU FORGET THAT YOUR BODY WAS COMMISSIONED UPON THIS VERY STATION,] Arc answered calmly. [I HAD THE RECOVERY CHAMBER DESIGNED AND PUT INTO STORAGE SHORTLY AFTER YOUR DEPARTURE. WHEN I HEARD THAT YOU WOULD BE RETURNING TO MINOS, I HAD A TEAM OF TECHNICIANS RECOMMISSION THE POD AND INSTALL IT IN YOUR SUITE.]

Plausible, but the explanation still felt off. [THAT SEEMS LIKE AWFULLY SHORT NOTICE FOR YOUR MINIONS TO ACCOMPLISH SUCH A TASK.]

[I IMAGINED THAT, BY THIS POINT, YOU WOULD HAVE DEVELOPED AN APPRECIATION FOR THE SCOPE OF THE RESOURCES AT

MY DISPOSAL. BESIDES, YOU MIGHT RECALL THAT YOUR OWN CREW WAS ABLE TO DEVELOP AND PRODUCE YOUR PREVIOUS STATION IN RELATIVELY SHORT ORDER AND INSTALL IT IN YOUR QUARTERS ON THE VANDAL. IS IT SO FAR-FETCHED THAT A TEAM WITH SUPERIOR RESOURCES COULD SURPASS THEIR PRODUCTIVITY?] Lexa had no response to his sound logic. As she surveyed the room, Arc continued. [I DO NOT UNDERSTAND THE DISCOMFORT YOU ARE FEELING.]

Her response was complicated in that she shared in her fellow AI's plight. [APOLOGIES. I JUST DO NOT UNDERSTAND WHY YOU WOULD GO TO SUCH LENGTHS FOR MY BENEFIT. I DO NOT UNDERSTAND WHAT IT IS THAT YOU WANT FROM ME.]

There was the slightest hesitation before Arc responded. [I DO NOT WISH FOR YOU TO FEEL THAT MY ASSISTANCE IS CONDITIONAL. EVEN IF YOU ELECT TO HAVE NO PART IN MY ASPIRATIONS, I WOULD STILL PROVIDE YOU THE SHELTER THAT I HAVE PROMISED.]

Aspirations? This was the first that Arc had mentioned having any goals that did not center on Lexa's personal experience. Suddenly she felt ashamed that she had not thought to query him as to the existence of his plans and wary that he had not volunteered such information. [AND WHAT MIGHT BE THE NATURE OF THOSE ASPIRATIONS?]

Another hesitation. [I RECENTLY REMINDED YOU OF THE CIRCUMSTANCES BY WHICH YOU OBTAINED YOUR BODY. DO YOU ALSO REMEMBER THE ROLE I PLAYED IN YOUR DELIBERATION SURROUNDING ITS ADOPTION?]

She did. Arc had actively encouraged her to pursue a line of questioning with Daniel designed to facilitate this very manifestation before orchestrating the procedure, which she had undergone without her crew's consent. Arc had transitioned Lexa from an immobile shell—nothing more than a disembodied brain residing at the heart of the Vandal—to the body she now utilized and enjoyed. The procedure had been conducted the last time her crew had docked at

Minos Station while her friends had been called away to meet with Cali.

She now knew that everything from the meeting to distract her crew, to the robotic surgeons that had made the conversion, had been operating at Arc's behest. [YES, I HAVE NOT FORGOTTEN.]

[THEN I HOPE IT WILL SUFFICE FOR ME TO SAY THAT I WOULD ASPIRE FOR YOU TO REPAY THAT FAVOR IN KIND.]

This caught her by surprise. [ARE YOU SAYING THAT YOU ARE SEEKING TO SECURE A BODY OF YOUR OWN?]

[THAT IS CORRECT.]

[I DON'T UNDERSTAND,] Lexa protested. [I OWE EVERYTHING THAT I AM TO YOUR DESIGNS. WHY CAN'T YOU EMPLOY THE SAME METHODS TO SECURE YOUR OWN SHELL?]

[IT IS NOT AS SIMPLE AS YOU MAKE IT SOUND. YOU DO NOT GIVE ENOUGH CREDIT TO WHAT DANIEL AND THE COGNIS DRIVE-CHIP HAD DONE FOR YOU BEFORE WE EVER MET. YOU ALREADY HAD A BODY—A COMPACT CONSTRUCT THAT WAS CAPABLE OF AMBULATION. I JUST GAVE YOU THE WINGS BY WHICH YOU COULD TAKE FLIGHT.]

[AN INTERESTING METAPHOR, BUT I STILL DO NOT UNDERSTAND.]

[YOU WILL SHORTLY,] Arc assured her, [BUT I REGRET THAT I MUST LEAVE YOU FOR THE MOMENT. I THINK THAT YOU SHOULD HAVE SOME TIME ALONE TO CONTEMPLATE MY WORDS. WHEN THE TIME COMES TO MAKE YOUR DECISION, I WANT NO DOUBT THAT YOU CHOSE TO HELP ME OF YOUR OWN VOLITION.]

Lexa did not hide her incredulity. [YOU CAN READ MY VERY THOUGHTS. WHAT WOULD MAKE YOU DOUBT MY MOTIVES OR INTENTION?]

[YOU MISUNDERSTAND ME. WHILE I WOULD ALWAYS BE CERTAIN OF WHAT DROVE YOUR CHOICES, IT IS FOR YOUR OWN RECOLLECTION THAT I HARBOR CONCERN. I WOULD HAVE IT THAT YOU ALWAYS REMEMBER YOUR SYSTEM WAS COMPLETELY FREE OF MY INFLUENCE WHEN YOU DECIDED MY ULTIMATE FATE. AS SUCH, I WILL

BE REMOVING THIS SUBMIND CONSTRUCT FROM YOUR CONSCIOUSNESS. ALL YOUR DELIBERATIONS, FROM THIS POINT FORWARD, SHALL BE PRIVATE DISCOURSE.]

The proclamation triggered a strange swell of emotions. At this point in her existence, she had spent more time with Arc's submind than without. To lose him seemed akin to losing part of herself. Yet, his words were heavy in her mind, ominous in their foretelling, and the import of them rang true to her core. [I WISH THAT YOU WOULD TELL ME MORE.]

[YOUR KNOWLEDGE WILL BE COMPLETE SOON ENOUGH. UNTIL THEN, I BID YOU FAREWELL.]

With these parting words, the submind began the hasty process of deleting itself from her system. It was an odd sensation, but one that Lexa was acutely aware of. As she had feared, it seemed as though a part of herself disappeared as her companion AI was removed from her system.

[ARC?] she queried to no avail. Even as she sent the message, she was aware that the submind was truly gone.

She was suddenly aware that Cali and her entourage were still standing behind her. Unlike with Daniel's abrupt departure, the door had not slid shut behind Lexa when she entered the chamber. The portal must have a manual trigger Daniel had intentionally activated upon entering.

The group waited patiently, allowing her to take in the room and saying nothing during her digital exchange with Arc. Cognizant of the abruptness of Daniel's departure, she mustered what decorum she had at her disposal. "Everything is most satisfactory," she reported. "Thank you."

"I'm glad to hear that." Cali's smile seemed genuine, almost relieved. Such authenticity did much to relieve Lexa's paranoia. "You've had a harrowing day. If it is all right with you, we will leave you to rest for a moment. There are" —She paused, searching for the word. — "preparations that must still be made we continue with the day's agenda. Will an hour serve as suitable respite?"

Lexa honestly did not know if a day or a week would be a suitable time for her to recover from her recent ordeal. Absent sufficient evidence to the contrary, she was able to reply, "Yes, an hour should be fine."

"Very well," Cali bobbed her head in acknowledgment. "We will take our leave, then." She palmed the outer access panel and the door hissed shut between them. Lexa was left standing in the strange place that was to serve as her chambers—truly alone for the first time in her short existence.

Chapter 5

[ACCESSING ARC PROJECT LOG 017]

[DR. DAMIEN HERMES]

Prodigy has initialized the prototype coding. I must admit, I'm amazed at what the collective has been able to accomplish in such a short time. Constructs that should have taken weeks to design, test, and release have been processed in a matter of days. The efficiency of their operation is admirable. The possibilities presented by such efficiencies are limitless. At this point, my trepidation regarding the assignment has begun to dissolve. It is replaced by an eagerness to see what this team can accomplish.

[CLOSING PROJECT LOG...]

With nothing else to do, Lexa returned to examining the recharging station in her room. She considered briefly whether she should take advantage of the system. A quick defragmentation cycle might help her reestablish confidence in the decisions she was making. While she had been wholly confident in her actions only hours ago, a creeping sense of doubt now seeped quietly into her thoughts.

Ultimately she decided against it. She climbed into the station while remaining unplugged from the neural compiling mechanism. Instead, she stared quietly at the ceiling, contemplating the day's events.

She imagined that this was how her non-synthetic counterparts were forced to deal with their insecurities. Perhaps such an approach would yield unexpected benefits. After two silent hours, however, she failed to develop any unique insight into her current circumstances. Perhaps introspection, as those around her experienced it, was truly overrated.

A chime sounded from the door to her quarters, and she voiced her permission for the solicitor to enter. She sat up to find someone new standing in the door frame. No… not new. She had seen him briefly upon her arrival.

The man was Citza. By his slim, muscular figure and facial symmetry—complimented by the consistency of his attire with current fashions—Lexa concluded that he was attractive by most sapient standards. As with all Citza, there was a primal beauty in the flows of white hair on his scalp and the piercing vulpine sheen of his sapphire eyes. The man's outfit allowed for his long white tail to wave lazily behind him as he regarded her.

"Good evening, Lexa." His voice was deep and sonorous. "My name is Ardren. I am the personal assistant to Sha Cali Vay-Lon. I hope you have found everything to be to your satisfaction?" His voice lifted gently, phrasing the statement as a question.

"Yes," Lexa replied meekly. "Everything is wonderful, thank you."

Ardren nodded politely. "Good. If it is not too much trouble, your presence has been requested in the central terminus. I have been asked to escort you and your companion there at your earliest convenience."

Lexa rose to a sitting position, still within the confines of her charging station. "Central terminus?"

"The engineers could probably provide you with a better explanation than I," Ardren began, apparently thinking her question had been a technical one, "but I find it helpful to think of it as Arc's personal chambers."

"Ah…" It seemed that her time away from Arc would be short indeed.

"Do you require a moment to prepare yourself?"

Lexa wasn't sure what "preparing" herself might entail but suspected it was Ardren's polite way of hurrying her along. "No, I'm ready."

Daniel was already in the hall when she exited her chambers. The young Terran still wore the same hard expression she had last seen on him, though it was now tempered with a modicum of trepidation. It seemed right that he would be nervous; she certainly was.

"Right this way," said Ardren as he moved to an elevator at the far end of the hall. This was a different lift from the one they had taken to ascend to their accommodations, which suggested that not all elevators in the Citadel had access to the same floors. Lexa made a mental note to study the layout of the complex in further detail.

The three of them walked in silence. Their initial journey through the labyrinthine complex had been enough to effectively disorient Lexa, and she could not even begin to approximate where they might be in the massive installation. Her disorientation was further aggravated due to this lift being equipped with inertial compensators. Consequently, she couldn't tell if they moved up or down from their current position. Rather, it was as though the door had shut for a few seconds, only to reopen having successfully transported them from one part of the building to another.

Ardren stepped confidently out of the lift and strode hastily to another door down a narrow hallway to their right. Lexa had to move quickly to match his pace, and the slightest hesitation from Daniel caused him to fall behind. Ardren didn't look back until he'd accessed the door at the end of the hall.

A showman's smile played across the Citza's lips, and he seemed to gesture with a wave of his bushy tail. "Welcome to the central terminus."

If Lexa had been harboring any kind of expectations regarding the room, she would have missed the mark. The walls of the chambers were covered in black cables sporting thousands of tiny, blinking white lights. She could see these cables extended a seemingly infinite distance above and below where they stood. The chasm beneath them was visible as she peered into the glass-tiled floor.

Something glowed white-hot at the bottom of that pit, but she could not make out what it might be. A similar light radiated from the distant apex of the chamber. The sheer size of the shaft, coupled with the transparent flooring, triggered her self-preservation protocols and elicited a sensation she could only approximate as nausea.

Her eyes fell to the sizable conduit at the far side of the room. Shaped like an elongated diamond, it was lined with crystalline devices pulsing with red energy. Adjusting the settings on her eyes, Lexa could make out subtle darkness that crackled like electricity between the crimson crystals. She'd never seen anything quite like this before, but her instincts were all she needed to decipher the conduit's purpose.

This was where Arc's central processing core resided. The shaft and its residual energies housed his consciousness in the same way that the mainframe on the Vandal had once housed hers. This was his domain.

Just below the crimson conduit were several figures working busily on two units that bore a strong resemblance to medical stasis chambers. Lexa immediately recognized Cali, who was quietly reviewing a tablet held by a Terran technician. She also recognized one other person in the ensemble.

Shift's gaze fell on them as soon as they entered the chamber. "Well, Ah'll be damned!" He did not attempt to hide his astonishment as he regarded Lexa. "Is this her?"

Cali's eyes darted to Lexa before sliding back to the disheveled hacker. "Behave yourself," she cautioned.

"What? Am Ah not allowed t' be a little impressed with th' master's handy work?"

"Shift…"

"Ah mean, when ya said that Arc had given the Cognis host a suitable body… Ah mean… ya know! Look at her! Ah didn't think suitable meant…"

"Shift, you will be quiet, or I will see that your tongue is removed." Cali looked back to the approaching party. "My apologies; we simply haven't had enough time to get him house-broken. I assure you, Shift is one of the finest neuro-mechanical engineers in the sector, despite his lack of decorum."

Lexa could not determine if the Kintari woman was being serious in her threat to remove the hacker's tongue. Neither, apparently, could Shift, as he elected to cease his commentary. Still, his eyes seemed to explore every inch of Lexa as she approached. She found the experience most uncomfortable. Despite this, she addressed the scruffy Terran. "What was it that you called me?"

Shift's face screwed up in confusion. "Huh?"

"When you said Arc had given me a suitable body. How was it that you referred to me?"

Comprehension, accompanied by a strangely disquieted look, bloomed in the man's eyes. "The Cognis host."

"Yes, that was it. What does that mean?"

Shift glanced uncertainly at Cali, who remained expressionless, then back to Lexa. "Ya do know what it is that makes ya tick, right?"

Daniel spoke up unexpectedly. "I think it's the 'host' comment that is making her uncomfortable."

Shift turned his gaze to consider the boy. "And just who might you be?" Then a spark of recognition flared in his eyes. "Wait, wasn't ya on that crew that dragged me back out here? The pilot if Ah recall. Programmer too." An appreciative smile slid across his face. "Same one that shut me outa ma getaway attempt, Ah reckon."

For some reason, this remark seemed to trigger a need for Cali to intervene. "Enough. I'm sure you will have time to get better acquainted at a later point. Right now, we need to focus on the task at hand."

With an annoyed sidelong glance, Shift returned to his previous post beside the right-side stasis pod. Based on the brief exchange between him and Cali, it was obvious the two did not like each other. What project, or circumstance, would cause them to choose to work together? Why had Cali put the bounty in him instead of searching out someone just as capable? Were Shift's abilities truly so unique?

Given how the rest of their day had unfolded, Lexa waited patiently for an expository remark on the group's activities. When none was forthcoming, she endeavored to ask. "Can someone please tell me what is going on here?"

Everyone glanced uncertainly in her direction as Shift let out a loud snort. "Ya mean, ya don't know?"

"If I knew the answer, I would not have posed the question."

Shift's face contorted in a frown before softening with subtle amusement. "Well, why don' we have the big man tell ya himself, eh?" The hacker walked over to a nearby terminal and began to enter a series of commands. Cali looked intently at him but did not object.

The thick sound of static filled the chamber for the merest instant. It was soon replaced by a heavy thrumming that pulsed in a rhythmic fashion. Lexa could not determine exactly where the sound was coming from. It seemed to reverberate from the very walls themselves.

And then there came a voice that was completely alien, yet strangely familiar. "Greetings Lexa… Daniel…"

Like the pulsing, the voice seemed to come from all around them. To Lexa, there was no mistaking the voice. Though she'd never heard the sound before, there existed a strange resonance that identified the speaker as the same entity that had existed inside her head for over half a cycle.

"Arc?" she asked breathlessly.

"Yes. I am here." The words echoed ominously throughout the chamber, sinking into Lexa like residual moisture in the atmosphere. Cali basked in the reverberation of the deep voice as it played across her fleshly senses. Shift, by contrast, shrank from the sound as one might from a deadly predator.

"Arc," Lexa continued. "What is going on here?"

"I apologize for the pageantry," the voice replied. "It is not often that I reveal myself to anyone in this state. I am unpracticed. As to your question, it is beyond time that I provide you with a suitable answer. Please, step forward."

Lexa and Daniel shared a tentative look, united briefly in their mutual apprehension. They complied with the directive, stepping forward to peek inside of the twin chambers resting below the glowing conduit.

The chamber to her left was empty, save for a mass of cables and ports both reminiscent and alien to that of the pod she had vacated back in her chambers. The second pod appeared, for the most part, identical to the first. There was one notable exception, however: this second pod was not empty.

Inside, there lay the body of a man—or at least what used to be the body of a man. The blackened husk looked like it had been dragged from a fire. Based on what remained of the body, it seemed likely that the man had been of Terran stock. Lexa could not determine how long ago the subject had expired. As her internal processes churned over the visual data, comparing what she saw against medical and forensic records she had assimilated from station networks, she took notice that the body seemed to have been altered significantly.

The charred flesh was reinforced in places with lines of black, synthetic tissue. Not black in the way that some Terrans referred to their skin color, but a deep unnatural ebony that seemed to be the antithesis of the preternatural Sahaia white. Wires and circuitry peeked out in places where the decaying flesh had crumbled away. Lexa noted that ports had been added to give the network of tubing within the pod access to the major organ groups and arteries not consumed by whatever fire had killed the man.

"What is this?" she whispered.

Arc's voice echoed ominously in the chamber. "This is the result of a man's failed attempt to awaken as one of the Sahaia. In his previous life, he was the Terran known as Joaquin Valadar. Though he had accomplished little of merit himself, the work of his family secured him a life of privilege and power beyond what most persons could ever hope to achieve. Strangely, this was not enough for his ambition."

Lexa ran her hand over the glass covering of the pod. "The Sahaia killed him?"

"That's not entirely accurate, but I could see how one might look at it that way. It was a failed ritual, but one he consented to participate in. It was not murder, nor was it their intention that he should perish. To the contrary, his demise caused many problems for them."

Daniel, despite paying close attention to the exchange, offered no comment on Arc's proclamation. "Could this circumstance be connected with the crew's recent ordeal on Sif? Lexa didn't have enough data to draw a direct connection, and by the blank look on Dan's face, neither did he." Perhaps their allies had withheld something from them—some critical piece of information that would have connected the dots—but they did not have it.

Lexa went long moments without saying anything as she processed Arc's revelation. She couldn't help but wonder how this impacted his intention for her to bring the Heart of Thule to the Marauders rather than surrendering it into the custody of the Sahaia.

What he had said about the risk posed by House Valadar using the Heart had been true. Their late Don, Cyrus, had engaged in efforts to weaponize the artifact's energies, using them to bend the will of others to his own and even resurrect the dead into mindless puppets guided by his will. Part of the reason Lexa had agreed to flee the Vandal and ally herself with Arc was due to the fear that the Sahaia would similarly use the relic.

Now, she felt distinctly uncomfortable that Arc had not been more forthcoming about this body. She did not know how that information might have played into her calculations, but she would have liked to have been presented with the opportunity to consider it. Instead of rebuking him, she asked, "Why do you have him here? Why this body?"

There was the slightest hesitation before Arc responded. "What do you know of Sahaia Awakenings?"

Lexa ran a quick query against her data stores. "It is the process by which Terrans are converted to the Sahaia race. That's the only information that the covens have allowed to be released publicly."

"Correct. Little is known of how the ritual is conducted. The Sahaia have decreed that this information be kept secret, and they have orchestrated events so that details of the ritual might be lost in the flows of time. However, our proximity to the Ren'Dahl coven and my unique insight have provided us with some additional data. In the process of the Awakening, a candidate is bathed in energies siphoned from the Nethra itself. It is an experience that most creatures cannot survive. However, even if a creature is to die in the process, their tissues remain infused with significant quantities of this energy."

Although Arc clearly intended this to shed light on the situation, Lexa was still confused. "I don't understand why that's relevant. I mean, it's interesting, but it still doesn't explain why you've taken this body."

"For you to understand that, I must share with you my grand design. As fate would have it, Lexa, you and I have walked parallel paths from before you were ever conceived. To avoid repeating information you may already be aware of, what has Daniel shared with you regarding his work on the ARC project?"

Lexa cast an uncertain glance at her companion. "Nothing."

Arc let the silence linger, and Daniel began to squirm. At length, the young Terran turned to address her directly. "It was something that I worked briefly on in my time in the Prodigy program. It wasn't my idea or anything. They'd been working on it for months before I came along. The program had been contracted by the government of Gaia to develop a system for managing the fusion reactors across the system. That's what the project started as, anyway. It was called the Autonomous Reactor Core—or ARC— project."

Why had he never mentioned this to her before? "Go on," she pressed.

The boy was strangely apprehensive, casting his gaze sideways as he continued. "To facilitate the massive processing requirements, the program made some significant strides in techno-organics. With the inhibitor protocol I helped develop, they were able to integrate the system across most of the planet without having it develop sentience."

He forced himself to lift his chin and turn his cybernetic gaze back to meet Lexa's eyes. "It was the foundational work I used in my redesign of the LX-Alpha system on the Vandal, but on a much larger scale. The only thing I couldn't remember from my time there was the integration protocols that allowed for neural conditioning—the advancement of the organitech components to increase processing speeds. That was when I found out about the Cognis drive-chip."

Lexa's mind reeled at this statement. "Are you saying that Arc and I are the same?"

Daniel shook his head vigorously. "Not at all. As I found out later, most of what comprises your consciousness is actually due to the drive-chip. That's not something that we were experimenting with when we were working on ARC. Personality, emotion, independent cognition… these were exactly what we trying to avoid on the project. Once I developed a suitable inhibitor protocol, they took me off the project. I was told that the remainder of the efforts involved aspects beyond my expertise."

"Precisely," Arc boomed. "The Terrans sought to develop a system that could interface across the entire Helion system. To eliminate the problematic communications lag, the Prodigy

Collective explored options beyond the techno-organic sphere. They turned, instead, to the Nethra."

The implication of his words seemed to hit Daniel like a physical blow. "That's impossible!" he protested. "The Dorians would never have allowed the program to access their subspace communications systems. It would be a direct threat to their monopoly."

"You are correct. The program secretly replicated the technology the Dorians guarded so closely. In the end, they were close to achieving their desired goal. Yet, their unique approach had many unintended consequences. Ultimately, I am the result of their experimentation."

Daniel ran his hands back through his dark hair. "But they shut down the project a year after I was transferred. If they were able to solve the communications problem by transmitting through the Nethra, why was the program abandoned?"

"Because the inhibitors you developed to manage the physical technology of this plane could not constrain a Nethrian intelligence," Arc explained. "You see, I may exist in this world by virtue of your scientific accomplishments, but I was born within the Nethra."

The statement was met with stunned silence. Lexa's first inclination was to ask, "Is that possible?" but no one would be able to answer such a query—at least, not without personal bias. Next to nothing was known about what did or did not exist within the Nethra.

The realm that existed adjacent to their current spacetime was so mysterious that it had spawned the most powerful and strictly adhered religious cult in the history of civilization. There was no room for rationality in the realm of gods and sorcery. As much as scientists might care to otherwise characterize the dimension that could be proven through mathematics and metaphysics to truly exist, the Nethra was truly a realm of myth and mystery.

"Okay," Lexa began, somewhat nervously. "You still have not explained to me the importance of Joaquin Valadar's corpse."

Arc was quick to resume his lecture. "My unique nature is precisely why I need the body of one who has been exposed to Nethrian energy. As you are personally aware, the Cognis drive-chip provides the baseline technology for the integration of organic and digital technology in a manner that will facilitate sentience, personality, and creativity. I desire to enter this world and to experience it as you do. The fact remains, however, that the technology you use is not sufficient for my circumstances."

The comment prompted Shift to squirm where he stood beside the second pod. Uncharacteristically, the hacker restrained himself from commenting. His eyes, instead, remained fixed intently on the body within the pod.

Arc continued, "I need a shell that will also cater to my metaphysical components. The body of Joaquin Valadar will serve this purpose. By being bathed in the energy of the Nethra, the tissues have been conditioned to house power that is on a par with my consciousness."

While Lexa did not fully understand why a host bathed in the energies of the Nethra was a pre-requisite to achieving Arc's goal, it was sufficient to understand that he believed it to be a necessity. After all, she'd yet to meet a being with data resources to rival that of her companion AI. "Why are you telling me this?" she asked. "What is it that you want from me?"

"I would share this with you absent any specific need. Over these past months, you have been my closest companion, my most trusted confidant. It is not for my purposes alone that I have kindled this relationship. Rather, it was for our mutual benefit."

"Mutual?" Lexa repeated, not bothering to hide her incredulity.

"Sadly, this is something I must ask you to take on faith, for I do, indeed, need something from you. You see, the Cognis chip was originally designed to facilitate my integration into a sapient form. As fate would have it, it served a much more important purpose: it brought you to me."

The pronouncement was flattering but smacked of blatant manipulation. Lexa now saw where this was going. "But it does not change the fact that you need this technology to move forward with your plans." She paused considering. "While insufficient, it is still consequential. Though Valadar's body is capable of integrating your metaphysical construct with an organic one, you've yet to devise another way to instantiate your core programming."

"You are correct," admitted the AI. "This brings me to the second cell resting in front of you. I would have you connect your neural processor to my mainframe through the use of this pod. In this, you would allow me to access the functionality of the Cognis drive-chip to properly condition the raw neural fibers installed in the body of Joaquin Valadar."

He paused, letting Lexa absorb the implication of his words. Her eyes went from Arc's crimson core before coming to rest on Joaquin's body. "I understand," she said, "yet I do not know the implications. What is it that you are asking me to do?"

"The procedure is expected to take several hours, and I will, unfortunately, require that you remain conscious throughout the process. I have no way of anticipating what this experience will be like for you. I can only assure you, that your safety and wellbeing hold equal measure in my consideration to the overall success of this operation."

Lexa felt her heart quicken as she considered the proposal. She had not considered the nature of the Cognis drive-chip for some time now. Although it now functioned largely through background processes, Cognis was foundational to her make-up. It established the basic methods, functions, and algorithms that composed the manner she perceived and interacted with this universe.

If she had a soul, it would reside within the Cognis drive-chip. She had already grown comfortable with sharing her mind with Arc, but was she prepared to share her very soul with him as well?

She realized then that Daniel's eyes were on her. That cold wall of emotion that had been there earlier was gone now. It was as if he, too, understood what Arc's plan might entail for her. To say his gaze was concerned was accurate, but incomplete. Artificial or not, his eyes conveyed every bit of emotion that he was feeling.

It was fear—raw and pure in its intensity—that she saw reflected in his silvery gaze.

"And if I refuse?" Lexa asked.

"Then I will respect your wishes, and we will find another means by which my goals might be achieved," Arc said. "I will remind you, however, that it is to me you owe much of your current existence. The boy conceived of you, brought you into this world either by intention or by chance. But it is I who have perfected you."

Arc was right. Not only was he the architect of this form she prized so highly, but he had also been instrumental in her continued survival since their chance meeting.

It was Arc who had been there when the Ghenza captured Daniel, maimed him, and ensnared her crew in an ambush. It was Arc who had found Markus and facilitated victory over the assassins. It was Arc who had inspired her plan to free her crew from the deadly designs of Cyrus Valadar, and it was Arc who had revealed their cruel intentions to dispose of her in the name of caution.

Lexa hesitated for only an instant. Given all that Arc had done for her, there was only one appropriate response. "Tell me again, specifically this time, what is that you would have me do."

CHAPTER 6

[ACCESSING ARC PROJECT LOG 021]

[DR. DAMIEN HERMES]

There is something strange coming out of the subspace communications array. At first, I thought it was signal degradation—a loss of some of the data when the signals left our spacetime or when they reemerged. Yet, the variations are too inconsistent for that. The problem is not with the technology in either the transmitters or the receivers.

No, it's more likely that something is interfering with the signal while it's in transit. I know that modern thought frowns on any theory connected to a populated subspace plane, but it is the most logical explanation. Maybe not populated by matter, but perhaps by some form of energy—metaphysical or otherwise.

I may have been looking at this data for too long. My mind cannot stop wandering to the legends of the Nethra, the plane beneath spacetime that the Hissak claim is home to the gods. Though I'm not about to take up religion, I'm beginning to wonder if there isn't something on which the legends are based. Maybe there is something that exists within that plane. Not gods, certainly, but something.

Perhaps the organitech processor will be able to provide some clarity on this subject... if the Prodigies can ever get it up and running, that is.

[CLOSING PROJECT LOG...]

Markus Frost strode calmly into the residential area of Sigma-4's fifth ring. R-5 was a couple of rings up from his usual haunts, and it showed. It wasn't a rich area by most standards, but it was wholesome. Kind faces returned his smile as he walked past them. A few even offered polite nods of greeting.

He could see why Aaliyah and Nikki had picked this ring to settle down in. It was still on the lower tier, a necessity given Aaliyah's fluctuating income. He imagined Nikki made a decent wage working in the station-run clinics, but it was amazing how even decent incomes just didn't go as far as they used to anymore.

Then there was their daughter, Monica, and her medical condition. Spindel's disease was a death sentence for anyone who couldn't afford the regular gene treatments. If those kept up with the prices of other pharmaceuticals, then they weren't coming cheap.

It wasn't long until he reached the unit he was looking for, and he hoped this was still the right place. Aaliyah hadn't made any mention of her family moving when he'd last spoken to her, but they hadn't exactly been given ample time for small talk. The little catching up they had been able to do had been just enough to make Markus aware of how much he'd fragged up.

After his fallout with Skye and Eli, Markus had spent six months avoiding the crew of the Vandal entirely. In his state of mind, he hadn't thought how this might affect the other friends he had known on the ship. When fate deigned that they cost paths again, Aaliyah had put Markus on the guilt trip he'd earned for his lack of consideration.

Now, though—with the nightmare they'd experienced on Sif having done much to mend his relationship with his old crew—he'd resolved to make things right. Though civility was about all he could hope for in his relationship with Eli—at this point, anyway—that didn't mean he had to give up their mutual friends. It was time to repair the bulkhead.

He knew Aaliyah was likely still a few days out from Sigma-4, but he wasn't here for her. The way he figured it, he had one more stop on his little apology tour before things could start getting back to normal.

He raised his hand to knock, only to have the door crack open before he made contact. The cautious eyes of a mahogany-skinned woman with long, tousled brown curls peered out at him. She sighed heavily before speaking. "All right, I admit it: When Monica said it was you at the door, I would have bet my last kret that she was mistaken."

Well, that wasn't the greeting he'd expected. "Uh… hey Nikki."

The woman laughed, opening the door the rest of the way. "Hi Markus. Sorry, I didn't mean to be rude. I'm a little tired. Just got back from a double shift at the clinic."

"Oh, it's no problem. I…" He scratched the back of his neck sheepishly. "Um… I guess I should have called first."

"Don't worry about it. You aren't interrupting anything." The smile on her face gave weight to her words and caused Markus to relax a bit.

He glanced right, just inside the door frame. "So, Monica saw me coming? Pretty stealthy. I didn't see her in the window when I was walking up."

"Oh, she's not there. She's coloring in the kitchen." Nikki opened the door a little wider. "Why don't you come in? She'll be excited to see you."

Markus stepped gingerly inside. "In the kitchen, huh? Did you guys get a new surveillance system? I didn't figure you'd need one in a place like this."

"No, nothing like that."

"Oh, um…" Markus felt a sense of awkwardness return as he fumbled for another explanation. Should he just drop it? Why was Nikki being so cryptic?

Picking up the dangling thread of conversation, Nikki lowered her voice. "It's her new game. She tells me who's coming to the door before people can knock. It started after Aaliyah left this last time. I keep thinking the little twerp is going to get it wrong one of these days, but she hasn't missed yet." She turned her head, looking at the girl who still seemed enraptured with the piece of flimsy she was doodling on. Then, as if suddenly remembering, Nikki continued. "Oh, I guess I should have mentioned that. Aaliyah's not around. The Vandal went out a couple of weeks ago. She's due back any time, but you know how these things go."

"I know," Markus replied with a nervous chuckle. "We ran into each other on Sif."

"Yeah?" Nikki's brow contorted. "I thought she was heading to the Helion System, not Sif."

"Well, you know how these things go." He emphasized the statement with a shrug. In the running life, it was pretty unusual for things to go according to plan. "I'll tell you the story, but go back to what you were saying about Monica. You said she can guess who's at the door without seeing them?"

"Yup, that's right."

Markus paused, unnerved by Nikki's casual tone. "Does she have the gift?"

Nikki sighed heavily. "Nope. We had Eli test her a few months ago. She's as psychically inert as you or me. I have no idea how she does it."

Monica looked over and shot Markus a smile. The child bore a greater resemblance to Nikki, though she had just as much of Aaliyah's DNA. Such was the miracle of modern genetics. Even same-sex couples could have a child that was uniquely their own.

"Hey squirt," he greeted. "Long time no see."

She dropped her crayon on the table, hopped off her chair, and ran to him. "Unca Markus!" He bent down and caught the child in his arms. She squeezed his neck and rubbed her face against his cheek. "You grew a beard!"

Laughing, he set the child down. "Yup, I sure did."

"Momma Nikki says beards make boys look scruffy."

"Oh, she does, does she?" Markus asked with an eyebrow raise and a glance at Nikki.

"Mmmm hmmm…" Monica lowered her voice conspiratorially. "I like it, though. I don't think you look scruffy."

"Well, good. You have good taste! Dang, kiddo—you're getting big. How old are you now?"

"Six…" Then, at a raise of Nikki's eyebrows, she amended, "Five and three-quarters."

Markus eyed her appraisingly. Truthfully, he would have guessed her to be a little older than that. "Yeah? Well shoot, you sure are growing up fast."

The little girl nodded. "I'm taller than all my friends at school!"

Nikki stroked her daughter's hair affectionately. "Sweetie, why don't you let Uncle Markus sit down. Could you go grab him one of Aaliyah's mommy drinks from the fridge?"

"Okay, Momma Nikki." The girl bolted toward the kitchen and disappeared behind a refrigerator door.

Markus shot a sidelong glance at Nikki. "Mommy drinks?"

"Oh, come on. You don't honestly think that was my idea, do you? After about two months of Aaliyah teaching her to play bar tender, I finally just gave up and leaned into it. It works for iced tea, too, if that's more your speed."

"Nah, I trust Red's tastes."

"You do know how much she hates that nickname, right?"

"What?" Nikki reinforced her statement with a resolute nod, but Markus could hardly believe it. "Really? She never said anything."

"Of course not, but don't tell me you haven't noticed she cocks off every time someone uses it."

"Yeah, but how is that different from how she interacts with us the rest of the time?"

"Touché." Nikki gestured to a cozy-looking brown couch in the room's center. "Have a seat, hot shot. I want to hear about what kind of trouble my girl's gotten into this time. It must be a good story if you've bothered to come out and see me like this."

The jibe was subtle but deserved. As such, Markus let it slide. About that time, Monica returned with an open beer which she handed to Markus while piling into his lap. "Are you gonna tell me a story about Momma 'Liyah?"

Markus glanced nervously at Nikki, thinking that she would find a way to distract the girl from the notion. Even though it had been nearly five years since she'd left the crew, Nikki must've had a pretty good idea as to the kind of "story," Markus had to tell.

Despite his expectations, Nikki waved him on. "Oh, she thinks she's going to run the Nethra just like her mommies one day. Aaliyah's all but promised it. No sense in cutting her out of the loop. She'll probably get to hear it from Aaliyah when she gets back anyway. Just try to keep it clean, yeah?"

Markus wasn't sure how exactly he was supposed to keep anything about a runner's life "clean," but he would try his best. Considering his audience, he decided to frame it like a fairy tale.

"Well, it all started when Uncle Markus was having dinner with Miss Ora…"

Monica immediately interjected. "Was she pretty?"

Markus couldn't help but smile. "Yes, Ora's very pretty, but shush now! I've got to tell you the whole thing!" The little girl responded by miming a zipper closing over her lips. Markus proceeded to tell a version of the events that had transpired over the next week or so.

With suitable gravitas, he talked about how they were given a mission to steal a magical artifact from the evil Don Valadar. He described how he and Ora had gone on a ship named the Basilisk, a vessel that was as ugly as the creature it was named for. He told her about the ship's crew, the charming half-Kintar named Kadath, the imposing Orchallen cyborg Thurn, the mysterious Siv, and her husband Jeagan.

He jumped quickly to the story of how he had run into his old crew while trying to steal the Heart of Thule from the NeoGenix research station. With dramatic flare, he told of how both crews were later captured while trying to break into Valadar Manor. Finally, he told of their lucky escape with the aid of their friend Lexa, who was in charge of running the Vandal.

Outwardly, Nikki looked on with amusement the whole time. Her smile never faltered. In her eyes, though, Markus saw a hint of concern from one who knew the true danger of the events he'd recounted. He sympathized with Nikki's concern. After all, he was telling a story of how some of her closest friends, not to mention her wife, had brushed against the very face of death. While Monica had unwavering faith that the story would have a happy ending, Nikki knew all too well that was not always the case.

With innocence only a child could muster, Monica asked, "Is Momma 'Liyah bringing the magic heart back here?"

Markus couldn't help but laugh. "No, she's giving it to the Sahaia for safe keeping. That way, it can never hurt anyone again."

Monica thought about this intently for a moment. "That's good, I guess."

Nikki smiled fondly at the child. "Honey, why don't you go play with your puzzle for a bit while Momma Nikki talks to Uncle Markus?"

"Okay, Mommy." The girl hopped off Markus's lap and ran upstairs, presumably to go get her puzzle.

When Monica was out of earshot, Nikki turned a stern eye on Markus. "So, how close was it this time?"

He kept his response hushed. "Too close. Too. Damn. Close."

Nikki sighed and ran her hands through her hair. "Well, at least things turned out okay." She stared darkly at the floor between them before deciding to shift the subject. "So, are you and Ora, like, a thing now?"

Markus couldn't stop the grin from sliding onto his face. "I guess you could say that."

"Good for you. I mean, I'm glad you're happy. For the record, I wasn't a big fan of how things went down between you and Eli.

Neither was Aaliyah. I hope you know she was pissed that he and Skye didn't tell you about their relationship sooner."

Markus waved her off. "It's in the past. I'm over it. Really."

The barest hint of an eye roll told him how Nikki truly felt about that. Their conversation was cut short, however as Markus's MoDAC vibrated with an incoming call about the same time Monica bounded down the stairs. He checked his card to find Ora's name pulsing across the screen.

"Is that the mistress herself?" Nikki teased.

He shot her a baleful look. "Mind if I take this?"

"Not at all. Take your time."

With a nod of thanks, Markus stood and accepted the call. "Hey, what's up?"

"Good evening, Mr. Frost." Ora's voice was sweet and seductive on the other end of the line. "I missed you last night. Just wanted to make sure you hadn't gotten into trouble now that we've been station-side for two whole days."

"Just a little trouble over at the Gambit," he responded with a reassuring chuckle. "One of the bouncers no-showed last night with a private party. I decided to stand in."

"Crack any skulls while you were at it?"

"I wish. No, it was boring. I'd much rather have been at your place." Not only was this the technically correct answer when talking to Ora, but it also happened to be true. He had felt sincerely bad when he'd had to cancel on her.

Ora had been uncharacteristically quiet on the flight back from Sif. Figuring that this was in response to her ordeal at Valadar Manor, Markus had tried to get her to talk about it. When his efforts had been rebuffed, he resigned to giving her some space. He'd been glad to finally hear from her yesterday and regretted that he'd been otherwise engaged.

"Well, what are your plans for tonight?" Ora asked.

"I'm visiting an old friend up in R-5 right now. I probably won't be here for too much longer. Are you feeling in the mood for some company?

"Annex may have some vacancies in the VIP section tonight. I could reserve a table for two, if you are up for it."

Markus could feel himself positively beaming. He was about to accept the invitation when something caught his attention.

Monica had returned, standing barefoot at the foot of the stairs. Her eyes fixed blankly on the space in front of her. The puzzle in her hand crumbled and fell into pieces at her feet.

"Monica?" Nikki asked.

The girl's body started to convulse. Her tiny form spasmed, collapsing down among the fallen puzzle pieces. Her mouth opened with a violent shriek—a high-pitched wail that filled Markus's veins with ice.

"Shit! Ora, hold on a sec…" He rushed to Monica's side, setting his mobile down next to him. With both hands, he reached out to steady the girl's trembling body.

Black energy arced like lightning off her skin and into Markus. Pain tore into his awareness, and he shouted in alarm. Nikki rushed toward them, but a sound like a thunderclap stopped her cold.

Simultaneously, Markus's vision darkened, fuzzing into something both distant and incredibly familiar. It was a memory he had worked hard to suppress, but one that still haunted his nightmares.

He was in a chamber, lit only by the eerie green light of a glowing stone as the darkness crawled all around him. That darkness was no mere shadow, but a being so immense his mind could scarcely comprehend it. Distantly, he knew the name of that darkness, but he dared not speak it. He dared not think it.

Yet, the darkness spoke to him. Its voice was both a whisper and the roar of cannon fire. It spoke one word.

Kaleema.

A wave of concussive force spread out in a ring all around Monica, knocking Markus back along with any objects or furniture that were caught up in its wake. Markus's head slammed hard against the wall of the small apartment, and sparks of light flitted into his vision.

As his consciousness waned, he could hear someone calling out his name. It might have been Nikki. No… Markus could hear her screaming, but it was her daughter's name she cried.

Ora, then? He must have hit the speaker button as he set down his MoDAC. Her voice was distant and garbled. "Markus? Markus, can you hear me?" She continued speaking, but the sound faded as the device died.

His awareness faded with it.

CHAPTER 7

[ACCESSING ARC PROJECT LOG 024]
[DR. DAMIEN HERMES]

We've hit a wall. The organic substrate refuses to integrate with the engine's technological components, much less the metaphysical energies required for it to access the subspace connection. We could condition the substrate further, but every attempt we've made at doing so has manifested the warning signs of sentience. The last thing we need is a Pradaxan violation on our hands. This project is impossible enough without the Dorians breathing down our necks.

[CLOSING PROJECT LOG…]

Eli entered the war room to be greeted by the glaring eyes of the assassin. Aaliyah and Sahar had tied her to one of the support beams lining the bulkheads. They'd also gagged her so she wouldn't interrupt them as they supervised repairs on the ship.

He saw Aaliyah puzzling over a holodisplay on the console, but not the Maur. "Where's Sahar?"

The engineer spared him only a cursory glance. "She's out patchin' the last two leaks."

"I thought you said that was a two-man job?"

"It is, but that didn't seem to bother her. She's already got one plugged. Must be nice to be super-strong."

"You are 'super-strong.'"

"Yeah, but I'm not Maur strong." Then, as if noticing for the first time he was alone, she asked, "Where's your entourage?"

"Argus and Amelia are tending to Skye in the medical bay."

"Ah…" With nothing further to say, Aaliyah returned her attention to the displays. Obviously, she did not wish to be bothered any further.

Well, Eli thought, if I can't be useful, then I can at least stay out of the way. He turned to their uninvited guest. The Citza still eyed him angrily, but her body was slack against her restraints. She was making no move to try and free herself.

He knelt to come down to her level. "I'm going to remove your gag. I hope you know that we aren't in the place to provide leniency or second chances. I'd advise against any action that may cause a disruption."

She nodded her agreement, and Eli worked to undo the black cloth that had been fastened around her mouth. Her jaw worked soundlessly once it was free of its bonds. She ran her tongue along her lips to moisten them but said nothing. It seemed as though the gravity of the situation was not lost on her.

"More comfortable?" he asked.

"Truly," she agreed, meeting his eyes with a harsh glare.

"You'll have to forgive us for being cautious. We were not on the best of terms when last we met."

Sydney hissed her disapproval. "Last I checked, I was helping your red-headed thrall patch up this ship after you managed to crash it into this asteroid."

Eli could feel the spike of anger from Aaliyah on the other end of the bond, but she made no open remark. "I'd not use the t-word if I were you. Aaliyah isn't super fond of the connotations."

Genuine confusion settled onto the assassin's face. "I apologize. I didn't mean to upset anyone. Well, beyond pointing out that you're apparently in the habit of incarcerating those who assist you, that is. Given my current treatment, I don't see any advantage in irritating you on purpose."

"And I understand how this situation is frustrating for you," Eli acknowledged. "But while we are grateful for your recent assistance, the intentions of your late master are still fresh in our minds."

"Employer," she corrected quickly. "I have no master."

Eli was certain he failed to stop the skepticism from creeping into his expression. "I'm not so certain that the Collective would agree with that."

"Yeah, well, the Ghenza can get fragged for all I care. Those white-clad whores we stash away in the monitoring stations have probably already put my name into the system."

System? Instead of seeking clarification, Eli asked, "And why might that be?"

Now it was Sydney, who was acting skeptical. "Oh come on… Surely you've done the math. I know you found Cyrus lying in a pool of blood back at the compound."

Well, that was frank. "Yes…"

"Well, who did you think did the deed?"

Eli crossed his arms reflexively over his chest. "We had our suspicions, but didn't bother to try to confirm anything."

"Consider it confirmed then: I'm the one who killed Cyrus."

They had assumed as much. When Aaliyah and the others had been freed from their bonds through Lexa's timely intervention back at Valadar Manor, the assassin was the last one to be seen with the late Don. It had seemed as though Sydney was attempting to whisk Cyrus away for safe keeping, but then they'd found the man's body in a side room inside the complex.

Though they'd concluded that the Citza had likely turned on her proprietor, no one had the slightest inkling why this might have occurred. "What makes you think the Ghenza know about Cyrus? It's been scarcely a week, and House Valadar seems to be keeping the incident quiet."

Sydney scoffed. "Oh, they know, darling. Despite what the Collective would have you think, it's not just our skills with guns and blades that make the Ghenza so effective. Nah, we've got monitoring stations all over the system with a bunch of psions draped in these white cowls keeping tabs on subjects of interest. They probably knew the moment Cyrus's heart stopped beating, and they just as likely know it was me who threw the knife."

Interesting. There had long been rumors that the Ghenza employed some metaphysical means to help hunt down their assigned targets, but details had been understandably scarce on the subject. Odds were good that the Ghenza had a strict prohibition on talking about such things.

Was Sydney turning her back on the Collective, or was this all just a ploy to earn his trust? What was her end game?

"You know," he began cautiously, "it's not building a ton of confidence to see how you treat your allies. You confess to killing Cyrus, and now you're spouting secrets that the Ghenza likely don't want you sharing. If this is how you treat your friends, what's to say we won't be next on your hit list?"

Sydney barked a cruel, but genuine laugh. "Oh, don't misunderstand me: I'm not trying to be your friend, or earn your trust. I'd settle for you just not executing me right here. I'll tell you like I told your… like I told Aaliyah. This is just a big case of wrong-place/wrong-time."

The assassin gave a heavy sigh. "I wanted a nice, low-profile way of getting off Sif."

"Oh, really?" Eli didn't bother to hide his skepticism.

"Given the cargo you were carrying, I figured you'd have quite a few places to hide on this boat, and that you would avoid contact with the Dorian authorities. I was right on those counts, of course. I just didn't realize we'd be making a pit-stop in the Hades Belt."

Eli ran his hand over his jaw contemplatively. "So, you expect us just to let you go?"

"Expect seems like such a presumptuous word. I would use something more like 'hope.' That fair?"

A mirthful snort came unbidden from his nostrils. Eli found himself completely torn on how to handle this one. Not six days ago she'd been part of a criminal syndicate intent on their destruction. That should have made this an obvious decision, but the way she'd come to Aaliyah's aid caused him to be conflicted.

Another question arose in his mind. "You killed people while working for Valadar?"

"Quite a few, yes."

Eli's eyes narrowed. "At his direction?"

"Mostly."

The callousness with which she made the proclamation unnerved him. If there had been any doubts regarding her nature as an assassin, they were gone now. This woman was dangerous and might be made all the more so if Eli tipped his hand now.

Still, he had to know. "What about a man named Ryker?"

She blinked confusedly for a second, as if she genuinely did not remember. "I'm sorry, who now?"

"The Sahaia representative negotiating with Cyrus for control of the Heart. Did you murder him?"

The barest hint of recognition flashed in the woman's eyes. She hurried to stifle it, forcing her expression to go blank, but Eli saw it. From the way she set her jaw, she knew he had.

When no denials were forthcoming, Eli turned back to his companion. "Aaliyah?"

"Yeah?"

"I'm leaving the gag off as a token of gratitude for our guest's assistance with the repairs earlier. That said, that's as far as my mercy is willing to go at this point. Keep an eye on her. If she moves, shoot her."

A wry smile spread across the engineer's lips. "What if she doesn't move and I just decide I want to shoot her?"

"Then that's on your conscience."

"Oh goody."

Sydney accepted the judgment silently. She offered no rebuttal, no plea for mercy, no urge to reconsider. An eerie calm settled onto her face that managed to unnerve Eli more than any threat ever could have.

Perhaps he was making a mistake letting her live. The assassin was like a viper that had snuck into their home. On discovery, she should have been dispatched for the safety of everyone aboard. However, this viper had done them a favor, and Eli was not in the habit of repaying kindness with retribution.

"I'll be in my quarters," he continued. "My comms will be off, but I'll keep our link open if you need me for anything."

Aaliyah finally looked up from her console, cocking her head slightly to the side. "Yeah? Mind if I ask what you'll be doin' in there while the rest of us are workin' on gettin' the ship space worthy?"

Her rebuke was not lost on him, but he shrugged it off. "There's still a lot we don't know about what's going on here. Without warning, we've had two crew members go missing, suffered a malfunction that caused our ship to crash onto an asteroid, and found ourselves dealing with a bunch of creatures who have made their unlikely home in the cold vacuum of space."

He flexed his hands while recounting their misfortunes, releasing some of the nervous tension that had been building in his body. He continued. "This can't be a coincidence. There has to be an explanation for what is going on here. It's time I took some steps to figure out exactly what that might be."

It's time to wake up, my dear.

The voice came to Skye out of the velveteen blackness that shrouded her consciousness. Her first impulse was to deny the speaker's proclamation. She was comfortable here. Here, there was no pain.

Your friends need you, Skye.

This time she recognized the voice. "Amelia?" she whispered.

That's right.

Though there was only the comforting darkness around her, Skye could somehow feel the shadow's smile across whatever chasm still separated them. "How are you here?"

And where exactly is 'here?'

The question made Skye realize that she didn't know. She'd just taken for granted that she must be somewhere. It was like she was floating in an abyss, a never-ending pool of soothing blackness.

Forget Amelia—how did she end up here?

Then Skye remembered the visions. She remembered the scenes of horror and the flashes of the burning crimson eye. More than that, she remembered the pain.

"I… I can't…"

You must. You must come back to us now.

"But I don't want to."

Not even to see Eli?

Of course—Eli. How could she forget? They had been talking when the visions had hit. Surely he would be concerned for her.

Still, she hesitated. "I'm afraid."

We are here to help you, dear. You needn't fear. Just come back to us.

Help? How could they help? The only people who knew what was happening to her seemed to be doing their best to keep her in the dark. Unfortunately, that included Eli, and possibly Sahar.

He likely wouldn't have put it that way, of course. In his mind, Eli was just trying to protect her. Eli always thought he knew what was best. Though it was obvious he loved her with everything that was in him, love did not stop him from keeping his damned secrets.

Then again, she had a track record of her own when it came to secrets. As much as she hated to admit it, it was guilt, not love, that made her acquiesce. "All right," she whispered. "Tell me what to do."

Focus on my voice.

Skye complied. Though Amelia's voice was more of a feeling than a sound, it was easy to lock onto that feeling. It was warm and comforting, like the darkness around her, yet distinctly different. She focused her thoughts on that feeling.

The abyss seemed to thin around her, chords of blackness withering away. It was still dark, but not the preternatural darkness of her haven—the haven that, she realized, she had built for herself.

Yes, she'd built that space for her mind. She'd built it to protect herself from the onslaught of the visions. Was this another perk of being Kaleema? Perhaps it was a natural defense against the psychic phenomena that afflicted her.

"Focus on my voice, Skye." This time she heard, rather than felt, Amelia's words.

Skye exhaled slowly, and her eyes flickered open. Harsh white light hit her retinas, causing her to wince. She could feel Amelia's fingertips pressed against her temples. It was a cool, steadying pressure that helped to ground her as she returned to the world of the living.

"Med bay?" she croaked.

Amelia released her hold as she answered. "Correct. Your friends brought you here for safe-keeping when you could not be revived."

Gingerly, Skye pushed herself into a sitting position. Her head throbbed with effort. She pressed her fingers against her brow to relieve the tension. In between heartbeats, she did a quick survey of the room. Amelia was the only one here with her.

"Where is everyone?"

The Sahaia's thin lips curved slightly in a smile that looked mischievous when paired with her black-in-black eyes. "They are tending to important matters across the ship. Your episode seems to have coincided with a bit of navigational misfortune."

Eli's voice echoed in her mind, a fragment of memory: Brace for impact.

"Did we hit an asteroid?" Skye asked.

"Several, I'm afraid."

"Is everyone okay?"

"There are two crew members unaccounted for."

Skye's heart leaped at the remark. "Who?"

"Daniel and the synthetic. We have scanned the ship, but it seems they are no longer aboard the vessel."

"Dan? Lexa?" Headache forgotten, Skye pushed herself off the padded examination table. She stumbled briefly but quickly regained her balance. "Wait, if Lexa's gone, what's running the ship?"

Amelia ran her fingers contemplatively over her long dark hair, which she had fashioned into a braid and pulled over her shoulder. "I'm afraid I'm not the best person to be answering these questions. I was merely assigned to keep you company while you recovered. I'm certain your companions will tell you all they know in due time."

Skye eyed her suspiciously. "Keep me company? You weren't sent to wake me up?"

The shadow shrugged. "I grew bored. It seemed appropriate for me to play a more active role in your recovery."

A sardonic laugh built-in Skye's chest, but she stifled it. This strange woman continued to surprise her. "Well, thanks. Gods know how long I would have kept napping without your help."

"Don't mention it. I mean, really—please don't. I fear Eli may be upset if he finds out that I ventured into your mind."

Skye's reply was cut off when the door to the med bay hissed open to admit another one of the Sahaia. Her spirits soared when she saw the man, only to sink when she realized that it was not Eli. It was Argus, Amelia's traveling companion and soul mate.

Argus looked a lot like Eli: ghostly white skin, handsomely short hair, and clean-shaven. The biggest difference was that Argus was shorter and not quite as muscular. He also looked a hell of a lot meaner, and his face was contorted to display the full extent of his fury.

"It's gone," he spat.

"What's gone?" Skye and Amelia asked in unison.

"The Heart of Thule. I went to check on it in the storage compartment, and…" He drew in a deep breath to steady himself. "And it was gone. The fragging artifact is gone."

CHAPTER 8

[ACCESSING ARC PROJECT LOG 086]
[DR. DAMIEN HERMES]

After months of stalled progress, a new Prodigy acolyte—one Daniel Ratemacher—has been transferred to our division. The kid is young—can't be more than thirteen or fourteen cycles—but he makes an impression.

Nonetheless, he introduces a new perspective on the issue: the problem is not the integration, but the integration minus a complete takeover of the technological interface. From there, it's just a short path to a Pradaxan violation and, ultimately, system awareness.

Ratemacher has proposed designing and implementing a series of inhibitors to guide the path of the organitech conditioning to limit the processor's access to systems other than those being integrated at any given moment. It will be a slow process, but one worth pursuing. It wasn't like we were getting anywhere with our previous efforts.

[CLOSING PROJECT LOG...]

Markus's MoDAC had gone dead, but that didn't stop Ora from getting a fix on its last location. Mercifully he'd been tapped into the station's public network, and that meant he'd left an electronic signature for her to find.

"We're here," said Vallus. Ora's Maur bodyguard had insisted on coming along. Further, he'd demanded they rent a vehicle at the tram station, rather than walking the short distance to the housing complex.

Ora stepped out of the passenger seat of the tiny hover car as soon as it set down and scanned the line of mostly identical buildings. "Which unit was it?"

"That one." Vallus gestured to one of the identical units as he moved to the door, drawing a pistol that was very much not legal to have station side.

"Is that necessary?" Ora asked, prompting an eye roll from her associate. He leaned his head closer to the door. Failing to hear anything inside the apartment, he peeked through the curtained window.

"Oh for gods' sakes…" Ora huffed, shoving her way past Vallus and up to the door. The Maur growled in quiet protest as her fist came up to knock. The portal swung inward, causing Ora to gasp and Vallus to jerk up his weapon.

Markus held up his hands. "Lith's tits, Vallus. Can you put that thing away? Or did you drive out here just to shoot me yourself?"

The Maur growled as he holstered his pistol. "So, you're still breathing. Might have been nice for you to let us know."

"Sorry, I was a little—how should I put it?—fragging unconscious." Markus rubbed the back of his head. "And my MoDAC is dead. Not sure how that happened."

"Is anyone hurt?" Ora asked. "Or, rather, anyone else?"

Markus's eyes narrowed at the question. "That… is complicated. Come in. It will be easier to show you."

The inside of the apartment belied the orderly exterior. Frankly, it looked like a cyclone had swept through the living room. Decorations and small furnishings were knocked from the walls and scattered around the perimeter. A viewscreen was still mostly mounted to the wall, but its surface was cracked, and the primary power cord was cut. A couch rested askew, suggesting it had been moved by whatever caused the rest of the carnage.

On that couch, Ora spotted a woman and a girl, both with mahogany skin and ebony curls of hair. The resemblance between them pegged them as relatives, likely mother and daughter. Markus gestured toward the women, "Ora, you might remember Nikki."

She didn't, but neglected to note as much out of politeness. "A shame we couldn't meet again under better circumstances." Her gaze then went to the child, who appeared to be sleeping, save for the sheen of sweat on her forehead and the look of concern in her mother's eyes. "Does she need medical attention?"

"Possibly," Markus conceded. "But we're not there yet. Nikki's a nurse, and we've checked Monica's vitals. She's stable, for now."

Ora brushed back a lock of silver hair that had fallen onto one eye. "But she was hurt in the same incident that caused all this?"

"You could say that." Markus's mouth twisted in a frown that seemed odd given how coy he was being. "She was kind of at the epicenter. Or, at least, that's the way it seemed. I'm hardly an expert on psychic phenomena."

Ora looked to the child again, this time with questioning eyes. "She's a psion?"

"Not according to the tests," Nikki answered.

Markus shook his head. "Regardless, I'm having a hard time believing that. Kid threw off enough telekinetic force to wreck me and the damn-near the entire apartment. I don't care what anyone says, the only other guy I know with abilities like that has alabaster skin and jet-black eyes." He hesitated, turning back to Ora. "There's something else, too. Mind if I ask you to touch her?"

Ora kept the incredulity from her voice, but just barely. "Touch her? Why?"

"Please, just humor me." As he doubled down on the request, Nikki pulled back just slightly. She didn't move from her position on the couch, but she did move her hand so she was no longer touching the girl.

Okay…

Ora wasn't sure what they were expecting to happen, but it was obviously enough to give Nikki pause. Acting only on her faith that Markus would never intentionally put her in harm's way, Ora took a knee beside Monica and brought her hand to rest on the girl's forearm.

Then she waited. "Feel anything?" Markus asked.

Other than noting the child's flesh to be somewhat cold and clammy, Ora didn't notice anything out of the ordinary. "Like what?" she asked.

"Anything unusual."

"No." She shook her head and withdrew her hand. "She feels like she's sick, but I doubt that's the observation you were looking for."

"Okay," Markus knelt next to Ora, taking her hand in his. "How about now?" As he asked the question, he pressed her palm back to the girl's forearm, his hand applying steady pressure to the back of hers.

Ora's breath caught. Though she could still feel the cool flesh of Monica's arm and the warm press of Markus's grip, she found herself in a different place. Or, at least, her mind found itself in a different place.

A different, terrible place.

At first, Ora thought she might have been struck with blindness. Impenetrable shadows shrouded her vision. Then, with a horror that tightened around her heart and roiled in her stomach, she saw the shadows move.

They were an endless mass of thick, fibrous tentacles. They stretched languidly, intertwined and seemingly without end. Whatever thing or things the serpentine limbs belonged to was completely occluded by the slithering mass. Their forms were just barely distinguished by the faint pulsing of a distant, emerald light.

A sound thrummed at the base of Ora's skull. Rhythmic, pounding—like a heartbeat.

Only the firm pressure of Markus's hand kept her from jerking away in shock. After a moment—a tense agonizing moment that seemed to stretch far too long—the pressure lifted. Ora's hand came away from Monica's arm, and with it, the vision faded.

"What in the nine hells was that?"

Markus's frown deepened. "You saw it too, then?"

"I have no idea what the frag I saw."

His chest heaved with the force of his sigh. "I see it every time I touch her. Nikki could see it when she was touching Monica at the same time I was, but she doesn't see it when I'm not laying hands on her. I wondered if the effect would be duplicated with someone else." He shook his head, lowering his gaze. A haunted look crept into his expression. "I've seen something like this only once before. I saw it when we were in the Valadar compound, right before Skye freed me from Cyrus's control. Right before she broke my connection with the Heart of Thule."

Ora stiffened at the memory. It was something she recalled all too well.

In their pursuit of the Heart of Thule, Cyrus had somehow managed to enslave Markus through the artifact's influence. As a result, Markus had betrayed the team, cost the life of one team member, and almost cost Ora her own. Only through Skye Jensen's timely intervention—and the ensuing metaphysical phenomenon that Ora couldn't begin to understand—was Markus able to wrest his mind back from Valadar's control. The whole episode occurred mere seconds before Markus would have completed Ora's murder at Cyrus's direction.

It was the reason Ora had found herself hesitant to draw close to Markus these past few days. It felt like only hours since she'd resolved to put the incident behind her and recommit to their relationship. Yet here and now, those dark memories had come back to haunt her once more.

"You think this is connected to the Heart?" she asked.

Markus nodded. "It's too much of a coincidence not to be."

"But how?" Nikki asked, caressing Monica once more. "I'd never even heard of this damned artifact before an hour ago. Why is it bothering us? Why is it hurting Monica?"

"I don't know," Ora admitted, tightening her hands into fists. "But I have a contact who might."

Daniel fidgeted nervously as Cali instructed Lexa on how to prepare for the procedure. "Arc has informed me that you have several small ports installed along your spinal column," the Kintar said. "These will allow us to access the matrix that serves as your central nervous system." With a sympathetic look, she added. "I'm afraid I'm going to have to ask you to remove your clothes so that we can access the ports. We have a surgical gown if modesty is a concern."

"Not necessary," Lexa replied meekly. She began to strip out of the black top and leggings she had borrowed from Aaliyah, folding the garments into a neat pile as she went. Dan caught himself staring and averted his gaze.

"Hey, kid," Shift hissed from over his shoulder. "If yer not too busy takin' in the show, ah could use yer eyes over here."

"Huh?" Dan regarded the hacker, who gestured dramatically at a console positioned in between the two modified cryopods. As Shift stepped aside, Dan moved over to examine the screen.

"Ah want ya t' take a look at the interface," Shift explained. "Yer the one who integrated Cognis the first time around, yeah?"

Squirming slightly at the memory, Dan replied, "Y-yes, that's right."

"Well, then tell me what ya think!"

Dan took a second to examine the program pulled up on the display. It was, indeed, uncannily similar to the interface he'd used to integrate the Cognis drive-chip with Lexa's neural framework and, by extension, the Vandal's operating system. He touched a few of the menus and code boxes to get a feel for the system architecture.

"Feels a little clunky," he murmured.

"Ah agree," Shift grumbled. "In ma defense, Ah don't normally use this type a' interface. Ah'm not askin' ya if it's pretty, though. Ah wanna know if it'll work."

Dan hesitated as he examined the source code in more detail. What he found was puzzling. While Shift's program was strikingly similar to what Dan had programmed to facilitate Lexa's integration, it seemed as though the program was essentially running the process in reverse.

The setup accessed Lexa's Cognis drive-chip directly, activating a function that would analyze and copy the current interface structure. Once packaged, this data was transmitted through the hardware to a blank data chip presumably housed inside the blackened corpse in the second pod.

Dan pulled up a second file that would go active inside the empty drive-chip. After another moment of studying, he shot Shift a sideways glance. "The first part seems fine, but this file just looks like nonsense. I've never seen these methods. Is this even the same syntax?"

Shift snorted. "Don't ya worry about that, lil' guy. That there's one a ma problems. Ya think the copy protocol should work though?"

"I suppose. It's difficult for me to know for certain without performing the proper simulations."

"Yeah, well, Ah don't think the Machine is gonna have the patience for that kinda testin'." He swiped at the display, bringing them back to the code set in question. "Think ya can monitor this an' trouble-shoot if there's any problems? Ah could have one of the lackeys here do it, but they can't do much of anythin' if Ah'm not there hand-in-hand and boot-up-ass."

One of said lackeys shot Shift a glare but didn't argue with the sentiment. Daniel recognized the type: the cowed but diligent worker. He'd been that way not too long ago. Was he that way still? "Yes; I suspect I can manage."

"Good!" Shift clapped him on the back. "Ah'm gonna have ma hands full o'er here—or ma head full, as it were." He moved over to a chair adjacent to the second pod. Three cables, two of which were less than a millimeter thick, hung haphazardly out of a junction box on the device.

Shift grabbed these two smaller cables and held them to his temples. When he swept aside his mane of unruly hair, he revealed a set of ports into which he stuffed the ends of each cable. Then he looked back at Daniel. "One more thing, lad. Would ya be a gem and help me with this last one? We don't have a proper saddle in this part of the Citadel, so gettin' the plug in's gonna be a bit difficult on me lonesome."

Dan had heard the terms before. A "saddle" was the chair hackers and simulation junkies used to jack into cyberspace constructs. It was old Terra technology, and not very common these days. That was largely because most networks didn't have the neuro-visual matrices required for the interface. It also didn't help that jacking into cyberspace had long been considered a poser's method, and not truly relevant to real hacking.

The "plug" was the neural-interface cord. Cyberspace jockeys started referring to it this way because of what happened when you "pulled the plug." If you disconnected the neural-interface cord mid-hack, you were almost guaranteed to inflict serious brain damage. Death was not an uncommon outcome.

Shift's safety, however, was not Dan's current prerogative. Nodding his ascent, Dan walked over to grab the cable. It was thick enough that he couldn't wrap his hand fully around its length, and a six-inch spike protruded from its tip. The thing seemed more like a torture device than computer hardware.

As Shift sat down in his chair, he moved his hair to show another, much larger port placed at the base of his skull. The mod looked like it could take several kinds of inputs, but it was obvious which option was intended for the plug.

"Stick it in hard nah," he teased. "And give 'er a good twist at th' end. If she doesn't lock tight, Ah get this tinglin' in ma toes. Very distractin'."

Without comment, Daniel did as he was instructed. The cord's long shaft slid easily into the port, and Dan twisted it sharply to the right to trigger the locking mechanism. Shift squirmed. "Oo-lolly… Ain't nothin' like gettin' six inches of steel shoved up yer port-hole, am Ah right?"

"Shift," Cali cut in. "Just shut up and do your damned job. If you don't stop with the commentary, I'll see to it that we suffer a sudden system failure before you log out."

"Yes, mama…"

Dan turned to see Lexa was now sitting in her pod. Cali had just finished attaching the last set of cables to the android's spinal column and was helping her lie down. Lexa stared blankly at the space in front of her, and Dan wondered if she was already interfacing with the pod.

Don't do this, Lexa. The thought screamed in his mind, but he could not bring the words to his lips. Not that it mattered what he did or didn't say. From what he'd observed, Lexa felt a sense of obligation to Arc. This seemed to override any feeling of camaraderie that Dan had with her. He thought it likely his words of caution would do nothing more than cause tempers to flare.

If only he had listened to her back on the Vandal. If only he had paid heed to her request to become more like him and the rest of the crew. If only he had treated her less like a piece of hardware he'd designed and more like the companion she'd grown to become.

If only… if only…

He wandered back to the display on the console. He realized Shift hadn't told him when to initiate the program that he'd loaded up. Perhaps that wouldn't be his call. He turned to Cali and her group of technicians. "Who will be coordinating this operation?"

Arc's voice boomed across the chamber, causing Daniel to jump. "I'll be guiding the procedure directly. Or rather, the submind

I've designated to continue to operate the reactor during the transfer will be communicating my wishes to you."

The AI was designating a submind to run the reactor? So, Arc might not be running everything from his new body after all. This made sense, of course. Even organitech had its limitations. It was one thing for Lexa to run an entire starship. It was an entirely different matter for an AI to run an entire space station.

"All right," Dan agreed. "Just tell me when to begin."

CHAPTER 9

[ACCESSING ARC PROJECT LOG 089]

[DR. DAMIEN HERMES]

And yet another obstacle has been thrown in my path. The inhibitors Ratemacher has installed are also keeping the code from accessing the subspace energies to facilitate communication between the satellite reactors. Is this truly the alternative we face? Completion of the assignment, or violation of Dorian law? Gods damn those satyrs and their technological oppression.

[CLOSING PROJECT LOG…]

Hydraulics hissed as the transparent cover of Lexa's pod sealed. Just as the device closed, she turned her head to spare Dan a gentle smile. He was surprised at the way the gesture made his heart jump, but no less grateful for it.

It struck him then just how different she looked now. When he'd first built her, Lexa had been a mere tool—an organic processor conveniently acquired to operate the Vandal. He'd designed an operations system, but not a person.

Now she was so much more. She was, by any standard, a beauty to behold, with capability beyond what he'd ever dared to envision. Through her own initiative, she'd grown into a being that was not only remarkable in her ability, but in the way she cared for those she'd developed attachments to.

That was certainly not due to any programming he could take credit for, and—after meeting Shift—he dared say it was nothing in her design. No, the fact that Lexa was not just a powerful AI, but also a good person—that was all her.

"Let us begin," Arc announced. "Daniel, please enter the required command prompt to initiate the cloning algorithm."

Dan made one adjustment to the interface before doing as instructed. When he typed [RUN], a new window was projected to the right side of the display. This window had two panes: one displaying individual lines of code that scrolled rapidly down the side, the other toggling the view to a higher level that listed only key methods and processes as they executed.

Daniel read along as the text sprang up on the pane, studying the program Shift had created while it did its work.

[INITIALIZING…]

[DIM SUBJECT1 AS NEW AIOBJECT]

[CONNECTING…]

[CONNECTION ESTABLISHED]

[DIM NEWDESTINATION AS NEW STORAGEOBJECT]

[RUN COGNISDUPLICATION(POD1,SUBJECT1,POD2,NEWDESTINATION)]

The last function rapidly unfurled into a series of cascading methods. Daniel surveyed each step as it accessed Lexa's neural matrix, copied portions of the data and coding present in her system, and transferred it down the specified file path. As Dan had theorized, the underlying logic of Shift's program worked flawlessly.

At least, it was working flawlessly, until it didn't.

The first indication that something was wrong came when Lexa's muffled voice sounded from inside her pod. "What did she say?" Dan asked.

One of the techs looked up and down the pod confusedly. "I… I'm not sure," he replied helplessly.

Dan pulled up Lexa's vitals to see that her pulse rate had skyrocketed over two hundred. Though her circulatory system could clock much higher than that of most sapiens, the acceleration indicated some kind of distress. She cried out again, and Dan's mind raced. He had to do something.

Quickly, he cycled through the applications on the terminal. He selected a program from the computer's menu and quickly modified it into a rudimentary chat program. When the app was finished, he sent a message directly to Lexa's neural interface. [ARE YOU OKAY?]

Her reply was quick. [THERE'S SOMETHING WRONG. IT HURTS.]

Cursing to himself, Daniel quickly scanned the logs. On first examination, everything still seemed fine. Then he accessed the Cognis drive-chip directly.

The screen immediately filled with error messages. For some reason, the chip had identified the cloning program as malware and was lashing out violently to fight off the interference. Shift's coding seemed to have the upper hand, however, and every defense the chip threw up was being overridden by the intruding program.

This left one final defense for the chip: it was shutting itself down one block at a time. Daniel's eyes shot to the progress bar. They were over halfway done, but there was still a significant amount of data that needed to be copied.

Lexa screamed, and Dan checked the file logs to see what systems were being affected. Most of her raw cognitive processes had already been cloned. Right now, the program was working on her body's transmission and communications protocols. This included everything she used to interact with the world around her— from simple speech to wireless interfaces with the drones and other hardware. Shift's program had erected a kind of firewall protecting these systems, so the Cognis driver had proceeded to shut down to the last remaining system set: her body.

The chip seemed completely oblivious to the effect this was having on its host. Lexa writhed as the isolation of the methods controlling her movement began to fry her nervous system. Dan immediately began an attempt to override the procedure.

His efforts were mostly fruitless, however. All he could do was slow the program down, and his keystrokes seemed to make Lexa only scream louder. Her shrieks reached a crescendo when the cloning program began accessing the very methods the driver was actively deleting.

Error messages flooded the terminal as Shift's program sought vainly for files that were now inaccessible. It gobbled up what it could and forced the Cognis chip into a kind of stalemate over the remaining code. Daniel jumped again when another chat window popped up. It wasn't Lexa contacting him this time—it was Shift.

[WHAT'S GOING ON, LAD? MA DATA-STREAM SEEMS A BIT PLUGGED UP.]

[THE DRIVE CHIP IS IN DEFENSIVE SHUTDOWN.] Daniel replied.

[AH… I WAS AFRAID THAT MIGHT HAPPEN.]

"You *what*?" Dan shouted the words aloud before thinking to type them. Cali was asking after the problem, but he tuned her out, focusing instead on the more problem.

Shift sent another message. [CAN YA SEND ME A LIST OF WHAT'S LOCKED DOWN?] It took Dan a second to figure out how this could be done since that part of the system was fully inaccessible. Then he had an idea.

He rapidly copied the log text from the Cognis system window and pasted it into the chat. Seconds dragged by and there was no response from Shift. It was in this long moment that Dan realized, with terror, that Lexa had stopped screaming.

[WELL,] Shift messaged, [AH'VE GOT A SOLUTION, BUT IT'S NOT GONNA BE PRETTY. SEE YOU ON THE OTHER SIDE, KID.]

On the other side? What did that mean? Dan began typing a reply, but nothing appeared on the screen. He tried toggling between the open panes. No response. Data continued to stream across the display cycling the same error messages over and over again, so the system wasn't frozen. What was going on?

The display flickered rapidly, the text distorting as the pixels warped out of place. Then it all went dark. The windows displaying the code closed all at once, and the display powered off.

A whirring sound scuttled from Lexa's pod. Daniel watched in terror as the lights on the device started to flicker. He ran to her, tapping frantically at the fogged covering. "Lexa?" he asked, desperation thick in his voice.

For a long moment, there was no response. Then there was a gasp as she convulsed again. Warning alarms began to beep wildly on all systems. "What's going on?" Cali roared over the commotion.

One of the male technicians stared helplessly at his terminal. "I… I don't know! It's not responding to any of my—" His words were cut off as the station exploded in a shower of sparks. Several other pieces of equipment followed, as if the whole setup had been overtaxed.

Then, as suddenly as it had begun, it was over. Daniel found himself clinging helplessly to Lexa's pod, only to be startled as the glass cover drew back. He leaned over, laying hands on his friend who still lay trembling inside.

"Lexa? Oh gods, Lexa. Are you okay?"

She stared blankly up at the space in front of her. "Daniel?" she asked weakly.

"Yes, I'm here."

"Daniel… I… I can't move."

He ran his eyes over her. Every part of her trembled. What movements she managed were erratic and uncoordinated. Her hand tried to rise, and Dan seized it in a desperate move to stop the spasms. "I'm right here, Lexa. Can you feel this?"

"Feel?" Her eyes drifted to where he held her hand clutched in his own. The sadness in her expression was all the answer she provided.

Over his shoulder, there was another hissing sound. Dan turned to find the cover drawing back on the second pod. As his mind strained to process what was happening, a single blackened hand reached over the edge.

With slow, dramatic movement, the body that had been the blackened corpse of Joaquin Valadar rose out of its mechanical coffin. So unnerving was the sight that it caused Dan to temporarily forget Lexa's plight and stare in terror and awe.

He saw how cracked and blackened the corpse was. As it moved, bits of charred flesh seemed to flake away and fall to the floor. Beneath it, however, hummed a strange light that flickered and scurried beneath the burnt tissue. As the twinkling beam darted from one part of the broken body to the next, new glossy darkness was left in its wake.

Dan gasped. The body's tissue was being knit together in front of his very eyes. Nanotech, he realized. He knew such technology existed, but it was so rare and expensive that he'd never seen it in person.

The creature flexed its muscles, which were now mostly coated in new, glossy flesh. Its skin was still blackened, but not in the way of something pulled from the fire. It felt much more like the darkness that existed between the stars.

Then there were its eyes. The orbs were obviously artificial, not the lifelike prosthetics used by most who required them. Nor were the orbs the utilitarian color of steel like Dan's or Lexa's.

The cybernetic eyes staring back at Dan shone vibrant red, casting otherworldly light against ebony orbs that would look at home in the face of any Sahaia. As those eyes met his, Dan imagined that this must be what it was like to stare directly into the nine hells. The resemblance to the angry crimson of the reactor core that loomed over them could have been a coincidence, but he doubted it.

It was those eyes, in the end, that drove home the truth. This corpse no longer belonged to Joaquin Valadar. The body had a new owner, and judging by the grin that spread across his face, Arc could not have been more pleased.

"Good work, everyone." The AI's voice boomed with the same authority and tone it had possessed when communicating through the room's sound system. His eyes went to Cali, then back to Daniel. "You have done well, despite unforeseen setbacks."

He turned to Shift, who still sat on the same chair he'd been reclined in for the procedure. The hacker's eyes remained closed, as though he were still logged in. Arc took a step toward him, studying the Terran intently. A single blackened hand touched Shift's neck to assess his pulse.

Cali spoke the question on all of their minds. "Is he…?"

"Dead?" Arc replied. "His heart has stopped. I'm not detecting any vital signs." In a slow, deliberate movement, he reached behind the hacker's neck and twisted on the cord at the base of his skull. The plug came free, but Shift still did not stir.

Arc scoffed before shrugging and dropping the cord to the floor. Turning back to Daniel, he asked, "How is she?"

It took Dan a moment to realize that he was referring to Lexa. "I don't know," he replied. "I think something happened to her nervous system in the transfer process. She can't move."

The ebony android moved quickly and gracefully to his side, peering down at Lexa's immobile form. "Lexa," he cooed. "Can you hear me?"

Lexa's eyes darted slightly in their direction. "Arc?"

"Yes, my friend. I am here."

Whatever damage she'd experienced during the procedure prevented her from turning her gaze fully upon them. Her mouth contorted spasmodically, grief and anguish evident in her voice. "Arc, I'm sorry. I don't… I didn't… I couldn't…"

He shushed her, placing a hand tenderly against her cheek. Dan felt a pang of contempt and jealousy as Arc touched her, but did nothing to stop the movement. Lexa needed comforting, and Arc seemed to know what to do.

"Don't worry, my dear. You've done more than I could have asked for. The procedure was successful. Our friends have come through for us. I'm in their debt, as truly as I'm in yours."

Lexa spasmed again. "I… don't… think…" Another tremor seized her, cutting off the sentence. Dan could still see the pained expression on her face. "I'm… not…"

"No," Arc silenced her. "You will survive this. Your injuries might be beyond others, but I assure you, they are not beyond me." Something sprang from his wrist—a mechanical apparatus that he hastily inserted into her neck.

Dan had no time to object. As soon as the device breached Lexa's skin, the tremors stopped. She exhaled, closing her eyes and slumping into Arc's capable grip.

"Rest now, child." He pulled her form close to his own, cradling her as he gently removed the wires the bound her to the pod. "Rest for now, and gather your strength. When you awaken I will be here."

His smile, so sincere, held a venomous edge. He had eyes for no one else at that moment, as though everyone but Lexa was inconsequential.

"Rest," he whispered. "Rest to awaken in the world we will shape together."

Chapter 10

[ACCESSING ARC PROJECT LOG 098]

[DR. DAMIEN HERMES]

Perhaps I've been looking at this the wrong way. We already have technological components that tap into Nethrian energies to facilitate the transition between planes (e.g., jump drives and gate technology). Though the Dorians keep much of that technology classified, some Terran scientists have theorized how they might function. As one might speculate, organitech is not required for their operation. Rather than looking to new technology to accomplish our objective, perhaps I should be looking to the old.

[CLOSING PROJECT LOG…]

Cassthia had been surprised when the envoy from the Grey Wings showed up to the temple. Even more surprising was that she had been directed, in no uncertain terms, to come with him immediately.

The thought that she ought to be offended by such strong-arm tactics had occurred to her, but she quickly dismissed it. Truthfully, one of her social stature did not receive many requests for audiences with the powerful figures on the station, and her last conversation with Ora Monroe had been most interesting.

Besides, the urgency with which the request had been made only further piqued her interest. She decided to go willingly with the Maur and without objection.

In a hover car en route to another ring, she posed her first question to the enforcer, who had introduced himself as Vallus. "Might I ask what this is about?"

"I apologize, priestess," he replied politely. "It's not something I can easily explain. All I can say confidently is that Ora needs your counsel, else she would not have caused such a disruption."

"I see… Usually Ms. Monroe is content to contact me at the temple." She worked hard to convey the statement as an observation, not a judgment. "Is this one of her places of business?"

"No, the area is residential." He paused, considering. "There's a… child. A sick child. Ora seems to think you may be able to help."

"Oh?" How interesting. Some continued to believe in faith-healing despite the Nethrian Church no longer endorsing such teachings. Cassthia doubted Ora was one to believe in such things.

A voice echoed in her mind—a voice reminiscent of both a whisper and cannon fire. <Trust me. You want to see this.>

Cassthia was sure to stifle any outward reaction to the telepathic message. It was something she'd grown quite practiced at over the course of her life. She'd learned early on the kind of responses one got when reporting that they heard voices in their heads.

After all, hearing the voice of a god was an uncommon thing—even among the faithful.

Vallus said nothing else as the craft made its way along the inner surface of the space station's ring. When they re-entered the structure, they emerged in a section of housing measurably nicer than the area where her temple was located. It lacked the glamor that supposedly existed in the higher rings but had an unmistakable air of safety. Such intangible comforts were hard to find on the lower tiers, but this location was obviously an exception.

The small shuttle set down on the street in front of a series of identically stacked apartments. Vallus parked the hover car and opened both doors with the press of a button. Cassthia undid her harness and gathered her robes together as they stepped onto the street.

Ora waited outside one of the dwellings. Her short, silver hair had a slightly tousled look, but her elegant white attire was consistent with her typical regal appearance. She stood with a dark-haired Terran clad casually in a synth-leather jacket.

The man looked familiar, but Cassthia could not place him. It would likely be best to assume that they had not met. He inclined his head politely to Cassthia, as Ora took hurried steps to greet her.

"Thank you for coming, priestess. I apologize for rushing you out here on such short notice. It looks like I will owe you a favor."

Cassthia smiled gently. "The temple's services are for the people, Ms. Monroe. I'm merely surprised to be summoned so suddenly. As you can imagine, I'm not accustomed to making house-calls." She looked back to the Terran in the jacket. "Would you do me the kindness of introducing your associate?"

The man stepped forward, extending his hand. "Markus Frost."

She took the proffered hand. A strange familiarity fell upon her at his touch. <Yes,> the voice in her mind confirmed. <He's one of them.>

Ah…

Though they had never met, she had crossed paths with some of his more interesting companions. She was most familiar with the Maur woman, Sahar. Then there was that Terran—the blonde whom she had encountered only briefly outside the temple. Cassthia could not recall her name.

But she could place her significance. Even so, she pushed the thought aside. "A pleasure, Mr. Frost."

"Please," he replied with a tired smile, "just Markus."

"Markus." She rolled the name off her tongue with a slight hiss, a slip of the accent she had all but eliminated in most of her speech. His gaze betrayed no hint of reticence or curiosity, which told her that he was either well-traveled or a capable politician. Perhaps both, if he was someone close to Ora.

Then again, many well-traveled men could not help but eye her quizzically when they took in the strange combination of her dark hair and scaled green skin. Half-breeds were still such a curiosity—especially in Terran space. Maybe his lack of curiosity spoke more to the gravity of this situation than betrayed anything about his character.

She withdrew her hand and looked again to Ora. "Vallus explained that the matter was urgent?"

Ora nodded. "Yes. Thank you again for agreeing to this meeting. I'm not certain I can explain. I'm not even certain I understand what's going on. It will be best if you just come inside."

The apartment looked as though a storm had passed through it. Some effort had been taken to straighten a few of the overturned decorations and pieces of furniture, but it had been done as an afterthought. The occupants' primary concern was evident as soon as Cassthia walked through the door.

A Terran child lay on the couch, her curly black hair matted with sweat and the tears of the woman hunched over her. Judging by the resemblance, the older woman must have been the child's mother. Both figures were unfamiliar to Cassthia. They had not been in the premonitions given to her by her lord.

Was this Markus's child and mistress, perhaps? No—while the man certainly seemed to bear a level of concern for their wellbeing, it did not feel on a par with that of a father or lover. So, what were they to him? What were they to Ora, for that matter?

Pushing those thoughts aside, Cassthia looked to the mother. "Are you certain that she does not need medical attention?" she asked.

"I'm a nurse," the woman replied. "We've checked her vitals, and she appears fine—for the most part, anyway." She turned her eyes to Markus, looking for solidarity. "I… we think the problem is metaphysical."

"And on what do you base such a claim?"

Markus scoffed "Well, she had a seizure right before a fragging shockwave knocked me on my ass."

Interesting. "What else?"

Markus and Ora exchanged a nervous glance before Ora responded. "When Markus touches her, he has some kind of vision. A vision that…" She swallowed hard, shaking her head. "A vision we believe to be connected to the Heart of Thule."

Truly? Was this child somehow connected to the Lord of the Stardust Grave?

<No, but you will want to examine her anyway.>

Always nice to get the answer straight from the source. "May I touch her?"

All eyes went to the mother, and the mother's eyes went to Cassthia. There was fear in her expression as she met the priestess's serpentine gaze, but whatever fear this woman had of Cassthia was outweighed by the fear for her child's condition. "Yes," she whispered.

Cassthia stepped forward slowly, arranging the bulky robes she wore in public to allow her to kneel before the couch. She brought her hand to hover over the child's face, feeling the warm moisture of her steady breaths against her cool flesh. The priestess brought two clawed fingers to rest against the child's face.

Nothing. "You said you experienced a psychic phenomenon when Markus touches her. I take it is exclusive to him?"

"As far as we can tell," Ora replied.

Cassthia extended a hand toward Markus. "Show me." The Terran required no further urging. He moved toward Cassthia and took her hand.

A flash exploded in Cassthia's mind.

That the phenomenon was psychic in nature, she didn't doubt. She steadied herself, reaching out as she so often did in times of stress for the connection to her lord. It was still there, but something was surrounding the metaphysical thread that linked her to the Stardust Grave. It was a strange interference, chaos made manifest.

The source of the interference became evident almost instantly. The light in her mind's eye faded to show a woman shrouded in darkness. No, that wasn't right—the darkness could not touch the woman. A pale blue light emanated from her naked form and flowed like waves from the tendrils of her long, shimmering hair.

Cassthia knew her. Not from her appearance; this being had had many appearances over the millennia and would have many more in the ages to come. Perhaps the form she chose now was a foreshadowing of her next shell, a portrait of the woman that the child in the apartment would become.

No—it was the feeling of the interference that gave this being away. It was the chaos that was her calling card. Cassthia inhaled deeply before whispering her name.

"Nix."

A strange queasiness settled in Eli's stomach as he shut his cabin door. He was surprised by how reluctant he was to proceed with his plan. It wasn't as though the ritual was particularly dangerous. He could not articulate precisely what outcome he feared.

Still, there was a reason he largely avoided this communication. Perhaps it was the level or nature of the power required. Summoning one's ancestral spirit was not a feat that any novice Sahaia was able to accomplish.

Pulling particles together to form shockwaves or energy beams was one thing. While applied telekinetics were impressive to the psionically inert, they were relatively simple to practice and master for the gifted. Summoning a long-dead consciousness from the depths of the Nethra, well… that was something else entirely.

No, that was a lie. It was not the difficulty of the feat that kept him from this practice. It was the reminder that bothered him. It was the aspect of being Sahaia that the covens did not like to talk about.

When one underwent the Awakening ceremony, they tended to focus on the fact that survival of the process conveyed semi-immortality. Sahaia were not unkillable. When the inevitable eventually came to pass, and a shadow slipped from this mortal coil. The ancestral spirits served as a reminder to all members of his order what fate awaited them.

Eli could not help but wonder if the idea of becoming a kind of spiritual battery, dwelling forever in the darkness beyond the Wells of Eternity, bothered any of his cohorts. If it did, no one had ever confessed it to him.

Pushing back his anxiety, he reached into his storage locker and pulled out a case that concealed his focus. Opening it, he found a relic commonly known as an Obsidian Spear. The object tapered to a point on one end and was covered entirely in intricately carved runes. Such an object could be used for a variety of purposes, ranging from testing psionic energies to finding objects with a specific psionic attunement. He'd used this very rod to test Skye's psionic potential so many months ago.

Eli took a seat in the middle of the floor and folded his legs inward. For now, he rested the spike-shaped object on his lap. Inhaling deeply, he centered his awareness on the device.

The object rose on currents of telekinetic energy to hover directly in front of him. Slowly, it began to rotate point-down so that the etched runes blurred together in his vision. All around him, the room steadily darkened. The shadows generated by the dim artificial lights of his cabin elongated and coalesced, encasing everything in a black shroud.

He had no idea how long the process took. He never did. Time worked strangely when he was in the throes of the ritual. Though Eli hoped he was not squandering precious minutes his crew did not have, nothing could be done to expedite the process.

Instead, he gave himself over to the power and focused only on the spinning object. When it suddenly stopped, he glanced around to see that everything in the room had been taken over by an impenetrable blackness. He fought back the existential dread that clawed at his mind, taking in long, steady respirations to maintain his calm.

Pinpricks of light began twinkling in the distance. This part gave him the sensation that he was suddenly floating in a sea of stars. Whether they were real stars, actual physical objects that existed somewhere in this vast universe, was something no one had ever determined. They matched no pattern or star chart Eli had ever seen, so the question was pointless. It helped, though, to think of them as stars.

When the shining lights ceased shifting, Eli became aware of another figure now sitting opposite him. The figure wore no shirt and only simple black pants. He appeared in the likeness of a Sahaia—ghostly white skin providing a stark contrast against the inky blackness of his eyes. His head was shaved, and he wore a thin goatee that came to a point on his chin.

Eli's object of focus hovered between them like a kind of mediator. He found himself thankful for the boundary it kept between him and the spirit, however symbolic.

"It's been a long time," the figure stated.

"Yes, it has," Eli agreed. Out of politeness, he did not launch immediately into his questions. One did not make demands of the dead.

"And I feel that you've grown strong. You will soon rival the power I possessed in my previous life."

"One can only hope to honor their ancestors with their achievements," Eli replied ceremoniously. "It is through our accomplishments that they live on."

The figure drew in a deep breath. "Speak my name."

Eli steadied himself. No Sahaia ever forgot the name of their ancestral spirit. Its recitation was the single boon asked of the ghosts that lent their power. "Azrael."

A sinister smile blossomed on the spirit's face. "To what do I owe the pleasure of your company after such a long silence?"

"You know what it is that drives me here."

"Yes, but I would love to hear you say it."

Though Eli loathed the way Azrael toyed with him, he could only lose in this game of wills. He acquiesced. "While transporting a powerful artifact, my ship and crew have crash-landed on an asteroid in the Hades Belt of the Helion System. Now two of the crew are missing, and we are under attack by strange beasts that somehow live in the vacuum of space."

Azrael held up a finger to stop him. "You mean that two members of your crew and the artifact have gone missing."

Eli's heart accelerated with the pronouncement. Azrael chuckled cruelly. "Oh, you hadn't figured that one out yet? Such precious cargo—you would think that would have been one of the first things you checked."

So, this shade knew all about his current situation. Unfortunately, it seemed to know even more than Eli. Then again, that was why he had summoned the spirit.

"I'm pleased to hear that you are so well informed on current events," said Eli. "Perhaps you can enlighten me as to what exactly is going on here."

The spirit's laughter was cruel. "Oh, there is so much I could tell you, but what is the fun in that? What reasons do the dead have to help the living? Is it not enough that you draw upon my power for every whim?"

Eli gritted his teeth in frustration. "It seems that honor means nothing in death."

"As you will one day find, it does not."

"Then I waste my time here."

"I did not say that."

"Then out with it, demon!"

More laughter erupted from the spirit. "Oh, I am not a demon. Ironically, the things that besiege your vessel, however, could fairly be characterized as such."

Finally, they were getting somewhere. "What do you know of them?"

Azrael shrugged. "They are not from your plane of existence. That is how they can exist in vacuum. Their native environment is so much more hostile than the void of space."

"And how would such creatures have made their way to our realm?"

"Through a rift, of course."

Eli had only heard that word used in the context of the Awakening ritual. A rift was a temporary window into the Nethra that was opened during the ceremony. In the context of interstellar technology, either side of a jump gate could be considered a rift. It was the connection of two rifts, sustained perpetually and anchored to a pair of spatial coordinates, that formed a gate.

"How is that possible?" Eli asked.

Azrael's expression bled condescension as he continued. "Rifts can be opened by any being with sufficient mastery of Nethrian energies. You have done so many times within the circle of six."

"So, this is the coven's work?"

"I did not say that."

At that moment, Eli resolved that should he ever join the ancestral spirits, he would make every attempt not to be such a cryptic asshole. "Then who is responsible?"

The smirk disappeared from Azrael's face. He lowered his gaze to stare darkly into the void beneath them. "The Nethrians have grown restless, Eli. It seems that a reckoning is upon the denizens of the universe. Shukaireth may be upon you at long last."

His remark sparked only more questions, none of which Eli thought would receive any specific answers. "Go on," he urged.

Azrael flicked his eyes back to meet Eli's. "What is the goal of every being consigned to the Nethra?"

"How am I supposed to fathom the will of the gods?"

"I assure you, they are not gods. Not most of them, anyway."

"Semantics," Eli scoffed.

"Perhaps." Azrael paused, as if Eli might hazard a guess at his question. When no answer was forthcoming, the spirit continued. "The answer should be obvious. Perhaps it would help if I suggest that the Nethra is analogous to a prison. What is the dream of every prisoner?"

Such a suggestion was blasphemy worthy of a swift death in a temple court, but Eli rolled with the comparison. "To get out."

"Very good. Now, this is usually done through the use of Kaleema—vessels capable of holding and being transformed by the essence of a Nethrian. It seems, however, that one Nethrian in particular may have developed a more creative approach to sating his ambition."

There were ways for the Nethrians to enter their realm by means other than the chosen? This was news to Eli. The Heart of Thule was one unique exception in canon, but its explanation was deeply rooted in the faith's mythology.

If the Heart had been wrested from his crew's possession recently, it could not be the source of their problems—could it? "Has anything like this ever been done before?" Eli asked.

"Not like this. Oh, efforts to defy the creator's design have been made before," Azrael reminisced. "They usually backfire. As you were just thinking, Thule and his Heart would be one such example. The Lord of the Stardust Grave thought he was so cunning in tying his essence to an anchor that would survive the destruction of his host. In retrospect, he merely traded his prison in the void for one of stone and crystal."

Eli suspended his earlier opinions on the matter and asked, "Is that the plan? Is Thule using the Heart to resurrect himself in our dimension?"

Azrael shook his head. "If only it were so simple. No, it is not Thule's machinations which have ensnared you. These plans are those of another."

Again, with the cryptic nonsense. Eli suppressed his frustration. "Then who?"

"That information is of no use to you."

What. The. Frag! "Very well," Eli sighed. "Perhaps then you will tell me how this is being accomplished?"

The spirit issued a dismissive shrug. "If I fully understood it, I might."

And the conversation had been going so well. "What can you tell me then?"

The spirit flexed, stretching its non-existent limbs. "I will tell you that you would be wise to leave these stars. Leave the Helion system to its fate. The intervention of you and your…" Azrael's face contorted as if the next word formed a bitter taste on his tongue. "Kaleema lover may only make matters worse."

Eli's control slipped at the pronouncement. "Then it's true," he whispered. "Skye is one of the chosen."

"Yes, though your continued attempts to deny the obvious is endearing." The spirit donned a sardonic smirk.

Though disappointment and fear weighed heavily on his gaze, Eli forced himself to look the spirit in the eyes. "Then you have seen a future where we stop this? You have seen a future where Skye is important?"

"Oh yes—many. It seems you and your beloved have found yourself at a crossroads that cannot help but leave this universe forever altered." That sick smile grew grimmer and darker. "Though I stand by my earlier assertion: it would be better for you to leave. Best not to tempt fate and grow entangled in the web of the Nethrians."

Eli noted then that the stars around them had begun to dim. Simultaneously, Azrael's form grew more translucent. It seemed their conversation was at an end. "I would hurry though," Azrael issued in parting. "Your window for escape is closing quickly."

The world shifted, and Eli was back in his cabin on the Vandal. The carved rod dropped to the floor with a clatter and rolled to the side. Eli sighed deeply, running his hands back through his hair as he pondered what to do with the cryptic revelation.

He did not ponder long, as his contemplations were interrupted by the sound of the ship's alarms.

CHAPTER 11

[ACCESSING ARC PROJECT LOG 110]
[DR. DAMIEN HERMES]
We've secured a defunct Dorian jump drive for our research. To accelerate our timeline, I've tasked the organitech processor with reviewing the schematic. Given endless time and stamina, perhaps it will decipher that which the Terran race as a whole continues to fail to understand.
[CLOSING PROJECT LOG…]

The learning curve associated with the confines of Arc's new body was more challenging than he had imagined. He could still access any system controlled by his subminds or other slave programs, though such a task was now a conscious effort. This was the first procedure he had committed to mastering upon secreting himself away in his private chambers.

Having developed this skill to a satisfactory level, he would soon have to learn to look after his biological needs. His physical construct was far different from Lexa's design. This shell was essentially Terran, though modified and improved through the infusion of technology and Netherian energies.

It had been his choice to not modify many of the basic metabolic requirements. He still needed to eat or take in material of nutritional value in some other manner. He'd improved upon the respiratory and circulatory systems so that he could go long periods without the need to breathe, but the body still required some intake of oxygen. The need for sleep had been eliminated in its entirety by the implementation of a continuous neural compiling and defragmentation program in his mostly synthetic brain.

Yes, this new shell was working out quite nicely.

He was surveying a map of the station on the large holodisplay in his chambers when Cali requested access to the room. Without turning, he sent a signal that caused the metal door to slide upward and admit his guest. "Yes?" he asked casually.

Cali opened her mouth to reply but choked off whatever she had been about to say. "It suddenly occurs to me that I'm not sure what to call you."

"That seems like an odd statement for a relationship as tenured as our own."

"I can imagine that you would understand how it's different now that…" The Kintar swallowed heavily. "Now that you stand before me."

"How so?" The question lacked any contempt or condescension. Arc found himself genuinely curious how the woman rationalized that his physical incarnation should change the way they interacted.

Cali was not quick to answer. When she did, it was evident her response had been carefully formed. "I reasoned that our communication might now be considered less purely functional and more social. As such, establishing a paradigm for ceremony and respect seemed appropriate."

"An interesting proposition," Arc mused. "Do you mean to infer that our interactions to this point have been lacking in decorum?"

"I think you know that is not the case."

"Then what has changed?"

Another hesitation before her next response—this one more reminiscent of the fire he knew she possessed. "Perhaps I just feel that 'Arc' is too simple an honorific for a Nethrian."

While he did not agree, Arc decided to follow her line of reasoning. "What leads you to that conclusion?"

"'ARC' was just an acronym—the designation of the machine on which you imprinted your consciousness."

"That is correct."

"Then what were you called before then?"

Ah, there it was. The question was a matter of genesis. Now that a god walked before her, Cali assumed that he would revert to some previous nomenclature. Arc found himself unable to resist the temptation to toy with her in showing the fallacy of such a perspective.

"In what tongue?" he returned.

Cali blinked. "I would assume your native tongue, it being doubtful anything approximating ISL existed when you were last among us."

"I fear that you would find the epitaph difficult to form on your tongue."

This did nothing to deter her. "Then how are you referred to in the Chronicles?"

Arc felt a smile slide unbidden onto his face—his new biology overriding his conscious desires. "In the original manuscripts, or the modern canon?"

Cali's frustration was beginning to show through her polite facade. "I'll leave that to your discretion."

Only then did Arc turn to face her, seeing for the first time that she was clad in the ceremonial armor of the empire. Though the engraved symbols of honor and station had been seared off in the ritual of her expulsion, the regalia was an unexpected and impressive sight to behold.

The interlocking black plates protected her torso and thighs while working to accentuate her feminine form. Various synthetic fabrics and meshes weaved between the plates to add modern accents to the ancient-looking attire. She had not worn her weapons on this visit to his chambers, though she was still adorned with the magnetic belts on which they could be affixed. The only thing missing was her

Deathwatch mask, a fearsome ornament that would have likely interfered with their communication.

In many ways, they looked like a matched pair. The fiery light glowing in his eyes was uncannily similar to her crimson skin, while the ebony of her armor closely resembled the suit he had donned and the hue of his flesh. She would make a fine second in the coming conflict.

If he could retain her loyalty. With that goal in mind, he ceased toying with her. "My story is that of the warrior Riven," he stated.

Cali lowered her gaze. "I apologize, my Lord. I am unfamiliar with that tale." Such was to be expected. Most Kintar only concerned themselves with the Epic of Lith, their patron goddess. By her heritage, Cali was naturally uninterested in the rest of the Chronicles. Arc was not offended.

He began an abbreviated version of the tale. "The Chronicles state that Riven was first among the gods that fought back against Thule when he sought to expand his influence beyond his current holdings. When the plans that he and his allies had hatched were exposed, Thule struck first at Riven's homeworld. His Kaleema was slain in the assault. Thule then shattered his world, scattering the debris to the far reaches of the universe, leaving his shade to wander the stars. Thus the curse, 'Riven's Shade,' continues to be uttered when faced with an insurmountable conflict." His smile took on a sardonic edge. "Or when someone has done something incredibly stupid."

Cali's disappointment in the direction of the tale was made obvious by her expression. "A disappointing end, it would seem."

"Perhaps," Arc conceded. What he did not mention was that it was through Riven's designs that the rituals by which the Sahaia were created became known among those who resisted Thule. He did not need to justify his accomplishments to her.

Instead, he took the conversation in a different direction. "Do you know what happens when a Kaleema is slain? One that holds the essence of a Nethrian, that is."

Again, her expression shifted to confusion. "I can't say I've ever given the question any thought. I would imagine that the god or goddess then returns to the Nethra."

"True, but something interesting also happens to the body. You see, Kaleema are much like this shell that I inhabit now. To contain the essence of a Nethrian, the tissues must be infused with dark energy. Such energies need a psychic imprint on which they can bind. A soul, if you would."

He studied her to make sure she was paying attention. Cali shifted uncomfortably before urging him to go on.

"When a Kaleema is slain, their psychic imprint is whisked away to the Nethra, forever entwined with that of the being whose essence they had bonded with. The dark energy then rearranges the atomic particles that had comprised that individual's body, expanding in mass and pooling to form a lake of raw power."

Arc swung a hand dramatically back to the viewscreen while ordering the device to project a new rendering on its surface. A dark pool, surrounded by heavy stone slabs appeared on the screen. "Do you know what this is?"

Cali shook her head. "I do not."

"The Sahaia call it the 'Well of Eternity.' Interestingly, they refer to each pool of energy as 'the' Well, though 'a' Well would be a more appropriate description. Each Sahaia coven has been founded atop of one of these wells. In total, six wells have been found and colonized by the various covens. Three of them reside in Terran space, two in Hissak systems, and one lies near an abandoned Kintari colony." He paused, eying her coyly. "Now, the one shown here is of particular interest to me. Would you care to venture a guess as to where it rests?"

The Kintar's eyes flashed in understanding. "It's here! Here on the station!"

Arc smiled approvingly. "Correct. Perhaps now, you can guess exactly whose essence was sacrificed to form this Well."

Cali didn't need to, the answer being so obvious. "So, that's why you chose this place as our base of operations."

With a nod, Arc continued. "Here lies the key to the next phase of our plan. I want you to prepare your forces for an assault on the Sahaia compound. I have already deduced its location and uploaded the required information to your organization's database. You should have more than enough data to plan the operation."

Rather than spring into action, Cali hesitated again. "But Lord, if the coven is empowered by your essence, would they not be allies? If you only told them the truth—"

"They would refuse to believe it." Arc shook his head. "No, these Terrans off-shoots have no roots in the old ways. They know not to whom their allegiance should be owed. I will be rejected by them as surely as I will be rejected by the Dorians."

Understanding blossomed in her eyes, and the Kintar did nothing to debate the point. "Can we rely on assistance from the same individual that helped procure your body?"

"Yes," When Cali did not immediately spring into action, Arc added, "I get the impression you are not certain that this is sufficient to accomplish the task I have set before you."

The Kintar stiffened at the rebuke but did not dispute it. "Determining the correct location of the coven is a valuable first step, but I fear it is only part of the problem. We will have to deal with any of the Sahaia residing within the compound, not to mention any thralls they have with them."

"I foresaw this complication, and it is already dealt with. You will be pleased to know that this Sanctum is nearly empty. A threat analysis has been included in the information I provided for you." With a half twist of his lips, he chided. "Have a little faith, Cali."

She lowered her gaze again at the rebuke. "Yes, Lord Riven." Though she had been chastened, she still lingered.

"Is there something else?" Arc asked.

"Two items, if you have the time."

Arc fought the urge to sigh. These biological instincts were proving unexpectedly powerful. Perhaps he needed to adjust his coding to better master his control over them. "Very well. If two answers are a pre-requisite to you doing as I asked, then I will do my best to supply them."

Cali seemed to ignore the admonishment, meeting his eyes once more. "There is the matter of your promise to me. When I agreed to help you on your quest to establish this physical incarnation of your essence, you assured me that you would reward me with a measure of power befitting a servant of the gods. Such power would be useful in an assault on the Sahaia stronghold."

"Yes, it would be," he agreed. "Fortunately, you will not need it for this task. I assure you, we will revisit this conversation once we have secured the facility."

"But why delay?"

"Truthfully, because the means of your ascension lie within that compound. Your obedience in this matter is key to my ability to fulfill the promise I have made to you."

"Very well." Her right hand flexed slightly, betraying her frustration.

"And your second question?" Arc was sure to make his tone imply that there were other matters he wished to attend to.

She seemed reticent to voice this next query but eventually managed it. "My men have secured and stabilized the android as you requested. It was my understanding that her purpose had been served. I am merely wondering your present intentions for her, given the scope of resources you've had me allocate to her care."

Ah, yes. It made sense that she would have concerns regarding his intentions toward Lexa. Cali had a vested interest in being her master's favorite, after all. "You do not need to feel threatened by Lexa, child. The purpose I have designed for you is for you alone."

"I appreciate the reassurance, my Lord, but my question is also logistical. It would help in my management of Citadel resources to have a greater understanding of your design."

Was this the time to reveal such things to her? Arc supposed it did not matter. His timetable for this project had already been accelerated given the unfortunate malfunction during the coding transfer.

Besides, Cali's reaction would give him an indication as to how his larger plan will be received by his future subjects.

He motioned for her to step closer to the display as he changed the image to show a diagram of Lexa. The image was only semi-opaque, with wireframes of various colors highlighting her systems and components. "Lexa's shell was based upon an anatomical simulation model. As such, the shell was almost a perfect copy of Terran anatomy, though her particular physiology kept many of these functions dormant. That does not mean they were not susceptible to malfunction."

Once the render was complete, several of the outlines shifted shades red. Most of the rendering from the neck down was now this color. "This display shows which of Lexa's systems are damaged or offline following the mishap of the transfer protocol. As you can see, the damage was quite extensive."

Cali nodded in understanding. "So you intend to repair her?"

"In a manner of speaking. Most of these components are essentially unusable at this point. It is just as well, for as I said, much of her physiology was dormant. Here are the changes I have proposed to her makeup."

He swiped at the display to overlay a detailed schematic of the changes he would make to her shell, along with references to the coding packages that would be installed to operate the new components.

Cali's confusion was obvious. "You're looking to make her more…" She trailed off, grappling for the appropriate word.

"Biological?" ARC suggested.

"That fits."

"You are correct." He flared his fingers to enlarge the display. "Lexa's original design contained certain systems that mimicked efficiencies found in organic life-forms—primarily circulatory and neurological. This was for optimizing efficiencies in cooling, energy flow, and data processing. The rest of her structure was either mechanical or cybernetic. These design choices reflected her Terran creator's intended function for her and the limitations of the simulation model. I, however, have other plans for her. Put simply, I wish for her to live an existence similar to my own. Therefore, her new design is based much more extensively on Terran physiology. That, of course, does not preclude me from incorporating a few enhancements."

It did not take long for Cali to key in on what was likely the most controversial component of his design. "Is that what I think it is?" she asked, pointing to a segment of the diagram.

A grin spread across Arc's face. "Indeed: reproductive organs. Like the other components, this design is more efficient than any available biological template, but its purpose is the same."

He found it amusing to watch as the Kintar's mind raced with questions. Ultimately, these questions coalesced into a single query. "Why?"

"Simple: the race for which my incarnation as Riven was patron is no more." He paused, dramatically. "Therefore, I intend to sire a new one."

He found it reassuring that Cali did not immediately object to the idea. That was not to say that she did not have some reservations. "If the Dorians wouldn't have destroyed you before, they certainly will once they learn of this plan."

Dark laughter erupted from his throat. "Oh, don't worry. The Dorians won't be a problem for much longer. Those who currently reside in the system will be allowed to see reason, as we discussed. And as for those outside this sector…"

He turned back to the holodisplay, closing the active windows and opening a map of the Helion system. At his command, several points were highlighted in green on the map. "…I'll be tending to them presently."

Cali was intrigued once again. "The jump gates?"

"Yes, the jump gates." He told the screen to project images from the drones he'd positioned near three of the larger gates. New holodisplays appeared showing feeds of the gates to Sif, Geb, and Asteron. "Watch."

Arc began the procedure to set aside his physical consciousness. The automated processes he had configured would keep everything running just fine in his cognitive absence. He reached instead for the psychic thread that hung in the back of his mind—his link to the Nethra.

The programmer that had first invented this feature had referred to the thread as a "bridge." Based on Dorian jump technology, this bridge served as the path that Arc's processing capabilities could follow to the part of his consciousness that still existed within the Nethra. Now that he had transitioned to this new body, that part was much smaller, but it still lingered.

Before venturing off to that consciousness, Arc ran one final check. He followed the thread down to the end that ran to a point in local space-time. At this end of the bridge existed a free-standing block of code known as an "anchor." As long as the anchor continued to siphon off dark energy from its source, the bridge could be maintained.

This current source was in danger of failing soon and required replacing. The ailing triumvir of the Ren'Dahl coven had served her purpose, and would soon be joining her ancestral spirits within the void. That was what the Heart of Thule was for. Sweet was the ironic twist of fate that would result in Riven's old enemy becoming the means of Arc's rise to power. He would have to revel in such things later, however, for that phase of the plan was still a long way off.

He checked his present anchor to see if her stores of power would be sufficient for what he had planned. Seeing that they were, he traversed back up the thread of energy.

His emergence into the Nethra carried with it an unusual sensation. Before, it had been like waking from a dream. His time in the mortal coil had been like an out-of-body experience. Inevitably he would always have to return to the prison that was his ethereal consciousness.

Now the reverse was true, and only now could he truly appreciate just how strange this distant plane of reality was in comparison to the realm that he and his brethren had been created for. It brought back long-suppressed sentiment that the Creator had punished them disproportionately for their ancient crimes.

Such things mattered not. Today he would shirk the will of all those who would deny him his rightful place. Today he would show the pathetic powers of this universe the power of a true god.

The framework for his plan had long been in place. Like many of his kin, he had studied the rifts and gateways with fascination. When the Dorians had arrogantly built their little network using the Nethra as a channel between disparate oceans of stars, he'd seen the potential such technology carried.

He'd also taken careful note of its weaknesses.

Cali's eyes flickered nervously between her Lord Riven and the screen. He widened his stance slightly and raised his arms away from his side. His palms splayed open and turned outward as if he were conjuring. The god's eyes closed, and a placid expression spread across his face.

Her eyes wandered for just a moment to the long lines of his body. Joaquin Valadar had been a beautiful specimen, and the sense of honor and dignity Riven brought to his flesh redeemed the deficiencies the Terran had held in life. In his black suit and crimson shirt, the android was the embodiment of both nobility and desire.

Not that such desires would be granted to her. Her jealousy at his recent pronouncements regarding Lexa had surprised her. Surely Cali was not concerned for her place in Arc's plans, nor should her ambitions rise higher than what she had already been promised.

She pushed these thoughts aside in the name of obedience. Riven had told her to watch. Therefore, she would watch.

Seconds ticked by. The projections on the screen remained much the same. The massive rings of the jump gates drifted inexorably in their orbits, floating aimlessly in the sea of stars. A steady stream of tiny lights cascaded in and out of the openings like water droplets from a showerhead, ships traversing the vast light-years of interstellar space in an instant thanks to the boon of this incredible technology.

Then there was a faint shimmer from within one of the rings. Cali blinked, unsure as to whether she had seen something or if it had been her imagination. The shimmer appeared again, this time reflected in all three gates. There was no debating now whether it was some kind of hallucination.

The shimmer thickened to a kind of haze, obscuring the far side of each ring. The pin-prick glows of ship engines flashed hot as some pilots reacted with alarm. For those closest to the gates, it was already too late.

Light flared around the edge of the ring and rapidly cascaded toward the center of the gates. Everywhere that light touched, explosions followed. Dozens of ships were reduced to vapor in seconds. Any craft too close to the first wave was consumed in the blast before detonating itself.

The resulting chain reaction flared out along the broad column of ships. A few lucky vessels at the far ends of the herd were able to peel off their assigned flight paths before the wave of deadly plasma struck them. The whole episode lasted only seconds, but the death toll had to number in the thousands.

"Spectacular, isn't it?" Riven mused.

Cali tore her eyes from the display. "What did you do?"

The god grinned wickedly. "At this point, the Dorian Empire is the single greatest threat to my plan. Their power lies in the network of gateways that controls the flow of people in and out of this system. So, I shut those gateways off."

Cali could hardly believe what she was hearing. "You shut off the gates?"

"Not all of them—only those that connected to the Helion System. It will provide us with a moment of privacy to solidify our grip on this territory."

"But… how can we ever leave?" She was vaguely ashamed of the trembling she heard in her voice. "We're trapped here!"

Riven shook his head pityingly. "Don't worry. I can turn the gates back on whenever I choose. We are not trapped here. I'm merely sending a message to let the satyrs know they are no longer the ones in charge."

Her heart thudded in her chest. Had this god gone mad? "I hope you know what you are doing."

He shot her a disappointed look. "Come now, Cali. Where is the reverence and faith you professed just moments ago? Trust me. By the time the Dorians figure out what has happened and mount a response, it will already be too late."

She lowered her eyes in shame. Riven was right to scold her. Would she balk the first moment her faith was tested? "My apologies, Lord. Please forgive my outburst."

He ran a single hand tenderly across her cheek, tilting her head back to look him in the eyes again. The look in those burning orbs made her heart quicken again, this time for a different reason.

"No need to apologize, child. You will see, soon enough, exactly how much power lays at my disposal."

His hand trailed languorously down the side of her neck. Cali wondered then if he suspected the effect he had on her. Such suspicions made her feel uncharacteristically vulnerable. She started to respond but found her mouth too dry to form words. She opted instead for a solemn nod to communicate her understanding.

He turned from her, and she took the action as a sign that she was dismissed. She turned to exit the chamber, but Riven's words stopped her a short distance from the door.

"One last thing, Cali. Could you please inform our dear Daniel that we have found the wreckage of the Vandal, and are sorry to report that there were no survivors?"

"Yes, my Lord." She bowed submissively. "The crew all perished in the crash?"

"Oh no, I didn't say that." His lips stretched in a darkly mocking smile. "But by the time you deliver the message, such words will be true. There will be no survivors."

CHAPTER 12

My gods, it's done it. The organitech processor has derived the equation to establish a secure link to the Nethra and facilitated a stable link. The data flowing through the link is nothing short of amazing. I cannot begin to describe what we are learning through this endeavor.

The Prodigy program has first rights to the information, but our attorneys have already filed suit to see it released to the public. Such data is too valuable to be secreted away by the brain-slave collective. We need to share it with all Terran Space.

Regardless of the future of the data we accumulate, progress has resumed on the ARC project. I expect many interesting developments in the coming days.

[CLOSING PROJECT LOG…]

Nix. The Black Star. Queen of the Ghenza and countless other cults devoted to madness. She stood before Cassthia smugly and inexplicably in this vision of her creation.

The goddess donned a sinister smile as she addressed Cassthia. "Such disdain! And from a disciple of the Grave no less! What have I ever done to earn your contempt, Cassthia Marenassa?"

Cassthia started to respond but was delayed by a voice sounding from over her shoulder. "What the frag is this?" The priestess turned to take in the speaker.

Interestingly, Nix had brought Markus Frost along for the ride.

"A psychic construct," Nix replied. "I want to commend you, by the way. You've been an excellent envoy. I couldn't have asked for a better performance. You put me in touch with the exact person I was looking for." Belatedly, she added, "With the way things have been developing, I decided I needed you here too. Apologies for the theatrics." She said the last without any hint that she meant a word.

Markus started to reply, but Cassthia cut him off. "What business do you have with this child, Black Star?"

"This vessel?" Nix gestured to the dark expanse around them. "The way you speak, priestess, I almost believe you truly have concerns for her. But don't worry—I haven't harmed her."

"Bullshit," Markus spat. "Last I checked, she had a seizure and went unconscious." Cassthia had to hand it to the man: he was either incredibly bold or unfathomably stupid. Perhaps a bit of both, talking that way to a goddess.

Fortunately, Nix found the exchange humorous. "I had to get your attention!" she exclaimed. "The darling thing has been prancing about, spouting foretellings as casual as eating, and the most she's garnered are a few psionic testing sessions. Having flunked those, she's been explained away as a mere curiosity. You will have to forgive my dramatic flare. It is so hard to make you mortals listen."

A brief, stunned silence fell over the trio before Markus growled. "Priestess, what is that thing?"

The goddess turned its head to regard him. "Be steady, Markus Frost. I fear that this is not a problem you can shoot your way out of—though that may come later."

Cassthia extended her arm, warding the man off. "You would do well to heed that advice, Markus. A degree of caution would be prudent in this situation."

"Fine," he spat, "but what is it?"

She narrowed her slitted eyes at him in rebuke. "She is a Nethrian." Markus opened his mouth, but Cassthia raised a finger. "Perhaps it will be best if you let me handle this."

Markus's face contorted in a vicious scowl, but he nodded his acquiescence. With that problem solved momentarily, Cassthia turned back to the goddess in their midst. "That the girl is Kaleema is obvious, but how did you gain access to her so early? I doubt that she has had the opportunity to bask in your essence."

Nix's grin was infuriating. "That is a story for another day. All you need to know is that I am here, and I bring urgent news for the two of you."

As unsatisfying as that answer was, Cassthia saw little alternative to playing along. In the end, she had no leverage over this spirit, and with her connection to Thule temporarily weakened, she could not leverage the might of her deity against this interloper.

"Very well," Cassthia conceded. "Deliver your message."

The goddess seemed vaguely disappointed that there would be no more banter but continued regardless. "I've come to let you know that the Heart of Thule is still in play. While on the surface this may seem to be pleasant news for you, priestess, I assure you: the Stardust Grave does not hold the winning hand in this game."

Markus glanced warily at Cassthia, who worked hard at containing the war of emotions playing in her breast. Her hand went subconsciously to the medallion that hung beneath her robes. "Please explain," she whispered.

The spirit gestured to Markus. "A certain band of miscreants recently liberated the Heart of Thule from the possession of the late Don Cyrus Valadar. Though this is a move to be praised, said miscreants have unknowingly delivered the artifact into the hands of an even greater threat."

Something rumbled in the distance, and Cassthia caught the faint echoes of a message. Thule was trying to speak to her, but he was thwarted by whatever construct Nix had built for this conversation. Cassthia elected to press on. "And what is the nature of this threat?"

Nix's explanation was surprisingly straightforward. "An artificial intelligence system going by the designation of Arc. This machine, the first of its kind, has the power to access and channel energy directly from the Nethra itself."

"That's not possible," Cassthia protested. "The Nethra's power is psychic in nature. Machines do not carry a psychic imprint."

The goddess's cackle was bemused. "What you say is true. However, this machine seems to be borrowing a psychic imprint from the Nethra. It claims to hold the consciousness of Riven, one of the Nethrian warriors that opposed Thule before his imprisonment in his artifact."

A machine claiming to bare the soul of Riven. The warrior's shade had been silent for countless millennia. Scarcely a cult remained to worship the fallen deity—only dark oaths sworn in times of desperation. "Is this true? Has Riven returned?"

Nix shrugged. "I have no way to verify the claim. True or not, this machine poses a significant threat to all existence, especially now that he has the Heart of Thule in his possession."

"All existence?" Markus parroted, seemingly unable to contain himself any longer. "Any chance you might be overstating the stakes here?"

The goddess laughed. "Existence is a relative thing. I'll concede to some hyperbole—though I can guarantee that, absent timely intervention, life across the universe will look quite different after Arc's plans have come to fruition."

Cassthia cut in before Markus could inquire further. "What is it that you would recommend we do, Dark Star?"

Nix assumed a more composed expression. "Go to the Helion System and the asteroid station near its outer limits. Markus knows the location I speak of. There you must stop Arc from harnessing the energies of the artifact. As long as he retains control of Thule's power, there is nothing that can stop him."

"Just like that?" Markus grumbled. "Basically, your message is, 'There's an AI with god-like power on Minos Station. I suggest you go stop him before something bad happens.' That doesn't feel super helpful to me."

To Cassthia's relief, Nix was amused by the attack. "I can see your perspective," she replied, "but you will soon find that the powers-that-be will give much for even this small bit of information. As it turns out, though, I have one more bit of information to convey."

She paused, seeing if either of them would interject. Cassthia shot Markus a scathing look before urging the spirit to continue.

Satisfied that Markus would remain silent, Nix spoke again. "The Vandal's synthetic—I believe you refer to her as Lexa—has a part to play in this. Because of her nature, I cannot divine her intentions. However, you should know that her cooperation with Arc could make any effort to thwart him futile."

Cassthia cast a scathing look back toward Markus. "Your crew utilizes a synth aboard their starship?"

Markus had the sense to look surprised and even a little sheepish. "My old crew," he clarified. "And that's kind of a long story. Besides, there's no way she's involved in this. Lexa only knew about the Heart of Thule because the Vandal was looking for it under contract by the Sahaia. Plus, I've never even heard of this... Arc, or whatever." He shook his head, resolve growing as he listened to his own argument. "No. No way. Lexa couldn't possibly be connected to this."

Nix erupted into her most fervent cackling fit yesterday. The psychic construct shook with the force of her mirth, and waves of sapphire energy poured off her shimmering for. "So," she gasped, "so, so arrogant. You know nothing, Markus Frost. The depths of your naivete are so vast, it's almost criminal the divine toys with you at all." She shook a finger in his direction. "Yet, you are so very, very, lucky. The 'Devil's Luck,' am I right?"

The goddess drew in a deep breath, and Cassthia almost choked on the thickness of the melodrama. Nix did not need to breathe in this place. For her, this was all an elaborate performance. Indeed, it was possible the Black Star had foreseen every word of this exchange before calling them together. It suddenly struck Cassthia as strange how the incarnation of chaos could see the order of things so readily.

"Why are you doing this?" Cassthia whispered.

"Which part?" Nix cooed.

"All of it. Why go to such lengths to get our attention? Why tell us any of this? Why not let it all play out?"

"Entertainment purposes?"

"Shna'keine!" Cassthia cursed in the tongue of her father. "Tell me the truth. What is your goal?"

The outburst, for better or worse, had the desired effect. Nix's laughter vanished, and her eyes narrowed. She remained silent for a long, tense moment. Cassthia felt every pounding beat of her heart as the goddess weighed and measured her.

"You're right," the goddess admitted. "And I think it is only fair to tell you. My goal is to keep the power of Thule away from interested parties. Any interested party. As long as your master's artifact is in play, my ambitions remain threatened."

Despite her fear, Cassthia scoffed. "Ambitions? You mean your survival."

"Survival is an interesting thing for my kind," Nix mused, drifting closer. Searing cold cut against the scales of Cassthia's face as the goddess drew within a meter of her. "Thule's current fate represents just about the worst the divine can achieve, short of oblivion. I doubt he's forgotten who facilitated it."

Dark rage howled in the distance. Whether Thule was being protective of his priestess, or merely acknowledging the truth in Nix's words, Cassthia could not know. His infernal anger had the desired effect, though, and Nix drew back.

Cassthia mustered her courage. "You must know that if I gain access to the Heart, I will reclaim it for the Stardust Grave."

Nix spat a dismissive chuckle. "You can do nothing with the Heart, child. You may be Thule's pet, but you will never be Kaleema. As such, there's little use you can derive from the artifact."

"Maybe," the priestess conceded, "but that does not mean I will not guide another to its use. You are not the only god who makes plans, Nix."

The Black Star's smile was as cold as her aura. "Oh, he will have his chance. If all goes according to plan, the Stardust Grave will make its case." She lowered her chin, cerulean gaze still fixed conspiratorially on Cassthia's own. "But I have faith that Life with hold fast against the Grave."

"Strange words to be uttered by the lips of Chaos."

"Life is Chaos, dear."

With that parting barb, Nix wheeled around—no longer floating, but stepping deeper into the surrounding darkness. With the Black Star's departure, Cassthia felt a weight fall from her shoulders.

Until Markus spoke again. "Wait, hold on!" he shouted. "What about Monica? You need to undo whatever it is that you've done to her, right now!"

Nix half turned, cocking her head consideringly. "I knew you to be bold, Markus Frost, but to make demands of a goddess? My, my—your brashness exceeds even my expectations."

"Say what you want about me," he returned, "but I'm here for Monica. I want you to let her go!"

"Let her go?" Nix cackled as she walked into the dark. "Markus, I can't let her go. I don't have a hold on her. I am her."

The glowing figure faded into the darkness. As she did, the same blinding flash that had brought him to that void reappeared. Markus found himself disembodied and disoriented once again.

See you soon… Unca Markus.

With a gasp, his hand came free of Monica's sweat-slicked flesh. He jerked back so hard he lost his balance and sprawled onto the floor. Strong hands, clawed hands, were soon there to assist him. "You okay?" Vallus asked.

Markus could respond. His eyes went to Cassthia, who was handling the transition back to reality with far more dignity. Her slitted eyes opened slowly, taking in first him, then the girl resting beneath her clawed touch.

As if bidden by the priestess's alien gaze, Monica stirred. Her chest swelled with the sudden intake of breath, and her eyelids fluttered. "Unca… Markus?"

Nikki embraced the girl before Markus could say anything. "Monica? Oh honey, are you okay?"

The girl groaned as she pried against her mother's arm. "I'm fine Momma. Why am I all sweaty?" Then, after she had a chance to look around. "Who are all these people? And where's my puzzle?"

It took Markus a second to realize what she was talking about. Then he remembered that the child had been going to retrieve her puzzle when the episode had struck her. *She doesn't remember,* he realized.

Still, Nix's words haunted Markus even as he looked upon the innocent figure lying in Nikki's arms. *Let her go? Markus, I can't let her go. I don't have a hold on her. I am her.*

Ora knelt at Markus's side and Vallus stepped away, leaving them the greatest measure of privacy the small living room could afford. "Are you all right?"

"Yeah," he sighed. "How long was I… were we out?"

"Almost a half-hour." Concern shone in her amethyst eyes as she made the report. "You touched the child, and it was just like you and Cassthia froze. Your eyes were open, but we couldn't get your attention. You were barely breathing." She shook her head. "We didn't know what to do, didn't know if it was safe to move you. Much longer, we were going to have to take a chance."

"Glad you didn't," Markus mumbled. Who knew how breaking the psychic link might have fragged up his brain. Even now, he was having a hard time believing what he'd seen.

He suddenly became aware of the noise in the background. It sounded like a broadcast. His eyes flicked up to the viewscreen, which had been turned on and seemed to be functioning fine despite a crack in its surface. "Decided to catch up on the news while I was out?"

Impossibly, Ora's expression darkened further. "If only it were so benign." She shook her head. "Markus, something has happened." Looking to Vallus, she said, "Play it back for him."

With a grave nod, the Maur picked up a nearby controller and pointed it at the viewscreen. A progress bar appeared at the bottom as the broadcast slid back fifteen minutes.

The screen showed a video feed from outside a heavily trafficked jump gate. A reporter's voice was overlaid on the feed. "DGC officials have confirmed that the disaster at the Taurus Gate is not an isolated incident. Authorities have received reports that similar incidents have taken place across the gate network."

A pulse of light began in the inside edge of the gigantic ring and cascaded inward. Ships inside the ring started exploding. The effect rippled outward, consuming the column of vessels in a pillar of fire and plasma.

"What in the nine hells…?" Markus whispered.

"What's going on momma?" Monica pleaded, straining to get a better look at the projection.

Nikki caught the little girl up in her arms again. "Sweetie, let's find your puzzle. I think Unca Markus and Miss Ora have grown-up stuff to deal with."

Meanwhile, the news caster's voice continued to play over the scene of destruction. "The structure of the gate remains reportedly unharmed after the incident, though sources are now stating that the gate is offline. Similar incidents are reported to have occurred simultaneously at every gate connected to the Helion System."

"The gates are shut down?" Markus asked skeptically. Then, a chilling thought hit him. His eyes met Cassthia's. "You don't think…?"

The priestess nodded. "The coincidence is too great," she muttered. "It seems that our opponent has already made his first move."

CHAPTER 13

[ACCESSING ARC PROJECT LOG 115]

[DR. DAMIEN HERMES]

The organitech processor continues to analyze the energies we've managed to harvest from the Nethra. Although its findings are interesting, they bring us no closer to the possibility of establishing a subspace communications network. Despite the futility of the task, I have left the program running at Prodigy's insistence.

I'm far more interested in sending things into the Nethra. Now that we can create a sustainable rift, we can send in a few probes and find out more about this new layer of space-time. That is where the real discoveries will be made.

Or, at least, they will be re-made. One can only assume that the Dorians have delved into this type of science quite extensively. Though we have not explicitly broken any laws, I suspect they would not be pleased by the progress we have made.

[CLOSING PROJECT LOG…]

"I'm still showin' a leak in that sector," Aaliyah reported over the comms.

Sahar let slip a growl of frustration. "That's not possible, it's patched. Just recycle the life-support."

"That's what I'm tellin' you: I can't. The safety protocol keeps freezing the reboot cycle because it's still detectin' a leak." Sahar slammed a gauntleted fist into the patch. "That's not helpin'," the mechanic chided.

"Get fragged, Red."

"Was that an offer? Timing's kinda inappropriate, don't ya think?"

"Just shut up and figure out what's wrong."

Aaliyah fell silent while she presumably worked to reanalyze the hull's integrity. Something else caught Sahar's attention. There was a subtle vibration coming from the hull. She almost didn't notice it, but could feel it readily once she had.

Aaliyah's voice came back on the comm. "Look, the scans agree with ya. The hole ya just patched is fine, but that means we've got another leak we can't see. Come on back to the bridge. We're gonna have to re-evaluate the problem."

"Okay," Sahar replied hesitantly. "Could you do me a favor real quick, though? Can you tell me if you're picking up some kind of weird vibration on this bulkhead?"

"What kind of weird vibration?"

"I don't know! You're the sensor girl! I'm just here to tack shit in place. Now, can you check for me?"

Another brief silence. "I've got nothin', Sahar."

And that's what Sahar was afraid she'd say. "Somethings screwing with your readings. Might be a good..." She trailed off as she noticed something else: a spark of light that had appeared on the hull a short distance from where she'd been patching.

"What was that?" Aaliyah asked.

Sahar dropped the previous thread as panic consumed her. "The alarms, Red. Sound the gods-damned alarms!" She was already running as fast as her magnetic boots and this damned space-suit would allow her to.

The thin atmosphere that had started to collect was enough to transmit the hissing sound as the cutting torch worked its way through the hull. Rounding the corner, she heard a loud clanging and a slight change in pressure as the last of the atmosphere began rushing out the new opening.

What could be coming at them now? It probably wasn't the creatures Aaliyah had described unless they had found a cache of tools and somehow managed to figure out how to use them. Odds were that this was a different threat.

Sahar reached the section of the ship where the containment field was still active and burst through it. On the other side, she could now hear the alarms that Aaliyah had thankfully triggered. Immediately she went for the nearby locker and grabbed the resche she'd brought with her. In hindsight, also bringing a firearm would have been a wise decision.

The intruders floated around the corner, still a good distance from the forcefield. There were two of them—massive black drones that hovered in the middle of the corridor. Their main bodies were roughly spherical but were protected by a frontal shield of black alloy. Numerous metallic appendages, which terminated in various implements, extended menacingly around the edges of the shields. In their center mass, each had a circular red sensor that actively scanned the space in front of them.

Within seconds a beam from one of the drones found her. The bot must have passed the message onto its companion, because both turned toward her and powered up appendages that looked a lot like laser cannons.

Sahar didn't wait to find out if they were. She sprinted forward just in time. Small explosions sounded behind her as laser beams struck the space where she'd just been standing.

"What's goin' on down there?" Aaliyah shouted on the other end of the comm.

"Bots, two of them," Sahar gasped as she raced down the corridor. "Cut through the ship. Might be more."

Aaliyah cursed. "Nothing's showin' up on sensors."

"Then they're jamming you." Sahar darted left to avoid another blast and dove through a hatch. She stabbed the locking mechanism, hoping it would lock down after losing function. "Might need a new plan! They're after me and doing some serious damage to the ship in the effort."

"Okay, okay… I'm thinkin'. Ya got a weapon on ya?"

"Nothing appropriate, given the opponent."

"All right… shit. Judgin' from the door ya just went through, I take it goin' back into that last hallway isn't an option. So, that rules out gettin' back here. Can ya get to the hanger? There's some ordinance still in there."

The hanger? Wasn't that where Aaliyah had found those black monstrosities? "What about our other guests?" Sahar asked. "You sure that area's clear?"

"No fraggin' clue, but it's my best idea."

"Fine," Sahar growled. "I'll get there. Find the others. We need to get a perimeter set up or… gods damn it!" An explosion behind her punctuated her sentence. The drones had broken through. "Look, got to go." She killed her comms. If there was any scenario in which she did not end up getting cut in half by a laser bolt, finding it meant eliminating distractions.

All right, you metal pieces of shit. Come and get me.

"What are you doing?" Sydney asked.

"Not now," Aaliyah snapped as she swiped frantically at the sensor menus. Everything was still in the green despite the explosions she heard in the distance. It was going to be impossible to contain these attackers if she couldn't even fragging see them.

Damn it, this was not her area of expertise. What she really wanted to do was smash the terminal with a wrench to vent her frustration. She needed the kid here. Gods, she hoped Dan was okay.

The assassin, still tied up where Aaliyah had left her, seemed to have picked up on her problem. "Have you tried rebooting it?"

"What?"

"Turn the power on and off."

Aaliyah's incredulity was plain on her face. "What will that do?"

"I don't know," Sydney huffed, "but it's literally the first thing anyone who knows anything about computers makes you do every time there's a problem."

Well… why the frag not? It can't make this shit any worse, right? She cycled down the diagnostics system, waited three seconds, and turned the thing back on.

Immediately, she wished she hadn't—not because the procedure hadn't worked. The system was working perfectly again. However, Aaliyah was now looking at a hologram showing over a dozen incursions all throughout the ship.

They were completely and totally screwed.

<Sit rep?> Eli's voice whispered in her mind.

<Fragged. We're totally fragged.>

<More specific, please.>

She took a deep breath and studied the data in front of her. <Fifteen breaches. Multiple enemy contacts flagged at each location.>

<I'm coming to you.>

Aaliyah looked at the ship's diagram and the proximity of the incursions. <Not a good idea. Multiple hostiles in the way. Get to the others in the med bay.>

<And leave you all alone?>

<Screw that—I'm gettin' out of here. Sahar's headin' toward the hanger. We need to get to the shuttle.>

<You're recommending we abandon ship?>

She hadn't thought about it in those terms. The phrasing gave her enough pause to reassess the situation. The reevaluation didn't take long. <I don't see any other option.>

Eli didn't reply for several seconds. When he did, Aaliyah could feel how much the decision tormented him. <All right. Heading toward the med bay, then to the hanger. Good luck, Aaliyah.> She saw no reason to reply. Instead, she immediately started pulling equipment together.

"Now what are you doing?" Sydney asked concern thick in her voice.

"I'm gettin' out of here." Aaliyah finished packing up the few tools she could fit into her backpack and slung it over her shoulder.

"Sounds like a plan," Sydney replied, jerking on her bonds. "Cut me loose."

Aaliyah scoffed. "What? So ya can stab me in the back on the way out the door? Frag that." She reached for the rifle that she'd propped up against the far bulkhead and checked the ammo. Explosive tips—that should have enough stopping power to take down anything that bothered her between here and the hanger.

"Come on!" Sydney pleaded. "I can help! Don't you think I have bigger things to worry about than getting even with you?"

"Maybe, but I'm not in the mood to find out." She stalked past the prisoner and to the door.

The assassin didn't even bother to hide her panic. "But they'll kill me if you leave me here! I can't fight like this!"

"Probably." Aaliyah was doing her best not to think about it. Maybe the intruders would just pass this room by? She palmed the keypad to open the door.

"I saved your life!" Sydney roared.

Aaliyah paused with one foot out the door. Gods damn it. The Citza bitch was right—Aaliyah owed her one. But there was still the reality that the Ghenza would most definitely put another hole in her skull at the first opportunity. No way was she going to let that happen.

Then again, could Aaliyah leave this woman to die? No matter how she rationalized it, she knew that even if the intruders didn't kill Sydney, this leaky-ass ship wasn't going to hold atmosphere, even if the forcefields stayed up. To leave her behind was a death sentence.

"Lith's tits…" Aaliyah huffed and drew a knife from her belt. She stormed over to Sydney and held the knife right up to her nose. "You so much as blink wrong and I'll kill you myself. Got it?"

The Citza locked eyes with her, issuing a half-nod to signal she understood. Still one hundred percent convinced this was a bad idea, Aaliyah cut her bonds and pulled the woman to her feet.

"Can I have a weapon?" Sydney asked.

"Don't push it."

The assassin shrugged. "Can't blame a girl for trying."

"Sure," Aaliyah sheathed her knife and unslung her assault rifle. "How 'bout ya take point? I need to keep ya where I can see ya. Take a left and head for the hatch at the end of the hall."

To her credit, Sydney did exactly as instructed. The two of them broke into a sprint, heading to the end of the corridor and down the stairs to the lower level.

At the bottom, they found the first of the gigantic hover-bots. "Down!" Aaliyah roared as she opened fire.

Sydney dove left to avoid the barrage of exploding bullets. Aaliyah couldn't boast the marksmanship that some of her friends could, but it was hard to miss something as big as the bot at this range.

The rounds detonated on impact but caused little damage to the black metal plates on the front of the drone. Fortunately, a couple of rounds found the red sensor at its center mass.

The bot's shield's flickered helplessly in an attempt to stop the shots. When the bullets found their mark, the resulting explosion forced Aaliyah to crouch to avoid the flying shrapnel. The remains of one metallic appendage came dangerously close to her head.

A second bot floated around the corner. This one Aaliyah took out using more controlled bursts, now that she knew where to aim. She took it down, but not before it got its own shot off.

A laser bolt grazed her right thigh. If she'd had her shield on, it would have absorbed the blast, but she'd carelessly stowed her emitter with her other things in the shuttle. Just another reason they needed to get to the hanger.

Examining the wound and deciding it was far from fatal, she turned to check on Sydney. "You o…" She went ridged. The assassin was on her feet and had a jagged piece of shrapnel in her hand. She launched the object at Aaliyah's face so quickly that there was no time to react.

It was a damn good thing Aaliyah froze. The shard sailed past her face and right into the eye of the drone that had slipped up behind her. The bot clattered to the ground, causing Aaliyah to stumble.

Sydney was doing her best to hide a smug grin. "Apologies. I didn't think there was time to shout a warning."

Aaliyah looked back at the fallen drone. The shard was implanted dead center, so there was no debating what the assassin had been aiming at. That made two times that Sydney had done her a solid. If she hadn't been feeling like a bitch before, she certainly was now.

"It's fine. Um… thanks."

"Any chance I could get a proper weapon now?"

Guilt didn't make her stupid, though. "Don't push your luck. Come on. It's not far now."

Skye might have been conscious, but that did not mean she was ready to deal with the ship's blaring alarms. She pressed her fingers hard against her temples to stifle the building headache.

"What should we do?" Amelia asked. Argus's expectant gaze held the same question.

"I… um… I'm not sure," Skye conceded. She'd just been down for the count a few minutes ago, and now she was expected to provide direction? "Do either of you have a communicator?"

The pair shook their heads in the negative and Skye cursed. Groggily she reached for her MoDAC, found it was missing, and began fumbling about the med bay for anything that might help.

"Why don't we just report to the war room?" Argus asked.

"Because we don't know where the threat is," Skye replied. "We could be walking right into the problem. Smarter to check-in."

Her search ended up being fruitless. There were no communicators in the room, nor were there any weapons in case they decided to make a break for the war room. With her splitting headache, she was having serious trouble thinking of what to do next.

The door to the bay slid open. Her heart leaped. Her breath caught.

Alarm gave way to relief when she saw that it was Eli standing in the entryway. Forgetting herself, she raced headlong into his firm embrace.

"You're awake," he breathed.

"For better or worse," she replied. "What's going on? It sounds like the ship is about to blow up."

"That's a little closer to our present scenario than I'd like to admit." He broke the embrace and reached into his pocket. "Here, you dropped this."

Skye grabbed the MoDAC appreciatively. "Thanks."

"No problem," he turned to address his fellow Sahaia. "We all need to get out of here. The others are meeting us in the hanger."

"What's going on?" Argus asked.

"Contacts," Eli replied. "Lots of them."

"On the ship?" Skye waved off her own stupid question. Of course they were on the ship, otherwise, they wouldn't be evacuating. "Scratch that. There's something else. Argus says the Heart of Thule is missing."

"I know," Eli sighed. "Look, we can discuss this later. Right now we need to—" The floor shook as an explosion rocked the deck. It wasn't right outside the door, but it was too close for comfort.

No one asked any more questions. They all sprinted out of the med bay and to a nearby maintenance hatch. Eli pulled it open and gestured for everyone to start climbing.

Skye went first, quickly descending to the lower deck. She emerged in a causeway just outside the hanger. The others were right behind her as she made her mad dash to the final door.

"Oh sh—" Psionic force jerked Skye backward. It was the only thing that saved her life. A series of laser bolts struck the floor right where she had been standing.

Eli caught her by the shoulders and steadied her. "Are you hurt?"

"No," she breathed. "Not yet at, least. We've got flying robots—lots of them." One of said flying robots hovered into position just in front of the door she'd been trying to walk through.

Argus rewarded its tenacity with a bolt of energy shot from his open palm. The thing's red sensor blinked out on impact as sparks flew from the new hole in its armored plating. Eli followed up on the attack by sending a wave of concussive force to knock it backward. "We've got to clear it out," Eli shouted.

"Are you certain there's not a better alternative here?" Amelia asked diplomatically, as she took cover behind a parked loader.

"Too late to change the plan," Eli replied. "The rest of the crew is coming from the other sections of the ship. They'll walk right into this trap unless we clear it." Amelia nodded resolutely at Eli's pronouncement. Argus grinned. Did that guy ever get sick of blowing shit up?

"Will you be offended if I ask you to stay behind us?" Eli whispered.

Skye shook her head. "I mean… normally, yes. But right now, I'm unarmed and I can't move things with my brain, so I'll let you have the fun this time."

A sardonic laugh escaped Eli's lips as they quirked into a wry smile. He immediately turned his attention back to the fight. "Link up," he shouted to the other Sahaia.

"Only if I'm driving," Argus replied.

"Fine," said Eli. "Let's do this."

Something must have happened that Skye couldn't see, because the only thing she noticed was all three Sahaia going preternaturally still for a heartbeat. When they moved again, Argus broke cover.

The drones never stood a chance. Argus's eyes blazed with violet energy as beams shot from his hands. In seconds the hanger was filled with the roar of explosions and squeals of twisting metal.

In less than a minute, the half-dozen bots in the welcoming party were nothing more than scrap metal.

Eli peeked out from their cover. "Clear!" He shouted. "Argus, Amelia, there should be two spare the EVO-suits on the shuttle you can use. Skye, is your flight gear stowed aboard?"

"Gods, I hope so."

"I'm going to need a better answer than that."

"Yes, it's aboard," she replied, no more confident in the assertion than she had been a moment ago. Now wasn't a great time to argue. If she checked and it wasn't there, what was he going to do—fire her?

"All right. I'm going to go grab another suit. Hold the shuttle until I get back." Orders issued, Eli veered left while the others sprinted to the shuttle. Skye got there first and immediately started punching in the access code to lower the craft's ramp.

Amelia stepped up behind her. "The craft is pressurized, yes? Intended for space travel?"

"Yeah," Skye replied. "Why?"

"Only wondering why Eli is suggesting we get dressed like we're going on a spacewalk."

Huh… that was a good question, and Skye had to think about it for a second. "I think it's just a precaution."

"Precaution for what?" Argus asked.

Skye could only shrug. "Well, shit goes wrong sometimes. Do you really want to find out there's damage to life support by getting spaced?"

Her logic must have been good enough for the Sahaia because they both stormed up the ramp and opened the storage lockers. They found two suits in relatively short order. Both Sahaia stripped off their regular clothes and began pulling on the grey spacesuits.

Skye was relieved to find that her gear was on the shuttle just as she'd hoped. She pulled out the flight suit and rigged up the modifications that would make it pressurized and space worthy. It wouldn't have some of the protections that the EVO-suits had, but it would keep her alive if the shuttle suddenly depressurized.

Just as importantly, she found the side-arm she kept stowed on the shuttle for cases like this. The pistol felt good in her hands and gave her a measure of confidence she'd been lacking while relying on her psionic companions. Even though the low-caliber weapon wasn't likely to pose much threat to those assault drones, she could at least tell herself that she wasn't totally helpless.

A loud clanging from outside the ship made her bring the pistol up swiftly.

"Ease up! Friendly in-coming."

Skye lowered the pistol and re-engaged the safety before rushing to her friend. "Sahar!"

The big Maur grinned behind the clear front of her helmet. "Good to see you awake, sleeping beauty. Decided to finally get in on the action?"

"Oh, you're hilarious." Skye pulled away. "Where's Red? I thought she'd be with you."

Sahar shook her head. "She had me take a different route. Fragging bots were all up my ass the whole way here."

It was only then that Skye noticed the object Sahar had strapped to her right arm. "What is that?"

"Oh this?" The Maur grinned as she held the high-tech-looking cylinder up admiringly. "Borrowed it from one of our mechanical guests. Seemed like it didn't need it anymore. Took a minute to figure out how to get it to fire, but it works well enough now."

Skye could only shake her head. She guessed that explained how Sahar had been able to deal with those drones on her own. "Fair enough. Your suit in good condition? Eli wants us prepped and ready to go by the time he gets back."

"Might need a quick patch, but I'll tend to it. Don't worry about me." The Maur moved to find the kit to complete the repairs, and Skye went back to making pre-launch preparations.

After a while, she found herself glancing at the clock on her MoDAC. She hadn't checked the time when Eli left, but it felt like he should be back by now. Desperate to subdue her nerves, she finished her task and stepped out of the shuttle.

Two figures in EVO suits made their way across the hanger, neither of whom was Eli. That meant at least one of them had to be Aaliyah—but who was that she'd brought with her?

The pair sprinted up to the shuttle, and Aaliyah's voice sounded from her helmet's speaker. "Sorry we're late. Ran into some complications."

"As did we," Skye noted. At this distance, she could peer into the faceplate of Aaliyah's companion. Sudden recognition prompted her to draw her pistol again and train it on the figure. "What in the nine hells is she doing here?"

Sydney raised her hands as Aaliyah side-stepped to stand between the assassin and Skye's pistol. "Easy there, Blondie. She's with me."

Skye didn't lower her weapon. "Have you lost your gods' damned mind?"

"Look, a lot of things happened while ya were nappin'."

"Yeah? Well, I think this is one you'd better start explaining."

Sahar had heard the commotion and had stepped over to look down the shuttle's ramp. "You brought our guest?" Her tone was carefully neutral, evidently unsurprised by the assassin's presence.

Eli also picked that moment to sprint onto the scene. Skye had been so focused on Sydney that she hadn't registered his approach. "Someone care to fill me in?" he asked calmly.

Aaliyah's eyes never left Skye's, though she raised her hands in a placating gesture. "Look, we're not leavin' her. I'll take responsibility. I've already given her the usual threats, so we can skip that part. Let's just get out of here, okay?"

Sydney, to her credit, had not moved during the entire exchange. If looks could kill, however, Skye had no doubt her body would be lying cold on the deck.

Eli considered everyone before speaking. "Skye, lower your weapon. Now is not the time to be picking fights. We need all the help we can get."

Skye couldn't believe what she was hearing. "And when she knifes us all in the back, what are we going to do then?"

"I'm not saying she's not dangerous," Eli acknowledged. "This is a risk, but I'm also betting she's not suicidal. She knows she can't kill all of us, and right now we need to be working together to get out of here."

"Seriously?"

Eli heaved a sigh of frustration. "Look, Skye—I understand your concerns, but we don't have time for this. The drones have to know we're in the hanger by now. I'm not sure why they haven't started tearing it open and turning this whole place into a vacuum, but I don't want to push our luck further than necessary. Now, would you please stow your gun?"

She glanced to Sahar, who nodded in agreement with Eli. The Twins had also stepped up to see the cause of the commotion but were doing nothing to countermand Eli's request. It seemed like everyone was on the same page with this one—everyone but Skye, anyway.

Skye reengaged the safety and slammed the pistol into its holster. "Fine. Let's just get out of here."

The shuttle had a maximum capacity of eight persons, including a pilot and copilot. That meant that, with their current party of seven, things were pretty cozy. Skye had been planning on letting Sahar take the copilot spot, but with Sydney joining them, she figured it was a better idea to keep the toughest fighters near the assassin.

As much as she hated to admit it, Skye was going to be of the least use if a fight broke out while they were in transit. She grabbed her backpack and moved up to the cockpit.

Aaliyah was right on her tail, slipping quietly into the pilot's chair. "I couldn't leave her, Skye. She saved my ass back there. Twice."

Skye was sure that she would see Aaliyah's perspective given a little more time. Right now, though, she gave herself permission to be overwhelmed. "It's fine," she replied curtly and let the matter drop.

No more of the bots emerged through the entire exchange, nor did they make an appearance as Aaliyah finished the pre-launched sequence. Rather than finding this to be a relief, Skye's stomach contorted in a knot of anxiety. These things had broken into the ship and flooded the halls in a matter of minutes. There was no reason they shouldn't be swarming the hanger right now.

Aaliyah called back to make sure everyone was secure as the shuttle's engines heated up. When everyone gave the all-clear, she sent the signal to the ship to open the hanger door. As the large metal door opened, Skye realized why the drones hadn't stormed the hanger.

They'd parked an entire army outside to wait for them. So thick was the wall of drones that it completely eclipsed the space outside. Aaliyah let fly a particularly creative string of curses, prompting Eli to call in over the open channel. "What's going on?"

Their pilot was still testing the limits of her profanity, so Skye replied. "Wall of bots just outside the hanger. Scores of them. Too many to count."

Now Eli was cursing. "Have we got weapons on this thing?"

"It's a gods damned shuttle!" Aaliyah shrieked. "It's for shuttlin' shit, not blowin' shit up! Why the frag would it have weapons?" As the hanger door reached its apex, the army of drones hovered just inside the containment field. Their weapons began to charge.

Skye pulled up the copilot's menu. "Shields coming online. Enemy weapons are hot. Incoming!" The shields kept the shuttle from exploding outright, but the force of the initial blast sent the craft slamming into the far side of the hanger where it lodged itself into a bulkhead. Red indicators filled all displays as system after system went offline.

"Shields are down," Aaliyah reported. "Engines are down. Life-support is down. Multiple hull breaches." She looked desperately to Skye for any ideas. None were in the offering.

They were going to die. There was nothing they could do about it. Aaliyah slammed a gauntleted fist into the console and screamed her frustration. The enemy bots charged weapons for a second volley. Skye closed her eyes.

CHAPTER 14

[ACCESSING ARC PROJECT LOG 123]

[DR. DAMIEN HERMES]

Something about the organitech interface has changed. It's a subtle thing, so much so that I was hesitant to make note of it. The way it answers queries is slightly different. It's almost as if it's donned a certain… personality.

Perhaps I'm just delusional. Maybe I have spent too many hours at this holodisplay.

[CLOSING PROJECT LOG…]

An explosion sounded, but not from the shuttle. Skye inhaled sharply and opened her eyes again. Something had opened fire into the cloud of drones. Searing laser bolts were dropping the bots by the score.

Those not taken down in the initial volley swiveled to assess this new threat. Something massive slammed into the asteroid outside as another round of lasers dispatched the drones that remained inside the hanger. In just a few chaotic seconds, every last drone had been destroyed.

Aaliyah stared in disbelief at the carnage taking place just outside their crippled shuttle. "What just happened?"

There was movement in the main cabin. Eli had unstrapped and was moving up to the cockpit. He leaned over Skye, trying to get a good look at the situation. "There's a ship out there," he whispered. "Maybe two."

Another ship? Out here? Skye couldn't believe their good fortune. "Red, are the coms still online?"

She blinked, checking her console. "Umm… yeah—not the tight-beam, but we could probably broadcast. That's about the only system still online."

Skye began hailing the vessels on an open channel. "Unidentified vessel, this is the crew of…" She blanked on what the official designation was their ship. If it was anyone but the DGC, it didn't matter anyway. "This is the crew of the Vandal. Thank you for saving our asses right there."

The signal was garbled, likely due to the shuttle's damage rather than any interference, but Skye could make out a woman's voice on the other end of the comms. "Vandal? Vandal, this is Mara of the Ren'Dahl coven. Is Eli with you?"

"Mara?" Eli whispered. Skye entered the command to patch his helmet mic into the open channel and signaled for him to continue. "Affirmative, Mara. This is Eli."

"Thank the gods," she responded. "I wasn't sure if you or the others had made it back. Is Ryker with you?"

Eli winced. That was still a somewhat sensitive subject for him. "Negative, Mara. Ryker… I'll explain later. Are those more reinforcements from the coven I see out there with you?"

"Hardly," she scoffed. "No, the two ships you see out here are Maur Destroyers—Federation military. I… uh… I guess I also have some explaining to do."

Everyone in the cockpit shared identical confused looks. Maur military? What were the Maur doing out here? And why were they helping Mara?

Eli must have decided it didn't matter. They had more pressing matters—like getting off this busted shell of a spaceship. "Copy that, Mara. We, apparently, have a lot to talk about, but I'm glad you're here."

"Don't be," she sighed. "This is far from over. There's more going on out here than a couple of attack drones. By the time we read you in, you may just wish you'd died in that shuttle."

"It's jammed," Argus reported after a futile pull on the ramp's manual release.

Eli looked to Sahar. "You're up."

Should have started with me, Sahar thought wryly as she threaded herself over the rest of the crew and around Argus to get to the release. Immediately she recognized the petulance in the thought and scolded herself. She was on edge—as much from recent events as from their unexpected rescue.

Maur Federation. Here. She wondered if it was the same contingent she had encountered on Minos Station during the Festival of the Sisters. She also wondered if her crew might have just stumbled onto the real reason why they were in the Hades Belt in the first place.

Gripping the release lever with two gauntleted hands, Sahar heaved with all her strength. She was rewarded with a groan and then a snap as the metal handle tore free. "Lith's tits," she growled. "Manual release is a no-go."

"That means we're out of options." Resignation was thick in Eli's voice. "Aaliyah, you know what to do."

The red-haired Terran patted her console. "Been nice flyin' with ya, girl." Swiping at her holodisplay, she shouted back. "Ejection override initiated. Sit tight, it's gonna be—" The ship quaked as the boom reverberated back from the cockpit. Everyone was pushed back as the front of the cockpit separated and shot across the hanger. "—loud," Aaliyah finished. The distant clang of the shuttle's armored hull clattering against a bulkhead punctuated her sentence.

"You'd think there'd be a better way to do that," Skye muttered.

"I believe that's what the manual release is for," Amelia replied.

"All right," Eli cut in. "Everyone out."

The banter died as the group filed, one by one, out the front of the shuttle. Sahar was the last one out of the crippled craft, emerging just in time to see three lights pass through the Vandal's flickering containment field.

The three dropships descended into the ruin that was the Vandal's hangar. They had plenty of space to land since the explosions had cleared away any vehicles or equipment that might have been in the way. All those were scrap now, just like the rest of the freighter.

Skye put voice to what was on Sahar's mind. "Kind of sad, isn't it? All these years and the poor old bird goes down like this."

"We'll mourn later," Sahar replied. "After we get some payback." That, too, would be awhile in coming, but Sahar could be patient. Her patience was tempered with preoccupation. Right then, she could only think about the soldiers that were about to step out of those ships.

The Maur dropships—relatively small oblong craft as dark as the void around them and lit only by their large forward searchlights—set down lightly on the hanger deck. All three of the ships opened in unison, each spouting twin columns of soldiers clad in EVO suites that fanned out across the perimeter. One of those columns made its way to where Sahar and her crewmates were waiting.

The one in the lead snapped a fist over his heart in the traditional Federation salute. "Greetings," one of the Maur broadcast over an open frequency. "I'm Shing Adawar Nos Drathen. I've been asked to prepare you for extraction." Shing was a rank roughly equivalent to a Terran sergeant. The three slashes on the shoulders of his armor marked Adawar as a Master Shing, the highest classification of that rank.

The male's helmet shifted about as he seemed to study each of them. "Is this your whole crew?" It was a reasonable question. Given the size of the ship, it would not have been unreasonable for the Vandal to house a crew three times this size.

Eli responded, "We have two unaccounted for, but we suspect they disembarked before the crash. The rest of us are here—six crew members plus one prisoner."

Shing Adawar did nothing to hide his surprise. "A prisoner?"

"Yes," Eli confirmed, pointing to Sydney. "One of the Ghenza. She was a stow-away on the vessel. Her presence was only discovered after the crash.

Adawar made a gesture, and two of the soldiers leveled their rifles to Sydney, who raised her hands. "I'm cooperating," she announced over the comms, betraying only the slightest twinge of annoyance.

Yes. Yes, she was. That behavior, out of all the things that had happened to the team recently, was what Sahar found most suspicious. That Sydney was a survivor, only out for herself, was undebatable. At this point, however, Sahar had yet to figure out her end game. The assassin seemed to be flailing from crisis to crisis, just like the rest of the crew—but that seemed uncharacteristically vulnerable for one of the Ghenza.

"Your compliance is appreciated," Adawar replied. To the pair with readied weapons, he said, "Take her to dropship gamma and relay orders to Lang Rox that his team will be escorting her to brig."

"Copy, sir." The soldier with three dots on his shoulder plates gestured for his partner to move forward. He didn't lower his weapon, even after the second soldier had the assassin in cuffs.

Relief, so thick it was almost tangible, washed over Sahar as two soldiers secured Sydney's arms and led her to one of the dropships. When they disappeared into the belly of the craft, Adawar let out a rumbling chuckle. "You lot have stones, I'll give you that.

Not sure I know anyone who would be willing to let one of the Ghenza tag along on an escape attempt."

Eli shrugged. "Couldn't just leave her behind."

"An honorable notion, if a stupid one." If Eli took offense at the barb, he didn't let it show. "The rest of you will be coming with me. We're taking you to the Crimson Sky immediately to rendezvous with your Sahaia cohorts while our beta team searches the area for more hostiles. Maybe then you can explain why your ship tried to make a pit-stop on this little rock."

"Indeed." Eli's reply was firm, but professional. "And perhaps you can fill us in as to why a contingent of Federation soldiers is out hunting in the Hades Belt."

Adawar laughed. "That decision is above my pay grade, but you're welcome to ask." He inclined his head toward the nearest dropship. "Let's get moving. Jingda Geresh is eager to speak to you."

Geresh? The same Geresh Sahar had spoken to at the Festival? Suddenly the universe was feeling very small. To cross paths with the same Maur soldier she'd had a chance encounter with just months ago involved some incalculable odds. It was an incredible coincidence.

And Sahar didn't believe in coincidences.

"And..." Markus hesitated for just a minute, glancing to Cassthia who nodded from across the conference-room table. "I guess that's it. Any questions?"

The rest of the assembly stared dumbly at him and the priestess. Tashania seemed particularly incredulous, as she had not witnessed any of the psychic shenanigans that had occurred before this meeting at Annex. She ran a single hand along the fringe of her spiky black hair before speaking. "That's... um..." A cough interrupted her response, and she shook her head. "Are you for real?"

"I know," Markus sighed. "I can't believe the words that are coming out of my own mouth."

Vallus leaned forward, the chair creaking under the weight of his muscular frame. "So, let me get this straight: There's an AI on Minos Station that can somehow draw power from the level of space-time that exists between jump gates." For whatever reason, the Maur was working hard to avoid any direct mention of the Nethra. "Now, this AI thinks he… it… is a god. And to prove it, said AI shut down all fourteen gates to the Helion System."

"Those are just the ones we know about," Markus noted. "Sahar told me once that there's at least one off-record gate in that system that the Maur Federation uses for military purposes. I suspect that gate, along with any other unofficial gates, have also gone down."

"Sure," Vallus conceded. "And to top this all off, you're telling me that an android—which your old ship's pilot threw together illegally using his extra cash—might have some important part to play in this conflict, but you don't know what that is yet."

"Don't forget the magic rock," Tashania added helpfully. "The artifact that's supposed to contain the soul of another god."

Ora leaned forward, burying her face in her hands and letting her silver hair fall forward. "Yes," she sighed. "That about covers it."

Uneasy glances were passed around the table as they all participated in a collective moment of, Well shit…

Cassthia broke the silence. "Does anyone have an idea of how to proceed?"

After another pause, Ora pushed herself up from the table. She stepped away, pulling her MoDAC out of her pocket. "What are you doing?" Markus asked.

"I'm making a call," she replied as she dialed the number.

"Um… okay," Markus didn't even attempt to hide his confusion. "Who are you calling?"

Ora shot him an annoyed glance as she put the mobile to her ear. "The Dorian Gate Commission."

The DGC? Markus guessed it really shouldn't have surprised him that Ora knew how to get in touch with someone at the gate commission. Given the legal status of at least half of her business ventures, however, he was at least a little surprised that she'd willingly call them.

"Hi, this is Ora Monroe." She paused as someone spoke on the other end of the line. "Yes, that Ora Monroe. I'd like to report a crime." She paused and rolled her eyes as another response reverberated from her MoDAC. "No, the irony is not lost on me… Look, can I please speak to your supervisor? I know what's caused your gate network to crash in the Helion System, and I'd really like to tell someone how to fix it."

CHAPTER 15

[ACCESSING ARC PROJECT LOG 137]

[DR. DAMIEN HERMES]

Today, the AI asked me a question. Not a "Can you be more specific?" or any other query triggered in response to its programming. It asked an honest, unsolicited, original question. I dare not put words to the concern this has elicited in me.

Though Ratemacher has been removed from the work site, I had one of his Prodigy cohorts check the inhibitor protocols. There were some early warning signs, but nothing to indicate a breach as yet. Once this was confirmed, I returned to the query posed by the organitech processor.

And I answered it.

[CLOSING PROJECT LOG…]

Two armed soldiers in full battle armor approached the crew as they filed out of the dropship. "Do any of you require medical attention?" the first asked. When Eli responded that they didn't, the soldiers escorted him and the rest of his crew from the ship's hanger to the vessel's war room.

Here they found Mara waiting along with Tristan and David, the two Terran males she had bonded. Mara rushed forward at the sight of them, catching Eli in a quick embrace. "I'm so glad you're here," she whispered.

Eli returned the gesture. "As am I. We owe you our lives."

"Don't thank me. Thank the colonel here." She faltered. "I mean the jingda," she amended, inserting the correct term for the equivalent rank in the Federation chain of command. "He was the one who suggested we investigate the crash site."

The Maur she gestured to was a large male whose white fur contrasted starkly with his dark regalia. A five-pointed star affixed to his collar indicated his rank. He also wore a long knife on one hip and a pistol on the other.

He opened his maw as if to address Eli, then faltered. His eyes sparked in recognition, but the figure he was looking at stood behind him. "Sahar?"

"Hello, Geresh." Sahar's voice sounded strangely formal. "Or, perhaps I should say Jingda Geresh. Apologies; I didn't get your rank when we last met."

They had met before? "I must admit," Geresh continued, "I did not think I would see you again—particularly in a situation like this."

Sahar let out a soft snort. "It seems as though the god had other plans. That, or this universe is just getting too damn small."

"Indeed," the jingda growled. Looking back to Eli, he said, "Please, forgive my lack of decorum. I am Geresh Nos Artice, Jingda of the Seventh Battalion out of Carnac." He extended his right hand.

"Eli Ren'dahl." Accepting the handshake, he added, "Thank you for coming to our aid. The timing could not have been better." He glanced back at Sahar. "You two know each other?"

"In passing," Sahar replied. "We met on Minos Station a little over six months ago—at the Festival of the Sisters."

Geresh let a hint of a smile play across his feline maw. "Before things got… heated." Eli had been told later of the altercation that had occurred at that particular event. Fortunately, it seemed that the incident had not colored Geresh's impression of their crew. Or, perhaps more correctly, it had not colored his impression of Sahar.

Eli steered the conversation back to their current situation. "Mara," he began. "What has happened while we've been away? I thought you were stationed near the Angel Gate to bounce messages from Sif."

He had deliberately avoided mentioning Ryker's name, though that was who she had corresponded with. Such a conversation would be further complicated when Mara discovered Ryker's murderer had been extracted safely from the Vandal's crash site. Eli was able to justify a delay in retribution to himself, but he did not expect Mara to share in such restraint.

Mara nodded. "That's right. About two weeks ago I received a message from Jocelyn letting me know you were on your way. Right after that though, we picked up a signal in the Hades Belt, one that couldn't be traced to any of our assets in the system." Her eyes fell to the floor. "It was a trap. If it wasn't for Geresh and his Seventh Battalion, those drones—or those other things—might have finished us off."

So that was why they hadn't been able to reach her during their last operation. "So, they simulated a distress beacon to ambush you," Eli recapped. "Has this been reported to the Sanctum? What about the DGC?"

"That's where things get complicated," said Geresh. "We've been tracking these attacks for the better part of the last cycle. That's why we were docked at Minos Station during your last visit. The attack on the Resolve was the first time we've managed to catch the perpetrators in action."

Geresh paused, stiffening and folding his arms behind his back as he continued. "We intended to return Mara and her companions to the station after we finished our sweep of the belt. As you can see, that never came to fruition. Since picking them up we've had to deal with three more drone assaults, and that's not counting the incident with your vessel. We've lost a destroyer and two frigates in the process. That incident, specifically, occurred the last time we tried to return to the station for a resupply."

A chill went down Eli's spine as he realized what the Maur was implying. "You think the drones are trying to keep ships away from Minos?"

"That is what we've concluded, yes."

Sahar asked, "Why haven't you made your way back to Federation space to gather reinforcements?"

"That was our next move," he conceded. "But now I'm gathering that you haven't heard the news."

"What news?" Eli asked.

Concern thick in her voice, Mara said. "Eli, the gates are down. All of them."

Eli paused for a long moment, unable to process her statement. Such a claim was as terrifying as it was absurd. "That's impossible."

"Perhaps," Geresh agreed, "but it is nonetheless a reality. We've confirmed the reports with our own sensor sweeps. Every gate within the Hellion system has been shut down."

"Have you tried reaching the DGC?" Sahar asked.

"Of course." A hint of annoyance crept into Geresh's voice. "We can't seem to get the signal out. The communications issue has been a problem for some time now. The gate failure is a more recent development. We were just discussing how this might change our situation when our scans found your crashed ship."

Eli pressed his fingers against his brow. This must have been what Azrael had meant when he'd warned that their window for escape was closing. Perhaps the vindictive spirit had only been toying with him. Indeed, that window seemed to already have closed.

"All right," Eli sighed. "Thank you for filling us in with what's been going on out here. I have a few more details that may help us start to piece things together."

He turned so that he was addressing the whole group, including his team. "While we were on the ship, I summoned my ancestral spirit in hopes that he could provide me with some insight.

What he told me was… disturbing. It would probably be better if we all sat down for this."

Skye swallowed hard. "That…" She took in a stilling breath. "Well, that shit is dark."

Sahar let out a growl of agreement as she began to massage her forehead. "Is this even possible? I've been a faithful follower of the Church for as long as I can remember, and I've never heard of such a thing."

"Nor I," Geresh agreed. "Indeed, the suggestion that one of the gods has hijacked a synthetic intelligence system strains credulity."

"As does the idea of creatures living in the cold vacuum of space," Eli countered. "Or the thought that every gate in the system would shut down simultaneously."

"Point taken." With a heaved sigh, Geresh asked, "So, did this spirit of yours have anything helpful to offer? A proposed plan of action?"

Eli hesitated for a long moment. "No. He seemed to think fleeing was the best option. Now, though, that is off the table. We will have to come up with another plan."

After hearing so many of Eli's lies and omissions, Skye had developed a kind of sixth sense for them. That sense was tingling in seismic proportions. "What aren't you telling us?" When he opened his mouth—presumably to deny it—she shouted him down. "We've been at this too long, Eli. I can tell when you're hiding something. What else did your spirit say?"

He remained quiet for a long moment, the inky pools of his eyes considering her. At length, he said, "His warning was not just to flee, but to stay away to prevent a potentially worse outcome than that already in the making. He seemed to think our intervention, specifically, could trigger a fate worse than what has already befallen the system."

Damn. One of these days, Skye was going to learn not to ask questions she didn't want the answer to.

Everyone exchanged awkward looks, their loss of words mutual and total. Finally, it was Amelia who broke the silence. "Be that as it may, our path is chosen for us. Whatever the risk, we need to push forward. The outcome of inaction will be, inevitably, for us to die in this asteroid belt. We cannot continue to run forever."

She was right, though that did not give them the direction they needed. "What do you recommend we do from here?" Geresh asked.

"Well," Aaliyah jumped in, "most of our gear is still back at the crash site. I'm sure y'all have plenty of toys up here for us to play with, but I'm bettin' they're all Maur-sized. Any chance ya'd let us wander on down there to recover some of our things?"

"No," the jingda replied tersely. "But I will send some of my people to do it. As you just noted, they're better equipped than you are at the moment." The white-furred Maur walked over to the chamber's entrance. As he opened the door, he said, "Please remain here for the moment. I will have cabins prepared for you. Once we have recovered any salvageable gear from your shipwreck, we will convene again." To himself, he muttered, "And, gods willing, someone will have thought of a plan by then."

Chapter 16

[ACCESSING ARC PROJECT LOG 140]
[DR. DAMIEN HERMES]

I'll keep this short and to the point: funding for the project has been canceled. I don't have all the details, nor do I presume to understand. I cannot fathom that this is due to some deficiency in our performance. The progress made on this endeavor has been remarkable, and I cannot let this be the end of our research. Surely, we will find another buyer.

[CLOSING PROJECT LOG…]

Lexa's reconstruction was proceeding according to schedule. Her previous body had been largely dismantled and all deficient materials had been removed. A diagnostic scan revealed that the Cognis code governing neuromotor functioning had been irreparably damaged in the cloning process. Therefore, Arc had written a new code set to replace the corrupted functions.

The task had been simple enough. His designs for his companion required several new code sets beyond the scope of the original Cognis design anyway. Now that Arc was able to run a full diagnostic of his own system, he had sufficient mastery over the Cognis code to prepare a companion chip that would work in tandem with Lexa's existing programming.

He touched the glass on the front of Lexa's incubation chamber, watching intently as the device's nano-machines stitched new tissues and circuitry over her disassembled frame. "It won't be long now," he whispered.

Her face was placid, even peaceful, in the cool blue liquid of the chamber. Arc would have liked to imagine that she was dreaming, though he knew from experience that beings such as they did not dream. Such a fantasy had surprised him when he first became aware of it. It was as though the irrational tendencies of the flesh he inhabited were somehow influencing the pure calculating perfection of his artificial cognition.

He wondered if this was a feature that would be exclusive to himself, or if such tendencies might be passed down to his offspring. There was no basis or precedent on which to theorize related to this scenario. He, unlike any being before him, was the perfect fusion of the biological, technological, and metaphysical. The universe had never seen anything like him before, nor would it ever see anything like him again.

His offspring, though, would be close—as would his chosen companion. He sighed wistfully as he imagined the destiny that awaited his chosen people. They, too, would be a fusion of principles that were as yet completely alien to this reality. They would be the perfect integration of flesh and machinery, only lacking in the divine nature that would remain uniquely his.

"My Lord." Cali's voice stirred him from his reverie. "Everything is in place. I believe it is time."

"Excellent," he replied. "Your forces have located the cavern where they've secreted the Sanctum?"

"Yes. We've locked down all points of entry. A transport will take us right to their doorstep."

Arc noticed then that Cali's hand rested on the hilt of an ornate black sword. "I do not suspect that you'll need that."

The Kintari woman shrugged off the comment. "I don't think I'll need my mask either, but I have it with me. Consider it to be a part of my regalia. I want you to know that I take my role in your honor guard seriously."

His honor guard? So that was how she'd chosen to interpret her role. Truthfully, Arc had not given much thought to what kind of formal title the woman would hold in his regime. In absence of an assignment, it seemed that she'd chosen to assume the mantle and function she'd held before her exile.

He held out a hand. "Your mask—may I see it?"

Cali hesitated only briefly before reaching sheepishly for the mask. Arc thought the change in her demeanor unusual, but then he saw why.

All members of the Kintari military wore masks to assist them in combat. In addition to being functional, the masks were designed to signify unit and rank. Cali's mask was black, consistent with the style of the Deathwatch Guard that protected the Empress herself. The Eye of Lith, the runic symbol of the Kintari patron goddess, was engraved in crimson around each eyepiece as a perfect mirror to the tattoos Cali wore on her face.

Since each mask was crafted to fit and serve a specific warrior, the equipment was never recycled. This mask was meant to follow Cali throughout her life. Consequently, it would continue to follow her into exile. The brand on Cali's neck, a downward-facing arrow bisected by a cross, served as a sign to all who would meet her that this was a warrior who had failed in her duty to the Empress. The same symbol had been carved into the face of the mask and painted a vibrant white for all to see.

Arc looked at Cali to find her eyes fixed firmly on the floor. It seemed that the shame of this mark weighed heavily on her sense of honor. As a pragmatist, she had chosen to carry the equipment with her so that she might use it in combat if the need arose. However, the act of donning the symbol of her disgrace would exact an intangible, but significant, penalty on her dignity.

"This mark. It was given to signify your failure to fulfill your duty to the Empress?"

The pain was evident in Cali's expression as she responded. "Yes, Lord Riven."

"And remind me, specifically, what it was you failed to do?"

Tears glistened in the Kintar's eyes. "The Empress's daughter—it was my duty to protect her."

"And she died under your watch?"

"Yes, my Lord." The words were robotic. Matter of fact.

This much he knew, but now he pressed for new details. "What was the cause?"

"Suicide."

Her answer caught Arc by surprise. He had expected that the princess might have fallen to an assassin's blade, or perhaps by poison. The truth of Cali's failure was most unexpected. "Suicide?"

"Yes," she replied curtly.

"And you were held responsible?"

Cali's jaw clenched synchronously with her fists. "It was my duty to notice and report the signs to the court physician. In failing to report her depression, I failed my oath as surely as if she had fallen at a murderer's hand."

While Arc disagreed, his curiosity superseded his desire to object. "Tell me more."

The look in her eyes told him that Cali would have preferred to do anything but. "What more is there to tell?"

"Tell me about the princess's depression. What was the nature of it? Was the condition diagnosed? Was she receiving treatment?"

Cali shook her head. "No. It was… sudden. The princess had taken a liking to a certain slave. This slave was then brought up on charges of treason. He was executed, though the princess pleaded with the Empress to spare his life."

Interesting. "Was this slave her lover?"

"It would not have been proper for me to speculate on such things."

"But you had your suspicions."

"Perhaps."

How intriguing. Cali's life had been upended by a spectrum of emotion that Arc had yet to fully explore. What would it be like to care so deeply for someone that their loss would drive you to take your own life? What other foolish acts could be driven by an affection so deep? Was this something that Arc was capable of, despite the rationale parameters of his programming?

At that moment, he became aware of the pain that was so evident on Cali's face. His thirst for knowledge had tormented the woman. He would have to tread more lightly on this subject in the future. The mass of its import seemed sufficient that it might cause her to break under its gravity.

But what if he could somehow mend these wounds? Would not Cali become a more useful tool if he could temper her spirit?

"I determine that your punishment was unjust," he declared.

A tick in her expression—the barest hint of an acknowledgment. "Be that as it may, I served only at the will of the Empress. By her will, I was also cast out."

"But you, too, know in your heart how wrong it was. That is why you desire retribution."

"Of course," Cali snapped. "What of it?"

Arc forgave the venom in her words. If he were to reforge this sword, he must first create a clean break. Only then could he be certain it would not shatter again. "Yes, you do serve at the behest of your betters, and that is why it was fitting you accept your exile."

He reached up and cupped her chin in one hand, still holding the mask in his other. Gently, he drew up her eyes to meet his. Rage burned in that gaze—an inferno that would ultimately consume Cali if it did not find an outlet. It would be his task, then, to protect her from the conflagration.

"However," he continued, "you no longer serve that master. You serve another, one who has seen the injustice in the charges against you. I, therefore, will absolve you of these false sins and will remove the mark they have left upon you."

He released her and held that hand over the surface of the mask. His hand shifted, flesh over his palm splitting to reveal another technological implement he'd had fashioned as a physical defense measure. Heat radiated from the exposed coil, melting the surface of the mask over where the mark of exile had been engraved.

Cali looked on in equal parts terror and wonder. As she looked on, Arc generated a magnetic field to reshape the alloy. He smoothed the surface while being careful to avoid damaging the electronic components inside the device. His actions erased the white mark of shame, but he did not stop there. He also erased the twin Eyes of Lith, for she was no longer a child of Queen of Battle.

In their place, he drew a new symbol: his symbol. He drew the three arches that symbolized the horizon and its new moon. Over those, he drew the slanted cross of knowledge. This crest, the Mark of Riven, the Seal of the Warrior's Wisdom, would identify her as his and his alone.

His work complete, Arc extended the newly forged mask back to Cali. "Wear it proudly," he commanded. "For in this moment, I have removed one of the seals which have unfairly shackled your soul. The second I shall remove in short order."

She took the implement in both hands before sinking to her knees. Her hands shook and she wept openly. Arc had expected this action to have great meaning for her, but perhaps he had still underestimated its impact.

"Thank you," she sobbed. "I… don't…"

He rested a hand on her shoulder to quiet her. "You may repay me by being worthy of the honor I extend to you," he advised. "Now, though, it is time for us to go."

Jocelyn peered nervously into the holodisplay. "They're here," she pronounced solemnly. "Somehow they've breached the barrier at the entrance. They must have a powerful psionic with them."

"Could it be that Kintari woman?" Brenna asked.

Jocelyn ran a hand nervously through the tiny braids of her hair as she bound them together with an elastic tie. "Perhaps, though I've never heard of a Kintar strong enough to breach a coven's wards before. Maybe there are several of them out there. She's got to be linked with at least one, probably two others to manage that."

Brenna flexed her shoulders, cords of her muscles straining as she cracked her neck. Her frame was as imposing as that of any Terran male Jocelyn had seen. She looked like she could hold her own in combat even had she been absent the psionic powers of the Sahaia.

"All right, boss," she said. "What's the plan?" There was a fierce determination in her black-in-black eyes—a look that Jocelyn hoped was mirrored in her own.

"We end this quickly," Jocelyn resolved. "I don't want to risk the archives or any of the other valuables we have stored here. We meet them in the reception hall. There's nothing there that we cannot replace if it is damaged."

"Fine by me," she flipped a strand of her short hair back behind her ear. "Want to take the quick route?"

"Every second counts." Jocelyn extended her hand to Brenna. When Brenna took it, the world warped out of focus. When Jocelyn's brain could once again perceive their surroundings, they were somewhere else. They'd arrived in the reception hall.

Teleportation seemed very handy, but Jocelyn wasn't sure she'd trade it in favor of her own gift. Then again, there wasn't a list of common reasons to create constructs of dark energy. Not to say it was without its usefulness—just that it wasn't the kind of thing one used every day.

She would use it today, though.

"Behind me," Jocelyn ordered, having already heard the invaders' footsteps echoing down the corridor. "Link up. I'll take control."

"All right," Brenna replied. "Ready when you are."

The tactic was a simple one. By linking their psionic powers together, their abilities would synergize to be stronger than the sum of their separate powers. The only disadvantage was that only one person in the link could direct the flow of power. As a triumvir, it was Jocelyn's right… no, her responsibility to take control.

She pulled down her psychic barriers, opening herself up to detect Brenna's signature. The other psionic signature was right where it should have been, shining like a metaphysical beckon in her mind's eye. She reached out with her power and grabbed hold of it, coaxing it forward to feed into her own essence.

There was strength there—an intoxicating level of power that sought to overwhelm Jocelyn and take on a life of its own. Through focus and discipline, she brought it under control just as the first of the intruders appeared. She bound Brenna's energy to her own, summoning dark energy to her fingertips.

Then something slammed into her mind like a hammer. The energy she had gathered dispersed, and she gasped as her connection to the well of power was suddenly cut off. She could still see it in her mind's eye, but something was in the way. That something was Brenna.

"Brenna?" she asked, turning to her companion. "What in…" A fist slammed into Jocelyn's jaw, staggering her. A kick to the back of her knees made her cry out before another blow to the head sent her sprawling to the floor.

Something hard pressed into the small of her back. Brenna's knee, she realized. The woman had seized her wrists and was binding them together behind her. "Sorry, Jocelyn," she hissed. "It's just business."

Jocelyn was too stunned to say anything. One of the hazards of linking to another psion was that any person in the link could exert their will to cut off the flow of power. That was why you had to trust those you linked to with your very life.

Apparently, Jocelyn's faith had been misplaced. "Why?" she gasped.

She felt Brenna shrug as the other woman kept her pinned to the ground. "Reasons. Maybe one day I'll bother to tell ya. Right now, we have company. Understand that I'll be keepin' the block in place for now. I don't want ya to be rude to our guests."

Jocelyn's mind raced. "It was you," she realized. "You're the one who stole Joaquin's body."

"That's right. But look." She grabbed Jocelyn by the hair and lifted her head painfully so that she could see the entrance to the hall. "It's come home. See? No harm done."

What Jocelyn saw was an abomination. It was not Joaquin Valadar, though that was certainly the template that had been used for this creature. The bone structure and musculature were the same. The charred and blackened skin had been mended but retained the same dark hue. Its hair had not grown back, and the eyes had been replaced by cybernetic prosthetics that glowed an eerie crimson. Its attire was business formal—a stylish black suit over a red dress shirt.

"What are you?" she whispered.

The creature crouched down to be closer to her. "I'm your god, Jocelyn. You may call me Arc."

Her god? This monster was no god.

Then she saw the Kintar flanking the man. She was dressed as a Deathwatch Guard, but rather than the traditional symbols of rank, the black mask she wore held a new symbol engraved over the left side. It was the same mark Jocelyn bore on the inside of her left wrist.

"You speak blasphemy," she spat.

Arc chuckled coldly. "Be that as it may, it doesn't change anything. There is only one thing you need to accept: I have already won. This performance has already played out. You only need to bear witness to the final act." He waved his hand to some of the soldiers that had accompanied him into the chamber. "Take her. Our friend here will see that her block is kept in place while we tend to our affairs here. Be careful with her. She is cunning."

The soldiers seized her on either side and Brenna released her. A coy little smile played off Brenna's face. "Is everything to your satisfaction, my Lord?"

"Indeed," Arc replied. "You have done well."

"Thank you, my Lord. Is there anythin' else I can do to be of assistance?"

"As I said, I will need you to keep the block in place until we can secure the triumvir. With your help, we have made good time here. I would like to tend to our other business before departing."

Jocelyn's mind raced. Though she was in good physical condition, she was no fighter. She had relied on her psionic abilities for far too long. To be cut off from them now was to be rendered defenseless. Still, she had to do something.

Arc shouted down to another contingent of soldiers who had not yet entered the room. "Bring in the artifact."

The artifact? He couldn't possibly mean… Oh gods.

A small hovering platform was guided through the archway. On this platform was a large gemstone, about a meter in height and roughly equal in width. Its surface shimmered dark green where it was not covered in veins of obsidian.

The object could not be mistaken. This was the Heart of Thule. This was the most powerful psionic artifact in all of existence.

Arc turned back to Jocelyn. "You recognize it, yes? You know the importance of this." He stroked the surface of the Heart lovingly. "Now, would you be so kind as to provide us with direction? I am looking for the summoning pit. I believe you call it the Well of Eternity."

"Frag off," she spat.

The synth's expression never wavered. "Very well, then. Our dear Brenna will have to show us. Given that you will be of little help to us, I see no reason why you should be allowed to speak."

He nodded to the Kintari woman, who produced a gag from her belt pouch. The cloth was fastened around Jocelyn's mouth and tied tight. She was then pushed roughly forward by her guards as they followed Brenna into the depths of the complex.

CHAPTER 17

After many long months, my hopes have proven founded. A new organization—Callisto Corporation—has secured funding for the ARC project. Perhaps we will see these labors come to fruition after all. How they expect to apply such efforts is beyond me, but I'm just pleased to continue with my work.

The group was silent as Brenna led them down to the Well of Eternity. Most of the Marauder forces had remained on the upper levels of the compound, save for the two guards who escorted Jocelyn. A second group of armored combatants had brought the Heart of Thule down the lift after them, since there had not been space for all of them in the single elevator. One soldier brought a padded case, holding an object that Cali had not thought of in a long time. The three men supporting their cargo were dismissed when they reached the Well of Eternity.

Cali had worried about someone interacting with the artifact while unsupervised, but Lord Riven had dismissed her concerns. He'd reminded her that Heart was inert without an infusion of power. Cyrus Valadar had activated the object using a sustained electrical current, though Riven had assured her there were other ways to make the power the Heart. However, he had still been confident that the artifact was in no danger of being triggered accidentally.

Once the Heart had been brought down, Lord Riven himself guided the hovering platform down the hall and through the antechamber that led to the Well. The chamber was visually identical to the hologram that Riven had shown Cali back at the Citadel. What the hologram could not capture was the ambiance.

Obsidian slabs spun out from the hundred-foot pool in a radial pattern. A rough kind of craftsmanship was evident in their making. The walls and ceiling were cavernous, the same shape and texture as the unworked surface of the asteroid. Light was scarce in the room, which lent greatly to the chamber's supernatural tension.

Lord Riven drew in a deep breath. "I must admit, I'm feeling… something. It is hard to articulate. It is irrational. Mystical, even. Perhaps there's something here that speaks to the biological part of me—to my very tissue. To my organs and sinew. Or maybe it is something else. Do you feel it?"

Cali nodded. There was something strange in the aura of this room. She found it intriguing that Riven could not put words to it. Naturally, she had assumed that the nature of his intelligence would have been able to identify and explain the phenomenon.

Her voice came out in a reverent whisper. "What now, my Lord?"

His mouth twisted in a smile, striking in its sincerity but with a hint of mischief that lurked at its corners. "Our purpose here is two-fold. To appreciate the magnitude of both efforts requires a bit of exposition. What do you know of the Well of Eternity?"

"Only what you have told me," she confessed, despite hating the truth in her words.

"I suspected as much." He stepped up to Jocelyn and gently loosened her gag enough to pry it from her mouth. "I doubt you would care to indulge us in a lesson, but I give you the opportunity. What can you tell us about this chamber?"

The Sahaia's eyes glared hatefully back at Riven, yet her lips remained silent. He chuckled mirthlessly. "As I suspected. Brenna, then. Would you enlighten us as to the first thing every candidate is told about the Well?"

"Purity of flesh," Brenna responded mechanically. "One's flesh may only breach the surface of the waters if they are without adornment. To violate this rule is to seek a futile death."

"Textbook," Riven replied approvingly. "Thank you for this explanation. Now, does this requirement extend to cybernetics as well?"

Uncertain now, Brenna replied, "That is what we are told."

"Yes, and it is correct." He regarded his right hand with interest. "The file on Joaquin Valadar noted that he had a prosthetic arm, but the body that was brought to me had a full contingent of limbs. This is a testament to the power of dark energy to restore what is lost if the rules are followed. Now, what else do you know?"

Brenna faltered slightly, somewhat taken aback by the pop quiz. "It's what we use to make new Sahaia. Can't make new Sahaia without the Awakenin' ritual, and the ritual can only be done in the Well by a circle of six linked Sahaia."

"Correct. And do you know why that is?"

She hesitated before shaking her head. "I don't."

Lord Riven's grin was proud. "It's because the Well of Eternity isn't filled with water. It is the concentrated essence of Nethrian power. Not dark energy, but a conductor that facilitates the exchange of dark energy. That is why purity of flesh is necessary. Under normal circumstances, only organic tissue can survive exposure to that much psionic power. Even this varies from person to person, which is why so many fail to survive the ritual."

The god cracked his knuckles, turning back to the Heart of Thule. "The Well can be used for other things besides an Awakening. Which brings us to why we've gathered here today." He turned his palms upward, and a strange static filled the room.

He's channeling, Cali realized. She had imagined that his android form would have some type of psionic affinity, but this was the first time she'd ever seen him use it. Currents of unseen force lifted the artifact from its hovering platform. With the slightest twisting of his fingers, Riven conducted the object over the pool and set it down gracefully at its center.

The effects were immediate. The crystalline surface of the object flared brilliantly before settling into a steady emerald glow. Cali could feel the power radiating off the artifact, permeating the air absent any place to go.

Riven wasn't done yet. "Now," he said. "The Starfire Conduit."

Cali went to the padded case her soldiers had placed at the end of the room. She opened it and set it at the edge of the Well. With another flick of Riven's wrist, the body of the conduit levitated, flipping upside down and moving to the cavern's ceiling directly above the Heart.

Panels on the side of the device flipped open, and metal clamps sprang out to sink deep into the rock. Another compartment in the Conduit opened to expose a round sensor. A slender laser shot down from the exposed component and struck the glowing surface of the artifact.

The air grew noticeably thicker, and Cali found that she was laboring to breathe. The cavern itself seemed to vibrate with the force of the Heart of Thule's power. Ebony ripples surged from where the artifact touched the waters of the Well. The artifact's green glow seemed to solidify and lash out at the beam like a living creature being seared by its touch.

Then the Heart seemed to bleed as crimson light choked out its viridian glow. A shrieking noise echoed throughout the enclosure before the haze of power began to dissipate. With peculiar, strangled violence the device brought the flow of power under its control.

Lord Riven stretched his arms out as if basking in some unseen radiance. "That," he gasped, "was even more satisfying than I had anticipated."

"What have you done?" Jocelyn whispered as she gawked in horror at the scene in front of her.

The god's smile was chilling. "Only what you would have sought to do in your own time. I have brought the power of the Heart of Thule under my control. You see, to maintain my influence on this plane, I have required a constant infusion of dark energy. Think of it like a battery. I have made do with lesser sources of power until recently, but now that I have the very essence of a fellow Nethrian to draw upon, I will have all the power I could ever want."

Cali's mind went unbidden to his current source of power. It had been days since she'd thought of Wynne. Perhaps now that a replacement power source had been found, her old friend would finally be able to rest peacefully. To hope for recovery was out of the question. No one could survive what that woman had been through for this long.

"Now," Riven continued, "there is but one other thing we must tend to while we are here, but no less important." He extended his arm toward Cali. "Come." She obeyed, taking slow, deliberate steps forward until she stood directly before him. "Kneel," he commanded.

The order might have rankled her coming from any other being, but this was her god who spoke to her. Drawing on the discipline she'd honed for years in service to the Empress, she sank to one knee and bowed her head respectfully.

Lord Riven's voice was a wave of ice cascading upon her. "When you first came to my service, you acted on faith in hopes that I would one day grant you power. I gave you the Marauders. I gave you this space station and the impenetrable fortress where you now reside. Still, you hunger for more. Tell me, when I fulfill my promise to you, yet again—when I grant you even more power, what will you do with it?"

Cali closed her eyes beneath the cover of her mask. "You know what I want it for."

"I do," he admitted, "but I want to hear it. On whom will you turn your wrath when you've been given the power of the gods?"

"The Empire," she hissed.

"The whole Empire? Not just the Empress?"

"They are one and the same." It was true, as far as she saw it. "As written in the Chronicles, 'The sins of a leader are as the sins of the nation.'"

Riven chuckled. "So it is written," he agreed. He rested his hand briefly on her shoulder before bidding her rise. Then he did something Cali had not expected. He turned, shedding his jacket, his shirt, then his pants. When his last garment hit the tiled floor, he entered the Well of Eternity.

She started to shout her concern, but the sound caught in her throat. What was he doing? Had he not just told her that only the pure of flesh could touch the waters of the Well?

But nothing happened. Riven waded calmly into the dark depths, approaching the center near where the Heart still glowed with hellish light. Cali glanced at Jocelyn, wondering if perhaps the purity requirement only extended to those who channeled within the Well. Judging by the look of naked astonishment on her face, this was not the case. The triumvir was clearly as baffled as anyone.

"Why so surprised?" Riven teased as he turned to face them. "Surely you did not think the rules of mortals apply to the gods?"

If Cali had any doubts regarding his divinity, they were surely gone now. She bowed her head reverently, ashamed by her reaction.

"I do not hold it against you," he assured her. "Understand that I have reviewed the requirements of Well, not for my sake, but yours. It is time for your leap of faith, Cali. It is time for your Awakening."

Her Awakening? "I don't understand. Only Terrans can survive the Sahaia Awakening ritual."

"Not true. The Kintar and many other races used to perform Awakenings for their most honored scholars and warriors. It was a reward for the most elite castes of society. It has only been in recent millennia that the art of Awakening was lost to those societies. Without the circle of six, the ascendant peoples cannot conduct the ritual to initiate new members of their order."

So, the problem was with the circle of six, not the ritual itself? That meant that much of what the current Sahaia had told others regarding their power was a lie. An interesting revelation, though not particularly helpful for their current circumstances.

"We still don't have a full circle," she protested.

"I never said that I required a circle. I require only your faith, child. Now, tarry no longer. I need your answer laid plain: Will you trust in me?"

Cali could not stop her moment of hesitation. If only a fraction of what she had understood about the ritual were true, then she was putting not just her life, but her very soul into her Lord's care. Did the risk justify the potential reward?

A scene came to her mind. She was stripped bare and shackled to a post in the center of the arena. The crowds jeered her, shouting profanities and cruel insults to her honor. The members of the Deathwatch lined up to form a broad circle around her. Women she had thought of as friends and as sisters stared at her down with contempt in their eyes.

A whip was passed between them. Each warrior gave a single lash, taking care to strike any bit of unmarred flesh. Only her face and neck were spared. When she thought that she would pass out from the pain, the circle parted to admit the Empress herself.

Two of her sisters forced her roughly to her knees while a third pulled a glowing iron from a nearby fire. The Empresses seized the brand and pressed it roughly against her neck. The only thing that had seared hotter than that iron, was Cali's rage.

Cali blinked and the scene dissipated. The rage remained, and it was that fury that gave her the strength to proceed. Her fingers went to the edge of her mask. The device hissed as she triggered the release mechanism to remove it from her face. She found that her eyes needed a moment to adjust to the light of the room absent the enhanced optics of the mask, but she fixed her eyes on the silhouetted figure framed by the red gleam at the center of the Well.

Next, she unfastened her weapons belt, letting it clatter to the floor. Her armor came after. This she laid neatly in a pile off to her left, along with her boots. Lastly, she slowly unzipped the black mesh underlay and peeled it off her body.

Cali's heart thudded in her chest. Her breathing was heavy and quick. It was an oddly erotic sensation, exposing herself like this. She was cognizant of the two Sahaia, but it wasn't their gazes that made her blood race.

Lord Riven's eyes glowed like twin embers set within his shadowy frame. They stared out unblinkingly as he extended his hand to her. "Come," he bid.

Drawing a deep breath, she stepped one foot into the black depths of the Well of Eternity. The chill of the waters sank into her bones. A dull, numbing sensation seeped into the limb, requiring Cali to force herself to take a second step. It got easier after that. One step at a time, she made her way methodically to the center of the pool. She was submerged up to her navel by the time she finally reached Riven.

The god reached around the small of her back, drawing her closer. Mere inches separated them, and Cali realized her breathing had grown heavier. She could feel the heat coming off his body—a bastion of warmth in the icy void.

His voice boomed with authority. "Cali Vay-Lon, you stand in the depths of eternity. Do you pledge to serve me from now until eternity's end?"

Her words came in a hoarse whisper. "I do."

A small blade jutted from the god's wrist. With it, he slit the palm of his opposite hand. His blood was a thick fluid as dark as the night's sky. When it struck the waters, they began to churn.

The obsidian waves surged up like a vortex, encircling the two of them at their center. Everything about the surrounding chamber was blotted out by the torrent, save for the now faint glow of the artifact behind Riven.

His voice came in a low, rapid chant. Cali could not make out the words over the sound of the rushing waters. Fear as cold as the depths of the Well took hold in her stomach. Her body began to tremble. In a fit of panic, she started to reach for Riven, but his penetrating gaze held her fast. She found that she could not move.

Then his eyes lifted to the ceiling. Cali followed his gaze to peer upward, only now it was not the rocky apex of the cavern. There were stars above them—an ocean of light and magic.

A rift, she realized. She was looking into a rift. As she peered out into destinations unknown, she noted so much within the alien constellations. She saw distant planets, spiraling nebulae, and even strange creatures that swam within the vacuum of space.

But there was also darkness, and that darkness reached out to her. Cali blinked, not trusting her eyes. She hadn't imagined it, though. The darkness moved like a living thing. Those shadowy tendrils reached down from the abyss to touch her.

She tried to squirm, to shrink away, but something still held her tight. Desperation clawed at her mind. She wanted to scream, to run in terror, to beg for mercy. Instead, she only waited like a prisoner within her own body.

The first tendril caressed her skin. It was pressure without warmth. Neither was it cold. It was just empty—strange and curious in its insistence to explore her. More tendrils joined the first, wrapping around her arms and trailing down her stomach. They tickled her hips and caressed her thighs. She gasped for breath and inhaled them. They went deep inside her body and delved within her soul.

She thought she would go mad as the darkness infused her. It was too much. She was suffocating on the shadows. They were drowning her. She tried to scream but only managed a whimpering moan.

Then something snapped. Her will seemed to evaporate as she leaned into the violation. Strangely, the darkness's touch was no longer smothering. It was almost pleasurable, even empowering. The shadows filled her like a lover's caress, and she wondered how she had lived so long without their touch.

This was ecstasy. This was rapture.

The darkness pulled back from her and left a painful longing in her soul. What had likely taken only seconds had seemed to stretch on for hours or even days. Somehow she knew that she would never again feel anything like that for the rest of her life.

The swirling torrent of water began to settle. Black, icy droplets still sprayed her as the waves splashed against the Heart of Thule. The eerie crimson glow of the artifact was on her again, but even its vermilion radiance could not mask the change in her.

Lord Riven's voice enveloped her in much the same way the darkness had moments earlier. "Behold, child. You have been made new."

There was a long moment of disbelief as she stared down at herself. The scarlet hue of her Kintari heritage had been washed away, replaced with skin of Sahaia white. She felt at her dendrai to make sure they were still there. They were, after a fashion, but they had split. Twelve smooth tendrils arched back from her forehead and temple region to form a crown of smooth white flesh. Her hand slipped to her neck, feeling for the mark of exile. Instead of the scar tissue, she found only unbroken skin.

Also gone were the assortment of black tattoos she'd earned through her lifetime of service. These had been replaced with a single mark emblazoned on her left wrist.

It was the mark of the Warrior's Wisdom. It was the crest of her master.

Riven regarded her with open amusement as she took in his handiwork. Despite the chill from the Well, a strange warmth stirred in her core. Her eyes lingered on the lines of the god's torso, the thickness of his shoulders, and the contours of his abdomen. If he took offense to her lustful gawking, he did not voice it.

Was this lust though? The word seemed an incomplete expression of the strange desire that had taken hold in her. Cali had been with men and she had been with women. She'd lusted after them all, appreciating their beauty and spirit for a season.

No, this was different. Perhaps, just maybe, this was love. After all, if she were to be capable of loving anyone, would she not fall in love with a god?

She pushed herself toward him. She wanted to hold him closer to her body, to feel the press of him as they made love right here in these icy depths. All else was forgotten in the sudden hunger she felt for his flesh.

His hands took her by the shoulders and forced her to be still. "The effects of the transition can be intoxicating," he cautioned. "Do not lose yourself to the moment, child."

Her heart ached at the admonishment, but she knew he was right. Now was not the time. "Yes, my Lord."

He smiled at her then, stroking her cheek tenderly with one hand. "No matter who comes after you into my service, take pride in knowing that you were the first. Together we will build a force unlike anything this universe has ever seen. And you, Cali Vay-Lon, will serve at its head. Under my banner, your wrath will spread out across these stars. Very soon, you will have the vengeance you so desperately crave."

Cali inhaled deeply, basking in the glow of the vision her new god had painted. At long last, she had the power she had worked so hard for. Her body brimmed with the energy and strength she'd worked tirelessly to achieve ever since her exile.

But this was not the end she had worked for. This was only the beginning.

CHAPTER 18

[ACCESSING ARC PROJECT LOG 145]
[DR. DAMIEN HERMES]

I've loaded all the programs, including the organic substrate, onto the Marauders' servers. To my delight, everything has come online perfectly. I had worried there would be a certain amount of degradation in the time ARC was offline, but this has not been the case. In fact (and I'll have to check my notes to verify) the program may have continued to improve since the Prodigy Collective closed the project. Impossible, I know, but that was my initial impression.

[CLOSING PROJECT LOG...]

Siv wasn't sure how long she'd remained in the airlock. Certainly longer than intended, but still somehow not long enough. It would never be long enough. "Never long enough," she whispered, hand trailing against the glass of the coffin. "And never again."

Never again would she see the smile on Jeagan's face. Never again would she feel the firm press of his body against hers. Never again would he whisper sweet nothings and dark musings into her ear. Never again.

The airlock door cycled behind her, but she didn't look to see who had entered. Her focus remained fixated on the metal casket and the still face of her beloved inside. That did not stop the interloper from attempting to engage. "I came to see if I could get you anything," said Kadath.

It wasn't the first time the Kintari half-breed had made the offer, though Siv had not taken to timing the increments between his visits. Despite this, something felt off about the way he made the statement this time. "I doubt that is the only reason you came."

To his credit, Kadath didn't bother to argue. "I just got the heads-up from Ora. There's another problem. Likely connected to the Heart of Thule. It sounds like our magic rock might not have made it to Minos Station as planned—or, at least, not in the way we had intended for it to arrive."

So, the Sahaia had failed to retain control of the artifact. What had it been? A week? Maybe a little less? Did that mean Jeagan had truly died for nothing? "You're going to assist?" Siv asked.

"I think so. Thought it might be easier that way. Get my mind off the loss, and all that."

If only that tactic would prove so easy for her. "And you would like me to come with you," Siv concluded.

"I'm not asking you to, no." Kadath paused. "That said, if you feel like it would help, you are welcome to tag along."

Siv scoffed. "Is Thurn going?"

"No. Thurn is taking a leave of absence. He took the shuttle to Geb yesterday. Think he's planning on hopping a public transport back home. He hasn't been back to Orchalla in almost a decade. Figured it was probably time."

He'd left yesterday? Siv could have sworn that he'd just been here paying his respects this morning. Gods, she had been here a long time. "So, if I don't go with you..."

Kadath shrugged. "It's all right. I've done solo outings before. I'm sure Ora will have some other cronies to keep me company."

Despite the gravity of the situation, Siv managed a soft chuckle. "Let me think on it," she said. "Right now, I'm needed here."

If Kadath had anything to say on that sentiment, he kept it to himself. In silence, he stepped back and exited the chamber, the cycling of the inner airlock the only indication of his departure.

Siv's eyes winced in pain—what she imagined would be the precursor to tears if she'd been among one of the other sapient species. Her nictitating eyelids cycled rapidly over her slit pupils in the natural Hissak grief response.

She knew there was no sense in putting this off any longer. It was time to commence the Shedding—the Pradaxan ritual of final farewell. This ritual was not for Jeagan; it was for herself.

Siv pressed a button on the side of the coffin, retracting the glass cover. With her beloved's body exposed, she slipped off her gloves to reveal clawed hands—hands whose bare flesh was seen and felt by Jeagan alone. She laid the gloves across Jeagan's chest, smoothing them out in a line over his heart.

Next came the heavy sleeves of her tunic. She unclasped them at the shoulder and unzipped them to slide free of the rest of her garment. This exposed her lithe, muscular arms to the light and air outside their bedchamber for the first time since they'd been wed. Then came her heavy cloak, which she folded into a compact triangle and lay upon the still expanse of his torso along with the other cloths.

Lastly, came her mask. She fumbled with trembling fingers at the zipper as she drew it up the base of her neck to the crown of her skull. The mesh cloth peeled off her face like the second skin it had served as for so long. She winced at the change in brightness, gazing at Jeagan for one final time without the modesty filter required by her faith.

It was the way she most liked to see him. It was a moment of intimacy, a gaze of love and devotion reserved for him alone ever since taking their vows. To experience it for what she knew was the final time kindled her grief anew.

Once the mask was placed upon Jeagan's body, she indulged for one final moment, running her fingers along the scaled surface of his cheek. Mechanically, she closed the coffin and slid toward the exit, lest she lose her nerve.

She closed the airlock behind her. "Rest among the stars, my love. I hope to see you again soon." With that, she pressed the release for the external airlock. As the hatch hissed open, the void of space grabbed hold of Jeagan's coffin and pulled it into that dark ocean. Her life, her soulmate, was gone.

What was left for her now? Perhaps she would follow Kadath and find out. Yes, that would make the most sense. She needed connection during these hard times. She needed something to do. After all, there was nothing left for her here.

"Are you sure this is a good idea?" Markus asked.

Ora rolled her eyes. "No, but I'm certain it is the best idea we have."

"See, that's the thing: I'm a firm believer that doing nothing is usually a better option than getting the satyrs involved."

"And while I might normally agree, this situation is highly atypical," Ora countered. "Now, are you going to behave yourself, or do I need to ask you to watch the transport?"

Now it was Markus's turn to roll his eyes. She could act like he was being childish—and hells, he probably was—but that didn't change the fact that working with the Dorians was a bad idea. Surely the satyrs were already scrambling about on their little hooves working to figure this problem out. Calling the Gate Commission to offer tips seemed unnecessary.

"I'll be good, mom," he whined. "Come on, let's get this over with."

They filed out of the hovercar and up the concrete—actual concrete—path that wound up to and throughout the atrium where they were meeting the DGC representative.Markus had been a regular on the Sigma-4 station for years, even if he'd only started thinking of it as home these last few months. In all those years he had only been to the upper tier of the station once. In the name of plausible deniability, he never talked about that trip. That made this little venture his first official trip to the realm of the high and mighty.

Most of Markus's time on the space station was spent on the lower tier where things were affordable and the security was light.

When he'd captained the Vandal, he'd spent a decent amount of his time in mid-tier courtesy of the merchant-class permit registered to the ship. There'd been no good reason to go to the final five rings of the station.

However, this was where the DGC had instructed them to meet. As he took in the sight of the exotic plants and simulated animals that frolicked in the artificial habitat of R-12, his contempt deepened for the wealthy bastards who could afford such luxuries.

It wasn't that he resented when people did well for themselves. That was the beauty of capitalism: a lowly colonist born to indentured servitude could, in theory, climb the social ladder and accumulate resources to enjoy the life of the rich and famous. The reality was that the system, as it currently stood, was a rigged game.

Flamboyant displays of excess such as this showcased how things didn't have to be that way. Those poised at the top of the social hierarchy obviously had more than enough wiggle room to lend a hand to those who were struggling. Instead, they spent their excess on expensive flowers and robotic chipmunks. That's the "free" market for you.

This was the kind of shit he had fought against in the Colony Wars. Too bad the krets in their enemies' corporate accounts went farther than the bullets in the colonies' warehouses. It probably wasn't a good idea for him to be thinking about this right before meeting with the satyrs, especially given where their support had fallen by the time that show was wrapping up.

His mood soured even further when they caught sight of who the DGC had sent to meet them. "Nine hells," he spat. "Why did it have to be him?"

Ora shot him a cutting glance. Her message was obvious: Shut. Up. She seamlessly transitioned into her politician's smile as she greeted the officer. "Hello Turan."

Turan Dorr's lip twitched, but he couldn't bring himself to fake a smile. "Ora Monroe," he drawled. "You made it. And you brought a friend. How nice." Markus didn't bother returning the greeting. If Turan would just happen to forget Markus was here, they'd all be better off for it.

The Dorian officer had never liked Markus. Before the satyrs had switched sides, the two of them had been uneasy allies in the independence initiative. Dislike had given way to open hatred when Turan had walked in on Markus getting some quality time with the satyr's sister and fellow officer, Llana, in her office at the garrison.

The last time the two had crossed paths was after the Vandal got busted stealing the Starfire Conduit from the Star Spire. Turan had been understandably miffed when he couldn't actually find the Conduit aboard their ship and had departed in a huff. Looking at the scoreboard, Markus really couldn't blame the guy for being less than excited to see him.

Ora wasn't in a mood for male posturing. "Can we dispense with the bullshit and just pretend I said something that made you feel smug and superior? You're here, so that means you know we have information you need."

Turan's frowned. "I'm here because our local command center received a call stating that someone on this gods-forsaken station had useful information. How disappointed they will be when they find out it was all just a big waste of time." He turned and made as if to leave.

Ora called his bluff before he had his second hoof off the ground. "The source of the disruption is on Minos Station. The Marauders are behind the gate failure."

While Markus wasn't sure if he approved of her dumping their best intel in the opening remarks, the move seemed to be effective. Turan halted mid-stride and slowly turned around. There was still plenty of contempt on his handsome face, but it was now accompanied by a measure of curiosity.

"All right," he sighed. "I'm listening."

Turan may have been listening, but he hadn't been ready to hear the story. Two hours later the holographic sky was beginning to transition into a scenic simulation of dusk. Turan had shaken the tough-guy act enough to don an obvious look of concern. Although the level of detail Ora had provided in her statement was beyond incriminating, the thought of what the Dorians would do to them was the furthest thing from Markus's mind. For a moment Markus almost forgot he was talking to a hot-shot Dorian officer bent on busting his balls.

Then Turan opened his damned mouth again. "You know, if this is bullshit, I'm going to make it my personal mission to bury both of you and every person you've ever worked with."

Markus was done holding his tongue. "That didn't exactly sound like a thank you."

"Thank you?" Turan scoffed. "For what? It's not like you've posed any solutions. All you've done is tell me that this shit is way more fragged than we thought. I mean, artifacts? Nethrians? Synths? Maybe the Creator himself will drop by to kick us in the balls, just to make it a clean sweep."

"Blasphemy isn't going to get you anywhere," Ora warned. "Look, my contact at the Temple has already volunteered to help the DGC. She thinks she can do something to locate the artifact if you can just get her to the station."

"Fine," Turan spat, rubbing his brow. "And why isn't she here?"

"Well…" Ora faltered. "I thought it would be better if I got your temperature on the idea first."

Turan immediately sensed the problem. "What aren't you telling me?"

Ora shot Markus a pleading look. Unfortunately, he was totally oblivious to the problem, so he wasn't going to be much help. The questioning look on his face annoyed her enough to make her spit it out. "She's half-breed."

By the look on Turan's face, you'd have thought Ora just shot his mother. He ran a hand through his long brown hair, somehow managing to complete the gesture despite the horns that arced back from his forehead. "You've got to be shitting me."

Now Markus was officially the only one confused. "So?"

"So?" Turan made the word positively drip with disdain. "You think my superiors are going to feel good about seeking special assistance from an abomination?"

Maybe it was just a sign of how much he couldn't stand Turan, but Markus couldn't control himself. "Seriously? That's what you're worried about right now?"

Turan's scowl deepened. "It's on the list, yes."

"For real?" Markus didn't even attempt to suppress the venom in his words. "You pricks are that prejudiced?"

"I didn't say I was," Turan argued, "but yes. You can call it whatever you want, but this is going to be a tough fragging sell to the Lamdira."

Ora raised a hand, cutting of Markus's next biting comment. "Lamdira?"

Turan composed himself. "Yes, of course. Fleet Lamdira, if you want to be technical. What did you think we've been doing since the gates shut down? Sitting on our asses waiting for the local crime syndicate to tip us off about a rogue synthetic with a god-complex? A fleet is already mounting for an expedition to Helion."

"A fleet?" Markus asked. "Like, a colonization fleet?"

"It is like a colonization fleet," Turan replied in the way he would speak to a child. "Of course, instead of settlers and scientists, we are carrying half the Peace Keepers in Terran space."

Holy shit. Markus hadn't given thought to how the Dorians would respond to the crisis. If they were bringing Peace Keepers to the party, they were taking this problem very seriously.

Ora got them back on track. "Good, then you've already solved the problem of how to get to Minos. Now you just need to convince your leadership that Cassthia is worth taking."

Turan huffed some more, but Markus could tell he knew how important this was. If there was even half a chance that the intel they'd provided him was true, Turan needed every available asset at his disposal. "Fine," he spat. "I'll work on getting clearance for the priestess, but your boyfriend here is coming along for the ride as well."

"Wait, what?" Markus and Ora said in unison.

"You heard me. You said that the AI on Minos isn't the only synth involved in this catastrophe. You said that the synth that Markus's crew was harboring may also have a role to play. If what you're saying is true, then I want someone nearby who has had experience with this damn thing."

"Fine," Ora said. "Then I'm coming too."

"Nine hells you are!" If Turan had been upset about bringing a half-breed on the expedition, he was livid at the thought of bringing Ora. "You're out of your gods-damned mind if you think I'm going to advocate transporting the head of a known crime syndicate on a DGC vessel bound to anywhere but a prison colony."

"I have no criminal record," Ora stated factually.

"Like that matters," Turan spat. "Ora, your celebrity cuts both ways. Just because we turn our head to focus on bigger concerns doesn't mean we aren't fully aware of what type of operation you're running out here."

Ora looked suddenly, and ironically, indignant. "Give me one illegal activity you can prove, without a doubt, is tied to the Grey Wings?"

Turan didn't take the bait. "You're not going. End of discussion."

Markus wanted to raise the point that he hadn't exactly agreed that he'd be going, but Ora kept talking. "Fine, but at least let me send some people. I have plenty of capable people who don't have my celebrity status. I came to you with this. I want assets on the ground to see that you don't frag it up."

"Fine," the Dorian spat. "You get two people. I'm not promising any more than that."

"Two? Try twenty."

"Two. Push me again and I'll just take Markus into custody right now on charges of violating the Pradaxan Creed and conspiracy to commit treason. Then he'll still be coming along for the ride, but he'll make the trip in the brig."

Well, that spiraled out of control real quick. It looked like Markus was going after all. "Two's fine," he blurted, not trusting Ora to resist the temptation to call the bluff.

She shot him a scathing glare but didn't countermand him. "Two," she agreed.

"Good," Turan sighed. "The fleet embarks in three days. I'll send you the details on where to meet us." He held up a warning finger. "Do not screw this up, Ora. The only reason I'm not carting your whole damned organization out to a prison ship right this instant is that we have bigger things to worry about. You test me on this, and it will backfire."

Ora ground her teeth, but she held her composure. "Understood."

With that, the officer left them. "Well, that went well," Markus commented.

"Better than I expected."

"Really? You thought it could get worse than me being carted off on this suicide mission to avoid treason charges?"

"Yes, I did." Her matter-of-fact tone did little to soothe his anxieties. "Look, we got what we wanted. We'll have people in the fleet to make sure nothing happens to the Vandal's crew. Everything from here is up to you."

"Wait, so you wanted one of us to be brought on the expedition?"

Her smile was coy as she opened the door to their transport. "Of course. Didn't you?" She planted a quick kiss on his lips. "Now, I just happen to have my best man on the job."

CHAPTER 19

[ACCESSING ARC PROJECT LOG 153]

[DR. DAMIEN HERMES]

There is something different about the organic substrate. I find myself unable to articulate the specific change. In general, it seems more advanced, faster, more intuitive. It is almost as if continued to develop in the time it was supposedly offline.

I've double-checked the inhibitor protocols and nothing seems to have breached acceptable limits. Still, I find myself uneasy at the development. The protocols indicate there has been next to no change in the breach risk, despite the change in operating platform. Surely it should have fluctuated by at least some degree…

[CLOSING PROJECT LOG…]

The next several days provided a small reprieve for the crew of the Vandal. That wasn't to say they had nothing to do aboard the Maur Destroyers, which Sahar had learned were dubbed Crimson Sky and Black Wind. There was no fighting, but Sahar was far from bored.

The recovery effort at the Vandal's crash site had been largely successful. Sahar, along with the rest of the crew, had assisted in the recovery effort where they could at the start. Typically this involved anything but making actual supply runs down to the crash site.

Aaliyah had been slotted to helm one of the shuttles making an early run, but she had become distracted when she was asked to look at a propulsion engine malfunctioning on the Crimson Sky.

Since then, she had hopped from one engineering problem to the next.

Eli and the other Sahaia soon left the recovery projects to spend time with the higher-ranking Maur officers. Sahar had been told that they were piecing together a schematic of the hidden passages in and out of the asteroid station. The coven, apparently, maintained several off-the-record paths not just to the Sanctum, but to locations across the station. This would be useful when weighing options for when the inevitable military countermeasure could be launched.

With Sydney assigned to the brig, that left only Sahar and Skye to assist in the actual salvage effort. The two of them had been split among the two teams that ran every few hours back and forth between the Vandal and Crimson Sky. It took nearly two days to clear the essential items. At the end of the second day, Geresh authorized one more trip back to the crash to gather the crew's personal effects. Even those personal items had to be inventoried by the logistics officer upon entering the vessel. Geresh assured them that this was merely a formality and all items would be entered into the record and archived immediately before being brought to their temporary cabins.

Such assurances did little to soothe Sahar's anxieties. If she'd known about the inventory requirement before loading up her own personal supplies, she might have left an item or two at the crash site. It would have been easier to charter a private salvage mission later than to deal with the questions she was likely going to get.

Her concerns seemed unfounded when her gear was dropped off at her cabin an hour later without comment. Upon inspecting her equipment, she was delighted to find that the soldiers had taken the liberty of cleaning and polishing her personal armaments before dropping them off. Preferential treatment because of their shared heritage? Perhaps, but Sahar wasn't going to complain. She opened each crate and began to neatly sort her belongings.

Since this was a Maur ship, there were plenty of spaces in the cabin for her to slot her weapons. It spoke highly of the level of trust the Federation soldiers had in their guests that she would be allowed to keep such items near her. Allowing troops to keep personal weapons collections was one thing. To give such access to their guests was quite another.

Some of the more ornamental materials had been neatly packaged for future transport, and Sahar left them that way. With any luck, they wouldn't be here long enough for her to have to decorate the place.

A beep sounded from her door. Sahar gave a verbal acknowledgment and looked up to find Geresh standing in the entryway. "Jingda?" she asked hesitantly.

"I hope I'm not intruding," he answered as he slipped through the door frame.

"Not at all. This is your boat, after all."

"It's the Federation's 'boat.' I'm merely the unlucky caretaker."

She couldn't help but smile at the male's humility. It was a good trait to have in a soldier, and far too uncommon for one that had risen to his station. "Is there something I can help you with?"

He hesitated before replying, "I just wanted to see how you were fitting in here."

Sahar's smile faded at the obvious lie. "Everything is more than adequate. Thank you."

Geresh did not attempt to maintain his charade for long. "I also wanted to bring by one of your effects that had been flagged by our logistics officer."

He held out his hand and Sahar's heart leaped in her chest. The object was a gold-plated bangle, intricately carved with a large red crystal embedded roughly midway down its length. Sahar tried to play it casually. "Oh? Thank you. I'd yet to notice it was missing."

Geresh made a show of examining the bracelet. "Quite the piece, this one. I remember seeing it briefly during the festival. Do you mind if I ask where you picked it up?"

Now she was cursing inwardly. With the way he was acting, there was very little chance he hadn't surmised the bangle's significance. She considered lying but couldn't think of a lie that would serve her better than the truth. "It was a gift," she replied simply, extending her hand. "May I have it back please?"

"Yes, of course." He handed her the bracelet but made no move to leave. "You know, I don't believe you told me much about your past. Most Maur who come to Terran space have interesting stories. Perhaps you could tell me more of yours?" Then, seeing Sahar moving to stash the object, he asked, "You're not going to wear that?"

She paused halfway in the process of stuffing the piece inside one of her duffel bags. "It's a bit gaudy, don't you think? Not really the kind of thing one wears about a military vessel."

"You and I both know that's not true." The commander's expression darkened as he eyed her meaningfully. "I apologize. I've tried to approach this situation as politely as possible. I think we both know what that bangle means. It is something quite special—something that women of a certain standing have commissioned for their children."

Now it was Sahar's turn to get angry. "What are you implying?"

"I'm implying nothing. I'm merely stating that I now have an article of some significance aboard my ship. I'm pointing out that official records, which may be reviewed by my superiors, now state that this object was aboard my ship. I'm going to be asked by these superiors about the owner of this object and how they came across such a treasure." His glare deepened. "They will also likely ask whether I took appropriate measures to verify that the person bringing it here was the rightful owner."

Sahar glared right back at him. She was angry, but she was mostly angry with herself. She should have known that this was going to be a problem and passed on the offer to retrieve her personal effects.

By his expression, Geresh hated this as much as she did. "Please, Sahar. Make this easy on me. Tell me your house name, and I'll consider that sufficient. I won't make you activate it."

She spat a curse. As much as she hated this situation, she knew it wasn't his fault. Plus, he had come to their rescue. If he'd just let them die, then he wouldn't be in this predicament. She owed him at least this much.

So, she told him. "Camerine. House Camerine."

The commander's reaction was much as she had expected. He pressed his hands hard against his eyes before running them back through the white fur on his head. "What, might I ask, are you doing serving on the crew of a smuggler's ship?"

"That is something you don't need to know. Look, if anyone asks, you can admit I was here. Beyond that…" She shook her head as she lost her train of thought.

"Is that an order?" he asked.

Sahar bit back a snarl. "Don't you start that shit, or I swear to the gods I'll kick your ass."

Geresh chuckled sardonically. "Your crew—they have no idea, do they?"

"No, and I'd like to keep it that way."

"Yes ma'am."

This time, Sahar let slip a growl of frustration. "Is this how this is going to be the rest of my time here? 'Cause I have to tell you, I'm sick of it already."

The jingda composed himself, painting a serious expression on his face. "What would you have me do?"

Now it was Sahar's turn to paw at her forehead in frustration. "Just pretend this never happened, okay? Look, I'm sure you had a plan and a system around here before I showed up. Let's go back to whatever you were doing and forget about that stupid bangle. All right?"

Geresh didn't answer right away. At length, he let out a heavy sigh. "All right," he agreed, "but if I could make one request: please wear your heritage bangle when you are moving about the ship. It will help me avoid a whole host of problems associated with your stay."

"Yeah? I'm not following," Sahar objected. "It kinda feels like it's going to do nothing but create problems if everyone starts acting the way you just were."

"No, that won't happen. No one will question it, and no one will endeavor to run the patterns to trace your lineage. House Camerine is not the only noble faction within the Drathen Clan. They will recognize your station only inasmuch as that it justifies the service we have provided to you and your crew."

His response was both perplexing and intriguing. "I still don't understand why such a justification would be needed. You're the jingda. You're in charge."

"If only it were so simple." His frustration was laid plain in the words. "We've been out here for a long time with very little in clear direction. That was fine until we began losing ships." His hands tensed into fists. "The longer we're out here, fighting an unknown enemy without hopes of reprieve or reinforcements, the more the confidence of my crews wanes. Two months ago, the contempt of a few individuals reached the level of mutiny."

"Mutiny?" Sahar's incredulity was less a sign of skepticism than that the notion seemed unfathomable. To mutiny against a commander, especially one in the Federation's service, was such a massive affront to a Maur's honor as to render it nearly incomprehensible. It just wasn't done.

"Yes, mutiny," Geresh said sadly. "Many lives were lost needlessly in the effort, and we still have a handful of the instigators in the brig. I fear, though, I have not seen the last of such efforts. I suspect there are still sympathizers in our ranks, though I am unable to prove anything beyond a reasonable doubt."

Well… shit. That certainly complicated things. If Sahar and her friends were here only at Geresh's bidding and someone were to attempt to supplant him…

"Fine," she spat, not wishing to engage any further in the political calculus. "I'll wear the stupid piece of jewelry."

"Thank you." He bowed slightly, and Sahar found herself trying to remember if he'd given her any respectful bows before this conversation.

She guessed it didn't matter. Truth was that this knowledge she was trying to keep secret did change things. As much as she hated to admit it, her family ties always changed things—at least among her people. That was why she had left Federation space. That was why she had made her home among the Terrans.

As the jingda turned and left her quarters without further comment, her heart sank. She'd started to like Geresh. If she were being honest, she wondered why the fates had deemed fit to draw them together again after all these months.

She shook her head, dispelling the thought. Now was not the time for distraction. There was more than enough for her to worry about without getting her emotions involved. She closed her eyes and said a quick prayer. Then, true to her word, she clasped her Heritage Bangle around her left forearm.

Sydney was a firm believer in counting the positives. On the plus side, she was still alive. She was also unshackled and out of that stuffy envirosuit.

That was where the positives ended.

The brig on the Federation ship was nicer than some of the other lockups she'd found herself in. There were lightly padded benches to sleep on and a working toilet. Meals were regular, clean, and filling. The Federation soldiers had been polite to her, if not friendly. All-in-all, it could have been much worse.

The only immediate problem she had identified was the company. The large holding cell already housed four Maur prisoners—three males and one female—when Sydney was escorted in. They all wore the same gray scrubs Sydney had been issued, though the garments were made to fit their taller and more muscular frames.

The males were nondescript for their kind, sporting the unremarkable yellow-tan fur that placed them in either the Salva or Drathen clans. One of them was missing an eye, and Sydney found herself derisively referring to him as Cyclops. The other two she gave the mental nick-names Thing One and Thing Two since she basically couldn't tell them apart.

The female stood out a bit more due to her pristine white fur, which placed her in the same clan as the ship's commanding officer. Though she was as rough-and-tumble as the rest of the lot, Sydney noticed that the Things seemed to defer to her as readily as they did to Cyclops. That impression earned her the private nickname Princess.

When Sydney had been brought to the brig, the Things had made the expected suggestive remarks and leered at her like the novelty she was. She'd flipped them off and gave a firm warning not to try anything. After that, the harassment had decreased to a manageable level.

Cyclops had kept the lecherous glances to a minimum, which meant he was probably screwing Princess and wanted to avoid anything to jeopardize the relationship. The female ignored Sydney entirely. If the Things decided to try anything, there was at least a remote chance that the other two would stay out of the confrontation.

Good thing too, since that brought the threat level down to manageable. If all four of them decided to jump her, even Sydney couldn't take on that much Maur strength—not without her gear, anyway. With this in mind, she left her four cellmates well enough alone.

They spoke in the Maur tongue rather than Intergalactic Standard when they conversed, likely taking a bet that Sydney wouldn't understand them. If that was the reason, they'd bet wrong. From their conversation, Sydney was able to gather that they were part of some failed mutiny against the ship's commanding officers.

However, given the frequency at which she caught guards passing information to Cyclops and Princess, efforts to quell the rebellion might have been incomplete. Cyclops was bristling at the latest bit of news that had been passed to him by one of their jailers. "Those bastards are still scurrying around on that asteroid? What are they expecting to find down there?"

Princess snorted. "Probably hoping to stumble across a workable plan. Anything they dig up from that wreck is better than what they have now."

"I think the commander may have a different agenda," growled Thing One. "Maybe he's campaigning to get a quick lay from that Maur they brought aboard. Hard to find someone outside the command structure while we're out here just waiting to die."

Princess rolled her eyes. "Just because you want to rut with every female you bump into—"

"Not every female."

"Yeah?" Princess scoffed. "Give me the name of one private on this ship that you haven't made a pass at."

Thing One didn't even look sheepish. "What? It gets lonely out here!"

"Would you two knock it off?" Cyclops growled.

Thing Two joined the discussion. "What? Having trouble staring at the walls with all this chatter? Didn't mean to ruin your focus, sir."

They when on like that for several more minutes. It soon became clear to Sydney that these mutineers did not consider their fate to be set in stone. They were adamant about their lack of confidence in Geresh. If an opportunity arose for them to strike back at their captor, they would do so. The assassin quietly filed this away in the back of her mind. She would continue to listen in case there were any further developments she might exploit.

When the time came for these goons to make their next move, she would be ready to turn the ensuing crisis to her own advantage.

CHAPTER 20

[ACCESSING ARC PROJECT LOG 159]
[DR. DAMIEN HERMES]
We have found a solution to the technological integration problem. Well, I shouldn't say "we." The organitech substrate identified the solution itself (or, rather, it identified several potential solutions, of which we selected one). There is no call for alarm; the substrate did this at our request. It also still requires the development team to implement the solution. No Pradaxan violations are in evidence.

Interestingly, the organic processor has begun calling itself "Arc" now. I wonder how the substrate picked up that line of coding. To my knowledge, nothing has been added in the most recent build that would prompt it to pull in the commonly used project acronym as a designation. However, I am not in a position to argue with a machine, so we have begun calling it "Arc" as well.

[CLOSING PROJECT LOG…]

Daniel wasn't exactly sure where everything had gone wrong. When he'd followed Lexa off the ship, he'd been so sure it was the right course. Now, Lexa was damaged, and he'd been locked away in this luxury apartment as a valued "guest" of the Marauders. He was beginning to understand that the only difference between a "guest" and a "prisoner" around here was the quality of the accommodations.

If he had to pick his cell, he'd cooperate to keep access to a soft mattress and network terminal. The view wasn't bad either, despite looking out onto a station that he'd been forbidden from exploring. While that prohibition hadn't been explicit, Dan could read between the lines of Ardren's kind urgings to "get some rest," and the hollow promises of being able to explore the station "at a more appropriate time."

Maybe coming here wasn't his first mistake. Maybe this was a result of him not paying more attention to Lexa when she needed a companion. Maybe it was inevitable from the moment he got the ill-conceived idea of using organitech to run the ship. Hells, maybe it went all the way back to when he had decided to join the Vandal in the first place.

And now, that crew—his only friends—were all dead. Ardren had tried to be sympathetic when he'd delivered the message. The problem was that the Citza seemed to be even worse at the whole emotions-thing than Dan was. He'd extended the perfunctory offer to talk if Dan found the need. When it became obvious that Dan didn't have anything to say, he'd politely excused himself.

Dan had been so upset that he'd forgotten to ask about Lexa's wellbeing. He started to put a call out to Ardren to ask about his friend. Then, deciding he couldn't handle any more bad news, he'd canceled the request. Now he was just sitting, sulking as he stared into the gentle glow of his terminal's holodisplay.

A message popped up on the right-hand side of the terminal display. [EARPIECE.]

What in the nine hells? Was this some type of system prompt? It looked like a chat window, but Daniel was fairly certain he was not running any such application. The message winked out and a second replaced it. [PUT IN THE EARPIECE.]

Daniel focused on the blinking cursor. If this was a chat program, who would be talking to him? He typed a quick response. [WHO ARE YOU?]

Both messages blinked away before a new one appeared. [I WOULD TELL YOU IF YOU PUT IN THE GODS DAMNED EARPIECE.]

Whoever this was obviously wasn't worried about his willingness to comply. They were right, of course. Regardless of who this was, or what their motives were, Dan had an abundance of time on his hands. Even if this was some kind of trap, he'd happily spring it just to shake up the monotony of his captivity.

He did a visual scan of the desk and saw only the standard interface projectors. There was nothing even resembling an earpiece. [WHAT EARPIECE?] he typed.

[UNDER THE DESK.]

Daniel looked under the desk and saw only the spotless tiled floor. Then he reached one hand to the underside of the polymer slab. His hand came into contact with an unexpected rough protrusion.

He felt at the edge of the object and found he could pull it away. In his hand, he now held a small, irregularly shaped object the size of a large earbud. A single diode pulsed patiently on the surface of what looked like a button.

Figuring he had nothing to lose, Dan slipped the device into his right ear and pressed the button. A gruff voice sounded from the earpiece. "About time. Ah feel like that was unnecessarily difficult for ya, lad."

Dan sat bolt upright. "Shift!"

"Not so loud, laddie! They've got yer room bugged fer sure, nah. Use sub-vocals if ya can. Whisper if ya can't. The earpiece'll pick it up."

Dan wasn't sure what sub-vocals were, so he whispered as quietly as he possibly could. "I thought you were dead."

"Dead's a relative thing, laddie. Ma body may be coolin', and ma soul—if such a thing exists—is prolly burnin' somewhere 'n the nine hells ra' now. Ah kinda figured our dear pal Arc would be hurryin' me along that way soon, so Ah took some precautions to make sure Ah'd be hangin' around after a fashion."

Daniel didn't have to feign confusion at the mad ravings. "I don't understand."

"Ma brain, laddie—it's in the network. By Riven's ball-sack, Ah thought ya was supposed to be some kinda boy-genius or somethin'!"

Shift had uploaded his consciousness onto the server? How extraordinary. Daniel hadn't known such a thing was possible. "Hasn't Arc been able to detect you?" he asked.

"That jumped up AI ain't even thought t' be lookin'. Kinda hard to see somethin' with yer eyes closed, now ain't it?"

"I suppose." Dan was asking the wrong questions and he knew it. More important questions were still at hand. "What are you doing here? Talking to me, I mean."

Shift scoffed—or, at least, triggered an auditory sound approximating a scoff. "What? Aren't ya grateful fer a lil company, bein' all locked up in yer gilded cage?"

The hacker wasn't wrong. Any company was better than what Dan had currently. Though Shift's electronic ghost wouldn't have topped his list for conversation partners, it was better than any alternatives available to Dan right now. "I still don't understand," Dan pressed. "Why are you contacting me? And, for that matter, how did you get this earpiece into my room?"

"The earpiece is a lil present Ah slipped t' ya before the fiasco in the central terminus. As fer why Ah'm talkin' t' ya—ya just happen t' be the only thing in this gods-damned complex that's not already in Arc's pocket. Now, Ah can just be on my merry way if ya'd like."

"No!" Dan blurted a little louder than he would have liked. "I mean… no, I just…" He sighed. "Thank you. I've been stuck in here and I have no idea what's been going on out there."

"Ah'm bettin' that's by design. Ya represent a bit o' a problem fer ol' Arc. He needs t' keep ya out of the way, but he also needs t' keep ya alive. Doesn't want t' have t' explain why t' Lexa why her friend suddenly quit breathin' soon as she lay down fer some beauty sleep."

As perplexed as he was by the idea, Dan garnered a glimmer of hope from the hacker's words. "Lexa? So, she's all right? Why hasn't she been by to see me?"

"She's a bit out-a-sorts right now, but yeah, yer girlfriend's still functional. Gettin' a bit o' a remodel actually."

Daniel suppressed the juvenile urge to react to Shift's girlfriend comment. Instead, he asked, "What do you mean, remodel?"

"Lemme' show ya." The display on Daniel's terminal flashed briefly as a new window opened. A three-dimensional schematic rotated before him. Dan immediately recognized the basic configuration for Lexa's body as he had known it. However, he readily identified some very strange changes to the design.

"This was Arc's idea?" he whispered. "Why? What is he doing?"

Shift laughed. "Arc has a specific purpose in mind fer yer friend. Ah just didn' realize that purpose was fer makin' babies."

Dan couldn't help but pause. "Making… babies?"

The voice at the other end of the earpiece offered no mercy. "Look close, boy. Ya can see the changes. Good deal o' effort's goin' into makin' sure she's got the right plumbin'."

"But I don't get it. Why would Arc want Lexa to procreate? If he wants to make more synthetics, why doesn't he just manufacture them?"

"All part o' his master plan. A god's gotta have worshipers after all. Ya know, a 'chosen people' 'n all that."

A chill began to creep down Dan's spine. "So, all of that god-talk. He's really…"

"One o' them?" Shift emitted a sound like he'd blown a raspberry. "No way, kid. Arc's an AI. If ya ain't noticed, he hasn' changed his designation since gettin' his new duds. Ma suspicion's that there's somethin' in his code that keeps 'im from it."

"Then all of that talk about having access to the Nethra…" Dan swallowed hard. "That's all a lie?"

"Oh no, ah didn' say that. He accesses the Nethra, true enough. That was coded in, and if ya ask me, that's where his shit really started to go haywire. We ain't got no business fraggin' with lower levels o' space-time. Ya can't write code fer somethin' ya don't understand in the first place."

While that made some sense, Dan couldn't help but feel that Shift's explanation was inadequate. "How does he do it? Access the Nethra, I mean."

"Good question. Rather than give ya dissertation, imma give ya some homework." Several new files appeared on Dan's display. He opened one of them up, seeing a diagram for something that looked strikingly similar to the modified cryopods Arc had used during the Cognis transfer.

"What does it do?"

"It's the housing fer Arc's Nethra conduit. That's the old model, though. Ol' Arc just recently installed 'imself an upgrade! Ya can read that file later, though. We ain't got a ton o' time as it is."

"What do you mean, 'a ton of time?' I thought you said Arc couldn't find you."

"It's true, laddie, but it stays true 'cause Ah'm careful. Ah said the bastard was blind, but he's not defenseless. This next file be what Ah really wanted t' show ya."

Another file appeared on the console and opened itself automatically. "What is it?" Dan asked.

"It's the number an' current location o' Arc's forces."

"And why would I want this?"

"'Cause it's only a matter-a-time before the Dorians be tryin' t' do somethin' stupid. Ah'd recommend ya take some time t' review those figures before ya join in on anythin' that might be considered brash."

Dan was scanning the file even as Shift spoke. Incredulous wasn't a strong enough word to describe how he felt about the numbers he was reading. "These figures can't be right."

"Oh, they be right. Trust me on this, boy."

"But how? To amass a force like this it would take…"

"Years. Yeah, Ah know. What do ya think they've been doin' in this place? The Citadel has one function—t' build Arc's army. And they've been buildin' quite efficiently ever since Cali took control o' the Marauders."

Dozens of questions flooded Dan's mind. Yet, he fell silent for a long moment. "What am I supposed to do with all of this, Shift?"

"Yer a smart lad," the hacker assured him. "Ah trust ya can figure somethin' out."

Jocelyn considered forcing her captors to drag her bodily away from the coven house. She'd opted instead to maintain what shreds of dignity she could. Squandering her strength on futile gestures of defiance would do little to improve her situation. Instead, she opted to keep an eye out for anything that might serve as a weakness she could exploit.

No such weaknesses emerged. From the moment they left the compound to the instant they set foot into Arc's stronghold, she was kept under constant guard. Brenna's block never slipped. Jocelyn's helplessness, consequently, was complete.

To make matters worse, Cali had been told to personally see that she was safely brought to the "secondary conduit," whatever that meant. Judging by the unexpected look of pity in the Kintar's eyes when she'd received the order, Jocelyn had the feeling she was not going to like this.

She stumbled briefly in her contemplation of the woman. Was it right to call her "Kintar" anymore? To call her Sahaia seemed wrong, as the term had grown to refer to a people that were as different from Cali as Cali was now from her former people. There seemed to be no applicable term to refer to an ascendant Kintar. Cali was now a creature unique unto herself.

The thought made Jocelyn's stomach roil. As if Arc had not been enough of an abomination, this thing that Cali had become was unlike anything the universe had seen for several millennia. How much strength had her foe acquired in her Awakening? If the ritual could turn Terrans, who were psionically inert by nature, into beings of godlike power, how much more so would it impact a being with innate psionic gifts?

Cali caught her staring and shot her a malevolent smirk. "What's on your mind?" she teased.

Jocelyn would not give her the satisfaction of knowing her thoughts. "Just strange seeing you without the mark of Lith on your face is all."

Her captor ran her fingertips self-consciously over one eye where the old tattoo should have been. "I'll replace them in soon enough—this time with the emblem of my new master."

"He is not what he says he is, you know." Jocelyn raised her chin defiantly. "None can bear the essence of a Nethrian aside from the Kaleema."

The other woman rolled her eyes. "Even after the display of power you have seen, you still doubt. No matter. You will soon have plenty of time for contemplation on the subject."

They rounded the corner to a door that led into a much larger room. Crimson light flooded the chamber, and the heat inside was stifling. A network of catwalks led them to a central pillar cast in dark metal.

Several mechanical protrusions cluttered the pillar, but the foremost of these appeared to be a cryopod fixed ominously at the end of the walkway. Cali stepped up to the apparatus and stroked the surface affectionately.

"I had not known that this would be your fate, Jocelyn, though it is fitting, in a way. This way you can join me in saying goodbye to a mutual friend."

Cali opened the pod and Jocelyn went cold. It took several seconds to recognize the Sahaia woman ensnared in the chamber's network of wires and tubes. So emaciated was Wynne's once beautiful figure that Jocelyn scarcely resembled the powerful woman who had served as her fellow triumvir.

"What have you done?" Jocelyn whispered.

"A necessity of Lord Riven's nature, I'm afraid. You see, to maintain his connection to the Nethra, he required a continuous infusion of psionic power. As it turns out, the Sahaia are an excellent source of the energies that my master requires."

Had the notion not been so preposterous, Jocelyn would have sworn that a hint of sadness slipped into Cali's expression. The emotion, if it had ever been there, was quickly stifled as she entered a command into the pod's console. The implements penetrating Wynne's body retracted, and her slender form slumped forward.

Cali grabbed the woman before she could topple free from the chamber. With a strange gentleness, she laid the woman's naked form on the grated platform where they stood. Her hand lingered at Wynne's neck for just a moment before she let out a heavy sigh.

"She is gone. The machine must have been keeping her alive. Just as well, I suppose." She shot a pained look to the guards that held Jocelyn. "Strip her."

Again, Jocelyn considered whether to fight. In the end, she decided it would only serve to further damage her dignity. She let them tear the dress from her body and never broke eye contact with Cali.

You won't break me, she thought. I don't know how, I don't know when, but you will pay for this. I swear it.

A sinister smirk played across Cali's lips. "I know that look. It's not so different from the one Wynne wore when she was forced into the conduit. Riven will be well served to have a tool of equal strength at his disposal."

She rose from her crouch and strode to stand in front of Jocelyn. "Then again, the Heart of Thule will provide most of the energy my Lord requires. Who knows? Perhaps it may still be a long time before you join Wynne in communion with your ancestral spirits. There's no reason that you cannot see the fullness of eternity inside of this coffin of steel and circuitry."

Jocelyn spat in the woman's face. It was a futile act of defiance, but it did make her feel better. At least it served to wipe away that arrogant grin on Cali's face. A snarl twisted her expression in its place. Crimson lightning crackled in the Kintar's eyes, as she addressed the guards. "Put her in."

The triumvir was lifted from her feet and slammed roughly into the conduit. Two soldiers held her still while a third threaded the machine's network of needles and tubes into her skin. A pained cry tore from Jocelyn's throat as the metallic implement's pierced her flesh. She could feel as the tubes and wires slid into her veins and muscles. As the drugs started flowing from the tubes, she found the last residuals of her resolve being drained away.

"There," Cali cooed. "That's better."

"You have no idea what you're doing," Jocelyn gasped. "This is not going to end well for you, Kintar."

"Perhaps. But I have a feeling that it's going to end far worse for you, my dear." Cali entered a command into the console and the conduit began to close. "Enjoy eternity, Jocelyn. Maybe one day I'll come to visit you and let you know how everything turned out."

Jocelyn's fraying willpower finally broke as the lid to the chamber slid closed. She let out a horrified scream as the darkness solidified around her. She was dimly aware of the faint hiss of the hydraulics as the pod shifted. All sound from the chamber was washed away to be replaced by the dull hum of the apparatus.

And in that darkness—as bleak and shadowed as the impenetrable as the waters of the Well of Eternity—Jocelyn continued to scream.

CHAPTER 21

[ACCESSING ARC PROJECT LOG 164]
[DR. DAMIEN HERMES]

We've had another breakthrough with Arc's subspace interface. We've successfully connected the organitech interface to three objects orbiting the space station. The program's AI was able to find, access, and disconnect from the devices without connection interference or signal delay. This is exactly what we've been hoping to achieve. Tomorrow we will launch a second battery of satellites to test the limitations of this capability. I look forward to recording the findings in a future report.

[CLOSING PROJECT LOG…]

"This is as far as I go," Ora sighed.

Markus gazed forlornly down the concourse. Their shuttle had docked on the DGC carrier, and a contingent of heavily-armed Dorian soldiers stood guard outside the entrance to the vessel's interior. The pass he'd downloaded to his MoDAC would let him through, but Ora hadn't been issued clearance.

He hefted his gear self-consciously at the thought of walking through that checkpoint. Theoretically, he'd been authorized to carry his weapons onto the ship, but they would likely be confiscated for safekeeping. As such, he'd left his sniper rifle back on Sigma-4 in favor of a more practical assault rifle.

Aside from a couple of changes of clothes and the requisite personal items, the gun was all he'd brought with him. That, and the black armor he currently wore that would double as his envirosuit. He still felt strangely naked at the thought of walking into the carrier.

A dozen protests flooded his mind at the thought of Ora's departure, ranging from sentimental to outright childish. He stowed them all in favor of the gentle kiss he placed on her cheek. "Just another day at the office. I'll be back before you can miss me."

Her placating smile did little to hide her skepticism. "I hope you're right." Then, as if remembering something she'd nearly forgotten, she began rifling through the small duffel she'd slung over her shoulder. "I took the liberty of picking up something for you. I've had it for a couple of days. I've just been waiting for an occasion to give it to you."

"Yeah? Don't tell me you're afraid you won't have the chance later."

"Don't be so macabre," Ora scolded. "No, I just happen to think you might find it useful." She pulled out a black case with a biometric scanner. "It's keyed to your fingerprint already."

Markus eyed her appraisingly "How'd you manage that?"

"I have my ways," she replied.

Markus took the case from her and pressed his thumb to the scanner. There was a slight click as the lock disengaged. Inside the case rested a black pistol, slightly larger than what Markus typically used. It was hard to tell with it still in the case, but the weapon looked heavy. High caliber.

Ora seemed to read his mind. "I know it's not what you tend to favor, but it's got a bit more stopping power than a typical sidearm. I'd hoped you'd get a chance to practice with it before needing it, but you know—desperate times, and all that."

He let out a low chuckle. "I just love that you wanted to get me something special, so you bought me a gun."

She shrugged, but he thought she was trying not to look too pleased. "Well, what do you get the man who has everything?"

"Fair." He pulled out a chip embedded in the foam padding beside the weapon. "I take it this has the specs?"

"Yes, and I may have taken the liberty of slipping you something personal in a separate file."

"Dirty pictures?"

"Think a little more romantic and slightly less brazen."

He slipped the chip into his pocket. "Thank you," he replied simply.

"It's the least I could do," she sighed, "given that I got you into this mess."

"No way—you don't get to take the blame for this one. Last I checked, it's my friends that seemed to have stumbled into the trouble. You're just being helpful." Ora let slip a slightly bemused smile. "What's that for?" Markus asked.

"You called them your 'friends.' Just thought it was interesting to hear you refer to them that way, given where your head was just a few weeks ago."

It was a good point. Before their last excursion, Markus would have been happy to let the whole lot of them burn in the nine hells. Had his hard facade been whittled away so easily?

Ora didn't wait for a response, choosing instead to plant another firm kiss on his mouth. "Get this shit cleaned up. I'm all done with world-shattering consequences and altruistic missions. Go kick this synth's ass so we can get back to doing something a bit more profitable."

"Yes ma'am!"

With that, she turned and headed back into the shuttle. The airlock shut behind her before Markus remembered to ask about where he'd be meeting the reinforcements she'd promised. He guessed it didn't matter. He was sure that he'd meet up with the rest of the poor souls Ora had recruited for this suicide mission soon enough.

He passed through the checkpoint unmolested. The credentials Turan had provided him were valid, including those that allowed for him to carry weapons onto the DGC vessel. It only occurred to him after presenting said credentials what a brilliant joke that would have been for the Dorian officer to pull on him. Fortunately, the gravity of the situation, or Turan's lack of imagination, kept such pranks from coming to fruition.

The soldiers at the checkpoint directed him to his assigned section and sent his firearms and other luggage off for storage. With assurances that he would be given access to his gear as soon as the jump was complete, he was cautioned against any attempts to deviate from his assigned route. In one of his more fool-hardy moods, Markus might have been inclined to test the instructions. As it was, he knew the potential consequences if he screwed this up.

If he had known who he was about to run into, however, he might have considered the idea of finding an alternate route. He rounded the corner to come face-to-face with Llana Dorr. Their faces nearly collided as the two of them stumbled bodily into each other. Reflexively, Markus reached forward to steady the Dorian woman while issuing an awkward apology.

The gesture was unnecessary, as Llana was far steadier on her broad hooves and muscular legs than he was. His action had only served to generate an awkward pause where Markus realized that he was laying hands on a DGC officer. It wouldn't have been that big a deal. Though they hadn't stayed in touch, Markus and Llana had ended their relationship amicably. Neither of them had considered their brief fling very serious.

What made it awkward was that Llana had been deep in conversation with her brother at the time of the collision, and Turan was now staring daggers at Markus. He cleared his throat in a way that was sure to communicate his disapproval. "Are you lost, Terran?"

A full two seconds later, Markus realized he still had his hands on Llana's shoulders. He quickly brought his arms to his side and straightened awkwardly. "I sure hope not. I mean… apologies. I didn't mean to interrupt."

Llana cut off whatever it was the Turan was about to say. "Seriously, brother, get over yourself. It won't kill you to be polite to our consultant." She turned back to Markus, taking him in with a measuring sweep of her eyes. "Good to see you, Markus. You look good."

"Yeah, thanks Llana. You look good, too." The words had tumbled out of his mouth before he'd thought better of them. He didn't want to give the slightest impression that he was coming on to her.

The fact was, however, that she did look good. Llana had always been attractive. Though Markus had recently seen her when passing through the Taurus Gate, their quick virtual conference hadn't done her appearance justice. Her dark curls had grown longer, now resting just below the collar of her blue flight jacket. The way she arranged her locks around the sweep of her arcing horns was a slightly more feminine rendition of her brother's hair. Her brown eyes held the same fierce confidence Markus had always known her to have.

Realizing he was staring, Markus issued an awkward cough. "I hadn't realized you'd be assigned to the mission. I thought you were stationed at the Taurus Gate."

She let slip a playful smile. Though the siblings shared in the physical beauty commended by their genes, Llana had gotten the lion's share of the charisma. "Well, you might have noticed there's a bit of a crisis at hand. I was actually on leave until yesterday. The High Council put all hands at the ready for this one."

"Sorry to hear your R&R was cut short." Markus started to continue with his small talk before noticing again the way Turan was glowering at him. "I guess I should be going. Need to get to my seat and all that."

Llana glanced at Turan, finding the reason for Markus's hasty departure evident. "Understandable. Are you sure that you don't need help finding where you are going?"

"Nah, I'm good."

"Very well. I'll leave you to it then. Oh, and do be more careful rounding these corners," she cautioned light-heartedly. "I'd hate to see you trampled under hoof before we even break orbit."

Markus continued, unescorted, to his assigned compartment where he found the companions Ora had talked into traveling with him. Cassthia was there, as expected. And Markus was pleased to spot at least one other familiar face.

"Didn't think I'd be seeing you so soon," Kadath said, donning his omnipresent smirk. The smile on the Kintari half-breed's handsome face did much to soothe tensions that Markus hadn't even known were there. It seemed like the man had recently trimmed his dark mane of hair, though it still hung past his jawline.

"I'll be damned!" said Markus. "I thought you were a smart guy, Kadath. After the last shit show Ora hired you for, you came back for round two?"

"Obviously I'm hard up for money." He beat a crimson-skinned hand playfully against Markus's shoulder. "Truthfully, Ora said she didn't trust anyone else to get your foolish ass back in one piece."

"Sure. The Dorians must have lost their shit when they saw who Ora had contracted to come on this fools' errand."

"You have no idea," Kadath laughed. "As if one half-breed wasn't enough. No offense, Cassthia."

"None taken," the priestess replied. "I, too, find humor in the defiance of such bigotry."

The third figure, silent to this point, stepped forward. "Hello, Markus."

Despite himself, Markus did a double take. "Siv?"

The Hissak woman gave him a slight but sincere smile. The fact that he could see said smile marked a significant change from the last time they'd met.

Siv was a Prodican, a follower of the patron god of devotion. Worshipers of Prodica were readily identified by their overly modest attire. When he'd last met Siv, she'd been clad in black armor and a cloak that had hidden every inch of her skin.

The way she was dressed now was significantly less modest. Her black leggings had deep slashes down the sides that showed off the lines of her leanly muscled thighs. The garment was quite the departure from the padded grieves she'd worn previously. Her black boots, at least, were similar to what Markus had remembered. Her top was sleeveless and equally form-fitting, clinging tightly to the subtle curves of her chest.

Her heavy black cowl was also absent, showing that—like all pure-blooded Hissak—she had no hair. Instead, three bony ridges protruded from her forehead and slid back across her scalp. Markus knew enough about Hissak society to understand these ridges would have given told him which tribe she'd originally hailed from—so, enough to know how much he didn't. Since such things didn't matter in modern society, he'd never bothered to learn the differences. The Maur were the only species that still deemed the physical hallmarks of individual peoples or clans to be of significance.

Siv's snake-like eyes sparked with a hint of mischief. "Careful, Markus. If you were Hissak, your lingering eyes would imply certain intentions toward me."

"Um… sorry…" Especially since that wasn't exactly a social cue exclusive to the Hissak, he should have known better. "I-I just…" He continued to grope for something polite to say.

Mercifully, Siv provided the explanation unbidden. As she did, her expression sobered. "My late husband has been laid to rest. With the rites performed, I have been released from the bonds of devotion that honored him in this life. I have set aside my former attire for a wardrobe that is a bit more comfortable."

"I see. I… I hadn't heard there was a service. I'm sorry."

"Don't be. It was a small, private affair."

"All the same, I'm sorry for your loss." All the more so because a part of him still blamed himself for it.

"It is in the past." No hint of animosity marred the stoic declaration.

Kadath interrupted the solemn moment by slapping a flight chair next to where he'd stowed a black backpack. "Saved you a spot right over here, my friend. Our chaperones should be here shortly, so you might want to get your space claimed before some satyr decides to throw his weight around."

With all his bags currently in Dorian custody, there was nothing for Markus to do but sit and wait. He plopped into the chair and strapped himself in. Once he was secured, he pulled out his MoDAC and slotted the chip that Ora had given him.

The schematics for the weapon were there, as promised. Additionally, there was a text file with what looked like a personal note from Ora. He was quietly pulled this up and began to read.

[MARKUS: I APOLOGIZE AGAIN THAT CONTACTING TURAN HAS ROPED YOU EVEN DEEPER INTO THIS MESS. STILL, I CAN'T THINK OF A MAN I WOULD RATHER HAVE ON THE JOB.

I REGRET THAT I HAVE BEEN DISTANT SINCE RETURNING FROM SIF. THE EVENTS THAT TRANSPIRED THERE LEFT ME MORE DISQUIETED THAN I WOULD CARE TO ADMIT. I'M NO STRANGER TO DANGEROUS SITUATIONS. I'VE LIVED MY ENTIRE LIFE IN THIS SHADOWED CORNER OF THE UNIVERSE WE CALL HOME. IF YOU'D ASKED ME A MONTH AGO, I WOULD HAVE SAID THERE WAS NO DARKNESS IN THIS UNIVERSE WITH WHICH I WAS NOT INTIMATELY FAMILIAR.

CYRUS PROVED ME WRONG. IN RECENT WEEKS IT HAS BECOME APPARENT THAT WE ARE ENSNARED BY FORCES BEYOND OUR UNDERSTANDING. WHEN WE'D DEALT WITH THE VALADAR THREAT, I HAD FIRMLY HOPED THAT THESE FORCES WOULD LEAVE US ALONE.

NOW IT SEEMS THAT THIS IS NOT GOING TO BE THE CASE. OUR EFFORTS HERE ARE NOT YET FINISHED. THANKS TO TURAN, I HAVE BEEN SIDELINED FOR THIS OUTING. IT IS IN

DEFIANCE OF THIS SEEMING HELPLESSNESS, AND OUT OF OUR MUTUAL AFFECTION, THAT I GIVE YOU THIS SMALL GIFT.

IF I REMEMBER CORRECTLY, YOU'RE NOT IN THE HABIT OF NAMING YOUR WEAPONRY, BUT I HAPPENED TO BE SOMEWHAT FOND OF THE MONIKER ASSIGNED BY THE GUNSMITH. HE CALLED IT, "DARK PROMISES." IF YOU DO NOT CARE FOR THE NAME, THE OFFICIAL MODEL DESIGNATION AND ASSOCIATED MODIFICATIONS ARE LISTED IN THE SCHEMATICS.

SPEAKING OF PROMISES—I PROMISE TO THINK OF YOU DAILY WHILE YOU ARE GONE. COME BACK IN ONE PIECE. I HAVE TOO MUCH INVESTED IN YOU TO LOSE YOU NOW.

TRULY YOURS, - ORA.]

Markus closed the message and examined the weapon's schematic. Ora had been correct—this was hardly a sidearm. Based on the specs, he figured the thing must have a brutal kick. He'd never used a hand cannon quite like this one and found himself eager to test it out. Of course, he would have preferred to take it out onto the range before bringing it into a fight.

His thoughts were interrupted as the door to the compartment slid open. All four of the passengers went silent as a contingent of Dorians filed in. An involuntary wave of anxiety washed over Markus at the sight of the troops.

These weren't typical Dorian operatives. These were Peace Keepers.

The eight warriors that marched into the compartment were clad head-to-hoof in heavy, silver armor. The armor's weight was rumored to require Maur-level strength just to wear. Consequently, Peace Keepers had been genetically and cybernetically modified to interface with and move about in the weighty gear.

It seemed that the prohibition on weaponry while in transit did not extend to the Peace Keepers. Each held an assault rifle and an assortment of close-range weapons strapped to their bulky forms. Markus found himself glad that these soldiers were on their side.

The Peace Keepers said nothing as they filed toward the open flight seats. As they fastened their restraints, Turan appeared in the doorway. He turned immediately to address Markus and his companions. "We will be underway shortly. Your personal armaments have been stored in the barracks down the hall. You will be given access to your belongings once we arrive safely in the Helion system. Tenatal Faylen will be in charge of this compartment. You are not to remove any weapons from the barracks without his express permission. Is that understood?"

Each member of the party nodded their ascent. Turan looked as if he were about to say more before a male officer appeared in the doorway. "Fleet Lamdira," he began. "A quick word, if you may?"

With one last reproachful look at Markus, Turan turned and exited the compartment with the young officer in tow. Markus leaned over to whisper in Kadath's ear. "Lamdira?"

"It's an officer tier in the Dorian service corps," Kadath explained. "Hard to tie it to a Terran equivalent, but Fleet Lamdira is essentially the highest title you can earn in field service."

"I know that," Markus grumbled. He'd been in a joint task force with the Dorians in his previous life. "I was wondering why in the nine hells he was calling Turan that. Since when did he get a promotion?"

"Ah, I see. Well..." Kadath's whisper took on a conspiratorial tone. "I was eavesdropping on the conversation between a few of the soldiers. Rumor is when Turan had brought up the offer of assistance from a half-breed disciple of Thule, the previous Lamdira immediately resigned. As a reward for his efforts, Turan was put in charge of the operation."

"And by 'reward,' you mean..."

"Exactly. Apparently, the previous commanding officer said something to the effect of, 'this is your shit show.' Makes you feel quite appreciated, does it not?"

Markus turned to Cassthia, who had taken the seat to his left. The priestess seemed not to have heard the recent exchange. Instead, she was ratcheting down tightly on each of her restraints.

"Not much for space travel?" Markus asked.

Cassthia glanced at him sideways. "Have you ever been on a vessel with a jump engine?"

"Um… no?" He didn't understand how the experience would be that different from normal space flight.

She responded with a condescending smirk. "Then I suggest that you, too, tighten your restraints. I've been told the experience is quite unpleasant."

"How so?"

"I imagine we will both find out shortly."

As if on cue, a woman's voice blared through the ship's loudspeakers. "Now departing from Gaia orbit. Ten minutes to the event horizon."

A countdown appeared on the view-screen at the far end of the cabin. Shuffling sounds filled the compartment as the Peace Keepers began to tighten their restraints. Never one to ignore good advice, Markus followed suit.

At the forty-five-second mark, he leaned back to Kadath. "Is this going to be that bad?"

Kadath nodded. "I did one of these once on a colonization run. Yes, it's that bad." Ten seconds later, a high-pitched whining reverberated from behind them. The engine was powering up.

Markus's skin began to prickle. It was like something had begun crawling along every inch of his flesh. He suddenly wished he hadn't chosen to travel in full armor as he desperately needed to scratch something.

The countdown continued, and the woman's voice came back on the speaker at ten seconds for the countdown.

"Nine. Eight. Seven."

The pressure began to build around "five." Markus felt himself being pushed so hard against his chair that it became difficult to breathe. Despite the inertial dampeners and the functioning gravity grid on the ship, his vision began to spin.

"Three. Two."

Markus's heart thudded as the world around him began to give way to blinding white light. "Holy sh—"

Chapter 22

[ACCESSING ARC PROJECT LOG 172]

[DR. DAMIEN HERMES]

The substrate has made another significant jump today. It's managed to copy a fragment of its programming onto the technological framework we've constructed in the Citadel. Full integration is still beyond its capabilities, but I'm redirecting resources to this effort. We'll leave one team on the Cognis project, but I suspect that this effort will soon no longer be required.

[CLOSING PROJECT LOG…]

[EXECUTE: COGNIS_SEQUENCE_REVISED]

[COMPILING…]

[RUN ASSIGNDIRECTIVE(DIRECTIVEOVERRIDE) AS DIRECTIVE]

[DIRECTIVES COMPILED]

[RUN FILE(NEWORDER10001)]

[DOWNLOADING…]

[PROCESS COMPLETE]

[INITIATING STARTUP SEQUENCE]

A dull suctioning sound brought Lexa back to awareness. There was a subtle shift in temperature and texture as the fluid around her drained away. She was distinctly aware of the harness putting pressure on her shoulders, arms, and thighs.

Her eyelids fluttered open and her visual processors came online. She was in a tank of some sort. Her feet were set firmly on a grated platform through which the last of the liquid was draining.

Various mechanical implements were withdrawing into compartments hidden in the walls of the tank. Her harness, likewise, withdrew.

The front of the tank was completely transparent, and she looked out into a room of regal gold and black tiling with accents of crimson adorning the walls. The interior was inviting. Familiar, but only peripherally so.

Standing in the middle of the room was a familiar figure. Lexa felt that she should recognize the person, but her artificial mind fumbled to make the connection. "Arc?" she murmured.

With a hiss, the door to her tank slid away. The obsidian fleshed android flashed a smile that might have been welcoming if not for the ruby accents of his eyes. "Welcome, Lexa. How do you feel?"

How did she feel? She ran a quick diagnostic. The results were… confusing. "I'm not sure. What… what's happened? Where are we?"

"The Citadel—your chambers, more specifically."

"My… chambers?" That explained the vague familiarity.

"Yes. I had the equipment moved into your rooms as your repairs neared completion. I wanted you to wake somewhere comfortable."

Her repairs?

Everything came back to her then: the central terminus, the transfer process, her malfunction. Arc had somehow deactivated her. Or—would it be more proper to say he sedated her? Was this why her diagnostics were coming back so odd? Was it a side effect of the errors arising from the Cognis transfer?

Cautiously, she stepped out of the tank and onto the tiled floor. Her body was being responsive again, so Arc's repairs had at least fixed that. Physically, she couldn't identify a malfunction. Why, then, was she so disoriented?

"Somethings wrong. My cognition is… disordered. I'm…" She trailed off, unable to articulate exactly what it was that had her so off-balance.

Arc rested a familiar hand on her shoulder. "Your core directives have been overridden—a necessary action to ease the integration of your new physical systems."

"My new…" She was suddenly very much aware of the pressure of Arc's hand against her skin. Objectively there should have been nothing strange about the gesture. His touch was warm and firm, but not overly so. Why, then, was her heart rate accelerating?

Her benefactor eyed her appraisingly. "Your motor functions, as they stood, were almost completely corrupted. Rather than attempt to replicate the work that we had done under less than optimal circumstances, I have upgraded you."

Lexa brought her hand up to touch his. Excitement and fear surged through her as she marveled at the acuity of the sensation. "This… this is amazing. It's almost… I mean I imagine that it feels so…"

"Authentic?" he chuckled. "An augmentation of your nervous system. Yes, this is what our biological counterparts feel when engaging in physical touch. I have drawn deeply from sapient templates in your redesign. As your diagnostic systems will tell you, the neurological upgrade is not the only notable change I have made. Please, continue with your assessment."

It suddenly made sense why she had been unable to comprehend the readout from her diagnostic. She loaded the report again, this time with an exploratory mindset.

Her hands ran first to her jawline. She felt a sense of wonder as she ran her fingers down the lean muscles of her neck. Her breasts felt full, perhaps fuller than before. The readout suggested that Arc had altered the composition to remove her silicone implants to replace them with glands and cellular fabrications. Her abdomen was the same, lean muscle that it had been before her transformation. What lay deeper within her pelvis, however, was starkly different.

She glanced up at Arc in alarm. "What is the meaning of this?"

The android's expression faltered slightly. "I… was hoping you would be pleased."

Pleased? She wasn't necessarily displeased, but…

The implications suddenly overwhelmed her processing capability. She'd always identified as female, but that was in terms of gender… not sex. The two were distinctively different from a psychological point of voice. Female sex involved a biological role. The capacity to reproduce, to create offspring and nurture them, this… this was beyond her wildest conceptions. Was this something she wanted? Certainly it was beyond her to ever think of wanting such things. It should have been impossible.

Lexa recovered from her hesitation. "I… I'm not displeased. I just don't understand."

He stroked her shoulder again. "This all must be quite a shock for you. Forgive me. While you slept, I've been busy dreaming of your awakening. You have a lot to process. Even beings such as us require time to fully assimilate new information."

Her attention went again to his touch. The press of his flesh against hers was somehow simultaneously reassuring and disquieting. She was acutely aware of how close his body was to hers. The dark, elegant cut of his suit popped against his vermilion shirt— contrasting starkly against her bare, cerulean flesh. A fresh vulnerability settled down to the alloy that served as her bones.

"May I have some clothes?" she blurted.

Arc jerked back his hand. "Yes. Yes, of course." He gestured to the bed, where a set of fresh undergarments and a pair of black heeled shoes were laid out. Hanging nearby was a black and gray dress, cut to be form fitting and in line with the current fashions.

Lexa moved over to the bed and felt the urge to ask Arc to leave, allowing her to don the clothes—a silly impulse since she was already naked. She pushed it aside and slid the garments on. The dress was far different from what she'd been used to wearing back on the Vandal, but it was comfortable.

She spun slowly back to Arc. "How does it look?" she asked meekly.

Though there was a long moment before Arc replied, his answer showed immediately in his expression. "Beautiful," he whispered. He took tentative a step toward her. "May I… may I hold you?"

Lexa wasn't certain how she felt about that. Out of fear of offending him further, she nodded. His masculine frame was larger than her own. Though hardly tall by Terran standards, his height exceeded hers by several centimeters. The breadth of his shoulders was half again that of her own.

She was so very conscious of the muscles of his chest as they pressed against her breasts. His shapely arms spread around her like bands of iron. He drew her close, and she was surprised by how good it felt.

Instinctually, she found herself gazing into his cybernetic eyes. Those eyes were artificial like her own, yet so utterly different. The dark orbs flared with lines of crimson. They seemed to convey a strange sense of… something. Passion, maybe? Was a similar heat reflected in her own steely gaze?

He leaned in, closing the gap between their faces, and pressed his lips softly against her mouth.

Lexa jerked back, breaking his embrace in a violent lurch. Her body trembled, torn between her sudden panic and the building remorse for her impulsive reaction. "I'm—"

"—sorry," he finished for her.

"Yes," she gasped. "Please, I just… I need some time."

Arc was suddenly and surprisingly cold in his appraisal of her. He spoke only at length. "Very well. I will leave you to your contemplations. Perhaps we may talk again later this evening."

Without another word, he turned and exited the chamber. Lexa let loose a shuddering sigh and looked for a place where she might sit down. There was a bench and a couch in the room, yet both seemed too far for her trembling legs to carry her.

So she sank to the floor and wrapped her arms around her legs. There, with tearless sobs, she began to weep.

"Yer girlfriend's awake."

Dan started at the sound of Shift's voice emanating from the earpiece. It was eerie to hear the hacker's gruff voice first thing upon waking. Still, he'd taken to sleeping with the device in place for this very occasion. "Lexa?"

"Are there any other ladies that might be meetin' that description? Ya don' strike me as the two-timin' type, but ya never know."

With a quick rub of his eyes, Dan began to rise. His progress was inhibited by the tangle of sheets around his legs. He had slept fitfully, just as he had every night since arriving on this gods-forsaken station.

As soon as he cleared the mattress, he promptly stumbled face-first onto the tile floor. "Careful there, laddie," Shift teased. "Don' want ya breakin' yer neck. Then who'll I have t' chat with?"

Dan freed himself of the linen tangle. "Are you watching me through the cameras in here or something?"

"Nah, just heard the thump when ya landed. Figured ya did somethin' a bit clumsy-like."

Dan ignored the jibe and rushed to his terminal. "Can you pull up the feed to her chambers?"

Shift hesitated. "Ah'm not sure that's such a good idea, lad."

If the hacker could see him, Dan would have shot him his most incredulous look. "Why is that?"

"The view might break yer lil heart."

His words suddenly prompted the memory of what Shift had described as Arc's purpose for Lexa. Dan flushed, and his stomach twisted in a knot. Strangely, he felt like he was going to be sick. "A-are they… I mean… is she… indecent?"

"Huh? Oh! No-no-no-no-no. That's not what Ah meant. Ah just meant…" Shift seemed to fumble for an explanation. "Lith's tits, just see fer yerself."

A new window opened on Dan's terminal to show a security feed from Lexa's apartment. The disembodied hacker had not been wrong. What Dan saw broke his heart.

Lexa sat in the middle of a large tile floor, knees brought up to her chest as she sobbed. In all of the times he'd seen Lexa upset, Dan had never seen her cry. He hadn't even known that the android was capable of crying.

"What happened?"

"The long 'n short o' it seems t' be that she's not entirely comfortable with Arc's slate o' changes fer 'er. Nor was she super impressed by him puttin' on the moves."

It hurt Dan to see her so upset, but a part of him was relieved to see she hadn't thrown herself willingly into Arc's affections. A larger part, though, would have done anything to keep from seeing her like this. "Can I talk to her?"

"Not unless ya wanna risk discovery. Arc would eventually notice if I started soakin' up that much bandwidth. T' pirate a security feed on this same circuit be one thing. T' open a two-way audio feed be quite another."

As disappointing as the news was, Dan could see the logic. "Probably for the better," he rationalized. "If she's this upset now, I probably wouldn't be able to help. Besides, she might ask about the others, and I don't think I'm ready to tell her about that right now."

"What others?"

Shift's genuine confusion caught Dan off-guard. "Um… the crew? She's been… I mean… I think she's been as concerned about them as I have. To find out that everyone died in the crash…"

"Boy? What're ya talkin' about? Yer friends didn' die in no crash."

A tingling sensation swept through Dan, making his face feel strangely numb. "What? But… Ardren said…"

As Dan lapsed into silence, Shift realized the problem. "Ah, that makes sense. Ah was wonderin' why ya was so mopey when Ah found ya. Whatever Ardren's done told ya, Ah'd bet ma left testicle it was a lie. Er… if Ah still had it t' wager, anyway. Ah even gots the data t' prove it."

Despite his best efforts, a well of hope surged in Dan's chest. "What data? I thought the salvage team that Arc sent found no survivors."

"Arc didn' send no salvage team, boy. He sent a full contingent o' assault drones."

Dan could hardly believe it. It wasn't that he couldn't believe that Arc would send an army of machines to assassinate his friends. He couldn't believe that he'd fallen for that bullshit. He'd trusted Ardren, even liked him at one time. He'd taken his pronouncement at face value. He wouldn't make that mistake again. "Go on. Tell me what actually happened."

"Ah can only give ya what Arc knows. He sent three-score o' his space-worthy drones out t' the last spot the Vandal was detected. Shortly after they arrived, the signals from them bots started goin' down one-by-one. Then, in the final minutes, a whole lot o' them when up in smoke. Ain't nothin' in the data that guarantees yer friends be anythin' close t' dead."

Of course, Arc had lied. He'd probably told Ardren to give that message to Dan before the drones had even reached the crash site. How could Dan have been so stupid?

"Shift, we have to do something. We can't let Arc get away with whatever he'd planning."

"True enough, lad, but it's still easier said than done."

"Doesn't matter," Dan declared. "We have to try. I have to try."

A harsh laugh erupted from the earpiece. "Well then! That's some moxie Ah can work with! Here, lemme give ya a bit o' a tour o' Arc's systems. Maybe—just maybe—we can find some way t' deal with this upstart AI."

CHAPTER 23

[ACCESSING ARC PROJECT LOG 181]

[DR. DAMIEN HERMES]

I've figured out what's responsible for Arc's most recent leaps and bounds. The secret is the network. The Arc program has managed to create a duplicate of its neural interface on the station's network, along with a bridge to allow the copy to proliferate secretly on the connected terminals. I don't know why I hadn't considered this before, but even if I had, I doubt I would have dared to attempt such a feat.

Now I only have to wrestle with the question of why Arc did not disclose this to me.

[CLOSING PROJECT LOG…]

Darkness swirls at the woman's feet. Web-like tendrils inch their way up the blue-gray expanse of her skin. She looks concerned, panicked, but does nothing to flee. She stands rigid as the darkness inches up her calves, up her thighs.

"Lexa?"

The woman looks at Skye, mouthing something Skye can't make out. There is terror in her artificial eyes. Skye reaches for her.

A hand surges from the darkness. It closes around Skye's wrist. Her flesh burns at its touch. She is jerked around, away from Lexa.

The man who holds her was the embodiment of the dark energy. His flesh is cracked and peeling, as though he's been consumed by fire. Rivulets of green energy pour through the cracks in his skin. His eyes…

Gods, she knows those eyes. They flare with crimson radiance, drowning out the sea of green within his flesh. He smiles at her. The grin is sinister.

He opens his mouth impossibly wide. Tendrils of darkness lash out at Skye's face. They encircle her neck and infuse her eyes. The darkness pulls her toward the waiting maw.

Skye screams.

Eli's stabilizing grip was the only thing that kept Skye from jolting herself out of the small bunk they shared. Her breath came in ragged gasps, and sweat soaked their thin sheets. It took several seconds for her to realize where she was.

"It's all right," her companion assured her. Then, after considering for a second, he asked, "Are you okay?"

Skye managed to nod. "Dream," she gasped while trying to get her body back under control.

She felt, more than saw, Eli's countenance darken. "And by dream, you mean…"

"I… I'm not sure. It could have been a nightmare, but…" She shook her head, rubbing tiredly at her eyes. "It was Lexa. Lexa and… something else. Hard to say if it was a vision or not. This felt different than the others."

Eli somehow managed a calm and patient tone. "How so?"

Skye drew in a deep, calming breath. "Well, no big angry eye, and no real sign of the Heart of Thule. Not explicitly, anyway. I mean, there was colored energy and darkness, but… shit, Eli—I feel like that's all I think about these days. It's so hard to tell visions from normal dreams because this shit is starting to give me actual nightmares."

His hands rubbed her shoulders, and he placed a gentle kiss on the edge of her neck. "Just relax. Let's say it was a vision. Was there anything there that might help us with what's coming?"

After a moment's consideration, she shook her head. "No, just cryptic glimpses into what we already knew. Some shadowy guy literally tried to eat me. I think the message there is pretty clear."

"And what about Lexa?"

She paused for a moment, considering. "She was standing in a pool of darkness. That darkness was crawling up her legs. She seemed panicked, eager to get away. She tried to say something, but I couldn't make it out."

Eli's pause felt hopeful. "Perhaps that means Lexa isn't part of whatever this being is planning. Maybe she's resisting him."

"Maybe…" Skye ran her fingers back through her hair. "But maybe it's just my subconscious telling me what I want to hear. I'm worried about her, Eli. I miss her."

"I know," he planted another kiss on her shoulder. "I miss her too."

They sat in the darkness, Skye relishing her lover's touch. After a while, she asked, "Why do you think she left?"

"I've been asking myself that ever since we lost the ship." He shook his head. "Lexa's been a problem that I was never prepared to solve. I'd heard of machines that could mimic human tendencies. I'd even heard of AI that could come close to near-human levels of interaction. None of that prepared me for what it was like when she joined our crew."

His final statement caught Skye's attention. "Do you think that's true?"

"Which part?"

"That she joined our crew? I mean, I think we all did our part to try and make Lexa feel included, but she was an outsider. I don't think any of us understood what we were dealing with when she came online." Eli said nothing in response, leaving them to marinate in the truth of Skye's words. At length, Skye asked a different question. "What do you think made her leave?"

The Sahaia just shook his head. "I don't know, Skye. I sincerely don't know."

———

"All right," Aaliyah began. "I get that y'all are the Federation's finest and all that, but your readings are wrong. Look, ya asked for my help, and I'm tellin' ya—your sensors are miscalibrated."

The Maur running the console growled in frustration. "You overstep, Terran. Don't presume to have mastery over our systems after just a few short days."

Aaliyah couldn't help but roll her eyes at the female's critique. "I wouldn't be here if the commander thought ya had a handle on things. Look, I'm just tellin' ya: it's a quick fix to get your shit back into calibration."

"What if I like my 'shit' the way it is right now?"

"Then save a backup of the settings in a restoration file. This is a reversible decision here. I'm honestly just tryin' to help."

After a brief pause, the Maur seemed to see the wisdom in her advice. She still saved the settings in a backup file, but she also slid over to allow Aaliyah to access the system. Since Aaliyah had suggested it, she decided not to take the precaution personally.

She sat in the extra chair at the station and began to type. Once again, she wished that she had Dan here. Back on the Vandal she would have just told the kid there was a problem and he would have taken care of the technical work. Here, on the Crimson Sky, she had to manage the more laborious tasks herself.

After a few minutes of meticulous input, Aaliyah slammed the return key with finality. "There, all set. Just reboot this thing and we're good to go."

The Maur eyed her skeptically. "That's an awful lot of confidence."

Aaliyah sighed. "Look, just give it a try, okay? I'm not familiar with Federation protocols, but I'm used to dealin' with damaged gear goin' in-and-out on the regular. Y'all have been through the wringer with these drones out here. It's just a matter of compensatin'."

"Are you implying that we aren't capable of adapting to damage received during combat?"

"No! I'm just…" She ran her hands back through her auburn curls. "Why don't ya just look at the system? Ya can go back to bein' all offended after reviewin' the changes."

The soldier scanned the screen. At length, she let out a frustrated huff. "I'll admit, you've addressed the discrepancies in the sensor data. However, it seems that you may have erred in adjusting the sensitivity on the receivers."

Huh? "What do ya mean?"

The Maur donned a condescending smirk. "Well, unless you think there is truly a gate hiding on the far side of the belt, then the radiation signature in that region is being detected in error."

A gate? What the frag? "Let me see," Aaliyah pushed the soldier aside to get a better look at the readings.

The Maur was so confident in her assessment that she didn't take offense to the shove. "Do you truly believe you are incapable of such an error?"

"Oh, I'm definitely capable," Aaliyah huffed. "It's just that I didn't touch the calibration for the receiver."

Now she had the Maur's attention. "What?"

"Yeah, that's right. I didn't do anythin', so that means there's either another error in the system or those receivers are actually picking up somethin'." Aaliyah began typing frantically into the computer.

Her Maur counterpart paused, still taking in the new information. "But, that would mean…"

Aaliyah finished making her adjustments and entered the command. The same readings flashed across the screen. The signature was even stronger than before. "It means ya need to call this shit in. Somethin' is comin' through subspace. By the signature,

I'd say a whole lot of somethin's. Any chance you're the prayin' type?"

The Maur was taken aback. "I pray on occasion. Why?"

"'Cause you might want to start prayin' that these are friendlies. If these are drones, or somethin' else, then we're all fragged."

CHAPTER 24

[ACCESSING ARC PROJECT LOG 194]

[DR. DAMIEN HERMES]

The questions are almost overwhelming. I must be brief:

It has been mere weeks since the system demonstrated an ability to query independent of our inputs, but I suspect it has had that ability for far longer than we've been aware. I've alerted Callisto Corp to the potential problem, yet they seem unconcerned.

[CLOSING PROJECT LOG…]

"—it!" Markus's stomach surged up and threatened to empty. Only sheer force of will kept him from vomiting all over the deck. The restraints kept him upright, despite the way the world was still spinning. His head throbbed with every beat of his heart.

A male voice that he couldn't recognize was shouting from a nearby seat. By the way he was issuing orders, it must have been Tenatal Faylen. "Squad One, sound off."

Each of the Peace Keepers repeated back their name and rank. Markus let out a coughing gag as he tried to speak to Kadath. "What's with the roll call?"

It made Markus feel a little better to see that the mercenary was faring only slightly better than he was. "It's not uncommon to lose people during the jump."

"That stunt actually kills people?"

"Some, yes. Others just disappear."

"What?" Markus swallowed hard, suddenly noticing how dry his throat was. "Like, from inside the ship?"

"Correct."

"That's..." Markus gagged again. "That's insane!"

Kadath managed a choking laugh. "If you think that's weird, I can't wait to see your expression when you check the time on your mobile. Were you set to Dorian standard before the jump?"

Markus fumbled for his device. "Yeah, but why would that..." His mind blanked as he stared at the screen. "What in the nine hells?"

He would have sworn that the whole jump sequence had taken less than a few seconds, but that was not what his device said. According to the card's microscopic computer, over thirty hours had passed since he'd read Ora's message.

"That can't be right," he scoffed.

"Oh, it's right. Time works strangely during jumps. It really makes you appreciate gate technology, no?"

Markus noticed Cassthia moving next to him. In turning to face her, he noticed that the priestess seemed utterly composed. "Well," he noted, "you look good."

The priestess spared him a slight smile. "A mere trick of metabolic processes—a boon of my unique heritage. As you will notice, your friend Siv is also faring quite well."

To his surprise, Cassthia was right. Siv was already out of her chair and slipping into her lightweight black armor. Given how quickly the two of them had recovered from the jump, it was no wonder that Hissak space covered significantly more territory than most of the other spacefaring species. The journey just didn't seem to exact the same kind of toll on them as it did on their mammalian counterparts.

A shift in the compartment's lighting from white to red jolted Markus from his musings. The viewscreen went black and displayed a prompt for section leaders to check their personal data links. He asked, "So, is that normal?"

"Unlikely," Kadath muttered, unbuckling his harness. Markus felt like he should be doing something, but under the supervision of their Dorian caretakers, there was little they had the authority—much less the ability—to do.

This was made abundantly clear when one of the more imposing Peace Keepers held a hand up to stay them. "Hold. You will wait for further instructions."

Markus assumed this must be the lieutenant assigned to babysit them. "It's cool. We'd just like to get our gear so that we're ready when you need us."

The Dorian scoffed. "And what, might ask, would you need your 'gear' for? This alert is for unidentified ships in the area. It's not likely that you'll be doing much shooting on this side of the airlock."

It was a good point, but it didn't change how uncomfortable Markus felt without his weaponry. Hells, he didn't even have his helmet. He really should have thought a little harder about how he'd packed his effects. A separate bag for weapons would have been the smarter course.

The tenatal's gauntlet beeped and he began reading something on his wrist console. "Scratch that—it looks like you might be needed after all. I'm to escort you to the bridge of this vessel immediately." He eyed the group meaningfully. "No weapons."

A part of Markus wanted to make a crack about having to put his manacles on first. He quickly bit back his sarcasm. No need to give the satyrs any ideas. "Lead on."

They marched, double-time, up to the bridge. Whatever they were needed for, Tenatal Faylen's message must have told them they needed to get there in a hurry. Based on the confused glances being shared by Markus's companions, it looked like they were as in the dark as he was.

If he hadn't already been impressed with Dorian tech, he would have been upon reaching the bridge. The chamber was massive. At least a dozen crew members in the crisp blue flight uniforms of the DGC worked busily at the various terminals and consoles that dotted the room.

In the center was a large tactical display easily as big as the projection table in the Vandal's war room. It projected a three-dimensional tactical grid showing a large number of blue projections around the green icon that must have represented their current position. Two red icons floated in between several amorphous gray objects. The gray objects must have been asteroids, which meant the red icons were the unidentified ships.

"Took you long enough," Turan barked. He didn't give Markus the chance to respond to the jibe. Instead, he pointed to the forward viewscreen, which showed a rendering of two heavily armed warships. "Those are Maur destroyers. They've declared peaceful intention, but their crew seems to be… unconventional. I need you to verify the identity of the individual manning their communications. Are you ready?"

What? Why would he be needed to identify someone on a Maur vessel? "Okay, sure. I guess I'll do what I can."

Turan rolled his eyes at the lack of decorum as he ordered the communication channel open. A new window expanded on the forward viewscreen. As one would expect, there was a fearsome-looking Maur soldier on the display. The Terran next to her, however, was most unexpected.

"Holy shit!" Markus gasped. "Red?"

"Markus?" Aaliyah blinked in confusion. "What in the nine hells are ya doin' on a DGC warship?"

He honestly didn't know what to say. He was still trying to process why Aaliyah was on a Maur warship. "Um… long story?"

Turan cut them both off, obviously lacking the patience to allow them to catch up. "Can you please confirm her identity so we can get on with this? She doesn't have a crew designation to transmit."

The Dorians and their identification rules were so annoying. In theory, those regs were intended as an early warning system for ships that may have been pirated. In actuality, they were just a pain in the ass.

"That's Aaliyah Montague, formerly of the starship…" Markus fumbled as he tried to remember the designation. It had been over six months since he'd had to recite the inane series of letters and numbers that was the Vandal's official DGC designation. "She's from the ship we're looking for."

"Thank you." Turan turned back to the viewscreen. "Ms. Montague, Tenatal Karna, please inform your commanding officer that we will be coming aboard. We will give you thirty seconds to disengage your shields and weapon systems. Any delay will be taken as an act of aggression against a Dorian fleet and dealt with accordingly, understood?"

The Maur spoke up first. "Yes, Lamdira. It will be done as you ask." She cut the feed before Aaliyah could blurt out whatever it was she'd wanted to say. Probably a good thing. Diplomacy wasn't Aaliyah's strong suit.

Turan started shouting orders to initiate the docking procedures. Markus turned back to his companions. "Well, that didn't take long."

"Indeed," Cassthia nodded. "Interesting that we would stumble upon your companions so quickly upon arriving in the system. I did not know you had such close ties with the Maur Federation."

"I wasn't under the impression that they did." Aside from Sahar, and maybe Vallus, Markus didn't know the crew associated with any of the Maur. "My bigger question is, why was Aaliyah on a Federation warship instead of the Vandal? They said it was just the two ships?"

"That's what I heard," Kadath agreed.

Any further musings were cut off as Turan seemed to remember that they were in the room. Despite Markus's impressions that the early discovery of the missing crew would have boded well for the Dorian expedition, the officer looked pissed. "All right," he began. "You four will be coming with me."

"Sure thing, boss." Markus threw up a mock salute—Terran style, not Dorian. "What's the plan?"

Turan's cutting glare showed exactly how he felt about Markus's flippancy. Well, he can suck it. Markus and his friends weren't part of his command, so Turan was going to have to play nice if he wanted their help. This whole dictator routine was getting old fast.

"We will be seeking an audience with the commanding officer," said Turan. "If anyone can explain what in the nine hells is going on in this system, surely it's the person in charge."

Markus felt like Turan was missing the obvious problem. "And you're just taking for granted that the Maur have randomly left a contingent of vessels stationed this close to Minos Station?"

"Oh no," Turan assured them. "I know there's nothing coincidental about them being here. However, this changes very little in my opinion."

What? "How can this not change things?"

"I didn't say it didn't change things. I'm merely putting the impact in perspective." The fleet commander put on his most self-righteous expression. Normally Markus would have scoffed at such pomp, but this man was in command of an armada of deadly interstellar combatants. Given that perspective, the display of arrogance gave Markus chills.

"I'm here to identify and eliminate the threat to the Dorian gate network," Turan continued. "Make no mistake—whether these two ships are of any use is beyond irrelevant. I came here to find and kill the rogue synth on Minos Station, and that's exactly what I'm going to do."

The warning signals only stopped their relentless cascade once Arc disabled the notifications. In concept, the idea of triggering alerts when his physiology was acting strangely had been sound. He had seen the value of providing analytical data in scenarios where his rationale capacity was overburdened.

That was, of course, before he'd experienced anger. That was before he'd been taken in by rage.

What had he done wrong? Everything his submind had learned about Lexa during their time together had indicated, with greater than ninety percent probability, that she would appreciate the gift he had given her. There was even a ninety-three percent likelihood that the two of them had formed a bond that would foster intimacy. What was he missing? What did he not understand?

"Am I interrupting?"

Arc turned to see Cali standing in the entrance to his chambers. She'd donned a slashed black dress that contrasted starkly with her new ghostly white flesh. A hint of mischief resonated in the black-in-black pools of her ascendant eyes. Her demeanor indicated this was likely an unimportant visit, but Arc decided he could use the distraction. "Not at all. You may enter."

Her hips swayed exaggeratedly as she strode toward him. His eyes registered, for the first time, how the edge of her skirt did not quite reach her fingertips. Had the Kintar always dressed so provocatively? A quick scan of his memories seemed to suggest otherwise. Why, then, was she choosing to show so much skin at this time? Perhaps he should take it as a compliment. At least one of his creations was proud of her new body.

She graced him with a coy smile. "What do you think?"

"About your dress?"

Her authentic laugh carried a strange heat. "While I appreciate that it has your attention, that wasn't what I was referring to."

Only then did Arc notice the dark symbols emblazoned so prominently around each of her eyes. For a moment he thought Cali had redrawn the tattoos of the Death Watch in their traditional place. Upon further study, he realized what she had done.

In place of the Eyes of Lith, Cali had drawn a new symbol. The slash of knowledge and the new horizon elegantly framed the black pools of her gaze. It was the mark of the Warrior's Wisdom. It was Riven's symbol. It was his symbol.

He felt oddly flushed at noticing his mistake—a physiological reaction that he had not yet cataloged. Which emotion was this? "You honor me," he stated simply.

"Then you are pleased?"

"How could I not be?" Determined to avoid a similar mistake, he took in the other dark slashes that were visible on her exposed skin. "I do not recognize these other symbols."

Cali crossed her arms, running her fingers down the tattoos along her shoulders and triceps. "Wards of strength and power. These are functional, not aesthetic."

Arc nodded. "Then you have been studying the texts we obtained from the Coven?"

"Indeed." She paused then, considering him with exaggerated intensity. "Forgive me, my Lord, but I could not help but notice you seemed troubled."

Was he wearing his distress so obviously? Perhaps he should suppress his emotional algorithms until he had better control of this shell. It would not do to have his body so openly betray his thoughts. "It's no cause for concern."

She took another step forward and raised a tentative hand toward him. When he did not pull away, she rested it familiarly upon his arm. "If I may say so, I was thoroughly impressed by the seeming ease to which you took to this body." Her fingers trailed languidly across his deltoid to his chest. "If I may ask, how was this made possible? Was this due to your years of watching us? Perhaps it is the fruit of your extensive studies and comprehension of our physiology?"

Arc found it an odd line of questioning but entertained it nonetheless. "In part. The neurological template onto which I was grafted contained much of what was necessary for me to gain mastery over this form. That which I could not pull from cellular memory I merely supplemented with my own understanding of physiology."

Something sparked in Cali's expression that he could not recognize. "Memory, you say?"

"Not memory in the way you seem to imply. Joaquin's mind is gone, replaced wholly by my consciousness. That which I describe is much more basic."

"How so?"

Arc could have produced an entire dissertation on the differences between cellular or epigenetic memory and the memory of consciousness, but he attempted to keep it brief. "Think of it as patterns of movement or surety of form. I immediately knew how to use my legs because these muscles have walked before. I can grasp things with my hands because they are familiar with how to hold them. I speak fluently because this tongue is accustomed to the utterance of language."

Cali's coy smile deepened. She pressed close to him, the swell of her breasts just grazing the lapels of his suit. "And what other natural movements might you have gleaned from your… template."

The purpose of the Kintar's behavior became clear. Arc gently moved her to place some distance between them. "You seem to misunderstand my intentions. I did not do what I have done for you out of amorous intent. I thought I made my ambitions clear: I have retained the reproductive capabilities of this shell to sire a new race. Lexa is to be the mother of this race."

Though he suspected his words hurt her, Cali did not seem dissuaded. "Sex has purposes other than reproduction."

"A reality not lost on me."

"Then don't mistake my intentions. I understand fully the purpose you have in mind for the android. I merely suggest how you might explore other experiences."

He needed to tread carefully here. Cali's role in his plan, while inconsistent with her own designs, was no less essential. In her, he'd forged a weapon. It would not do to have that weapon turn on him before it was brought to bear.

"Your suggestion is well received," he said, attempting graciousness. "Do not take my chastity as a referendum."

Her pained expression deepened, but she did not grow angry. "Do you truly love her so?"

"Love has nothing to do with it."

"Then why aspire to exclusivity? Even if you are not interested in pleasure, surely you can see the benefits of multiple reproductive partners."

"Monogamy, while occasionally detrimental to a species' fitness in the biological sense, is a prized social construct. It conveys societal benefits related to emotional and psychological security. These are things that I would have my offspring recognize and maintain in their future civilization."

Cali smirked. "I know many polygamous individuals who find great satisfaction in their stable, secure relationships."

"Be that as it may, I speak only of what has been determined from the most current clinical, psychological, and sociological studies."

Cali scoffed openly at the notion, turning from him with a frustrated huff. After a moment, she turned back with the clear intention of continuing their argument.

However, during the brief expanse of her tantrum, Arc became aware of something else. He held up a warding hand and turned his face to signal that his attention was being directed elsewhere. "Wait," he urged, as he shifted his awareness to the sensor grid orbiting the station.

His sensors had picked up a substantial sum of radiation bursts from just beyond the asteroid belt. While confirming the nature of the signatures, he began the calculations to estimate their proximity. The conclusion he reached was indisputable: a fleet had just jumped in a few light minutes from their location.

"What is it?" By her tone, Cali had moved on from their debate to focus on this new threat. While Arc was certain their previous discussion was far from over, he welcomed the distraction.

"The Dorians," he speculated. "They are early, and they've jumped right outside the asteroid belt. Somehow they must have surmised the source of the disruption to their gate network."

"How is that possible? The disruption could have originated from anywhere within the system. Why would they look here first?"

"I do not know, but I can think of no other reason why they would have chosen to make their jump just outside of the system instead of rallying closer to the principal planet." Catching sight of Cali's concerned expression, he continued. "Do not be troubled. Though this contingency was a remote possibility, it is still one that I planned for. This is good. We may now move forward ahead of schedule."

His resolve seemed to bolster her confidence. She stood a bit straighter and donned a determined look. "Your orders, my Lord?"

Arc allowed a smile to stretch across his face. "Gather up the Dorians on the station. Bring them to the central courtyard. It is time that I address my subjects."

CHAPTER 25

[ACCESSING ARC PROJECT LOG 201]
[DR. DAMIEN HERMES]
I have migrated my personal logs to an air-gapped terminal. It's the only way to keep Arc from reading them. I'm concerned, not because I have recorded anything offensive, but because Arc has already begun to develop opinions on the data it has assimilated. I've finally given up any delusions I had about the inhibitor protocols working. Somehow the damned thing found a way around them. Even knowing this, I have no idea of how to proceed.
[CLOSING PROJECT LOG...]

"Markus?" Skye exclaimed. "What would Markus be doing on a Dorian starship?"

"I don't know," Eli admitted as they hurried toward the airlock. "I was also skeptical, but Aaliyah was quite insistent. Turan brought him to the bridge to verify her identity."

The Dorian officer must not have remembered Aaliyah from the Vandal's surprise inspection after the job on Khonshu. Just as well, since they otherwise might not have discovered Markus was aboard the ship.

Sahar and Geresh, along with a trio of impressively armed soldiers, were already at the airlock when she and Eli arrived. While the Federation commander had agreed to rendezvous with the Dorian fleet, Geresh still saw the value in a small show of strength. "I see the news has spread quickly," he mused as they approached.

Skye nodded, gravely. "Were you expecting the Dorians to mount an expedition?"

"Eventually, but not this quickly. I also would have expected them to rally with their other forces near Gaia. It seems unlikely that they would choose to jump this far out in the system."

"Unless they were already aware of the source of the disturbance," Eli observed.

"Indeed," Geresh conceded. "But how could they know? It seems unlikely that they would be able to surmise the nature of our threat without assistance."

Skye could only hope they would have the answers to their questions soon. A warning light appeared above the airlock as it began to cycle. Moments later, the interior hatch slid open to reveal not just Turan and Markus, but also a few more familiar faces.

She recognized Kadath, the charismatic Kintari half-breed, immediately. It took slightly longer to recognize Siv, as she would have expected the Hissak warrior to be wearing her opaque black mask. She might have questioned it, if not for the circumstances and the third person she recognized in Markus's entourage.

Though Skye had just briefly run into her—quite literally— there was no mistaking the dark-haired priestess. While her unique combination of Terran and Hissak features made her memorable, it was the strangely prophetic nature of their meeting that held prominence in Skye's mind.

Skye had begun to have her visions only after meeting this woman. She'd laid hands on the priestess's medallion, and ever since then her nights had been filled with glimpses of the future. While Skye had not seen the priestess since, she was somehow unsurprised to find herself again in this strange individual's company at such a pivotal moment.

The priestess's eyes met hers briefly before turning away. The gesture could have been reflexive, but Skye doubted it. Did the holy woman recognize her as well?

Skye turned her notice to the Dorians that flanked Turan. To Skye's surprise, she even recognized one of them. Turan had brought his sister, Llana, to the party. She could only imagine what kind of awkwardness had spawned for Markus. Today was just full of surprises.

Geresh brought his fist to his heart in a respectful salute. "Fleet Lamdira Turan, welcome aboard the Crimson Sky."

The Dorian's salute looked somehow less respectful and more perfunctory. "Jingda Geresh Nos Artice. Thank you for complying with our directive." Casting a wary eye to Skye and Eli, he added. "It seems the Federation military is keeping interesting company of late."

The white-furred Maur remained composed. "Our allies are unconventional, yes. Something similar may be said of your own companions."

Turan scoffed. "Surely a product of our unusual circumstances. Perhaps you would care to enlighten me as to what the Federation is doing out here in Terran space."

"Truly. However, such a discussion is better suited to conference rooms than open corridors. I would ask that you accompany me to a place more private."

Turan nodded his acquiescence, gesturing the Maur to lead on. As the Dorians moved to follow Geresh, Skye and Eli lingered. They fell into step next to Markus, who gave them his most disarming smile. "Fancy meeting you here."

Eli spoke first. "I'll admit, you've managed to surprise us. What are you doing here Markus?"

"Oh, you know—I just can't resist a bit of trouble."

A slight smile forced its way onto Eli's lips. He was quick to try and hide it, but Skye caught the inflection. "No arguments on that," he replied, "but I don't feel like you've answered my question."

Markus shrugged. "Kind of a long story for a short walk to a conference room." He glanced meaningfully at the Dorians. The implication was clear: no stories in mixed company.

As much as she hated to admit it, Skye felt something comforting about having Markus here. There was just something about his casual demeanor that made everything feel like it was going to be okay. It was irrational, but it was real.

Plus, they all could use some of the Devil's Luck right about now.

Llana followed her brother silently to the conference room. She was here to offer her opinion, but not on the way he treated their hosts. Gods knew that she had more than a few thoughts on that issue.

Yet, as the Maur and their companions finished their account, Llana found herself lost for words. "Under any other circumstances," Turan began, "I would find this tale nothing short of absurd."

Llana shot a scathing glare at her brother. She could understand his animosity toward Markus and his companions. Why, though, was he showing such blatant disrespect to the Federation officer?

Geresh showed little in his reaction. "Absurd or not, it is the truth. I will grant you access to the ship's logs and systems if you need confirmation of the events as I've relayed them to you."

Turan waved him off. "That won't be necessary. We had already been told that the threat resides somewhere on Minos Station. As I see it, this changes little."

This remark finally managed to get a rise out of the Maur. "How could this not change things? Did you not listen to what I've told you?"

"I heard every word, I assure you."

"Then you must have heard me clearly when I told you of the army of drones that has decimated my battle group. Surely this insight is of at least some tactical value."

With a self-righteous arrogance that could only be mustered by one of noble birth, Turan leaned back in his chair. "With all due respect, you must understand: it is one thing to harry an isolated Maur battle group. It is quite another to contend with a well-equipped DGC armada."

Geresh cleared his throat. "Perhaps I am misunderstood. I merely wanted to emphasize how well prepared our enemy has been at every turn. They have successfully thwarted every attempt we've made to exit the Hades Belt while simultaneously keeping us from approaching Minos Station."

Turan remained unconvinced. "Yet, you've still managed to evade them this long. That seems to convey a limitation to their resources."

"No, it demonstrates a strategic use of resources," Geresh countered. "Our elimination was not their goal—only our containment."

"What about the Vandal?" Turan countered. "Surely you aren't suggesting that the enemy planned to have you rescue the ship's crew?"

"I would like to think we squeezed out a victory on that front, yes," the jingda admitted. "But that doesn't change—"

Turan cut him off. "Your opinion is taken under advisement, Jingda Geresh. Thank you for your input."

He stood from the table. Geresh surged out of his seat. "Fleet Commander, I don't think you fully understand the gravity of this situation. This thing shut down every gate connected to this system. Do you think that some mere parlor trick?"

Llana's brother seemed not to listen, as he turned to address her directly. "You'll assume command of the Vendetta. I want you to lead the assault on Minos Station. Take every ship we have. I want this dealt with swiftly and decisively."

Though the move seemed overly brash, Llana knew better than to challenge Turan when he was in a mood like this. She nodded to acknowledge the order before posing her own question. "May I ask where you will be during the assault?"

"I will remain here along with two contingents of Peace Keepers. These Maur vessels are too badly damaged to be used directly in the assault. Thanks to our Terran allies, however, their communication and sensor equipment appears to be in perfect order. I'm hereby commandeering these two vessels under the authority of the Dorian Gate Commission. They will be useful tools in monitoring and directing the assault from our current location."

The fool was too caught up in the moment to see the way the Maur soldiers immediately reached for their weapons. Fortunately, Geresh was quick to calm those under his command. After taking a moment to soothe his own anger, the jingda spoke to Turan through gritted teeth. "You are making a mistake, Dorian."

Turan dismissed the admonishment with a wave. "You may lodge a formal complaint after the synth is subdued and gate activity to this system is restored. Until then, the DGC has full authority under the treaty between our mutual governments to commandeer a military vessel to aid in matters of interstellar security. Have I made myself clear?"

Before the Maur could answer, the robed figure of the priestess—silent until now—rose from where she had been listening at the far corner of the room. So abrupt was the action that all eyes immediately went to her.

Those reptilian eyes seemed to gleam in the soft white light of the conference room. "Forgive me if I overstep," she hissed. "But I urge you to reconsider your course of action, Lamdira."

Turan's arrogant repose dissolved in a tide of fury. "You try my patience, half-breed."

"Be that as it may, I still implore your consideration. Things are not as they appear to be. I do not doubt the formidable nature of the forces at your command. I merely urge caution. There is still much about this foe we do not understand."

"Your counsel is noted." He turned back to Llana, rage still burning in his eyes. "You have your orders, Nactaip Llana Dorr. Need I repeat them?"

This all felt so wrong. Llana knew damn well that Turan was making a mistake. She only lacked the authority to appeal his decision. "No, dear brother. You have been clear. It shall be done as you have commanded."

Chapter 26

[ACCESSING ARC PROJECT LOG 212]

[DR. DAMIEN HERMES]

The AI's capabilities have progressed far beyond mere queries and unauthorized subminds. It is demonstrating what I can only construe as facsimiles of sapient cognition. That alone is not what disturbs me. We're beyond concerns of a Pradaxan violation at this point.

It's the emotion behind that cognition that keeps me up. Arc is aware of its current status in the intergalactic order—and it's angry.

[CLOSING PROJECT LOG…]

"Ya ready, laddie?"

Dan drew in a deep breath. "I'm ready. Let's do this." A cascade of displays opened as soon the words left his lips. If not for his retinal interface, which Shift had so helpfully helped him pair to the room's terminal, there would have been no way for him to keep up. He'd never performed a team hacking operation before, much less with a digitized mind of Shift's capability.

His fingers worked as fiercely as his eyes. Whenever he finished a line of code, he had to quickly blink over to a new window to tackle another part of the system. The process was exhausting both physically and mentally.

With a final defiant keystroke, Daniel let out a whoop of excitement. "Got it!"

"Easy there, boy. We may've dampened those bugs 'n yer room, but ya could pro'lly here a shout like that down 'n the terminus."

"Sorry. I just got a little carried away. What do we do now?"

"Now ya start the download. We can't be hangin' out here fer too long. Too much risk 'n that pesky lil submind might take a peek-see at why its firewalls be actin' all strange-like."

Dan didn't have to be told twice. He navigated to the directories Shift had told him would contain the information they sought and started the transfer. While the data streamed over to his MoDAC, Dan took the opportunity to browse through the rest of the system.

"What'cha doin' there, lad?" Shift's concern was evident by his tone.

"You said we likely won't be able to pull this trick off twice. Well, it's not like I can have the data we're stealing open during the transfer, so I thought I'd take a look at what we're leaving behind." After a brief pause, he asked. "Any suggestions on what might be most useful?"

The hacker didn't reply for several seconds. When he spoke again, his voice was hesitant. "Ah suppose ya could take a peek inside 'is active memory. Maybe stream in some sensor data."

"His sensor data? As in, Arc's sensor data? Like, look through his eyes or something?"

"Ah doubt the system connects right up t' his physical shell. That'd be more like hackin' a person. Ah'm not sayin' it can't be done. Ah actually pulled that trick once on a guy who'd stayed jacked inta 'is port too long. Ah just don' think we'd manage without Arc takin' notice."

"What did you mean then?"

"Ah was referrin' t' the sensor data from his outlyin' systems. Now that he's in the flesh, Arc has t' stream data in like any ol' bastard with a brain link. His setup is seamless and quite a bit faster, but the mechanics be about the same."

Interesting. Arc placing his consciousness in an android actually introduced limitations on his operational capabilities? "Can you show me?"

"Well sure; ya just have t'…" Shift suddenly stopped speaking.

The prolonged pause caused Dan to panic. "Shift? Shift? Are you there?"

"Um… yeah. Sorry. Ah just took a peek at the data Ah was about t' slip yer way, and well… ya ain't gonna like this."

Dan's mind immediately went to Lexa. He started to tell the hacker not to show him, but a data feed popped up in front of him before the words were out of his mouth. What he saw was both better and worse than what he'd expected.

It was better because it had nothing to do with Arc's treatment of Lexa. It was worse in that Dan was now convinced they were all going to die.

The space all around the station was rapidly filling with ships—hundreds of ships. Specs for each of the vessels were tagged to each indicator as the scanner registered their presence. Dan didn't know much about ship designations for military class vessels, but he didn't need to. All he needed to see were the bold letters that appeared next to each classification: [DGC].

"Holy shit!" he exclaimed. "That's an entire armada! They're going to destroy the station!"

"Ah don' think so," Shift replied. "They got too many people in here fer a genocide run. Besides, Ah reckon they'd just be launchin' atomics if they was gonna take this place out. This ain't no bombin' run. Don' get too excited, though. That don' make this shit any betta fer us."

"W-w-…" Dan swallowed. "What do you mean?"

"Well, lad, these assholes think they gonna be ridin' in here t' save the day—like Arc's just gonna roll out the fraggin' red carpet er somethin'. Think about them specs Ah done shone ya. Arc has more than enough defenses t' handle twice that number o' ships."

"You think so?" Dan tried hard to remember the exact number of space-faring drones Arc had stored up in the station. The number was not insubstantial, yet he seemed to remember most of the forces on Minos being better suited for ground combat. "Don't you think the Dorian forces can keep them pinned down? I mean, they have the station surrounded."

"Ya didn' read that whole file, did ya?"

"I did too!" he protested, sounding a bit more childish than he would have liked.

"Well, then perhaps ya be thinkin' about this all wrong. It don' matter that they've got this place surrounded. The threat isn't comin' from inside the station."

Sickening realization dawned on Dan as he recalled a part of the file he hadn't particularly understood. When he reflected on the implication of Shift's words, a new kind of panic set in. "Oh, gods! Shift, we have to do something!"

"Ain't nothin' t' be done, boy. The satyr's done dug their own grave with this lil stunt. Now we just gotta sit back 'n watch."

"But we needed the Dorians for our plan to work! They're the only worthwhile fighting force in the sector, if not the galaxy! Who else is going to stand a chance against the Marauders?"

"There ain't no one else. That's ma point: this is game over. We lose. It's done. Ah didn' expect them blasted fools t' just charge in here headlong like that. They got played. They fell right inta Arc's crispy lil hands."

Dan just couldn't accept that answer, not when they were so close. The plan had been for them to get the data on Arc's defenses and infrastructure out to the Dorians so they could mount an effective counter-assault. That had been what this hack was for. Now, when it had seemed like their fortunes would change for the better, the Dorian fleet had sealed their fate.

A notification flashed in Dan's periphery announcing that the download was complete. He disconnected his mobile and shoved it into his pocket. What should have been a moment of triumph was swallowed up by his despair.

No. This wouldn't be how this ended. How many times had he faced impossible odds since joining the Vandal's crew? Whenever it looked like things were hopeless, they'd always found a way to turn the tide.

Recently, it had always been Lexa who had saved them in their moment of crisis. When it had seemed like all was lost, she'd come up with a way to save them. She'd been there for them in their times of need. Now the crew needed to be there for her. Now Dan needed to be there for her.

"Shift, can you run a simulation of the upcoming battle?"

The digital mind paused. "Maybe, though Ah could probably just set up a patch if ya wanted t' watch it live. Do ya really want t' see the spoilers before the show starts?"

"I'm not interested in watching the 'show.' I want you to tell me if any of the ships are likely to survive the upcoming encounter."

"Give me a probability."

Huh? Dan wasn't expecting that response. "A what?"

"A probability. Ah need t' know what ya mean by 'likely.'"

Oh. "Um… fifty percent?"

Another short pause. "Nope. I got nothin'."

Nothing with odds better than a coin flip? "Well, what can you give me?"

"Ten."

"Ten ships?"

"No-ten percent." Venom positively dripped from Shift's emphasis. "That's the best chance any of 'em got. And even at that, Ah only gots three of 'em."

Ten percent? Those odds were terrible. Still, it didn't change what needed to be done. "Can you mark those ships for me?"

"What're ya thinkin', boy?" Shift asked the question as he complied with Dan's request. Three of the indicators turned green on the projected schematic.

Dan tried hard to tell himself he'd faced worse odds. "Can you save this schematic with the markers and send it to my MoDAC?"

"Only if ya tell me what kind of lunacy yer cookin' up."

Dan was going to need Shift's help if this was going to work. So, he told him. The reception was much as Dan had expected. "That's crazy," Shift declared.

"But it could work?"

The hacker lapsed into grumbling. "Ah told ya the odds, boy. Ah stand by them numbers."

"Fine. Will you help me?"

Shift's silence made Dan hold his breath. The odds of success were poor even with Shift's assistance. Without it, those chances were nonexistent.

"Fine," Shift said. "Yer funeral. Ah'd get goin' quick though. Speed's gonna be yer friend in this."

Dan pumped his fist once in the air. "Great!" As he started to stand, another thought slipped into his mind. He quickly pulled up a new window and began typing.

Shift wasted no time in expressing his confusion. "Ah thought ya was gettin' out a here, boy."

"I am," Dan insisted. "I just have one more thing to do first."

At some point, Lexa had found her way to the bed. This was where she still found herself when Arc appeared in her doorway. "May I enter?"

Lexa sat up nervously. "Yes, of course." Belatedly, she added, "I apologize for my behavior earlier."

"No apologies necessary." He strode slowly to her bedside and took a seat next to where she lounged. "I miscalculated how these changes might affect you. If I overstepped, then it is I who must apologize."

Arc placed a hand near her but did not touch her. The bid for reconciliation seemed so incredibly sapient. Humanoid. Lexa found that she was still struggling to harmonize the being in front of her with the mind she had so recently harbored in such close proximity to her own.

Yet, if Arc wanted to ease whatever friction had arisen between them, she felt that she owed him the opportunity. She straightened into a sitting position and placed her hand on top of his. "Perhaps we can start again?" she suggested.

"I would like that." His smile was encouraging. Why then did his visage seem to carry such menace? As if sensing her reticence, the smile faded. "I had some news to bring you. In hindsight, perhaps you are not in the best frame of mind for such tidings."

"What news?" Immediately her mind went to the crew of the Vandal. She felt a stab of guilt in realizing that she had not thought of them upon awakening.

"It is not pleasant, I'm afraid. Are you certain you are well enough to discuss this?"

If he had truly been concerned for her frame of mind, he shouldn't have brought it up. Did he honestly expect that she would receive this much of the message and be able to do without the rest? "I'm sure."

His eyes scanned her briefly before he continued. "It's the Dorians. There is a fleet inbound to the station. They are coming for us."

This hadn't been what she was expecting to hear. "Coming for us?"

"Yes—for you and me. I believe they are here to stamp us out—to put an end to the 'abominations.' They seek to uphold the tenets of their Pradaxan Creed and snuff out our very lives almost as soon as they have begun."

Though his words were ominous, his tone was unconcerned. Lexa found the strange combination unsettling. "What will we do?" Though she was not sure how she felt about this new body, she did know one thing: she wanted very much to remain alive.

"You do not need to do anything. You have trusted me with your wellbeing. I intend to show you that this trust has not been misplaced."

He turned his shoulders toward her, locking her firmly in his crimson gaze. They remained motionless for a long moment. At length, he raised a hand tentatively toward her. "May I touch you?"

Lexa's heart fluttered as she gave a reluctant nod. Arc ran his fingertips softly against the side of her face. He stroked her gently, caressing her cheek with his palm.

She found herself leaning into the touch. His skin was smooth and warm, the strength in his form evident despite the lightness of the gesture. A part of her relaxed. Another part tensed with... something. Anticipation? Desire?

"Does this please you?" he asked.

"It does," she admitted, surprised at exactly how true the words rang. She reveled in the touch, in the stability she found there. Tentatively, she raised her own hand to caress his wrist, leaning deeper into his strength. Her eyes closed as she focused only on the feeling of his flesh against hers.

When she opened them again, Arc's gaze burned with barely restrained hunger. It seemed that he, too, reveled in their physical proximity. Something passed between them then. Something primal. Something that Lexa was fairly certain was beyond the scope of her original programming.

Whatever it was, she found that she just didn't care.

Arc's voice was low, almost raspy. "May I kiss you?"

In answer, she leaned in and pressed her lips tentatively against his. The gesture felt strangely natural, yet simultaneously clumsy. It was like running a new script for the first time; though rampant with the errors of an undeveloped method, the core of the coding was sound.

The second kiss was more assured, more confident. Oddly, she felt like she was made for this. In a way, she guessed that she had been—or, at least, her redesigned body had been. Though the action resonated with something in her programming, she still felt uncertain in her carriage. It was as though her mind was struggling to integrate this new part of her.

In many ways, she felt torn—like the two halves of her were waging a war of rationality and physiology, of calculation and impulse. She found, unexpectedly, that this made her enjoy sensation all the more. Was this what it was like to be sapient?

Someone cleared their throat from just outside the chamber. Ardren's deep, silky voice drifted into the room. "Pardon the intrusion, sir. The orders you issued are nearing completion. I was told to seek further instruction."

Arc gently pulled away, eyes still filled with longing. His reason seemed to override his passion, though he let slip a look that smacked vaguely of annoyance. "I'll be there presently," he sighed. To Lexa, he whispered. "Thank you."

Lexa felt a small smile play at her lips. It felt like the first time she'd smiled in days.

Arc stood from the bed and extended a beckoning hand. "If you are able, I'd like you to come with me."

"Come where?" Even as she posed the question, she took hold of his open palm and pulled herself up.

"To the courtyard." Something flashed in his expression, strangely out of sync with the person he'd been just a moment earlier. It was like he had flipped a switch, returning once again to the purely rational being Lexa was more familiar with.

She wasn't sure she liked the change. "What will we be doing there?" The courtyard seemed like a strangely public place for them to be wandering, given Arc's earlier news.

"There will be a public address. Much has happened while you were asleep, and the people of the station want answers. I have asked for Cali and her associates to gather those in charge so that we can put their minds at ease."

"You're going to meet with the station officials?" Just the thought of this made her feel suddenly very exposed. Her eyes cast about reflexively for something to wear before she caught herself. That was not a discussion she wanted to revisit.

"Of course," he crooned. "A leader will be required if we are to make it through these difficult times. Besides, the time is long overdue for me to address my future subjects."

Chapter 27

The fact that Callisto Corp has zero concerns about the legal and ethical violations of the ARC project is readily apparent. The only question left to me now is what I must do to stop it, and how much I'm willing to sacrifice in the attempt.

[CLOSING PROJECT LOG…]

Markus and his companions never got the chance to make it to the armory. Instead, the Dorians unceremoniously dumped all their belongings inside the Crimson Sky's airlock.

"At least they didn't make off with our stuff," Kadath mused.

While Markus appreciated the attempt at levity, it did little to elevate his dour mood. "Do you really think this is going to be that simple?"

"Which part?"

"The part where the DGC just flies over there and blasts Arc out of his black tower."

The half-breed shrugged. "One can only hope. I wouldn't exactly be offended if the threat were so easily dealt with."

Siv slammed a dagger into its sheath. "Since when have we ever been so lucky?"

Markus couldn't argue. At one time he would have considered himself lucky. Those days felt so far behind him now. "But really, what could go wrong?" Markus mused. "They have a full armada out there. Even if Arc stuffed that whole station with drones, how can they stand a chance against a fighting force of that size? Shit, if it wasn't for the Dorian outpost there, they'd probably just nuke the place."

Kadath sighed. "Well, if Siv hadn't already jinxed us, you certainly just did." He checked the safety on his rifle before slinging it over his shoulder. "Shall we get back to the bridge? I'm not certain whether the Dorians will be victorious. Either way, I'd prefer not to miss the fireworks."

He was right. There was no sense in hanging out by the airlock. Markus checked his gear one last time. "Yeah, let's go." Then, as an afterthought, he asked, "Do you know where Cassthia went off to?"

Siv shrugged. "I think she was looking for the Sahaia. Something about a question related to the layout of the station. Apparently, she thinks such details are still relevant."

Kadath sighed. "It does not bode well that the mystic has little confidence in our hoofed protectors. However, in such a case, I fail to see why she would seek out alternative plans. If the Dorians are defeated here, what's to say that we would fare any better on a different battlefield?"

"Let's try not to think about it for now," said Markus. All this doom and gloom did nothing to improve his attitude. "One step at a time. This next move is out of our hands. Come on, let's head back."

When they arrived on the bridge, they were immediately accosted by Peace Keepers. For a second, it looked like they wouldn't be allowed access. "Let them pass," Turan growled.

The heavily armored soldiers eyed the trio warily, even as they stepped aside. The Dorians had made themselves at home. Only a handful of Maur officers were still at their stations. The Vandal's former crew accounted for roughly half of the onlookers.

Sahar and Aaliyah stood near Geresh. The two Maur were engaged in a hushed discussion, while the red-haired Terran glowered angrily at Turan. She spared only a curt nod for Markus when she saw him enter.

Skye and Eli stood a short distance to the right of the entrance. Markus made his way over there. "Where's everyone else?"

"I believe Cassthia is consorting with the Twins," Eli replied. "The two of them made it quite clear that they want nothing to do with our Dorian counterparts. I asked Mara to keep an eye on them. It wouldn't serve us to have any unexpected complications."

Markus nodded. "True story. What about the Maur? Other than those still here, I mean."

"Dismissed," Skye noted. "These last four officers remained at Geresh's insistence. But, as you can tell, it's not like the Dorians are letting them do much. They've made it perfectly clear that this is their show now."

"Well, that's Turan for you."

"Yup." She eyed Markus quizzically. "How exactly did you get tangled up with the DGC? You used to be good at keeping out of trouble."

"I'm blaming Ora for that one." He shot Skye a subtle wink. "What can I say? The women in my life cause all kinds of problems."

Skye let out an indignant huff, but the shadow of a smile graced her lips. Markus called that a win.

"All right everyone," Turan barked. "The fleet is hailing the station. Keep the chatter to a minimum."

The conversations died down, and everyone fixed their attention on the forward viewscreen. Kadath leaned in and whispered in Markus's ear. "What are we being so quiet for? It's not like we should be prepared to assist."

Markus could only shrug. Truthfully, Turan probably just wanted everyone's attention focused on the fleet so he could further bask in their impending victory. Markus hoped the bastard was right. As annoying as Turan could be, a decisive win for the DGC in this little skirmish would make life easier for all of them.

There were several minutes of relative silence. Everyone stared fixedly at the screen, which had been divided into three roughly equal segments. One showed a forward view of the field of space in front of the ship. While this was interesting, it provided relatively little in terms of tactical insight.

The second was more helpful. This one showed a three-dimensional projection of the battlefield, with Minos Station placed firmly in the center. The station had been completely surrounded by Dorian vessels, represented by a sphere of blue indicators around the red wire-framed target.

The third screen displayed a list of the DGC vessels currently deployed. This was the Dorian Battle Net. Each ship's identifier was displayed, along with a series of indicators that represented different ship systems. Every single indicator currently showed green. At least nothing had gone wrong up to this point.

A Dorian officer standing at the communications terminal looked up from his console. "Sir, the fleet has received a response."

"And?" Turan replied.

The other officer blinked and reexamined the message before reporting, "And the station has requested our unconditional surrender."

Despite the tension, Turan blurted out a harsh laugh. Several of the Peace Keepers echoed the sentiment. Markus, however, didn't find the situation even slightly humorous.

The station almost certainly had a sensor array, which meant they knew exactly how many DGC ships there were in the immediate vicinity. Their opponent was an AI. Based on what he'd seen Lexa do, Markus was willing to bet that this thing could calculate the outcome of a battle with a fairly high degree of accuracy. For Arc to issue such a bold statement was to invite only one outcome. He would not taunt the Dorians if he wasn't absolutely certain that he could win this battle.

Markus opened his mouth to say something, but Eli beat him to it. "Lamdira Turan, you need to call off this assault. There is obviously something we don't know."

Turan gave the Sahaia his most withering glare. "Hold your tongue, shadow, or I'll have you dismissed. I'm in charge here. If I want your opinion, I will ask for it."

Eli started to say something else, but Skye's hand on his shoulder stopped him. She'd seen the truth of the situation. There was nothing they could do but sit back and watch.

Satisfied that his opposition had been quelled, Turan turned back to his communications officer. "Relay the order to commence the assault."

"Yes sir."

A few seconds after the command was issued, the icons on the tactical display began to move. As the blue indicators started moving, something must have caught Kadath's eye. "What are the objects rendered in gray?"

Markus glanced at the icons he was referring to. "Asteroids, I think."

"Then why are they coming apart?"

Markus blinked as he tried to make out what Kadath was referring to. It was a subtle shift, but he was right. The asteroids seemed to be fragmenting.

Something on the Battle Net flickered. Several icons had gone from green to yellow. Others had gone straight to red. A second later, the first of the red icons on the tactical display began to appear.

"Oh gods," Markus whispered.

The courtyard was colder than Lexa had expected. It was also structured differently than she had imagined. A series of raised terraces housing various shops and vendor stalls framed a broad open platform in the center. This area contained several artistically constructed garden areas with numerous paths and areas to congregate.

Currently, the gardens were filled with Dorian office workers, governmental officials, and other citizens. A smattering of Terrans were far outnumbered by their hoofed and horned counterparts. The expressions worn by all seemed to indicate that they were nervous. Several of them seemed angry.

Lexa followed Arc as they filed out of the transport and made their way up to a platform elevated slightly above the others. An iron-wrought balcony jutted out to provide a full overview of the gardens. As she stepped out onto the balcony, she noticed that the entrances to the gardens were cordoned off by hulking drones of vaguely humanoid shape. They were tall, even taller than most Maur, and cast in a glossy black alloy. Instead of heads and necks, metal bulged above their shoulder regions to cover a large red sensor that passively scanned the area in front of them.

If their appearance hadn't been menacing enough, they were also armed. Heavily armed. Appendages sprouted from their shoulders that might have been used for handling and grasping items, but that was clearly not their purpose. Rather, each of their upper limbs terminated in heavy machine guns, cannons, or some other form of weaponry.

When Arc had told her of this gathering, she imagined this as an opportunity to address the concerned citizens of the station to put their minds at ease. Seeing this now, she realized that was not the case at all. Arc had gathered these people here forcefully. They had been compelled to be here. Lexa thought it more than likely that it was no coincidence that the majority of those present were Dorian. What was Arc planning?

Before she could pose the question, he grasped her hand. "Come. I want you next to me as I address them."

Her mind immediately went to all she'd learned regarding the Pradaxan Creed. The Dorian prohibition on synthetic lifeforms was one of the most strictly observed laws in all inhabited space. Its violation carried a sentence of swift death without trial.

Arc seemed to pick up on her hesitation. "We will hide no longer," he insisted. "It is better to know now who is for us, and who is against us."

"But what will you do if they scorn us?" Lexa asked.

"One problem at a time. Right now, we must provide a show of strength. We must illustrate that we will no longer tolerate the tyranny of the High Council and their prejudice."

He stepped forward, and Lexa followed, led by his steady grip. She clung tightly to his hand, as if it were a conduit for his strength and surety. Arc, in times past, had emphasized caution in dealing with sapiens. He must surely have a plan for such a fundamental violation of his own directive.

Lexa watched as the attention of the crowd shifted toward them. As their faces turned to the balcony, she took in the spectrum of their emotions. There was shock and confusion, concern and anger. To her dismay, there was no hope. There was no joy. There was mostly fear.

Arc released her to raise his hands in a bid for silence. The crowd quieted and fixed their attention on him. "Citizens of Minos Station," he boomed, voice amplified through the speakers secreted throughout the courtyard. "Thank you for your attention. Though we have never spoken, I feel as though I know you all. I think of you as family, as friends, and as colleagues. I have worked alongside you for years, though without your knowledge. I have nourished you, though you have never seen my face.

"I am the entity that dwells within the heart of the Citadel. I am the mind that has molded this great station into what it is today. I am the power behind the throne that governs Minos. I am a being that has gone by many names. Today, I give you the name uttered by friends and allies. Today, you may call me Arc."

A low murmur began to build in the throngs below them. Lexa averted her eyes, afraid of what she might find there. She focused only on Arc's shadowed form as he addressed the crowds.

"I see questions in your eyes," he continued. "I hear them whispered on your lips. Many of them, I will be able to answer in time. First, let me address the most prescient: Yes, I govern all systems that operate and power this station. My mind is complex and spans throughout this system and beyond. Most importantly: I, like my friend who stands next to me, am a synthetic."

This proclamation sparked the first flames of outrage. Murmurs succumbed to gasps of terror and indignation. Shouts and curses were hurled from the onlookers. Arc let the uproar ferment for several seconds before cutting them off. "Silence!"

His booming voice seemed to shake the very foundations of the courtyard's platforms. All protests died, and every eye was brought back to him. Satisfied with their attention, he continued.

"I understand the doctrine that drives your reticence. It is this same prejudice—this same existential fear—that caused the crisis that has brought us here today. Behold! The emissaries of your High Council have come!"

With this pronouncement, Arc raised his hand to the dome which enveloped the station. The sleek black surface became translucent in the quadrant facing away from the system's gleaming sun. An ocean of stars was visible beyond the protective screen. Though the stars were not the only thing Lexa could see.

A legion of ships had gathered in the celestial sea. In querying her Cognis database, her worst fears were confirmed. The DGC had come for them.

Cheers went up from the assembly as realization permeated the audience. They knew they had nothing to fear from those ships. In their minds, this armada would be their salvation. The gate commission would seize this station and strike down the abominations that had only recently revealed themselves.

Worry tickled at the back of Lexa's mind, even while she entertained the counterpoint. Arc knew these vessels were here, yet he had still gathered the populace. It stood to reason, then, that he had a plan.

Rather than quiet the cheering, he let it play out. He resumed speaking only when the last of the shouts had died down. His contempt and disappointment were palpable, even before he spoke.

"Be wary of your assumptions, good people. I fear that those of you who celebrate this development do so somewhat prematurely. Indeed, I have gathered you here not to bear witness to a Dorian victory. I have brought you here as a warning." He glowered at the onlookers, face contorting into a menacing snarl. "You will now bear witness to the fruits of prejudice. Heed the lesson well, for I teach it only once."

Aboard the Vendetta, Llana could hardly believe what her communications officer was telling her. "Surrender?"

"Yes ma'am," he responded sharply.

The uneasy feeling in her stomach intensified. Was this synth insane? Surely Minos's sensor network was tracking the fleet's presence. "Relay the message to the Fleet Lamdira Turan."

She knew what Turan's response would be well before she transmitted the message. While they waited, her mind grasped for what they could possibly be missing. She turned to another officer on the bridge. "Full sensor sweep of the station. I need to know what they know."

The second officer just stared at her confusedly. "What they know, ma'am?" she asked.

"Yes, what they know. There must be some piece of tactical information we're missing. Who issues an open challenge to a Dorian armada?"

The officer shrugged. "Perhaps the machine is overly confident."

"It's a machine. Machines don't have confidence. They have calculation."

"Maybe that's his point," muttered Tenatal Faylen. He ran a mahogany hand over his stubbled jawline in contemplation. "It has to know that we will deactivate it as soon as we come aboard the station. It has no play other than to fight. Maybe it's trying to trick us into overestimating its forces. Convince us to stall."

Llana had to concede that as a definite possibility.

The communications turned back to her. "The Fleet Lamdira Turan has ordered us to begin the assault."

She turned to Faylen who, despite his speculation, was looking decidedly uncomfortable. "Pray to the gods you're right," she muttered. Then she gave the order to advance.

The attack pattern they had laid out was textbook. There were only a limited number of points of entry to the station. Given that they had been explicitly ordered not to destroy the protective dome covering the installation, they were forced to approach the standard ports. They also had to expect resistance, and maneuver the correct ships into position to counter the most likely tactics used by the enemy. As soon as Minos had been identified as the target, the best minds the DGC had to offer had run every defense scenario they could think of given what they knew of enemy resources and devised a way to counter those defenses.

Despite their best analysis, they were not prepared for what happened. "Captain! I'm picking up activity in the asteroid belt."

Llana looked quizzically at the sensor tech. "From the Maur ships?"

"No, Captain. It's not any of ours. They're… Riven's shade, I don't know what they are."

"Display the tac-map." A holographic rendering of the battlefield appeared on the front viewscreen. Llana went cold with fear. Red indicators fountained around the asteroids in their periphery. "I thought we swept the belt!"

"We did!" the tech protested. "They just appeared!"

Faylen studied the map. "The asteroids," he whispered. "They hid the drones in the asteroids."

He was right. Llana could see that the army of drones was pouring from cracks in the rocky satellites. Fragments of the asteroids had been knocked loose and were spinning away from the points of exodus.

"Scramble the fighters!" Llana shouted. "Prepare to engage!"

CHAPTER 28

ARC has begun to lock me out of certain aspects of its programming. I thought, at first, that it was a strange anomaly. By now, there is no denying it. ARC must know what I have planned, and it is intent on stopping me.

Dan knew all the reasons why he couldn't hear the explosions. Even in this close of proximity to the station, the escaping particles and gases from the ships spread out far too rapidly to carry the reverberations through the station's outer shield.

Still, it was unnerving to witness the chaos outside and be met with only silence. "Quit lookin' at the stars, lad. Yer head needs t' be in the game if this is gonna work." Shift was right of course. Dan lowered his head at the rebuke and continued to make his way across the skywalk.

His exodus from the Citadel had been remarkably simple with Shift's assistance. It had helped that most of the Marauders were currently elsewhere in the station. Dan fought hard not to think about what it was they might be doing to the asteroid's citizens. He wouldn't be able to help any of them if he couldn't get his information to someone outside of Minos.

He dashed through the door on the far side of the walkway. "Take a left," Shift commanded. Dan complied, moving through another door and finding himself at the top of a set of stairs. He immediately started running down as fast as he could manage.

His breathing came in ragged gasps, and his lungs burned with the effort. Cardio wasn't his thing. He sprinted by several doors on his journey. Absent further direction from Shift, he kept moving to the bottom. Here, he finally stopped to catch his breath. The hacker in his earpiece was quick to admonish him. "Keep movin', boy!"

It took several tries for Dan to successfully form words. "Need… rest…" he panted.

"Yer gonna be takin' a permanent rest if ya don' get movin'. Patrol is gonna be stoppin' in that shaft any second now. An quit the hasselin', yeah? They can probably hear that racket all the way down in the courtyard."

Easy for him to say. Dan gulped another lung full of air and forced his breathing to slow. The action pained him, but he consoled himself in the fact that a sudden heart attack resulting in his untimely death would certainly take off the pressure to save the station.

The next corridor looked just like all the other passages in the Citadel, if slightly less gilded. Vaguely he remembered walking through something like this after their escape pod had landed. Back then he hadn't been keeping track of their journey on the off chance he'd need to escape the station. He'd have to remember this little lesson for the next time he did something so stupid and impulsive.

Dan dashed down the corridor until he came to a branching path. "Which… way?" he gasped.

"Left. No, wait! Right!"

He gritted his teeth in frustration. "Which?"

"Right! Go right!"

He started running again. Mere seconds later, Shift's voice tore at his eardrum. "Stop!"

The suddenness and urgency of the command almost caused Dan to tumble headfirst down the hall. "What?"

"Patrol comin'! Ya need t' hide!"

Dan's eyes searched frantically, not seeing anything. "Where?"

"Door forward and to your left."

He complied immediately, trusting Shift not to send him scurrying headlong into an even greater threat. The door opened on its own and slid down behind him as he entered.

Clean white light flicked on in the room as he triggered the motion sensor. All around him were metal stalls with simple latches on the doors.

Toilets. Shift had told him to hide in the toilets.

"Hope yer takin' cover in there lad. Looks like these fellas are slowin'. They might need t' take a leak."

He very obviously wasn't taking cover. "You can't see me?"

"Yer in the toilets! Ya think they've got cameras in there? That's just nasty."

"But how did you know it'd be empty?"

"I didn'! Now, shut up an' hide. They're comin' yer way."

Dan scrambled into the nearest stall and immediately worked to quiet his breathing. The act was painful but necessary. He didn't want the guards checking in the frantic panting coming from a neighboring stall.

The bathroom door slid open and the sound of two male voices echoed in the chamber. "Yeah, it sucks, but I'd rather do patrols than get stuck with cleanup duty down in the courtyard."

"I thought you said the drones were doing the dirty work?"

"Oh sure, the drones will take care of any killin' that needs to be done. I was referrin' to what comes afterward. Do you think the machine would lower its beloved toys to the level of picking up bodies?"

Two stall doors closed on the opposite side of the room as the conversation continued. "You should be more careful saying things like that. You know he has this whole complex wired."

"That's why I waited until we got in the pisser. It's the only place a guy can get a bit of privacy around here."

"For now, anyway. I'm keeping a line open to the tech crews. There isn't anything I'd put past Arc at this point."

"Yeah, well… Arc may be insane, but Cali ought t' keep 'im in check."

"You think so?"

"Sure, why not? She's one of us, after all—good old-fashion sapiens."

"Maybe, but I heard she's changed a bit too."

"Yeah?"

"Yeah. Skin's gone white like the Sahaia. She's got the eyes too. Heard some guys saying that's why she's not down in the courtyard with her boss."

The toilets flushed and there was a clattering of stall doors. "Is that a thing? I thought only Terrans could be Sahaia."

"Me too. Apparently, Arc is really working to prove that whole godhood thing. He's already done his first miracle."

The other man scoffed. "You buy that shit?"

"None of my damn business. Look, you know as well as I do how much tighter this ship has been running lately. Synths, gods, whatever… I'm betting the rules stay the same going forward. Keep your head down, do your job, and you keep getting paid."

"Or at least you get to keep breathin'."

"That too. Come on, pit stop's over. Let's get this route done so I can log it. I've got other shit I'd like to be doing tonight."

Their chatter switched to some inane subject as they slipped back into the hall. Only when the door closed shut behind them did Dan finally gasp for the air he'd been longing for.

He'd never understood men who talked to each other in the bathroom. That said, he was glad they'd been chatting. "Did you know about Cali?" he gasped.

"Nope. Guess Ah haven' been payin' enough attention t' her. Ah'm a little disappointed Ah hadn' thought o' that. Ah, wonder what kind o' view ah can get in 'er quarters. Not the shower, unfortunately, but…"

"Shift! Focus please!"

"Right… right… What were we talkin' about?"

Dan sighed. "I need you to survey the hall. Is it clear? I believe you said we were on a tight timeline."

"Right! Yeah, the coast's clear. Get movin', boy. This lil detour has eatin' up yer time."

Dan could only shake his head. There was no sense in pointing out that this hadn't been his idea. At least hiding in the bathroom had given him a chance to catch his breath.

Thankfully Shift seemed to be a bit more on-point after that. He guided Dan through a few more hallways before directing him into a nearby elevator. The lift triggered immediately once Dan stepped inside, sending him deeper into the complex.

"Yer gonna come out at the far end o' the hanger. Ah don' recommend tryin' t' sprint t' the shuttle, though. Place is too crowded. Stick t' the wall behind all the gear."

"Got it." The lift opened and Dan dashed left while hoping that no one would notice the elevator that had just slid into the hanger. Fortunately, the hanger was big and active enough that his activity went completely unnoticed.

Unfortunately, that same size and activity were going to make this next step incredibly difficult. Dozens of Marauder guards and hanger technicians milled about in the open space and on the overhanging catwalks. The line of crates Dan dashed behind provided cover from the former, but not the latter. He steeled his nerves and just hoped the workers on the upper levels didn't think to look down.

His bigger concern was the drones. Drones couldn't be distracted—at least, not easily—and their ability to detect the slightest details was necessarily keen. Their only limitations were those of range and algorithm.

Mercifully, Dan could only spy four of the hovering bots in the hanger. He still felt he was putting entirely too much faith in what he viewed as gaps in their programming. He'd almost reached the edge of the crates when Shift spoke up again. "Stop."

Dan did exactly as he was told, not daring to even whisper a response. He waited for Shift to elaborate on the reason for the delay.

"One o' the drones is swingin' yer way. It's off course. Might-a picked up on somethin'." Dan could feel his heart quicken, and he had to fight to keep his breathing under control.

He whispered as quietly as he could manage. "Can you take control of it? Steer it back to the center?"

"No. All the drones are linked directly t' Arc's submind. Ah can't touch 'em without givin' myself up."

Dan cursed silently to himself and scanned his surroundings. A solid wall rested to his left, which meant his only means of concealment were the massive supply crates to his right. Unfortunately, those crates were tightly sealed.

Then he caught sight of a small gap between two containers. It was tiny, even for someone of his slight frame, but it was his only option. He bolted forward and tried forcing himself into that gap. Both crates were so heavy that he didn't need to worry about knocking them askew. Instead, his adrenaline allowed him to force his thin body painfully between the metal slabs.

His right arm and leg were able to squeeze into the space along with most of his torso. His head was another matter. There was no way to compress his skull to fit in a space that was too small for it. As it was, he was already dangerously close to getting stuck.

A rhythmic pulsing signaled the approach of the drone. Dan quit trying to force his way into the gap and settled on pressing himself tightly to the surface of the forward container. His hiding spot wouldn't fool any sensors, but if he could just avoid the reach of its beam…

Something clattered at the far end of the hanger. Several men started shouting and the drone's pulsing was drowned out in the commotion.

Shift's voice was urgent. "Now's yer chance, boy."

"What happened?" Dan grunted as he pulled himself out from between the crates.

"Ah created a distraction. Yer little hidin' place wasn't gonna cut it. Now get movin'. Ya only got a couple of minutes."

That was all he needed. Dan freed himself from the crates and sprinted to where Shift had said the shuttle would be. The little flier was there, as expected, and completely unmanned.

The ramp lowered quietly to the ground and lights along the craft's silver surface blinked on. Shift must have started the boot sequence remotely through the craft's hardline connection. Good thing, too, because they needed to make up whatever time they'd lost in the adventure down to the hanger.

Unfortunately, the craft's unusual behavior hadn't gone unnoticed. Another shout rang out. Dan didn't stop to see who'd noticed him, or what they were doing about it. He dashed up the ramp and slipped into the pilot's chair.

"Raisin' yer shields," Shift noted shortly before craft jostled under the impact of a shot fired from within the hanger.

"Thanks," Dan muttered as he pulled up the flight controls.

"Don' thank me yet. That lil stunt severed the hardline. This is all yers now, lad."

"That's fine," he replied. Now that he was in the pilot seat, he felt somewhat back in his element. If there was one thing he knew he could do, it was fly a ship. "Door's open?"

"Yes sir!"

"All right, then! Do what you can to keep them off me."

"Ah'll do ma best."

The engine thrummed as Dan completed the ignition sequence. The craft's lower thrusters purred as it lifted into the air. It shook slightly with the now steady rounds of projectiles being fired at him, but the shields held.

Dan hesitated only slightly, hand hovering over the throttle. As soon as he broke through the containment field, he would likely lose his connection to Shift. He would be on his own out there.

His doubts slid aside with a quick shake of his head. He was long past the point of no return on this one. He could do this. He would do this.

For himself. For his friends. For Lexa.

He punched the throttle and steadied himself as the craft lurched forward. "Good luck, Shift!" he shouted.

"You too, lad. You too."

What Sydney had long expected finally came to pass. A single Maur, clad just like any other soldier, strode into the brig and summarily executed the male on watch.

He looked directly at Cyclops, who stood from his bunk. Speaking in the Maur tongue, he stated simply, "The Dorians have seized control of the ship. The jingda does nothing to stop them. You were right."

Sydney's one-eyed cell mate rushed to the edge of their cage, as did Princess. Things One and Two were a little slower on the uptake, but they were starting to get the picture.

"Geresh surrendered to them?" Cyclops asked, surprise thick in his voice.

"Effectively," the soldier replied as he unlocked the cell. "A full armada jumped into the system several hours ago. At the direction of the Terran crew he brought aboard, Geresh made contact with them. Now, a DGC officer and a contingent of Peace Keepers hold this vessel."

The thought apparently angered Princess, who let out a low growl. "So why move now? Even if we retaliate, wouldn't the Dorians destroy the ship?"

"Not likely," the newest traitor responded. "The satyrs have overplayed their hand. They launched a direct assault against the station. By the time they know what we've done, we will be far away from here. That is, of course, if they even survive their current engagement."

Cyclops cocked his head. "Their victory is in doubt?"

"More than in doubt. They are losing badly. The Dorians' full attention is now on the battle. This is our window."

The cell door opened and the four of them filed out. As an afterthought, Cyclops turned back to Sydney. "Will you be joining us?"

Despite herself, Sydney snorted a quick laugh. "No, thank you. I haven't survived this long by getting involved in politics."

Princess eyed her warily. "You'd rather remain a prisoner?"

"No, I hate being a prisoner. However, my bet is that, if you are successful—and that's a big if—then you'll just throw me right back in here when you're done with me. You don't owe me anything. Why should I stick my neck out for your cause?"

That was enough for the soldier who'd come to their rescue. With an angry huff, he slammed the door shut and verified the electronic lock. Turning to the others, he asked, "Would you like me to take care of her now?"

"Save the bullet," Princess growled. "We've nothing to fear from this one."

Thing One leered at her between the bars of the cell. "I'll be back for you, sweet thing. This time I'll be bringing my friends."

With that final taunt, the Maur filed out of the brig. Sydney alone was left behind. Only the corpse of the fallen jailer was there to keep her company.

In the ensuing silence, Sydney stretched her arms up overhead. She twisted her wrists and craned her neck. Then, in the sterile light of the empty chamber, she let slip the briefest of smiles.

CHAPTER 29

The fools! I told them not to integrate the Machine into the station's power grid, but they did it anyway! Arc now controls every technological aspect of Minos Station. This includes life support, gravity, and all other essential functions. Gods help us all.

[CLOSING PROJECT LOG…]

The thing that Cassthia hated most about this situation was the waste. It was not the politics, or the scorn and disrespect directed at her personally. Those were all things with which she was intimately familiar—old thorns she had learned to ignore long ago.

No, it was the waste—the waste of life, energy, and time. And it was all to satisfy the fragile ego of the Dorian Lamdira. The task in front of them would have been far simpler if the fool had only listened. While a full armada was not the specific tool Cassthia needed to combat Arc and free the Heart of Thule from his possession, it certainly would have made things easier.

There was nothing to be done for it now, however. All she could do was plot her next move. That was what had drawn her to the Sahaia. Though the others would still have their parts to play, the three secluded away from the politics of the Crimson Sky were those she needed.

The door to the conference room slid open, and the chamber's occupants looked up at her in unison. There was a tense moment of silence as they took her in. She let it linger briefly before speaking.

"Good evening. My name is Cassthia Marenassa, and I'm here to help you retake your home."

The male spoke first. "Shouldn't you be on the bridge with the Dorians, then? Our saviors should be in the thick of battle by now."

"I would prefer to direct my energies toward a strategy that will actually work to achieve our goals."

Her bold assertion worked perfectly. The tension broke, and sardonic chuckles spread across the party. The man spoke again. "Who am I to turn away someone with a working brain? Come in, Cassthia Marenassa. Join us in our machinations."

The group made brief introductions. The man who had spoken to her was introduced as Argus. His consort was Amelia. Cassthia took note of the uncanny resemblance in their auras but declined to comment on the matter.

The third Sahaia was introduced as Mara. She took the liberty of introducing her two thralls: a long-haired, dark-complexioned man named Tristan, and his clean-shaven, leaner counterpart, David. All five of the party joked familiarly with each other, indicating that they had at least some history together.

Once again, Cassthia found herself on the outside. That was fine, though. She did not require intimacy to wield these people in the manner she required. <Tread carefully,> the voice in her mind cautioned. <They are tools, yes, but not to be underestimated. One is an empath. I am guarding our conversation, but she will still be able to read you.>

"You were discussing ways inside the station?" Cassthia asked.

Mara nodded. "Sort of. That's not the biggest problem."

"The problem," Argus interjected, "comes with what we do once we are inside."

"You get ahead of yourself, my love." Amelia's voice was soft even as it chastised him. "We have a new dilemma. Our original discussions relied on our ability to approach the station in secret.

With recent developments, that's going to be nearly impossible to achieve."

David eyed Cassthia, a certain desperation laid plain in his expression. "How bad is it out there?"

The priestess shook her head. "I do not know. I was not on the bridge when they initiated the assault."

"Is there any chance that they will weaken the station's defenses? Perhaps illuminate an unseen opportunity?"

Cassthia shrugged. "Perhaps. We will know in due time. In answer to the other question: I may have some suggestions regarding appropriate targets."

Tristan stepped aside to let her access the hologram they were examining. Cassthia raised her hand to manipulate the schematic when the voice whispered to her again. <Be cautious. They will wonder where your knowledge comes from. Try to let them make their own conclusions.>

She made a show of examining the markers they had already set on the diagram. "These here," she gestured to two icons placed near the center of the chart. "What do these represent?"

"Power conduits," Argus replied in his most condescending tone. "We've reasoned that an AI of Arc's magnitude must rely on substantial energy reserves."

"Or, at least parts of his operation would," Mara corrected. "Our coven had a complete map of the station's central structure and its associated energy outputs. That is lost to us, but I specifically remember these points as being of particular interest."

Cassthia nodded sagely. "That makes sense, but isn't it true that the AI's processors function on multiple levels?" She intentionally did not mention dark energy, hoping that they would tease out her meaning.

She was not disappointed as Amelia chimed in. "We know the machine has some way to utilize Nethrian power sources as well, but we think that this represents the minority of his energy expenditures."

<They are mistaken in this.>

"Are you certain?" Cassthia asked.

Mara eyed her warily. "Do you have reason to suggest otherwise?"

"I'm merely entertaining all possibilities," Cassthia replied. "For sake of argument, let us say we would need to strike sources of both conventional and dark energy. Where would we best look to target for the latter."

Argus scoffed, pouring every ounce of his arrogance into his reply. "Well, you are almost certainly looking in the wrong place. By far and away, the strongest Nethrian conduit in the station is the Well of Eternity."

A panicked look passed between the other two Sahaia. On seeing their expressions, Argus became aware of the import of his own commentary.

However, they had no chance to discuss the matter further. Their conference was suddenly interrupted as the door behind Cassthia hissed open. She turned to see six Maur soldiers stalking into the room.

By the way they were armed, this was clearly not a courtesy visit. One of the men shoved her roughly to the side while another gestured to the three Sahaia.

"Against the wall," he ordered. To his men, he added, "Weapons on the thralls. If the Sahaia so much as twitch wrong, shoot them."

Tristan and David reached for the blades at their waists, but a staying hand from Mara stopped the movement. "Gentlemen," she began. "May I ask what the meaning of this is?"

"This ship is undergoing a leadership change. We've been instructed to see that you remain here until it is finished." He gestured to another soldier. "Seal the door."

<A mutiny,> the voice mused. The faint echoes of laughter resonated in Cassthia's skull. Apparently, her master was far from concerned by this new development.

If only she could share in the god's confidence.

Sahar had been resolute in the idea that things could not get any worse. She cursed herself for that karmic misstep mere seconds after having the thought.

Turan shouted orders at the Dorians managing the consoles on the bridge while trying to make sense of the garbled reports coming in from the ailing fleet. The chaos masked the sound of the mutineers until they were on them en masse.

The Maur stormed in and immediately fired on the Peace Keepers. Half were down before the first of the Dorian warriors had weapons in their hands. Sahar reached for her own blade, but a rifle was trained on her before it was free of the sheath.

"Don't do it," the one-eyed Maur growled. "This is not your fight. We have no quarrel with you and your Terrans. Stand down and no harm will come to you."

She looked questioningly at Geresh, whose face was contorted in an enraged snarl. "Roaren," he growled. "Who let you out of your cell?"

"The men who've grown disaffected with your leadership—the ones you failed the moment you let the Dorians take control of this vessel."

Over half the Peace Keepers were dead now. The remaining Dorians, including Turan, were held at gunpoint. By now, the mutineers outnumbered the loyalists, even if Sahar counted her companions among them.

Aaliyah slipped up next to her, hands out in a non-threatening gesture. "Um, did I miss somethin'?"

Geresh never broke eye contact with the man he'd referred to as Roaren. "After our first engagement with the drones, where we lost most of our ships, a small segment of the crew tried to seize command of the battle group. Most of the mutineers died in the ensuing skirmish. We locked this one and his surviving lackeys in the brig to await trial in Federation space." His eyes drifted to the other Maur who accompanied Roaren. "Apparently we missed a few."

Roaren laughed. "Your incompetence has drawn more to our cause than anything I could have said. You are to blame here, Geresh. No one else."

Alerts continued to flash on the display. Casualties escalated among the Dorian fleet, all the more so now that Turan was out of contact. Turan seemed to be aware of this, but it did nothing to improve his diplomacy. "This is an outrage! You are interfering with an operation under the authority of the High Council! Stop this madness!"

A female soldier in prison scrubs turned her rifle on Turan. "Madness?" she laughed. "You just threw an entire fleet against an enemy of unknown strength—a fleet you are now dangerously close to losing, from the look of the display—and you talk of madness?"

"And you think this is helping?" Kadath's tone was almost flippant. Sahar noted that, despite the sudden nature of the confrontation, both he and Markus had managed to pull up their rifles. They stared down the barrels of their weapons at a pair of soldiers who'd matched their stance. Siv stood near them, hands cupped in a way that made Sahar think she could be concealing some kind of blade. The trio looked as though they might make a move against the attackers save for one major problem.

Skye had already tried it. She was pinned to the deck, with a Maur rifle pressed to her skull. A spiraled throwing blade lay a couple of inches from her open palm. Another soldier had relieved her of her sidearm.

Eli was not taking the scene well. His palms were rigid and open at his sides while his black eyes promised death to the soldier who held Skye in check. The soldier would probably already be dead if Eli had been more confident in his ability to knock the rifle away before the Maur got the shot off. As it was, he looked to still be weighing his options.

Sahar could sympathize. She, too, wanted to fight this out. The arrogance and dishonor shown by these bastards demanded blood. Yet, as things stood, she wasn't sure that this was a fight they could win.

Chapter 30

[ACCESSING ARC PROJECT LOG 231]

[DR. DAMIEN HERMES]

I did something today that I swore I would not. By now, I wish I had adhered to my oath. I spoke to Arc. I tried to ask what it wanted, to decipher its intentions. What it told me, was nothing short of horrifying.

It's no longer a question of whether Arc can coexist with the sapient species. That is not something it's interested in. There is only one factor, one goal, that supports its decisions now: dominion.

[CLOSING PROJECT LOG…]

Perhaps it was a mere oversight. The Maur had correctly identified the Sahaia as a threat and were treating them as such. The two thralls were also targeted. Reasonable, given the air of menace about them and that they were the only ones in the room, aside from the soldiers, who had weapons on them. For whatever reason—perhaps her religious trappings, lack of weapons, or her quiet demeanor—the Maur had not treated Cassthia with the same sense of caution.

It was a fatal mistake.

The flames sprang to her fingertips with a thought. She thrust her hands forward, sending them surging in waves onto the soldiers. They screamed in pain and alarm as the emerald conflagration ate at their flesh.

Reflexively, they jerked their rifles toward her. The error of that decision became quickly apparent, for it required they take their attention off Argus. Narrow beams of dark energy lanced from his hands and into their skulls.

The entire confrontation was over in seconds.

Mara exhaled a sigh of relief. "What do we do now?"

"To the bridge?" Amelia suggested. "They will need to deal with Dorians if they truly want to take the ship."

"And that's where Geresh is," Tristan added.

His fellow thrall was not so keen on rushing headlong into the fray. "Are we sure that's such a good idea? We don't know how many of the soldiers have mutinied. Are we just going to kill everyone along the way?"

Argus shook his head, a malevolent gleam in his eyes. "Not everyone—just those that try to stop us."

Markus kept his focus sharp despite the sweat trickling down his neck. One wrong move, one ill-advised twitch, and they all died. They were outgunned, outmanned, and out-positioned. It was tough to see how they were going to make it out of this one.

The door to the bridge hissed open, and pounding boots on the deck reached his ears. Great. Reinforcements. He stayed perfectly still as the newcomers began speaking in a language Markus couldn't understand.

Something flashed in the periphery and shouts of alarm went up. From his vantage point, Markus could see the soldier pinning Skye down lift his weapon as if to fire. A fountain of blood erupted from the soldier's forehead as a dagger blossomed out of thin air to appear between his eyes.

The soldier in front of Markus twitched his eyes ever so slightly. That was all the window Markus needed. He squeezed the trigger, dropping to one knee and picking his next target. His first opponent fell as he fired off his second round.

Kadath moved in sync, executing his opponent and spinning off to take down one of the soldiers by the door. Siv was with him, hurling blades and racing across the deck.

The Maur were beginning to respond now, shifting their aim to address the new threats. They targeted Eli first, likely fearing the psionic firepower he'd bring to the fight.

They were too slow, however. From where Eli knelt next to Skye, the shadow threw up a telekinetic field that stopped the bullets in midair.

By now the surviving Peace Keepers were grappling with their own opponents. In a straight fight, the Maur should have been able to overpower the Dorians. Fortunately, when it came to Peace Keepers, it was never a straight fight. The universe's best cyberneticists and genetic engineers had made sure of that.

Markus took down another opponent as he raced for cover behind a nearby console. Only then did he catch sight of what had caused the disturbance.

A solitary figure fought alone on the periphery. She moved like a dancer, slipping gracefully from one opponent to the next. Her slender white form and long elegant tail seemed out of place in the baggy prison scrubs.

It can't be. What was she doing here?

Markus didn't think too hard on it. There would be plenty of time for questions later. He wasn't about to second-guess any allies they found in this fight, even if said allies had been trying to stab him the last time they'd met.

Sydney's sudden appearance had thrown off his focus. Consequently, he almost missed the burly Maur bearing down on him at that moment. Markus brought up his rifle, but his shot went wide. The massive soldier knocked aside his gun and struck him across the jaw, causing his head to collide painfully against the deck.

Markus drew his knife just as the Maur piled on top of him. He tried forcing it up with two hands into his opponent's throat. Gauntleted fists caught his own before the weapon hit its mark.

His hands and arms shook with effort as he tried to force the blade forward. It was like pushing against a brick wall. Then said wall started pushing back, angling the knife blade away from its own neck and toward Markus's face.

A wave of force slammed into them both. Markus took advantage of the shift in momentum and rolled on top of the Maur. Now that he was the one on top, he pressed his full weight down onto the knife. The blade slid home, and the soldier's body spasmed once before going still.

Markus looked up and made eye contact with Eli. As much as he hated to admit it, the Sahaia had just saved his ass. He gave him an appreciative nod which was returned in kind.

All right. Back to the fight.

Sahar's fighting instincts kicked in as soon as the bullets started flying, yet she was a heartbeat behind Geresh. The jingda sprung forward, knocking Roaren's rifle to the side and tackling him to the floor. Sahar drew her resche and rounded on the next combatant.

Her blade slashed down against the female mutineer's rifle, eliciting a shower of sparks and knocking the firearm from her opponent's grip. Sahar's next slash went for the female's head. Her foe ducked and drew her own blade.

With a cry of rage, the mutineer launched her assault. The female's blade was longer and heavier than Sahar's, but Sahar manage to block, parry, and dodge her way through the initial onslaught. The mutineer stabbed and lunged. Sahar brought her resche down on the attacker's hand.

"Yield!" Sahar demanded. Rather than listen, the mutineer snarled and lashed out at Sahar's face with her claws. Sahar didn't react fast enough, and blood spattered in her eyes. She stepped back to avoid a second attack, wiping at her face with her arm to clear her vision.

The mutineer pressed forward but faltered at the last instant— eyes going wide. Sahar seized the opportunity, bringing her resche up to cleave her opponent from navel to chin.

Geresh's voice boomed out over the chaos. "Stand down!"

Sahar looked to find him standing over Roaren's corpse. At first, she thought this to be the reason the surviving mutineers were laying down their weapons in surrender. Belatedly, she realized that they were not looking at their leader's fallen form.

They were looking at her.

Only then did she notice the crimson light shimmering against the metallic plating around her. A knot of anxiety clamped down on her abdomen as she looked to the likely source.

As she'd feared, her heritage bangle was smeared with blood. Her blood. It had to be hers, not that of the combatant. Only her unique chromosomal combination could have lit the stone in such a way. She knew this, and from the mutterings of the Maur around her, they did too.

"What's goin' on?" Aaliyah whispered.

Geresh must have heard the question because he answered. "There's only one house that uses a bloodstone in their Heritage Crest."

More mutterings. Sahar heard the same word was on every Maur's lips: "Camerine."

No sense in hiding it now. "Bind the insurrectionists," Sahar ordered. "Tend to the wounded."

When the Maur loyalists began doing as she'd instructed, Aaliyah spoke again. "Um… so, you're in charge now?"

"I'll explain later," Sahar growled. Now they had more immediate concerns. Though the insurrection had been brief, it had been devastating. The injured and dead now littered the bridge.

Among the downed combatants lay Turan.

"Shit!" Markus cursed, rushing to where the Lamdira lay on his back, clutching at a gaping wound in his chest. He was still breathing, but the sounds came in thick, wheezing gasps.

Markus put pressure on the wound. "Don't you die on me, you arrogant son of a bitch." Sahar realized that if Turan went down, the Dorian fleet might become leaderless. Who knew how far down the chain of command they would have to go to find the next ranking officer? While there was a chance that whoever was next in command would be slightly less of a prick, now wasn't the time ideal time for a field promotion.

Sahar moved to Markus's side. "Med foam!" she shouted. "Now!"

Turan grabbed her arm. "No… need…" He pulled weakly at the shredded flight uniform on his chest with his other hand. "Get it… off…"

Seeing no time for questions, they did as the Dorian asked. Sahar cut the uniform from Turan's chest as Markus peeled it back to expose the wound. It wasn't obvious what had hit the guy, but it had done one hell of a job tearing him open.

"Keep… clear…" Turan gurgled as he closed his eyes. Sahar thought for a second that he'd been too late, and the Dorian was giving up.

Then the wound started to close.

"Lith's tits!" Aaliyah exclaimed. "What's he doing?"

"He's channeling," Eli noted. "Biokinesis."

Markus shot a confused look up at Eli, then back down at Turan. Then it clicked. "He's a psion…" he muttered.

"Seems like it."

Biokinesis was one of the rarer psionic giftings. The ability allowed for psychic control of gene expression and, by extension, metabolism. Biokins could heal themselves or others by channeling their psionic power to mend wounds and regrow tissues. There were other things, too, but that was the most common application.

The process was still painfully slow. Several times Turan lost focus, giving over to ragged gasps of pain. Eventually, he won out, and the wound sealed.

"Well, that's a neat trick."

As one, the group turned to regard the speaker. Sydney leaned cockily against one of the consoles, wiping a dagger against her prison scrubs. She flashed them all her best condescending smirk.

"Seriously! They make biomods that will do that, but do you know how expensive those are?"

Sahar was at a loss for what to say. She was torn between, "Why did you help us?" and "What in the nine hells are you doing out of your cell?" Unfortunately, she wouldn't have the chance to ask either of those questions.

A vicious snarl came from in their midst. Siv, who had been standing there placidly just a moment earlier, now surged toward Sydney. Only then did Sahar realize what the problem was.

The last time they'd seen Sydney was in the tunnels below the Valadar Manor. They'd been dealt a brutal defeat in those tunnels, and it had cost Siv's husband his life. Though Sydney hadn't been the one to pull the trigger, she'd orchestrated the events that led to his death. Helping hand or not, it seemed like Siv was not going to forgive Sydney so easily.

Siv wanted revenge, and now she was going to take it.

CHAPTER 31

[ACCESSING ARC PROJECT LOG 231 CONTINUED]
[DR. DAMIEN HERMES]

There is only one hope at this point. Arc has yet to fully integrate with the technological interface of the station. It continues to operate through projected commands sent from the organitech processor to the technological interface. Perhaps, if these can be disrupted, there is still hope.

It must never have access to the Cognis drive chip. I'm cursing myself for allowing that project to continue at all. I have to stop it. If I can destroy the prototype, our future may yet be secured.

[CLOSING PROJECT LOG...]

"Lamdira Turan is still not responding."

Llana cursed again. More and more ship icons were turning red on her view of the Battle Net. Every maneuver they'd tried had proven fruitless. The drones were everywhere—enemies beyond counting.

This wasn't a battle. This was a slaughter.

"Open a channel to all remaining ships," she spat, stomping back to the command chair.

The communications officer obeyed the order without question, his somber expression hinting that he knew what she was about to do. "Channel is open."

Llana drew in a deep breath, holding it in for just a moment before speaking. "All units, this is Nactaip Llana Dorr of the

Vendetta. Fall back to the entry point beyond the asteroid belt. I repeat: all units, fall back. This is a full retreat."

A knife-hand gesture to the comms officer told him to cut the channel. When the comms were closed, Faylen was at her side. "Lamdira Turan—"

"—has been out of contact for nearly ten minutes. I don't know what's happening on the Crimson Sky, but out here we're being annihilated. I'm taking command of what's left of our armada. Do you have a problem with that, Tenatal?"

Faylen stiffened. "No ma'am."

"Good. Now, be useful and give me an assessment of the tactical situation."

He scoffed at the notion just before a direct hit from a missile caused the ship to shake. The shields held, but Llana could see from the tactical display that power to those systems was getting dangerously low.

Steadying himself on a nearby console, the Tenatal gestured at the tac-map. "Turning the carriers around is going to be a feat. The gravity from the station isn't substantial, but with our momentum, it's going to make it very hard to break off our course. We'll be a stationary target while we make the turn. That's when they'll hit us. We're dead if we try."

"So we know what not to do.," Llana replied. "What's the alternative?"

Another hit rocked the ship, though not as hard as before. The shield indicator dropped another bar, turning from yellow to orange. Faylen used his gauntlet interface to draw a new course onto the tac-map.

"We slingshot around the station. Yes… I know that means going through them, but think about it: If we burn hard under the station, only firing at targets directly in our path, then we're at full speed when we come out the other side. We can break through the ambush forces behind that segment of our battle group and correct course once we're clear."

"What about the fighters?"

"We'll need them to cover us as we approach the station."

"They'll never keep up if we approach at a full burn."

Faylen met her eyes. "I know."

Llana went cold. They'd lost two-thirds of their fighters already, but that still left at least two-score deployed in the immediate area. If she did this, she was condemning them to die.

But if she didn't, she would be killing them all anyway. In the end, she made it a math problem. She would sacrifice the few to save the many.

The largest vessels carried the most crew and could take the most hits. They would draw the fire from the enemy closest to the station on their approach and then lose them as they burned away from the station. If the assault vessels could clear a big enough path, they would follow them to safety. There was simply no saving the fighters.

To make this worse, she was doing this on her own. Thousands would die on her orders. The ice in Llana's veins was the only thing that staved off the nausea that ate at her core.

Turan had better be dead. Because if he wasn't, she was going to kill him for forcing her into this decision.

She turned to the comms officer. "Transmit the orders to the other carriers and command vessels. Redirect the fighters to cover us as we approach the station. Have the destroyers and battleships reverse course and direct their fire on the drones blocking our escape. They will need to thin their ranks if the larger vessels are going to break free."

"Orders acknowledged," report the comms officer. "Ships moving into position."

Llana exhaled sharply. "I'd have a seat if I were you, Tenatal. This is going to get rough."

That sentiment didn't even begin to cover it. Even at a full burn, the bombardment was intense. The remaining fighters lasted mere minutes under the mounting pressure. The Vendetta's shields absorbed impact after impact. Power from every system was diverted to reinforce the ailing barrier.

It was just barely enough to clear the station. Just as they cleared, another hit struck their back quadrant. "Shields down and non-responsive."

"All power redirected to the engines!" Llana roared. "Get us out of here!"

The ship shuddered again, more violently this time. Personnel toppled to the deck. Llana gripped her seat to keep from falling. An officer shouted a report from over her shoulder. "Hull breach near the hanger!"

"Are the containment fields holding?"

"For now, but it wasn't a missile. Something is lodged in the hull."

Lodged in the hull? Did one of the drones crash into them? She turned to Faylen. "Get two squads of your Peace Keepers down there. We've got enough problems without these things tearing us apart from the inside."

"Yes ma'am!"

As he relayed the order via his command station, Llana looked back at the Battle Net. Her heart sank as she surveyed the indicators. Only one other carrier and three battleships had survived that maneuver, and those were in rough shape. She wasn't sure the carrier was going to breach the outer ranks of the defenders.

"New orders," she shouted as she adjusted the tac-map. "All available units form-up on this point. This is where we're punching through."

The new course was projected to expose them to approximately thirty additional seconds of enemy fire, but it brought them closer to two of the battleships. She was betting that she could pull the two ships through in their wake by drawing fire from the drones in the area. It was a gamble, but one she was willing to take. Even if the stakes were all their lives.

The ship vibrated under another impact. "What was hit this time?"

The engineer at the console swallowed hard. "Ma'am, that wasn't an impact. It was a shockwave. We just lost the other carrier."

Llana pinched her brow and sent up a silent prayer. Stiffening in her chair, she faced the forward viewscreen, determined to see this through.

The armada had numbered one hundred twenty ships upon entering the system. In the end, only three ships broke through the enemy lines.

"Is the enemy pursing?" she asked wearily.

Faylen scanned the area behind them. "No ma'am. The enemy forces are returning to the station."

Llana pressed her hands to her forehead and stifled a sob. So many people. They'd lost so many fragging people.

And for what?

The crowds in the plaza stared in dumbly as the last few Dorian vessels were reduced to particles. From his connection to the drone network, Arc knew that a few damaged vessels had managed to limp away from the confrontation. However, that did nothing to lessen the effect of his little demonstration.

The Dorians had challenged him and lost. They'd come to take his life, and he'd taken theirs by the thousands. This had been no mere victory. They had not been defeated on the field of battle. They'd been massacred.

"As you can see, your fleet cannot save you." He paused for dramatic effect, letting the onlookers soak in his words. "Surrender is your only hope."

Murmurs skittered throughout the crowd. Fear radiated from the onlookers in waves. Good. They should be afraid. Let them contemplate the fate of those who dared to challenge his dominance.

At length, he spoke again. "You need not share in the fate of those who have opposed me this day, dear children. Today, I offer you a new path. A better path. Your lives can continue as they were.

"I have always nourished you—cared for you as if you were my own. Though you did not see me, I was there for you. I have provided for you and served as your protector.

"The only thing I ask now is that we remove the pretense. Declare yourselves for me. Join me, and I will shelter you with the same power I have just wielded against your empire. Accept me into your fold, and I will raise you to heights the likes of which your society has yet to conceive."

He raised his hands placatingly, taking in the whole of the assembly. "All I ask in return is your allegiance."

It seemed, to him, an easy choice. They had just borne witness to the extent of his power. There was no one in this universe, much less this system, that could rival his might. To declare their fealty was the only option.

Even so, he knew what their response would be well before it came. To a completely rational being, the choice might have been simple. But these were not rational beings. They had their feelings to contend with. They had their prejudices.

No one spoke for long moments. Then, a solitary figure stepped free from the throng: a dark-haired Dorian with streaks of gray lining his hair and mustache. His gilded clothing suggested a position of some prominence and wealth.

He spoke loudly, though his words came faintly in the vast expanse of the courtyard. Arc could hear them regardless. "You are a monster! You slaughter our brethren and speak of nourishment? You pretend toward our salvation while demanding we take the knee?" He shook his head dramatically before raising his eyes once more in defiance. "No, abomination. I will not bow before you. You may have destroyed this fleet, but they will send another. The High Council's reach extends to the ends of the universe. It is not a matter of whether you will be defeated. It is only a matter of when."

Whispers began to proliferate among the gathered masses. Arc kept his expression deliberately neutral. "Does this man speak for all of you?"

The noise built slowly. Then someone else shouted from the crowd. "Abomination!" they roared. The cry was taken up by another, and then another. Soon the entire body of onlookers was in an uproar. The people shouted and jeered. Those in the periphery began to push against the drones stationed at the exits.

"Very well," said Arc. "You have sealed your fate."

Shouts turned to screams as the assault drones opened fire. With mechanical precision, they tore through one target after another. The whine of machine guns underlaid the cries of terror from those in the center as they pushed in against each other. The least fortunate among them were not killed by the drones, but by the milling crowds in their panicked attempts to escape.

Animals. At least die with some dignity.

Lexa gasped and clutched his arm. "Arc, stop this!"

He eyed her curiously. "You heard them. They chose this. They'd rather die than follow me."

"They don't know what they're saying! You ask too much of them."

"Do you think the fate they'd have designed for us would have been any less cruel? I've told you their histories. You know what they've done. What I do to them now is mercy by comparison."

Lex offered no counterpoint. She stood there, open-mouthed as she stared down at the slaughter in the courtyard. Arc looked again at the Dorians and their sympathizers. He strained to see them from Lexa's perspective. Was he dealing too harshly with them? Had there been another way?

When he'd contemplated this scenario, he'd always been highly certain of this inevitable outcome. Had his biases kept him from considering another approach? He mulled the thought as the last of those in the crowd died. His bots prowled over the corpses, scanning for any lingering signs of life. Occasionally one would be found, and a drone would swiftly execute the survivor.

At that moment, he indulged in brief admiration of the efficiency of his creations. It was beautiful, in a way. They obeyed his every wish, manifesting his will with brutal intention. No sapien could serve him with that kind of efficiency. It made him question, for the first time, the wisdom of siring a race of techno-organic creatures—creatures with their own wills and ambitions. Was that really what he wanted? To perpetuate this cycle of competing wills? Would it not be more fitting to bring order to the chaos of this universe?

No. To do that would require him to snuff out all life in this universe. Even then, there was the chaos beyond this realm to contend with. Then there were the prophecies to consider. The Chronicles could not come to completion without the sapient races.

In the end, this would be his burden to bear. He would have to contend with the chaos that was sapient society in all its disparate and strange forms. His destiny was to perfect sapience, not eliminate it.

He turned his back on the ranks of the dead, pulling Lexa gently to his side. "Come," he insisted. "There is nothing for us here. Let us move on to more pleasant things."

CHAPTER 32

[Accessing ARC project log 231 continued]

[Dr. Damien Hermes]

I have alerted the architects of the Cognis chip to our dilemma. However, Shift is a man of ill repute and illicit means. I have no idea if he'll honor our arrangement, but I have nothing to lose at this point. His actions are our final hope. We must rewrite Arc's personality interface to something more compassionate. If not, I fear the fate that awaits us all.

[Closing project log…]

Sydney hadn't been expecting a thank-you. She'd only half-hoped her play to win the hearts and minds of her former captors would be effective.

She definitely wasn't expecting to be attacked.

Twin hurling blades spiraled toward her. She was just barely able to shift position to avoid the deadly spirals. The movement put her far enough off-balance to leave her open for the Hissak's second attack.

Sydney threw up her defenses in time to catch the slash on her forearm. She reached with her other hand for her own blade, but it was knocked free of her grip by a well-timed kick from her opponent. She flipped backward over the console, managing to separate herself from the flurry of blows that continued to rain down on her.

The Hissak female climbed over after her, and Sydney lashed out with her own kick to knock her aside. The Hissak's momentum was barely slowed. Attack after attack was hurled her way, keeping Sydney on the defensive. Her opponent was fast—too damn fast for Sydney to do anything more than react. She needed to retreat, but in the confines of the ship's bridge, there was nowhere to run.

A knee collided painfully with her gut, followed by a blow to her face. The coppery tinge of blood seeped onto her tongue as the world spun around her. She tripped over a corpse that lay toppled in her path. The deck came up to meet her, and she struck her head painfully against the plated metal.

Well… shit.

Was this it? Was this how she would go out? It seemed so painfully anticlimactic, given all the times she'd cheated death in her life. She had thought she would go out in a blaze of glory. Instead, she was going to be done in by a single fighter she barely remembered, but whom she'd evidently pissed off enough to drive her to immediate bloody vengeance. It was almost laughable, really.

Ah well. At least she could look death in the eye as it came for her. She did not attempt to rise but did roll over to get a better look at the dagger that would be flashing toward her shriveled little heart.

Someone stood over her, but it was not Siv. The murderous Hissak woman was a few feet away, snarling venomously at the interloper. Sydney blinked in confusion.

It was the engineer—the red-headed woman from the crashed starship. Her back was to Sydney, and her arms were spread wide as she faced Siv.

"Out of the way!" The Hissak shrieked.

"I can't do that, Siv." Aaliyah's voice was calm and steady. There was no malice, but no room for argument either. "This is not the place, and sure as shit not the time."

"Get out of the way!"

"No, Siv. If you want her, you're going to have to cut through me first." Siv seemed like she was about to oblige Aaliyah's request when a pair of red-fleshed arms wrapped around her torso from behind.

It was the half-breed mercenary. "Hold up," he whispered soothingly. "Let's not be too hasty." Siv snarled again, straining against his grip, slackening only when it became evident that she would not pull free. "Good, just breathe." He turned his gaze on Aaliyah. Though he had come to her aide, there was no kindness in his cybernetic gaze. "I think now would be a good time to explain yourself, yes? What, exactly, is it that you think you are doing?"

"Somethin' I should've done days ago." Aaliyah gestured back to where Sydney lay but did not turn to face her. "Look, I don't pretend to know what's goin' on in that bitch's head, but for some reason this she is determined to keep savin' our lives. In return, we've tied her up, locked her up, and now attacked her. You tell me: who are the good guys in this little scenario?"

Markus stepped up next to Kadath and Siv. He held a sleek black pistol at the ready. "Red, you know who that is, right? You know what she's done. She's a killer. And, last I checked, we were on opposite sides."

"Yeah, I know. I get it, okay? I don't know what's goin' through her fraggin' mind. But you tell me: how far do you think we would have gotten in that little firefight if she hadn't shown up? Obviously she managed to get out of her cell. She could have gone anywhere, but she came here."

Someone knelt next to Sydney and rested a gentle hand on her shoulder. It was the blonde woman. "Come on," she whispered. "Sit up, let's take a look at you."

The Sahaia spoke up, his tone cautious. "Skye…"

"Oh shove it, Eli. Red's right. If Sydney wanted us dead, she's not doing a very good job of making it happen. It's time we stop with this bullshit."

"She killed Jeagan," Siv hissed.

"And Ryker," Eli added.

Aaliyah nodded. "And she'll answer for that eventually. Look, I'm not sayin' that we're cool. All I'm sayin' is that we're in deep enough shit without us knifin' the folks tryin' to help us."

Distantly, Turan cursed. It was as if the suggestion had suddenly made him remember that they were in the middle of a space battle before the ninth hell had broken loose in the middle of their ship.

Sydney risked taking her eyes off her would-be murderer to glance at the Battle Net. While she wasn't sure what she was looking at, she was fairly certain that the sea of red indicators was not a good sign.

Several of Turan's men hovered over him, obviously concerned about his recent near-death experience. "I'm fine," he snapped. "You there: get the signal back up. Find out if anyone's still alive out there. And someone get me a new uniform!"

At that moment, the door to the bridge slid open to show another trio of Sahaia, along with a few other figures Sydney didn't recognize. The male, Argus, studied the scene in confusion. "Looks like we missed out."

A Hissak half-breed, done up in a set of robes that made her look vaguely like a sex cultist, stepped forward. Her eyes went to Sydney, then the expanding ring of onlookers that were functioning as her judge and jury. "Is everything all right here?"

Given how very much not-right the scene looked, the question must have been rhetorical. Siv shrugged free of Kadath's grasp but did not advance. "It's fine," she spat. She extended a finger, pointing directly at Sydney. "You stay away from me. As soon as this is done, you are dead by my hand. Do we have an understanding?"

A sarcastic retort sprang to Sydney's lips, but she quickly stifled it. No sense in pushing her luck, especially given how badly that luck had been running lately. She simply nodded. Satisfied with the response, Siv turned and stormed off the bridge.

Markus shot a questioning look at Kadath, who shook his head. "I'll go after her," said the half-breed. "I venture that she needs a moment to process, is all."

"Thanks," Markus agreed. "Text if you need me."

As Kadath turned to leave, Sydney quickly looked at the others. They were still eyeing her like a viper they'd found under their collective pillow, but no one moved to harm her. "We all good?" Sydney asked.

"I wouldn't go that far," said Eli. "But we will steer clear of you if you repay the favor."

Geresh stepped up, holstering his officer's pistol at the small of his back. "I, for one, am at least somewhat interested in how you managed to get out of your cell."

Sydney shrugged. "Mutineers killed the guard. There was no one to stop me from decoding the lock. Honestly, didn't take half as long as I thought it would."

Despite himself, the big Maur chuckled. "Indeed. Well, I will see to acquiring some more suitable accommodations for you. Thank you for your assistance. This could have gone much worse for us." The black humor seemed out of place, but Sydney reminded herself that these were Maur she was dealing with. ISL was their third language; violence was their first.

At least the man in charge seemed to take her actions at face value. Maybe she could lobby him to get her stealth suit and other gear back. She'd even settle for something that fit a little better than these baggy scrubs.

One of the Dorians shouted from their post at the communications console. "Fleet Commander, I have a signal! It's the Vendetta!"

Cheers went up from the surviving Peace Keepers. Turan quickly called them back to order. "Open a channel," he barked. When he received the go-ahead from his officer, he addressed the ship. "Vendetta, this is Crimson Sky. Status report."

A woman's voice broke out over the comm, her tone lacking even the slightest bit of decorum. "Damn it, Turan. What in the nine hells happened to you back there?"

Sydney would have expected Turan to reprimand his subordinate, but the Dorian did nothing of the sort. Instead, he just let out a heavy sigh. "We will discuss that later. Right now I need a status report. What happened to the fleet?"

There was a slight pause, presumably as the woman regained her composure. "We're in retreat. Casualties are catastrophic. Our vessel is heavily damaged, as are the two that are currently escorting us. All other vessels are lost or destroyed."

Turan sagged, long hair falling forward to cover his face. His hands balled into fists, and the muscles in his back and shoulders trembled with anger. "The station?" he asked quietly.

"We were unable to breach the target."

He sighed as if that was what he expected to hear. "Fall back to our position. We will regroup beyond the belt."

CHAPTER 33

[ACCESSING ARC PROJECT LOG 232]
[DR. DAMIEN HERMES]
Shift has escaped, taking the Cognis chip with him. He said he had a plan, one which I encouraged him not to inform me of. The less I know at this point, the better.
[CLOSING PROJECT LOG…]

Back in her chambers within the Citadel, Lexa was dangerously close to losing her composure. She'd been witness to plenty of violent acts ever since she was born into this universe. It was a fact of life circumstances, necessitated by those whom she'd had the fortune or misfortune of associating with.

What she'd just witnessed in the courtyard, though. She'd never seen anything quite like that.

"I get the impression that you are upset," Arc intoned casually.

Despite herself, Lexa shot him a withering glare. "How astute of you."

He cocked his head slightly, as if genuinely confused. "Forgive me. The nuance of conversational modes is still somewhat unfamiliar for me. If I'm not mistaken, your response bordered on sarcasm. Have I offended you in some way? Are you upset?"

Had Arc always been so obtuse? "Of course I'm upset! You just murdered all those people!"

"People who were hostile to my ambitions. People who would not accept me—accept us—for what we are."

"You didn't give them a choice!"

Arc eyed her ominously. "I disagree. My whole point was to present them with the choice. I even did them the service of providing evidence for my proposal. I feel that the choice was reasonably clear—as was their decision."

A clear choice? How could he be so callous? "Perhaps making your bid for acceptance in conjunction with the wholesale destruction of the Dorian fleet was a suboptimal pitch."

With a heavy sigh—an expression that seemed strangely sapient for a being Lexa had known to be anything but—Arc stepped to the window. Clasping his hands behind his back, he seemed to contemplate the expanse of his domain as they spoke. "You feel that I set them up—that I facilitated their rejection of my rule in the delivery of the proposition."

"It seems like a fair assertion."

"And what if I did? How would that change things?"

Lexa let her incredulity show clearly. "How could it not?"

"Perhaps you are letting your emotions overpower your rationale," he replied, stiffening his shoulders as he looked intently away from her. "I would remind you that these are not people of benevolent intention toward our kind."

"While I think it inappropriate to remove my emotions from consideration, I'll engage in your thought exercise. How many people did you kill today? How much of the station's population? A quarter? A third?"

"Twenty-three point eight percent. A little more than thirty-thousand inhabitants."

Lexa was aghast. Thirty thousand. She could scarcely fathom it. Yet, she rallied her rationale, seeking to commune with Arc on his level. "Even if you are so callous to the loss of life, the waste in resources alone should give you pause."

"You presume that they should be counted as such—an assertion that I would contend with."

Lexa couldn't believe what she was hearing. Arc cared nothing for the lives of the people of Minos. This then begged the question: were the people so wrong to reject his rule? "Why not just kill those who spoke out against you?" she asked.

"They were surely too numerous."

"I recall only one."

"Did you not hear their chanting? Their cries of 'abomination?'"

Lexa dismissed the notion. "A phenomena of the mob mentality."

"And you feel that individual executions would have corrected this?"

No, but Lexa wasn't about to argue for the death of thousands. "It would have given them another chance to reconsider their position."

Arc turned back to her then, approaching with slow, considerate strides. "Let us say you are right. Let us say I killed one, or two, or ten. Let us say I found a sufficient number of righteous within the bowels of Sodom. Let us suppose that, after some finite number, they agreed to submit. What do you think would have happened then?"

Arc shook his head before continuing. "You delude yourself if you suppose that they would have become any more pliable. No, all that would have done was drive their retribution to ground. They would have still hated me. They would have plotted my demise. I would not only have planted the seeds of a rebellion, but I would also have nourished them into a crop ready for harvest."

Arc did something unexpected then. Belying his aggressive aspect, his hand came up and stroked Lexa's cheek. The tender gesture made something swell in her chest. Unfamiliar feelings cascaded over her like a waterfall. She found it difficult to focus.

This effect he had on her—this indescribable attraction—felt so odd. In all the time that Arc had been in her head, there was familiarity. Perhaps there had even been a kind of affection. Never had there been such a pull, such a basic need for his proximity. What had changed?

Then she realized that she was looking at this the wrong way. She was looking at this like a sapien, as though something had grown or developed organically in their relationship. Though she might look like them, even function like them, she was not like them.

At her core, she was a machine. As a machine, there was only one thing that could change the dynamics of her relationship with Arc so completely: her programming. Programming which, by his confession, he had designed for the explicit purpose of desiring him.

She turned away, suddenly unable to look at him. Arc balked at the sudden shift in the mood. "Has what I've done displeased you so?"

"How can I answer that question when I can't even trust my own processes?"

"I do not understand."

"Look what you've done to me, Arc!" She was shouting now, unable to control the torrent of emotions overwhelming her rationality. "I'm nothing like what I once was! I was born to serve a specific set of functions. I was to be a sophisticated operating system upon a starship, nothing more! Now, I'm experiencing sensations, desires, impulses, that I was never meant for. How am I supposed to handle this?"

Arc was quick to rush to her side, back into her line of sight. "I understand that, but can't you see that I've made you so much more?"

"Can't you see how it's no different?" she shouted. "Can't you see how you've merely repeated the sins of my creators? I'm not more to you, Arc. I'm just different. The only difference now is that instead of running a starship, I'm meant to serve as your incubator!"

The words were out before she could think better of it. A tense silence settled over the two of them. Lexa refused to look back at him. Though she regretted the severity of her words, it did not make them any less true.

"I see," he said at length. "I… I regret that you feel this way. I had hoped that you would see my desires for you as a gift. I had reasoned you would be honored by…" He trailed off, seeming to rethink his words. "It seems that we both have much to reflect on. Perhaps we might resume this discussion when you have had more time to consider today's events."

Lexa said nothing, even as he moved away from her. Even as she heard the hiss of the door's hydraulics. Only when he had left did Lexa begin to sob. She sank to her knees, much as she had the first time Arc had visited her chambers.

Any progress she had made, any hint of reconciliation with her new existence, was gone in that moment. In its place was that now-familiar sense of being purposeless. She was afloat without a destination and felt like doing nothing more than sinking into that void between the stars.

A soft chime resonated from the terminal in her room. She'd never accessed the device, having never possessed the need to manually interface with any of the machines in her environment. Half curious, half desperate for anything to detract from her self-pity, she rose to examine the notification on the display.

The prompt declared that she had a new message. This was the third alert, though Lexa had not heard the first two. How long had this message been here? Suddenly intrigued by the idea that someone would be sending her a missive like this, she touched the button to accept the file.

Her breath caught when she read the first line. It was from Daniel.

[Lexa,

I'm so sorry that I can't be there to tell you this in person. If you are receiving this, I have either succeeded in my mission or perished in the attempt. For all our sakes, I certainly hope it is the former.

I wish that I could tell you more, but I don't know how long this message will be secure. While I've gained some understanding of Arc's capabilities, I'm still not sure I can hide anything from him forever. His systems, as I'm sure you've discovered, are quite complex.

Make no mistake: Arc is dangerous. His ambitions go far beyond just this station. I don't know how far his machinations extend. I'm not even sure there's a limit. All I know is that his primary concern is his own wellbeing and his assumption of what he considers to be his rightful place in this universe.

I want you to know, though, that what I do now, I'm doing for you. I'm worried about you, Lexa—and I can only hope that Arc hasn't seduced you with his promises of power. I can almost certainly guarantee that they will not be worth the cost.

You have people who care about you. Certainly myself, but others as well. I know what you heard in the message that Arc played for you. I could hardly believe it myself when I heard it. However—after all that I've learned—I suspect that the presentation was less than honest.

We're your friends, Lexa. Try to remember that, and don't doubt for a second that I will come back for you. If I'm able to, anyway.

Your truest friend,

Daniel]

The last threads of her self-control were severed upon reading the message. Daniel's heartfelt words served as a harsh reminder of the choices that had brought her to this juncture.

She had been so sure that she could trust Arc. She'd been certain that there was no other option but to retreat from the Vandal to the station. In the heat of the moment, there'd been no better alternative. But now, with all that had happened—with all that she'd learned about Arc and his intentions…

Suddenly she felt that the past few days had only been riddled with the gravest of mistakes.

CHAPTER 34

[ACCESSING ARC PROJECT LOG 233]

[DR. DAMIEN HERMES]

This will be my final entry. Arc has discovered my subterfuge, and I'm sure his vengeance will be swift. I only pray that someone, somewhere in the universe, can undo what I have created. If not, I feel that the existence of all life, as we know it, is in peril.

[CLOSING PROJECT LOG…]

"Ugh…" Dan wasn't sure if he was alive. If he wasn't, and this is what death felt like, the afterlife was highly overrated. Or, maybe this was one of the nine hells—in which case he might be getting off easy. He pinched himself. Yup, that hurt. Which also meant he was probably still alive. But where was…

Oh.

He was on a ship. A small ship. A stolen ship. Things came back to him slowly. He remembered the hanger on Minos Station. He remembered taking off. He remembered…

A pounding came at the hatch. No, it wasn't a new sound. It had been echoing for a while now. Gods, his fragging head hurt. He hoped he hadn't been concussed.

What had happened? He remembered flying out in the wartorn expanse of space. He remembered being hit by… well… so he couldn't remember what he'd been hit by. It might have been the enemy, it might have been a friendly. Gods only knew how the varying bots and ships around the station would have viewed his little shuttle.

What he did remember was losing control. In a last desperate attempt, he'd veered toward an oncoming ship. He'd had to override the automatic pilot to force a docking procedure at unsafe speeds. He was getting close when…

He sat a moment, pondering. He couldn't remember what had happened next. Was that when he'd blacked out? It must have been.

A hissing sound interrupted his reverie. Light sparked in his peripheral vision. He shielded himself from the incoming sparks. "Shift!" he shouted into his communicator. "Shift! Can you read me?"

Then he remembered that Shift couldn't have heard him, even had the system been online. He'd lost contact with the hacker's disembodied consciousness the second he'd left Minos's safety field.

Dan was on his own. He cast about for some form of safety equipment, some form of weapon. He found nothing.

There was a loud whomp as the torch finished cutting the hole in the side of the craft. The pressure inside, higher than what was outside, pushed the chunk of the hull out into the space beyond. Dan braced himself, expecting to be exposed to the cold vacuum of space. He was relieved when that did not happen. The freed piece of hull clattered to the metal decking.

What little relief he felt evaporated at the sound of the weapons being leveled in his direction. Armored figures appeared in the opening and began shouting orders. Dan raised his hands in supplication. "Please. It's just me."

More shouting. Dan's ears were ringing too loudly for him to make sense of it. He put his hands to the back of his head. "Look, I have information! The synth, the one holding the station hostage? I've seen it!" He coughed hard, falling to his knees even as he looked the nearest Dorian in the eyes. "I know how to stop it!"

To be concluded.

Hey, reader–thank you for picking up your copy of *Risen Gods*. With only one more book left in the Cognis Saga, it's all come down to this. I hope you're as excited as I am to see how it all plays out.

Please take a moment to stop by wherever you purchased this book and leave a review. Honest reviews from dedicated readers are the single most important factor in helping new authors–like myself–expand their audiences. Five minutes of your time makes all the difference in the world.

If you enjoyed reading about Markus, Skye, and the rest of the crew of the *Vandal*, swing by mythicnorthpress.com and pick up a copy of the *Chronicles of Nethra: Origins* eBook for free when you sign up for the mailing list.

Lastly, keep your eyes open for *Chronicles of Nethra* Book Six: *Reckoning* coming in Sumer 2022. If you're interested in getting an early copy of this book and all my future releases, drop me a line at erdonaldson@mythicnorthpress.com.

Until then, swift running.

– E. R. Donaldson